Praise for *Your Presence Is Mandatory*

"At once a historical epic, an engrossing family saga, and an astute examination of morality, survival, hope, and love, *Your Presence Is Mandatory* is a stunning feat. The emotional impact of reading Sasha Vasilyuk's gripping debut is immense. I sat with the vivid characters Vasilyuk has created for hours after reading, and I continue to think of them. *Your Presence Is Mandatory* is a book to last generations, and one I won't soon forget." —Lara Prescott, *New York Times* bestselling author of *The Secrets We Kept*

"Journalist Sasha Vasilyuk works magic in the gray areas of history, weaving her compelling debut historical novel out of the shadowy overlap between survival, secrecy, and guilt. Ukrainian Jewish Yefim Shulman fights through his time in the Red Army, but war and captivity will leave him with secrets he cannot tell his family. Struggling to build a life postwar in a regime where the wrong lie—or truth—means exile and death, Yefim makes choices that echo through the decades and generations to come. *Your Presence Is Mandatory* is an important, moving read that will resonate long in the reader's memory." —Kate Quinn, *New York Times* bestselling author of *The Alice Network*

"Wonderfully written, elegiac, and necessary. Sasha Vasilyuk uncovers the history behind the recent headlines with great skill and grace." —Gary Shteyngart, author of *Our Country Friends*

"This extraordinary debut is the best kind of historical fiction—an emotionally complex and heartrending saga that takes us to unfamiliar places in unfamiliar times and makes them feel known and lived." —Meg Waite Clayton, internationally bestselling author of *The Postmistress of Paris*

"In this piercing tale of a family struggling for compassion and understanding in the face of a seventy-year-old secret, Sasha Vasilyuk nimbly lifts the historical Iron Curtain to reveal the physical and psychological toll of war and autocracy. The character Yefim Shulman's tortuous and traumatic coming-of-age story during and after World War II is told with precision and heart; his return to the Donbas is a gut-wrenching illustration of loss and survivor guilt. But what Vasilyuk captures so meticulously is the suffocating lifelong burden of pretense Shulman must pull off in order to avoid the gulag and protect his family from a shame that makes no sense but is a cornerstone of the Soviet Union's moral code. *Your Presence Is Mandatory* is an outstanding novel of sacrifice, love, and forgiveness. If you have any confusion about the current conflict between Ukraine and Russia, this illuminating story will clarify so very much. It did for me." —Susanne Pari, author of *In the Time of Our History* and *The Fortune Catcher*

"*Your Presence Is Mandatory* is a powerful story of a Jewish Ukrainian family told in alternating time frames that stretch from WWII Germany to twenty-first-century Ukraine. In masterfully crafted prose, Sasha Vasilyuk examines the harrowing choices her characters have to make to survive during and after the war. With a cast of memorable characters, *Your Presence Is Mandatory* is a poignant and formidable tale of grit and guilt set against the harsh realities of state-sanctioned cruelty and indifference. You won't be able to put this book down, and it will stay in your heart long after you finish reading. Riveting and unforgettable." —Elena Gorokhova, the author of *A Train to Moscow*

"Captivating and suspenseful, Sasha Vasilyuk's novel is a tender tribute to the human spirit, a fresh and moving look at the nature of guilt and memory and one man's desire to survive at all costs. The characters loom off the page, so real, that I was quickly absorbed into this tragic yet life-affirming tale." —Kristina Gorcheva-Newberry, author of *The Orchard*

"This novel is a masterful exploration of the weight of secrets, generational divides, war trauma, and the search for home and belonging within one's own homeland—a subject that feels more urgent than ever. *Your Presence Is Mandatory* should be mandatory reading for this time of crisis." —Maria Kuznetsova, author of *Oksana, Behave!* and *Something Unbelievable*

"An engrossing family saga and a secret key for anyone who wants to understand how history has brought Ukrainians and Russians to where they are today." —Boris Fishman, author of *Savage Feast*

YOUR PRESENCE IS MANDATORY

Sasha V.

YOUR PRESENCE IS MANDATORY

A NOVEL

SASHA VASILYUK

BLOOMSBURY PUBLISHING

NEW YORK · LONDON · OXFORD · NEW DELHI · SYDNEY

BLOOMSBURY PUBLISHING
Bloomsbury Publishing Inc.
1385 Broadway, New York, NY 10018, USA

BLOOMSBURY, BLOOMSBURY PUBLISHING, and the Diana logo
are trademarks of Bloomsbury Publishing Plc

First published in the United States 2024

ISBN: HB: 978-1-63973-153-4; EBOOK: 978-1-63973-154-1

LIBRARY OF CONGRESS CATALOGING-IN-PUBLICATION DATA IS AVAILABLE

2 4 6 8 10 9 7 5 3 1

Typeset by Westchester Publishing Services
Printed and bound in the U.S.A.

To find out more about our authors and books visit www.bloomsbury.com and
sign up for our newsletters.

Bloomsbury books may be purchased for business or promotional use. For information
on bulk purchases please contact Macmillan Corporate and Premium Sales Department at
specialmarkets@macmillan.com.

For my grandparents

YOUR PRESENCE
IS MANDATORY

Chapter 1

2007
Donetsk, Ukraine

N ina watched her husband fish out a heap of papers from his leather briefcase and lock himself in the bathroom. She heard Yefim strike a match and soon smelled the sweet smoke of old paper burning.

Nina didn't stop him. What was the point? She liked her room neat. She, too, had been getting rid of things. Whenever their grandkids or her former students came by, she gave away Pushkin tomes or the rare rocks she'd collected on her paleontological expeditions throughout the USSR. But since no one would care for a dying man's documents, he may as well burn them. He could have of course just tossed them and spared their daughter, Vita, the worry that he might set fire to the apartment, but Nina liked Yefim's sudden penchant for the dramatic. In his own mind at least, his life must have seemed more interesting.

It wasn't easy watching her husband of more than fifty years turn smaller, more fragile, more erratic. After destroying his papers, it was as if he'd given up. Soon, there was no more going to the bathroom by himself, only the plastic toilet in the middle of the room that he'd nicknamed his "throne." The worst was when he rolled off the bed and howled, "Don't hit me!" in this pitiful voice she'd never heard before. Nina was relieved when he was more lucid on Victory Day so the great-grandkids could congratulate him properly. It was important for this pampered twenty-first-century generation to remember that Yefim was a war hero. But soon after, he got worse again until one morning when Nina awoke with her usual "Rise and sing, Fima!" and he didn't respond. His silence felt like a slap.

She cried almost nonstop over the next two days of preparations. The tears weren't only for Yefim. She cried for herself, too: she would be next. At eighty-two, she had seen so much death that she probably should have been looking forward to the darn thing. And yet, when she put on her black cotton dress to say goodbye to the man she knew best, she trembled.

As she and her son, Andrey, led their small procession past the Donetsk cemetery's flower seller with her plastic wreaths that shimmered in the sun, Nina dreaded the rectangle of scorched sandstone soil waiting for her next to Yefim. It was hundreds of kilometers away from her parents and sister, who rested in a beautifully overgrown cemetery in Kyiv.

Nina's hair quickly grew sweaty under her black beret. Andrey fanned her with a handkerchief he'd brought with him from Moscow as they turned right toward the newest section. With her one good eye, Nina saw the crosses, the gravestones inscribed with unfamiliar names, and the occasional black-and-white portrait of the deceased staring back at her. She tried not to think of them as her future neighbors.

At their plot, two gravediggers leaned on their shovels. Nina sat on a plastic chair and the rest of their group crowded around her: Andrey, Vita with her husband, three of the grandkids, and a couple of Yefim's former geology colleagues. It made her sad that the other two grand-kids were too far away in California and that Yefim's niece, the only survivor from the Shulman side, was stuck in Germany. But she knew Yefim wouldn't have held it against them. As everyone laid flowers on the grave, she imagined him cracking a joke to cheer them up. That silly husband of hers: how she would miss him.

They had no rabbi or priest since Yefim was a Jew and like most Soviet people an atheist. However, Andrey, who'd worn his Christlike beard ever since he'd gotten baptized despite her and Yefim's objections, still read a prayer. Nina didn't think God had done much for her family or anyone else in the country, but she still said "Amen" to please her son.

After the prayer, Vita put on her reading glasses and stepped up to recite a Yevtushenko poem she'd loved since high school. Her voice quivered when she got to the lines "What do we know of our own father? / Seemingly everything—yet nothing at all."

There wasn't much to know, Nina wanted to tell her. But then again, she herself never stopped wondering about her own father: he'd died during the war, followed by her mother, orphaning her at sixteen.

Nina wanted to wipe her daughter's tears as they fell onto the gravestone, a coarse-grained gray granite they'd chosen to honor Yefim's career in geology. In a year or two, once the earth settled, they would put up a simple black granite monolith with his name and dates. No laurel leaves, "Defender of the Motherland," or, God forbid, Soviet star like the other vets. He may have fought the whole war from day one all the way to Berlin four years later, but the man hated all things veteran. Didn't even write down a single war memory despite years of nagging by both Andrey and Vita. A truly impressive stubbornness.

After Vita's recital, Nina rose from the chair and, taking a rock she had been clutching in her right hand, placed it at the head of Yefim's grave. It was a piece of limestone from the quarry where they had met that summer more than half a century earlier.

For the wake their family squeezed into Vita's living room. This ninth-floor apartment in the center of Donetsk where Nina and Yefim had been forced to live since she had the stroke and he started shaking from Parkinson's had a view of the city all the way to the slag heaps on the horizon.

As the setting sun turned the flowered wallpaper orange and the evening breeze cooled the living room, they ate blintzes, drank cold berry kompot, and told stories about Yefim.

How he got lost in Siberia and then shrugged it off as if surviving alone in the taiga for days was no big deal. How, when Andrey and Vita were little, he'd saved them from a crazed mare that careened toward them, frothing at the mouth. Vita remembered how later he'd also saved her from being kicked out of university for losing a map—those ridiculous Soviet maps that were considered top secret—by splitting a bottle of cognac with her professor. How he had a way with everyone, even the authorities. People talked over one another, one anecdote leading to the next, and Nina listened and laughed and wondered whether she would have loved Yefim more if all she knew of him were these stories.

After Andrey flew back to his professor life in Moscow and Vita returned to work, Nina found it strangely quiet in the apartment. She was used to Yefim coughing and sighing on his bed in their narrow bedroom. Every morning she woke up expecting to find him there and briefly worried he'd escaped again like that one time when passersby found him clawing through bushes. Then she would remember and start counting how many days were left until they could take the towels off the mirrors.

Nina got herself through the forty-day mourning period with the help of soap operas and audiobooks, but the whole time she was itching to start cleaning. Before Yefim passed, she'd begun every other morning by dusting their bedroom: the desk, the TV, the nightstand, and the glassed-in bookcase with Yefim's small brass mug from the war. Twice a week she had Vita bring a red plastic bucket with warm water and got down on her knees, where she felt more stable, to wipe the room's linoleum floor with her husband's old shirt. While Yefim was alive, he wasn't allowed to get down from his bed until the wet streaks had disappeared from the floor. Now she could practically feel the dust gathering around her.

Finally, on the fortieth day, Vita uncovered the mirrors. It was a hot July morning, with a lavender haze settled over the slag heaps. As Vita packed Yefim's clothes and bedding into two large bags—one for the poor, the other to be burned outside the city—Nina began dusting. After all the usual places were clean, she crouched in front of Yefim's bed. From underneath it, she pulled out the leather briefcase he'd lugged around since the 1950s.

"We can finally get rid of this old thing," she told her daughter.

She remembered how when they first moved in together to that little house on the outskirts of Kyiv, he'd brought this briefcase along with a small bag of clothes and the oddly shaped brass mug, his only possessions. He told her right away that the briefcase had his private papers, and she understood that she wasn't to open it, not that she was curious.

Now Nina wiped the dust off its leather and checked to make sure it was empty before adding it to Vita's growing pile.

The inside smelled of the last century, of diesel, trains, iodine, and ink. She was about to close the flap when she noticed the spine of a thin beige envelope in one of the compartments. He must have forgotten to burn it.

She pulled it out. If this was one of the soap operas she liked to watch, inside she'd find something exciting, like photographs he'd hidden away or maybe even a love letter from some adoring woman. Instead, she found a dull yellowing photocopy filled with Yefim's immaculate cursive. Though she couldn't make out the individual words, it certainly didn't look like a love letter.

"Read this, Vitochka," she said. "Make sure it's nothing worth saving."

Vita put on her glasses and took the letter.

"It's from April 1984," Vita said.

Nina remembered 1984 was the year Chernenko became the general secretary, just for one year, before he died and Gorbachev stepped in to finish off the country they'd all stopped believing in. Nina wished she could stop associating time with general secretaries, but there was no changing how Soviet memory worked.

"You better sit, *Mamochka*," Vita said in a hollow voice. "It's addressed to the KGB."

Nina began to feel a little clammy.

"What would the KGB want with your father?"

She crawled toward her bed and pulled herself up onto the edge of her mattress, the dustcloth still in her hand.

Vita began to read aloud:

To the head of the Regional Committee of State Security,
I am writing to address the inconsistencies discovered in my military service
record. However, I must first say that my children and grandchildren love
me very much and it would be a big psychological trauma for them to find
out what I'm about to report.

Chapter 2

June 21, 1941
Šilalė, Lithuanian Soviet Socialist Republic

The shortest night of the year cast its pale blue light over the artillery base as Yefim sat in front of the fire, scraping the last bits of canned beef stew.

Their regiment had brought a lot of noise to this quiet corner of Lithuania, dragging their big guns past the scowling villagers, converting an old barn into barracks, pitching a kitchen and medical tents, running a telephone wire, and building stables for the horses.

The Germans were positioned less than an hour west, and it was unclear what would happen next. Stalin's latest order was to be combat-ready while taking every precaution not to provoke Hitler. No one wanted war.

Yefim licked the beef grease off his spoon. Tomorrow morning, he and Ivan would need to tow the big olive-green field gun they'd nicknamed Uska two kilometers west to join the rest of the battery. He considered which horses to take for the job. Definitely Neptune, his favorite. A chestnut-colored heavy draft stallion, Neptune reminded Yefim of himself: muscular, with sturdy legs, he could endure hours of heavy labor. He supposed they had both been bred for work in the fields but were lucky enough to end up in the army.

Yefim put the empty mess kit on the log between him and Ivan and grabbed his aluminum canteen. Tonight's beer had been specially trucked in because a dozen men in his division were celebrating the end of their tour of duty. They sat around him, drinking and talking of going home next week.

"Once I get home, I swear I'll never have canned beef again," said Anton Lisin, a slightly pudgy soldier who ate his stew as if he were in the czar's dining room. "Only borsch and beef Stroganoff and chocolates."

"Mmm, chocolates," the others nodded.

As the bitter beer bubbles tickled Yefim's tongue, he felt glad he wasn't going home yet. With two more years in the army, he still had a chance to return home the way his oldest brother, Mikhail, did— broad-shouldered and confident, with medals gleaming on his chest. He'd never forget how the whole village had gathered to greet Mikhail as their mother stood proud like an ancient Jewish queen.

"Chocolates are for kids," Regush said with his signature pretty-boy smile gleaming from the other side of the fire pit. "My first order of business will be between Svetochka's thighs."

"To thighs!" someone proposed, and Yefim was suddenly annoyed at these older guys bragging about something he and Ivan couldn't have.

"Oh please, Regush," he said, feeling loose-tongued and warm. "I guarantee you'll be missing us after a week with your Svetochka."

"Don't be jealous, dear Shulman, you'll always be my number one girl," Regush said, getting up and trotting toward him with his greasy lips pursed for a kiss.

Everyone burst out laughing as Yefim picked Regush up like a bride and carried him around the circle. The soldiers banged their spoons on their metal pots and hollered, "Gorko! Gorko!" as they did at weddings. He deposited Regush back to his seat and returned to his spot next to Ivan.

"I certainly won't miss this nonsense," Lisin said. "I'm going to Moscow after this. Gonna study geology."

"Who the hell will let you into the capital?" Regush asked.

"My sister lives there, if you must know," Lisin said. "Works at the Central Telegraph."

"Then why study geology? Can't she score you a job at the Telegraph?"

Yefim smirked. "In the absence of Svetochka, rocks are Lisin's best option," he said.

The soldiers sniggered.

"Someone like you, Shulman, wouldn't understand," Lisin said, waving his spoon in the air like a conductor and making Yefim wonder if *someone like you* meant what it usually meant: Jewish. "All you want to do is kick ass. But the Soviet Union's real power lies not in soldiers but in raw materials and our brainpower to wield them. Just look at the trainloads of wheat and coal we send to Germany. That's one solid guarantee the Fritzes won't start a war."

Yefim hated his arrogant tone. Lisin was a total *shvitzer*, as his brothers would say. Too bad Ivan didn't know such juicy Yiddish expressions.

"But if there is a war, Lisin won't mind if we get all the fun and glory, while he studies rocks in some dusty lab," said Yefim.

"To fun and glory!" someone toasted as voices hooted around the fire, and Yefim knew he'd won the crowd.

He raised his canteen, when Ivan whispered into his ear, "Except if they attack, we're screwed."

Yefim shook his head, glad no one else heard him. If they were alone, he'd tell Ivan that Hitler may have trampled Paris, but the Soviet Union wasn't France. They were a superpower. They had nothing to be afraid of.

Ivan was a damn good artilleryman, but sometimes Yefim wondered why, after a year in the service, his best friend still took every opportunity to take a dig at the Red Army. They had first met at the regional military commissariat in Kozyatyn, which was in the middle between their two villages. Yefim had been glad to reach conscription age and finally try himself as a soldier, following in the footsteps of his older brother and his father, who'd served in the czar's army. But for Ivan it was a way to escape from his dad, who'd turned into a drunk after Ivan's mother died during the famine.

Yefim had immediately liked Ivan's wide, jovial face and the warm gray of his eyes under his barely visible blond eyebrows. Though his rosy cheeks gave him an innocent look, he was wiry and strong in the way of a stray—he knew how to hit back if needed. During training, they were both placed in the artillery unit due to their strength. Working the horse-drawn divisional guns together, he and Ivan quickly grew close. They told each other all sorts of stories from their childhoods, avoiding only the worst horrors of the famine they'd both survived. Yefim trusted him so much that he even told him how he'd once pissed himself in the synagogue because the service was so long. Unlike some other guys at the boot camp, Ivan didn't seem to care that he was a Jew, nor that his skin tone was deeper and his last name decidedly not Slavic. He even got offended on Yefim's behalf whenever he heard a joke about a Yid.

When training was over, Yefim had brought Ivan home with him to say goodbye before they shipped out to serve here in the Baltics. His family had welcomed Ivan like their own, although he'd looked like a white crow sitting among the loud, dark-haired, brown-eyed Shulmans. It was too bad that Ivan didn't get to meet Mikhail, who lived with his wife and daughter in Kharkiv, but at least he got to meet Yakov, Naum, and Georgiy as well as their sister, Basya, whose long black hair and dancing eyebrows Ivan had clearly appreciated from his side of the table. His cheeks had glowed red.

Mother took to Ivan the same way Yefim had. Upon learning that Ivan's mother had died and he'd grown up alone with his drunk father, she said she would have been glad to adopt him. Georgiy, never one to keep his mouth shut, said Ivan could have been little Fimochka's best friend since Naum, who was closest in age, was usually too busy with the gaggle of girls that followed him. The brothers laughed, while their father mumbled, "Another mouth to feed," in Yiddish, and Yefim, who'd often been called that himself, remembered why he wasn't going to miss home.

Once their unit was rolling through the small towns of Latvia and Lithuania, Yefim enjoyed every minute of being in the army. He even liked the way the townsfolk looked at him with trepidation and closed their shutters against the ruckus his unit made as their horses dragged the huge Soviet guns. The power of it. He doubted his father ever felt this way. The old man had never talked about his time in the army and seemed to care only about the horses in the stables and God, always God. As if praying ever saved his ancestors from the pogroms or fed his family during the famine. Father revered Stalin the same way he used to revere the czar: as God's deputy. He refused to see that it was *the people* who were the true Almighty now. People like Yefim and Ivan and their whole generation who would build a grand Soviet future where no one fought over which God they believed in and everyone was equal. A brighter future made of steel and fast cars and tall buildings. A future that Yefim was tasked with protecting on the western border of his powerful country.

As he drank to "fun and glory," a part of him wished the Germans would attack already so he could finally show everyone what he was made of.

After dinner, they drove into town a few kilometers down the road. It was Saturday and two fiddlers and an accordionist played at a roadside tavern as couples danced on the lawn. There was no way the Lithuanians would let a bunch of Red Army soldiers dance with their girls, and Lieutenant Komarov had told them, "Don't start any trouble with the locals. We'll need them if the Fritzes decide to attack." So he and Ivan stood to the side with the others, watching. Filling their imaginations.

Across the lawn, Yefim spotted a lovely dark-haired girl leaning against a tree, wistfully looking at the dancers. She was surely Jewish: he'd heard more than a quarter of the town were his people. She tugged at the corner of her shawl as if ready to throw it off the moment someone invited her to dance. Except no one did.

He decided talking to a Jewish girl wasn't starting trouble and headed toward the tree. When he approached, he saw she was younger than he'd realized, no more than sixteen.

"I'm sure you want to dance, but unfortunately I am terrible at it," he said with a smile. "A bear stepped on my ears, as my mother likes to say."

The girl stared at him in silence, a small panic forming in her brown eyes.

"I'd only embarrass us both," he explained.

She grew red in the cheeks and said something in Lithuanian, pointing to the dance floor. He wanted to smack himself for being such an idiot. Of course she didn't speak Russian. They'd been Soviet for less than a year. He tried in Yiddish, though the only words that came out were *dance* and *can't* and he was pretty sure they were in German, which he'd studied in school.

She laughed.

Her name was Eva. She spoke Yiddish freely, the way his mother used to when he was little, before Shabbat was outlawed and the nearest synagogue got converted into an administrative office of the regional kolkhoz. He understood some of what she said and replied using Ukrainian, German, and a lot of gestures. She told him she was here with her older sister, that she loved to dance, and that she didn't think the Germans would attack, or at least that's how he understood it. He tried complimenting her eyes, but all that came out was a linguistic mess devoid of delicacy or humor.

The band started on a folk song and Eva ran to the dance floor, joining other local girls in a circle. They tapped their feet and circled back and forth in a slow traditional dance. They reminded him of how the girls danced in his village, Basya among them with colorful ribbons in her silky black hair.

On the other side of the lawn, his buddies whistled and hooted as Ivan and Regush, both good dancers and both a little drunk, started to dance the *hopak*. Yefim didn't know where Ivan had picked up such moves. He and Regush squatted and threw out their legs. Yefim noticed the local men glaring at them, then approaching. Soon there was a brawl. Yefim ran toward them as a beefy local wrestled Ivan to the ground. He tried to separate them when Ivan flipped his opponent, ending up on top. Yefim grabbed his friend.

"We've got to go!" he yelled, pulling Ivan, all red in the face, away from the lawn. Not only were they going to get in trouble with the lieutenant, but tomorrow they also had Uska to deal with, not to mention getting up at 0500 hours to head off in their vehicles in the direction of the border. He felt bad that he didn't say goodbye to Eva, but he would definitely try to find her next weekend. If they were allowed back in town, that is.

That night he woke up with a full bladder, but, hoping to fall back asleep, continued lying on his upper bunk to the snores and sighs of the men in the barracks.

This far north, summer nights were brief, but cold all the same. He was glad for his wool socks. The Baltic forests were nothing like Ukraine, with its steppes that kept the heat all the way until morning. Here, even the summer solstice wasn't warm enough to sleep barefoot.

Yefim liked the wool socks because Basya had knitted them for him before he had shipped off to the Baltics last fall. Every time he wore them, he thought of her in their small hut that smelled of cloves, wood, and boiling milk. Basya had knitted the same socks for Mikhail, Georgiy, Yakov, and Naum when it had been their turns to serve. Now Yefim washed them every week, making sure to be careful with the wool because it linked him to all of them from this corner of Lithuania to the heartland of Ukraine.

He'd need to write Basya about Eva and how odd it was to hear someone from their generation speaking Yiddish. His sister would probably answer something cheeky about their mother approving of the match. He remembered how disappointed Mother had been when Mikhail married a Ukrainian shiksa. She'd taken offense when the poor daughter-in-law had served rabbit stew, not having a clue that rabbit was as unkosher as pork. Two months ago, Basya had written that Yakov—who was the intellectual of the brothers and looked the most like Yefim, with prominent cheekbones and a high, stubborn forehead—married a Jewish girl who worked in the theater and whom their pleased mother described as "the perfect match for our Yakushka." She would definitely think someone like Eva was the perfect partner for Yefim.

His bladder felt like it was about to pop, so he hopped down from the upper bunk and pulled his tarpaulin boots right over his long johns. The bluish morning light peeked through the cracks in the wooden barracks. In the bottom bunk, Ivan slept peacefully despite the battle order, the beer, and the brawl. He must have learned to shut everything out during his father's drunken binges. At least his own God-fearing father wasn't a man of the bottle.

Outside the barracks, the dawn was hazy and grayish yellow. Nothing moved. Even the small dark clouds, gilded on one side, seemed to stand still in the pale blue sky. An early bird cooed in the trees. Yefim inhaled the cool, wet air that smelled of pines and thought of Eva. How good it would have been to kiss those soft lips.

He took the trail past the firepit that still smoldered from dinner. Remembering last night's banter, he didn't regret making fun of Lisin. That know-it-all had it coming. Just because his dad was the party secretary in some Russian town didn't mean he got to lecture the rest of them on raw materials and brainpower. What a schmuck. If a war broke out, he wouldn't last a day.

Inside the rickety outhouse, Yefim aimed for the dark pit and felt himself relax. A mosquito began to whine near his left cheek. He slapped it and then all was silence. He noticed the mosquito had left a red smudge on his fingers and wondered whose blood it was.

On the way back, he passed the stables and paused by Uska, dreaming her bellicose dreams under a tarp. He wondered what it would be like to fire her up and aim at the Germans. Just last month, Stalin had made a speech calling the artillery "the god of modern warfare." When Yefim heard those words, his chest had filled with pride. He wished his and Ivan's fathers had heard that speech too, but neither owned a radio. It wouldn't have made any difference anyhow. Those men lived in their own worlds.

He patted Uska and, looking at his hand on the tarp, smiled at how lucky he was to be an artilleryman. After all, shelling a tank from hundreds of meters away was so much more advanced than, say, shooting a man with a rifle. Though even if he had to shoot someone point-blank, of course, he would.

Especially if they were fascists.

He still remembered that film he and his brothers went to see in '38, *Professor Mamlock*, about a Jewish doctor in Nazi Germany. He never forgot the chill he felt during the scene when Professor Mamlock was led from the hospital onto a crowded street in his white robe with *Jude* written across the front. If that's how the Germans were, he'd gladly fire a rifle or, better yet, Uska's powerful barrel. He would not let them turn his country into the sort of place where Jews were led down the street like cattle.

Behind him, one of the horses nickered in the stables, and Yefim hurried back toward the barracks. He could still get a little sleep before the alarm. The bird that had been cooing earlier was gone. Reaching for the door, he paused, filling his lungs with the morning air before entering the stale room where three dozen men slept on sweaty straw mattresses.

Suddenly the door swung open and Ivan emerged, his rosy cheeks puffy with sleep. He startled when he saw Yefim and asked, "You coming or going?"

"Coming."

"Ah." Ivan smiled with the envy of a man with a full bladder and trotted toward the outhouse.

Yefim took another deep breath. His legs felt sluggish in his long underpants and he looked forward to climbing back into bed, even if for a bit. He really shouldn't have had that last beer.

Behind him, a truck rumbled around the bend of the road, skidding toward the command post tent. He stood, listening. The distant chatter sounded quick, tense. He wondered what could be so urgent. Then he saw Smirnov, who had been on watch that night, sprinting toward the siren post. Quickly, he wound it until it howled, waking up soldiers and horses and all the living things in the surrounding field and forest.

Yefim yanked the door of the barracks. Inside, men were already scrambling up. They belted breeches, pulled up jackboots. He rushed to his bunk to get his uniform. Ivan's bunk was empty and he thought maybe he should grab his friend's things.

From far off, he heard thunder. For a moment everyone froze.

"What the fuck is that?" someone yelled.

"Is it a drill?"

"Those are bombs, moron!"

The men began to stream outside. Yefim was hurrying to pull on his *gimnasterka* tunic when he heard an approaching shriek. It grew into an ear-splitting roar.

"Take cover!" someone screamed.

Yefim ducked next to the wall, wrapping his arms around his head as the bombs dropped with blood-chilling shrieks. The barracks with its beds and boots and men shuddered and lurched forward with a groan. He was hurled upward. Everything grew hot, dark, deafeningly quiet. He flew, then skidded for what must have been an eternity. In the haze, his limbs seemed unreachable. His head was a spiky, compressed ball. It cut through the heat until his back slammed into something with a thud.

When he opened his eyes, he was clutching a piece of the wall's wooden beam. It had splintered and now revealed its unspoiled, cream-colored innards. The earth convulsed, showering him with dirt and shards. The piercing clanging in his head blocked out all sounds. His skin stung everywhere: on the tip of his nose, on the back of his head, and even, despite the wool socks, on his shins. It was as if he'd landed in a beehive. He wheezed, trying to breathe.

His lower body was buried by dirt and debris. Beyond them was only black smoke. It bit his eyes, scratched his throat. Never in his life had he been this afraid. Not even during the famine. He hugged the wooden beam tighter as if it were a raft. Out of the smoke, a soot-covered soldier with wild eyes crawled past him, climbing over what couldn't be a severed leg oozing blood, and disappearing again into the smoke. Yefim wished he could disappear too.

Above him, something dark and towering gushed flames. The barracks wall. It leaned over him, threatening to collapse. He hurried to sit up, but his legs and hips were caught. He rose on his elbow and shoved at the debris, but it wouldn't give. His foot had twisted under something and he couldn't get any leverage. He looked up. A huge burning board splintered in half, dragging the wall toward him.

He heaved himself, grunting, when someone grabbed him under the armpits and pulled. The wall tumbled to his right, sending fireworks of sparks into the air. Above him was Ivan. He seemed like a pre-death mirage, but the black specks of dirt trapped in his invisible eyebrows looked too real. Ivan dragged him away from the fire, then patted him up and down, opening his mouth like a fish. His lips moved urgently, but he didn't seem to be saying anything, and Yefim couldn't understand why his friend was whispering now of all times.

Ivan stopped patting and drew his face closer to Yefim's. He pointed to his ears and shook his head, and Yefim understood that the explosion must have knocked out his hearing. He thought he recognized what Ivan was mouthing: *Voyna*. War.

Yefim sat up. The planes had left and the smoke was clearing. Though his head was spinning, he could see that the barracks was now a burning pile of wood. And something else fleshy . . .

He retched.

That cleared his head. He remembered their battle drill and scrambled up. He felt foolish in his muddy long johns torn at the knees with a big red stain on his right calf that, as far as he could tell, wasn't from his wound.

No, Ivan was wrong: this couldn't be war.

Stalin would have warned them, given them proper orders. This was just a provocation. They'd been told it could happen. Somebody somewhere fucked up and now their regiment was paying the price. He needed to find a uniform and everything would get sorted out. Maybe he'd even get his first medal for braving through this mess. Once this was all over, he'd write home, and his brothers would see he wasn't little Fimochka anymore.

Ivan pointed toward a shell crater behind them. Someone's hand was moving from below the ground. Quickly they dug him out. It turned out to be Regush. Half of his face was scraped off to the bone. His left leg was broken, but he was still alive. He and Ivan lifted Regush out of the crater, trying not to look at his blue eyes blinking helplessly on a ravaged face.

"Svetochka!" he screamed.

Yefim's hearing was coming back, though the sounds were muffled as if he were inside a hay bale.

"You'll be all right, Regush," Yefim lied. "You'll see her soon."

They carried him away from the field, his body dangling between them, until they came across medical staff with a stretcher.

As they were placing him on the stretcher, a horse galloped past them into the woods. Yefim could hear a far-off grumbling—German artillery in the west.

War or not, they needed Uska.

He and Ivan ran past the burning stables. Several horses lay dead; others were gone. Neptune wasn't there. But at least, on the other side of the flames, Yefim found Uska's olive-green body. She was no longer covered by a tarp but was unharmed. He felt the reassuring curve of steel under his palm. Uska weighed as much as three hefty cows, so there was no way of moving her now that the horses had been spooked by the bombing. They had to locate the ammo and be ready for another attack.

Parov, a forward observer, ran up to them and said, "We've lost communication with HQ. They've sent a runner to rewire, but for now, there are no official orders. Except not to fire."

"Not to fire?" Ivan yelled, his cheeks reddening as if he was going to tear poor Parov's head off. "Great! We'll just get a tan while those bastards reload. We're at war, for fuck's sake!"

"You don't know that," Yefim said, his hand on Ivan's twitching shoulder. "Parov, go get us some ammo in case they let us return fire."

While Parov ran off in search of ammo, Yefim and Ivan found a shovel and began to hack out a trench next to Uska's right wheel. They piled parapets around the gun and deepened the ramp.

"This can't be war," Yefim said. "The Fritzes aren't that dumb."

"But why would they ambush us unless they were damn sure they could finish us off?" replied Ivan, his face red and sweaty from the digging in the morning sun.

"Well, that's exactly it. If this was the big showdown, we'd know about it."

"By 'we,' you mean Stalin?"

"Sure," said Yefim.

"Maybe he does know about it."

"Then why wouldn't he have warned us?"

He didn't like what Ivan was implying. Stalin couldn't have known about the attack and left them without orders like sitting ducks. He could be harsh but only with those who wanted to harm the country, not the Red Army. The army was everything to him. He had just called the artillery "the god of modern warfare." He'd never abandon them—to Hitler no less.

Parov reappeared and said the closest crate of shells was buried in the explosion, but a cart with more ammo was supposedly on its way.

"Let's hope it gets here soon," Yefim said.

"Either way, can't shoot without orders," Parov replied.

"They'll goddamn eat us alive before we get either," Ivan snapped.

Ivan was right. Even if this was just a provocation to lure the USSR into declaring war on Germany, he hated the idea of sitting and waiting like scared little rabbits. He wanted to load Uska and return fire.

He heard a buzz of planes coming from the Soviet side.

"Finally!" Parov cried out, waving at the three ground-attack planes high in the morning sky. "Show those fascist dirtbags where the crayfish winter!"

Ivan stopped him. "Look at the crosses. Those aren't ours."

"What the fuck were they doing on our territory?" Yefim asked, a cold, leaden weight in his chest.

"What have I been telling you," said Ivan.

They stood and watched as Hitler's planes receded toward the German border. Yefim suddenly felt as though Ukraine weren't hundreds of kilometers away but right here, just behind this Lithuanian forest, with its straw-roofed hut where Basya lived with their aging parents. She had probably just gotten up and was braiding her long black hair before heading out to Kateryna's two houses down to buy fresh milk from her cow. Were German planes flying over her too?

By the time the ammo cart appeared, it was almost noon. He and Ivan were helping the two carriers unload the crates when they were called to line up with what remained of their regiment.

Major Fedorenko told them that the telephone wire had been fixed and they had finally heard from Moscow. People's Commissar Vyacheslav Molotov announced that Germany had declared war on the USSR and that fighting was happening all along the border, from the Barents Sea to the Black Sea. And it wasn't just the border. The Germans had bombed Kyiv.

Yefim didn't hear what else the major said. He saw his mother's eyes, bleak with disappointment, the way she looked at him during the Great Famine when he ate a piece of bread crust that she'd meant for all of them to share. He was supposed to be this powerful artilleryman, a god of war sent here to protect his country. Instead, he was still little Fimochka, a useless son who only talked about fun and glory but didn't see war when it was staring him in the face.

"Things are developing faster than anticipated," Fedorenko was saying. "German tanks have broken through the border and are on their way here. Our job is to stop them with what we've got left."

No, he wasn't useless. He still had a chance to prove himself.

On their way back to Uska, Ivan said, "What the fuck did they think this was, morning exercises?"

"We've lost so much time," Yefim said, still baffled that Stalin let them get ambushed and then didn't let them respond when they could have had an advantage. "Why didn't I see it?"

"Because you love to believe that our high command can do no wrong."

The ammo carriers were gathering to head back when incoming shells began to scream into the camp. Yefim and Ivan dove into their foxhole. Around them, shells raised plumes of dust and soil. Out of a corner of his eye, Yefim saw one of the ammo carriers torn to shreds.

In the foxhole, he covered his head. He tried to focus on his sense of duty, on what must be done, but everything raged above him and thoughts refused to form. His body shook uncontrollably. He shut his eyes and out of the howling darkness saw Basya running out of the house barefoot to greet Mikhail, who'd returned from the army. Mikhail had lifted her on his shoulder and Basya's feet, dusty from the village road, had dangled above Yefim's head.

Yefim's shaking turned more and more violent until he was filled with fury: at Hitler for wanting a land that wasn't his to want, at himself for not being as brave as he'd thought. He turned to Ivan and shouted into his ear: "We've got to stop pissing our pants and give them hell!"

They crawled back out. Yefim grabbed onto Uska, peering through the sights and trying to find something big and specific, something to absorb his fury. But all was chaos. There was too much smoke and flying debris. While he manned the gunsight, Ivan took out a shell, cradling it like an infant.

Finally, good old Uska found her target: a brand-new, dark gray German tank rolled right into her sight.

"Load!" Yefim shouted.

Ivan chambered the shell. The gun lock clanked. Uska fired.

It felt good to finally be doing something. To be one with this machine, to feel the artillery's power course through him. The air rumbled with the roar of blasts and the gnashing of metal. Ivan loaded the next round. Yefim shot again, and again.

By early evening, Uska's barrel was red-hot. Yefim could see her paint peeling and bubbling. Ivan had burned himself on the oil that over-heated in the recoil mechanism and oozed through the screws. Yefim was afraid she was about to burst.

They had shot an armored vehicle, maybe something else; he wasn't sure. On their end, their position looked like a scorched, uninhabited planet covered in craters and mounds. Nothing was left of the camp. The ammo carriers were both dead. Parov had been wounded in the leg. Somehow, he and Ivan were still in one piece, but their arms trembled, their backs ached, and their faces were covered in soot and sweat. Yefim's throat was so parched, he'd stopped swallowing.

As the sun began to roll behind the trees, the Germans slowed their barrage. When it stopped and they could finally leave the foxhole behind Uska, they learned the grim news: most of their men were dead and the telephone wire had been botched. Once again, they were on their own.

That night, a strange hush gripped them. They talked little and only in whispers.

"I haven't thanked you yet," Yefim said as he lay next to Ivan, the smell of smoke and dirt etched in his nostrils. "I'd be a charred corpse if you haven't pulled me out. I owe you."

Ivan stayed quiet for a while, then said, "I know how you'll pay me back."

"How?"

"Once we get out of here, you'll write your sister about your infinitely selfless and fearless friend Ivan."

Yefim smiled, trying to imagine Ivan as his brother-in-law.

"Fair enough. Just don't let it get to your head, Fearless Friend."

The next morning the Germans attacked at the first inkling of light. He and Ivan had only one crate of ammunition left and within two hours it was half empty.

They were ordered to spare the ammo as there was little chance of a new delivery. They tried, but the Fritzes had clearly been told to spare nothing because the rain of shells seemed inexhaustible. By noon the enemy was no longer firing from the west, where the border was, but from the south. They were being surrounded.

With his hands sore, his eyes glazed, and his shirt soaked from sweat, Yefim held on to Uska, wondering how much more she could take before she burst.

"What the hell are you two still doing here?" he heard. It was Lieutenant Komarov crawling toward them.

"We're almost out of ammo!" Ivan yelled.

Komarov ducked behind Uska.

"You and everyone else," he said, and handed them two rifles. "Here, take these. Our orders are to—"

A deep, resonant blast cut off the rest of his words and all three of them dropped into the foxhole, covering their ears. It detonated close to them on the right, sending a tall black tornado toward the sky.

"We're surrounded!" Komarov shouted. "Lithuanians have declared independence. I heard they are arresting the Jews in town. We're going to try to get out of here in small groups before it's too late. You two follow me."

Yefim watched Ivan crawl after Komarov but couldn't get himself to move. He thought of Eva from the dance, rounded up in the town square, and then pictured Uska abandoned here as he fled, an artilleryman without artillery, a useless son.

"Leave the fucking gun!" Komarov yelled, pulling him by the collar. "That's an order, Shulman!"

Yefim tore himself away and ran. There was a bang that he knew was bad news. He ducked. Then he was speeding through the air until he thumped back on the ground and was covered with earth.

So this is what it's like to die, he thought, his eyes shut, his tired body still.

Then there was nothing.

And then something. A piercing fear that if the Germans found him alive, they'd make him a prisoner. Prisoners were quitters, cowards; everyone knew that. Better to die here on the battlefield.

The fear blocked his throat, not letting him breathe. He sat up, choking and spitting out dirt. He tried wiping his eyes but felt an immense throbbing in his right hand. He wiped his eyes with his left hand, lifted his right and saw that his thumb and index finger were two shortened stumps oozing blood around the whites of his bones. The upper phalanges were no longer there.

Yefim felt light-headed but couldn't look away. He stared at the two fingers—his trigger fingers. The meaning refused to sink in.

Chapter 3

Nina turned onto her stomach and carefully put her glasses on the grass. After a hot day of lugging, sorting, and packing core samples, the shade of the willow tree and the cooling smell of the river were a godsend. The willow leaves moved lazily in the breeze, and shadows leapt across the pages of *The Lady with the Dog*. It wasn't smart to torture herself by reading about love, but what else was an unmarriable girl to do on a lazy afternoon?

As soon as they arrived at this dig site in the Donbas three days ago, her friend Ludmila complained that there were only two males here out of a dozen grad students: George and that undergrad collector. But Nina hardly noticed. It was no different than their school. When she got into the Kyiv State University's school of geology—the only place that would accept her, with her stain of living under occupation— she wasn't surprised they had no male students. It was 1944 and all the boys were at war. Once the war ended, however, she had hoped more men would return and she could find someone who wanted to start a family as much as she did. Instead, her classes continued being filled mostly with girls—girls who were mostly prettier than her.

If Mama were still alive, she'd tell her to gain at least five kilos to get some curves on that scrawny body of hers. Or maybe she'd alter one of her old dresses to fit Nina. Not that it'd make any difference. Mama had always called her a "blue stocking," worrying that plain, nearsighted Nina would probably never marry since she had more interest in books than in boys. That was her biggest concern up until she died. It didn't even help when her older sister, Vera, who was fatter, prettier, and married, had defended her, saying Nina's reading would get her into a good university where she'd easily find a quality husband. Anyway, Vera had been wrong. At twenty-five, Nina was still a virgin, eons closer to a PhD than to having babies. Especially if she continued pining for the Professor.

The Professor was different from guys her age. He spoke in the deliberate, literary Ukrainian of her parents, with none of that proletarian jargon. He wasn't in a hurry to gallop into the happy, Communist future. In fact, as the head of the paleontology department, he wasn't interested in the future at all. She supposed that's what she liked most about him: he was unlike the young geologists who were eager to help build the country, expand its natural resources, and bring the riches of the land to the masses. A noble goal, sure, but one she couldn't get herself to care about. Left without parents or her home, it was the past she longed for. In that way, they were alike, the Professor and her.

Nina swatted a fly from her arm and stretched her calves. Her muscles ached pleasantly after the morning of collecting fossil samples. Her dissertation on corals was going to work; she was sure of it now. Papa would have been so proud of his little Ninochka. She wished she could tell him how the Professor was convinced that with her good memory, speed-reading skills, and knack for organization, she'd make an excellent researcher and maybe even professor. How it was he who had fought for her acceptance into the graduate program despite her tarnished record.

She wished she was with him on his Crimean vacation instead of his wife and daughter. If only she could tell someone, but she couldn't imagine uttering his name to Ludmila, who lay next to her under the willow.

Nina tried to reengage her attention on Chekhov, but in the heat her stubborn mind wandered back to last summer when she was helping the Professor lug a heavy backpack full of rocks, sharing meager provisions, running from the rainstorm, even surviving an embarrassing bout of diarrhea together. He never touched her during those weeks, not in the way she wanted him to. But that one evening when they lay down on a grassy hill to rest and he put his arm under her head, the energy between them was electric. They watched the sunset in silence and when they got up to continue their long walk, she was in love.

"That was quite a performance last night," someone said, and Nina turned to see the undergrad collector sit down not far from her on the grass.

Last night, at the campfire, she had recited *Eugene Onegin* in full. She hadn't seen the collector there. She had taken off her glasses and knelt in front of the fire, transporting a bunch of forever hungry Soviet students who'd seen little other than collectivization and war to the heyday of Pushkin's St. Petersburg, long before it became Leningrad, longer still before the Germans starved the soul out of the northern city. Too bad the Professor hadn't seen her. She probably looked almost beautiful with her face lit up by orange flames.

"*Dyakuyu*," said Nina, grateful for the compliment. She was a touch embarrassed in front of Ludmila, who pretended to continue reading even though she was clearly listening. "I didn't realize you were there too."

"I'm not much of a poetry buff, but I think I came a few stanzas in," he said as she tried to remember if his name was Yegor or Yefim. "How long did it take you to memorize it?"

"I've read it so many times that it just lives in here," she said, tapping the side of her head, where a pin held up her bob.

She put down her book and sat up. Yegor/Yefim looked a few years older than her. His tan face was hardened, his strong chin covered in black stubble. He wore dark brown pants and a white polo shirt that, though loose, revealed his taut biceps. He looked tough, like a miner or someone who could work all day and sleep on the floor. She recalled the Professor saying something about sending the best collector at the institute, Shulman, to the Donbas dig.

"You remember other things by heart?" he asked.

He wrapped his muscled arms around his knees.

"Sure. More Pushkin, some Lermontov, Shevchenko. I used to know Heine, too, but I've made myself forget it. Can't stand hearing German. *Onegin* is my favorite. My father used to read it to me before . . ."

And then she was flooded with the smell of Papa's beard as he read Pushkin to her for the millionth time while she put her head on his shoulder, closing her eyes so as not to cheat and look at the words on the page.

She tried to hold off the tears welling behind her eyes and tickling her nose. She wasn't going to cry in front of this Shulman. He'd think her ridiculous. After all, everyone had lost someone in the war.

Ludmila came to her rescue. "Ninochka, let's go for another swim?"

"No, I'm all right," she said, her voice firmer. "You go if you want."

When Ludmila left, Yefim—she was pretty sure that was his name as Yegor would have been too folksy of a name for a Jew—edged closer to her side.

"I'm sorry," Nina said, quickly wiping a tear from under her glasses. "Both my parents passed away before the war, so I get upset when I remember."

"You all alone, then?"

"I have an older sister, Vera," Nina said, not wanting to mention her older brother, whose arrest in '37 broke Mama's heart and led to Papa's illness. "Are your folks still alive?"

"Just my mother," he said, looking toward the river where Ludmila and a few others were splashing. "Father died in the ghetto."

She was surprised that he said it like that, so coldly but also so frankly, considering the awful campaign against "rootless cosmopolitans," as Jews were increasingly called. She liked that he trusted her with something this delicate. They fell silent for a moment, not looking at each other. It was a strangely intimate conversation. She usually didn't ask

Jews or vets—and she guessed he was both—about the war, but since they'd somehow ended up in this territory, she thought they might as well get it out of the way.

"When were you drafted?" she asked.

"Summer of 1940," he said, a wrinkle forming on his high forehead. "We were stationed in Lithuania when the Germans attacked, close to the border. That's where I lost these."

He extended his right hand and she saw that his thumb and forefinger were stubs. She felt bad that she hadn't noticed.

"How did you fight after that?"

"Had to pretend I was a lefty. Took a few weeks, but then I got used to it."

"Well, if that's the worst of it, I'd say you're pretty lucky."

She liked how honest he was. Most vets she had come across didn't talk about the war with such ease. Usually, they avoided any mention of it and she didn't dare ask because in front of them she often felt ashamed that she had lived under the Germans. With Yefim, on the other hand, the thorny subject didn't seem painful or sacred, just a matter of fact.

"Lucky, yes," he replied. "Even got to Berlin."

She stared at him, wondering if he was pulling her leg. She'd never met anyone who had served through the entire war, from its first day to its last, and survived to talk about it. He must have been one lucky son of a gun. A real war hero. Her sister would tell her he was the perfect husband material, though Nina felt ridiculous for even thinking it.

She was about to ask him more when Ludmila ran up, spraying cold water on Nina's sun-warmed body from a bucket that George was lugging. Nina squirmed, raising her hands in protest as they continued splashing her. With a jump, Yefim yanked the bucket out of George's hands and, lifting it above him and Ludmila, poured the remaining water over their heads. At first, they gasped like two fishes. Then, as soon as they wiped the water from their eyes, they burst out laughing from the unexpected turn of events. Nina thought it strange and wonderful that they weren't mad at Yefim.

As Ludmila and Nina squeezed the water out of their black shorts, George extended his hand to Yefim's, saying, "Serves me right to go against our collector." With his glasses sliding off his lightly freckled nose, George looked like a goofy high school kid next to Yefim.

"I saw you loading all our core samples onto the truck like they were feathers," George continued. "Those boxes must be at least 150 kilos each."

"No, 120 tops," Yefim said, looking embarrassed but pleased.

He had a great wide smile, with a dimple on the right cheek and a golden tooth that shone in the sun. Smiling, he looked like a movie star.

"No wonder you made it to Berlin," said Nina, wanting to show him off.

"Oh my! We've got ourselves a war hero?" Ludmila chirped and gave Nina a sly, approving look.

She noticed Yefim wince. His jaw tensed and his eyes hardened.

"No, no, I'm no hero," he objected, and she saw something in him shut down. It occurred to Nina that perhaps he didn't talk about the war to everyone and had only told her in confidence, and here she was running her big mouth about it. She felt bad for putting him on the spot like that. She didn't want him thinking he couldn't trust her.

"You must have a lot of medals, then!" Ludmila said.

"They were stolen," he said flatly, and looked out at the river in a clear sign he didn't want to talk about it, but Nina's friends pressed on.

"Stolen? How?" they asked.

"On the train back home," he said with an exaggerated shrug as if he wanted to show them that he didn't care for any medals.

"Some people have no respect for our veterans," George said.

They were all silent for a moment while Nina tried to think of a way to get out of this conversation.

She picked up her towel and said, "Say, can you really lift 120 kilos?"

"Only when poor tired grad students leave me no choice," said Yefim with a wink.

Over the next few days the four of them became friends. They had begun to call Yefim "Hercules." Though he was the only undergrad, at twenty-eight he was the oldest among them. Soon they took a truck down to Stany, a village near another well where they were hoping to find more samples. Nina was hunting for fossil corals for her dissertation, while Ludmila and George were looking for Devonian flora.

At Stany, a widowed schoolteacher named Marusya took them in. She was in her midthirties, rosy-cheeked, with an easy laugh. Her husband had died at the front so, she said, she was glad to have the company of young, educated people from Kyiv, and they were glad to stay in her warm, tidy house after three weeks in tents.

One day, Yefim found Marusya's husband's old fishing rods and invited Nina to the river. "Let's see what this city girl is made of," he said.

She had learned to fish during her first summer dig as an undergraduate back in '45. Their group had been all girls, as most guys hadn't yet returned from the front. It was a very hungry summer: their diet consisted only of young cucumbers they stole from the nearby kolkhoz and bread received on ration cards. But their camp was on the Dnipro River, so soon they figured out how to fish and made themselves fatty fish soups that kept them going through the summer.

As she and Yefim walked to the river in the quiet hours of the early morning, Nina decided not to tell him any of this.

At the river, the water was warm, and a thin layer of mist covered the surface. On the opposite bank, frogs were starting their morning song among the cattails. River eels snaked through the gentle water, and occasionally a carp poked up and dove back in with a splash. Yefim had dug up a couple of worms, but when he handed one to Nina to hook, she squirmed and he said, "A true lady, are we?" She liked that he was this strong, simple man from a village who'd done brutal, manly things and had a damaged hand to prove it. Next to him, she could be a damsel in distress, a spoiled little woman from the city, something that she—an orphan who'd had to feed herself through the war—never got a chance to be. She let him hook the worm and hand her the pole.

They sat on an old, faded dock, staring at the water, and she liked that here her love for the Professor seemed like something she'd read in a Chekhov story.

Yefim caught two roach and a small carp, while she caught nothing. When they brought the metal bucket with the fish back to Marusya, she asked which of them were Nina's and he lied: "All of them. I didn't catch a thing. You should have seen her!"

Marusya laughed and said, "Beginner's luck."

Nina was surprised at this show he had put on, yet she enjoyed being in on his little white lie. She'd never seen anyone make things up with such charm. It made her wish she were a better liar herself because in their country it was usually honesty that got you into trouble.

Over the next weeks she found that she and Yefim worked well together. They were both willing to stay the extra hour despite the heat or walk the extra kilometer toward the farther side of the quarry.

They'd walk there early in the morning before the steppe became sweltering. Above them, skylarks swooped through the air, singing under a bleached blue sky. The quarry was almost five kilometers away, along a dirt road that glistened with limestone. To reach it, they wound past Lovers' Hill, which Marusya told them was where local couples traditionally ascended when they got engaged, past the kolkhoz sunflower field, across a dry creek bed overgrown with rose hip thickets and young hazel that by mid-July had only one small stream, and through the untamed steppe that struck Nina with the intoxicating smell of thyme and sagebrush, its endless green horizon of flowering fields dotted by balls of tumbleweed.

On the way, they talked about their childhoods, friends, the war. Nina told him that her first friend was a black chicken that lived in their yard, and it turned out he also had had a pet chicken, named Bek-Bek, and, like hers, it had met an unfortunate end. His other close friend was Ivan, who had served with him. He said that he'd made buddies in Kyiv, but no one as close as Ivan. She agreed there was something special about a wartime friendship. She missed her small crew of friends from those years. They were her life after her parents died: Galina, who worked at the chicken plant with her, and Vasya Varavva, who helped out the partisans. After they were liberated, Galina moved east to Vladivostok, where her uncle was based, and Vasya, poor, brave Vasya, joined the army in early '45 and was killed in Berlin.

At first, she felt shy talking about life under occupation to someone who had survived four years on the battlefield, but he seemed genuinely curious about her experience. She got a feeling he wanted to know what he had missed.

"Before they entered the city, our German teacher, who was a Jew, kept telling us, 'Finally, the cultured people are arriving. Just look at their writers, musicians, philosophers. They are an honest nation; no one steals there. It can't be true that they kill Jews,' " Nina told Yefim as they walked to the quarry one morning. "And he wasn't the only one who talked like that. Many people Mama knew were saying that too. So it was a shock when the Germans came. They built themselves toilets and used them with doors open in front of everyone; they farted in public, often while eating; they laughed at our clothes and shoes; they harassed women. The 'cultured people' turned out to be smug brutes."

"Soldiers have to be assholes when they are sent to occupy."

"You don't think that's how all Germans are? I mean, they were from different classes, different towns. It's not like they were bred to be soldiers."

"Yes, but they were at war. And that changes you. You think Russians acted any better in Germany?"

"I'm sure they didn't go around harassing civilians."

"Of course not. They were angels."

She wanted to ask, *And you?* but decided against it. Not knowing was probably best, just as it was better that he didn't know about all those times she got groped by her German boss or the time a Nazi officer who brought bread to their building suggestively pulled out a condom. As Vera once told her, a woman should have her secrets.

Instead, she told him how she almost became an *Ostarbeiter*, one of the millions of forced laborers that Germans shipped from the Soviet Union to help support the Reich.

"I thought I was finished when they called me to the *Ostarbeiter* office. I'd heard they throw you straight onto the train and ship you off with no goodbyes. I felt like I was walking to a guillotine. My only hope was my mother's chest X-ray. She died from tuberculosis. When I came in with this X-ray, the woman working there turned out to be an old friend of my parents. She recognized me and told the German doctor who was inspecting everyone that I'd had tuberculosis since I was a kid. So he shooed me away. Imagine my luck! When I got back home, my friends and neighbors greeted me as if I'd risen from the dead. It happened only a month before Kyiv was liberated. I still shudder when I think that I could have ended up in some German labor camp. Those ostarbeiter girls sure had trouble when they came back home."

She thought he'd marvel at her good luck, but he was quiet. He looked off somewhere, a crease forming on his forehead. She wondered if she'd said something wrong, so she asked, "Have you had anyone save you when you least expected?" and then realized that was probably a dumb thing to ask a soldier.

But he said, "I was saved by cheese once," and, with his dimpled smile, told her a funny story of finding a dairy farm when he was on the run from the Germans.

She liked the way his brown eyes twinkled as he talked. As the weeks in Stany passed, Nina was getting used to having Yefim by her side, and anytime he took off his shirt in the hot sun, something fluttered inside her while she, embarrassed at the fluttering, tried not to stare.

She liked that he was a quick study. She showed him which coral varieties she was after and he replied, "Got it, boss!" Still, she was surprised when he kept bringing her the right ones, never once making a mistake. He had a sharp eye, something that had probably come in handy during the war.

Once they gathered a big enough pile of fossils, she identified them and they prepared them by chipping off the sediment. She didn't trust Yefim with the chisel: the strike had to be precise in order not to damage the fossils. She'd seen the Professor do it many times but she was never that great at it. Still, she kept trying so they didn't have to drag the unnecessary weight to the village. She told Yefim his job was to mark and wrap the specimens, and carefully load them into the backpack.

But after she struck her finger for the nth time, Yefim grabbed the chisel and demanded she let him try. Unlike her, he quickly mastered the skill, and, watching him work the chisel, she told herself, *Here is a man who'll rescue me.*

Every day she wondered when he was going to make a move, but though during the hot afternoons they napped near each other in the shade behind the rocks, the distance between their bodies never shrank.

One day, on the walk back, Yefim told her about a girl he loved.

"She had these gold-speckled eyes that looked like everything surprised her. Kind of like a child. I fell for her, hard."

Now she knew why he hadn't tried anything with her. Apparently, he saw her as nothing but a pal, someone you talk to about other girls. What a fool she'd been to think something might happen between them. Still, in a voice that came out too cheery, she felt obligated to ask, "Where is she?"

"I don't know. We got separated during the war and I never saw her again."

They walked for a bit in silence. Nina tried to rid herself of the illusion she had built. She felt like a fool for thinking Yefim could want her. Of course he wasn't going to fall for her. There were so many girls eager to marry; why would he ever choose her? As the sun set behind the forest, Nina grew angrier and, having nothing to lose, told him about her crush on the Professor.

"He is so passionate about paleontology that he made me fall in love with it. He also has a great sense of humor and—"

"Isn't he married?" Yefim interrupted, and she immediately regretted telling him anything.

"Well . . . ," she said, swallowing hard, not looking at him.

Yefim stopped in the middle of the road. His eyes turned dark and flat like pebbles at the bottom of a river.

"Passionate about paleontology—oh please! He walks around the school as if he is better than the rest of us. But really he is just an old scumbag who saw a girl with no parents and conveniently forgot all about his wife. And you? I would have never thought you the kind of girl to fall for that."

"I'm not, I didn't," she objected. "He believed in me. I wouldn't be in the grad program if he didn't stand up for me."

"Clever way to make you feel like you owe him."

"I don't feel like I owe him—not in *that* way."

"Are you really that naive?" Yefim said, and kicked a rock, breaking it in half and raising a plume of dust. "Nothing I hate more than two-faced men."

It was their first fight. That evening they avoided each other, which wasn't easy in Marusya's small house. Nina was confused by Yefim's unexpected fit. She shouldn't have blabbed, but then he shouldn't have gone on about the golden-eyed girl. Lying on the mattress in her corner of the hut, she thought of the Professor, of how safe she had felt next to him. Maybe she should wait for him after all. Maybe one day he would leave his family to marry her and she would bear his children. Nina cried quietly in her corner.

No, Mama was right. No man would ever want her.

The next day Yefim went off to help Ludmila and George, and Nina, dragging her feet after a restless night, went to the quarry by herself. She stayed for only half a day and then returned to the village with a headache. That evening her friends came back from the field cheerful and Yefim joked loudly, while she just wanted to go to bed. After dinner, she came outside to the garden in the back of the house to wash up in the outdoor basin. It was a moonless night and she waited for her eyes to adjust to the darkness. The air was nice and cool on her face.

"Nina."

Yefim emerged out of the shadows. He gently took her by the hand and led her toward the dark open fields. She followed him, stepping lightly, confused and afraid to make too much noise in case she spoiled whatever had made him come to her. The grass grazed her legs as they walked under the inky sky. Here the sounds of the village grew fainter and she could hear the night, its crickets and frogs awake in the cooling steppe. He stopped, turned to her, and carefully took off her glasses.

The stars and fields grew blurrier. His face drew near. Her breath quieted down as he stroked her cheeks. His fingers were full of life. She waited for him to say something. Instead, he pulled her toward him and kissed her.

They didn't mention the girl or the Professor again. For the next two weeks, when they lay down in the quarry to rest, she rested her head on his chest, inhaling his musk. She wished Mama could see her little Nina working toward a dissertation with a brave, strong veteran by her side.

At one point, a small stray dog started tagging along with them down the road. Every day it would follow them farther and farther, until it ended up spending the day with them at the quarry. Yefim gave it part of his food, even though Nina didn't think he should.

One afternoon, when they were chiseling a core sample, a loose rock rolled off a cliff and they heard the dog's yelp ricocheting across the well. Yefim dropped the chisel and ran toward the sound. She followed him. The dog was curled up on the ground, whimpering. Blood was pooled between the claws of its back paw. Yefim picked up the dog and, cradling it in his arms, rushed back to the village.

By the time Nina made it back to the hut, the dog was resting on Yefim's lap, washed and bandaged. As he patted its small head, he looked up at her and said, "Shhhh. He's sleeping."

She didn't care one bit for the stupid dog, but she couldn't help noticing how gentle Yefim was, how paternal. She walked outside to wash her dusty face in the basin when Marusya came up to her.

"If he treats a dog like that, I bet he'll treat a wife even better," she whispered, and Nina knew it was true.

A few days after that, in early August, as they were lying down on the cool rocks after lunch, he said, "You know what I was thinking? We should get married and start our own family."

Nina shut her eyes, afraid to move while her heart beat a million beats a second. *Our own family.* The one thing she so wanted, that the Professor could never give her. His words blended in with the warm, fragrant air and she knew her dream was going to come true. She was going to be a wife and a mother. Nina turned to him, tears clouding her eyes, and smiled.

That same evening, along with Marusya, Ludmila, and George, they caught a bucket of crayfish, opened a bottle of local rowan liquor, and had a small feast in celebration of their commitment. Afterward, tipsy and happy, they followed Stany's tradition and climbed to the top of Lovers' Hill to seal their new union, knowing that that summer was one of the happiest of both of their lives.

Chapter 4

_____

August 1941
Latvian SSR

For the past few weeks Yefim and his seven-man platoon walked only at night. They were hiding from two enemies: the advancing German army and the Lithuanian partisans hunting down stranded Soviet soldiers. Lieutenant Komarov's plan was to catch up with the Red Army corps, but by August their progress had slowed and there was still no sign of their troops. It was clear that if they didn't want to end up rotting in enemy prison camps, they needed to hurry east.

That morning they rose before dawn to try to make it across a large pine forest to the Latvian border by nightfall. In Latvia, they hoped to find food and information about the whereabouts of their troops. For breakfast, they had a handful of blackberries and the last baked potato, which they carefully split into seven slivers.

"This Baltic diet is a luxury compared to '32," Yefim said, savoring every bite.

"*Da*," Ivan agreed. "In those days one could be killed for a potato."

"Every night, I dream of cheese," sighed Anton Lisin, the only survivor from the dozen men who were supposed to finish their service and go home. Yefim noticed that lately Lisin no longer talked about his plans for Moscow or geology—only about cheese.

A couple of weeks ago, they had come across a small abandoned dairy plant with a neat row of cheeses, yellow and smooth, just waiting to be plucked. Yefim still smiled every time he remembered how Ivan tried to stuff two heads of cheese into his coat and one would always fall back out, plopping like a big rubber ball and rolling away from him as he tried to chase it. Yefim had told him to try out for the circus after the war.

"There will be cheese once we're in Latvia," Komarov promised, and Yefim pretended to believe him. "Let's pack up and head out."

They set off through the colonnade of pine forest, foggy and hushed in the morning mist. The pine needles made walking so soft that Yefim kept wanting to take his boots off and lie down, lulled by the dizzying smell of tree sap. He'd been more and more tired in the past days, his mind often slipping into a not unpleasant fogginess.

Though no one said it out loud, it was clear that he had the worst injury of them all. Lisin walked with a slight limp after he busted his knee on the first day; Gurov had a burn mark on his arm; and Lieutenant Komarov got a cut from a small piece of shrapnel on his left cheekbone, which had all but healed by now. Everyone else, Ivan included, had nothing of significance. That was why they always had Yefim walk in the middle. And though he didn't object, this special treatment unnerved him. He couldn't help thinking they did it out of preemptive guilt, as if they knew he wouldn't last long and wanted to assure themselves they'd done all they could before he was killed.

He'd need to prove them wrong. After all, his left hand was already much better with the rifle. What he really needed was to be back with the artillery. Behind Uska was certainly a better place to be than in this forest, running from the Germans and having nightmares about being led away, his hands raised, a shame burning through him like a fever.

Meanwhile, he was grateful that at least he got to walk behind Dmitry Gurov, the elder of their group, who'd fought in the last big war and told many stories. It reminded Yefim of trotting behind Mikhail back when he was a head shorter than his big brother, feeling like no one in the village would dare mess with him.

A decade older, Mikhail had been more of a father to him than their father had. He always found a way to motivate, to make Yefim feel seen. Now Mikhail had surely been drafted, having to leave behind his post as chief accountant along with his beloved four-year-old, Lyubochka, the only grandchild in the family. Yefim missed Mikhail's cheerful, booming voice. He would have probably made a better commander than Komarov, though Yefim supposed they'd made it this far, so Komarov wasn't the worst, either.

"Do these Lithuanian fuckers really think they'll be better off with the fascists?" asked Sergey Kosar, a Ukrainian from the Donbas, where his dad was a miner.

"The problem is that one year under our hammer and sickle isn't going to change the fact that the Balts are actually more culturally similar to Germans than to us," said Lisin.

"Bullshit," said Gurov. "In '14, we had a Latvian in our unit. Crazy Kristaps, we called him. He hated the Germans as much as anyone. Knew all sorts of jokes about them. I remember watching him sprint across a field, yelling, '*Fuck the Germans!*' when a mine got him right in the middle of the word, so all we heard was, '*Fuck the Ger—*' "

They all fell silent.

"To Crazy Kristaps," said Gurov, raising his canteen.

The fog had dissipated into a sunny morning. The smell of pine resin pierced the warming air. It was going to be another hot day.

"I wonder how the fascists rank the Balts," Kosar said. "Don't they have a system of who is highest on the totem pole?"

"All I know is that they're higher than the Yids, but then again, who isn't, right, Shulman?" said Lieutenant Komarov with a snigger, and turned to wink at Yefim.

He hated when the lieutenant got like this. Yet it was hard to deny that he was indeed lowest on the totem pole, no matter how you looked at it. He wasn't just a Jew. He was a Jew with a busted shooting hand.

"If the Fritzes catch us, the totem pole won't mean shit," Yefim said, wiping the sweat off his forehead. "We'll all be screwed."

"And if we ever make it back home, we'd still be screwed," murmured Ivan from behind.

"You really think we'd get punished for getting captured? It's not like we're running toward the Germans."

He said it loud enough for Komarov to hear, hoping the lieutenant would reassure them that Stalin wouldn't hold whatever happened to them against them. Instead, Komarov barked, "I don't want to hear any goddamn talk of getting captured, all right? Latvia is not too far now."

"Sir, yes, sir!" Yefim said. "I look forward to finding our army and kicking some German ass!"

"Attaboy."

Yefim could hear Ivan muttering something to himself in the back, but there was no point in arguing. They weren't going to get caught. They couldn't afford it.

The August sun was beating down hard now. His water was almost gone, and the back of his head itched from the sweat tickling his scalp. His hair had gotten too long. He'd need to find a way to cut it, even if it was with a knife.

"This might be the hottest day we've had yet," he said, reaching to scratch his head.

Rifle shots cracked through the forest.

"Partisans!" Komarov cried.

There was a thump and Yefim's face was sprayed by something warm. Gurov's body fell to the side, a hole in his head. Yefim ducked as shots echoed through the forest. He slid toward the nearest tree.

"Four of them!" Komarov yelled from somewhere on the left as bullets whistled past.

Yefim crouched behind the trunk of a thin pine, trying to flatten himself by squeezing his shoulder blades. His face was covered in Gurov's blood. It was pungent and viscous.

Out of a corner of his right eye he saw Ivan. Then a bullet hit the trunk next to him, sending wood chips flying in all directions, and Komarov screamed, "*Davai!* Fire! Fire!"

Yefim's bandaged hand shook as he tried to hold the long rifle stock in place. Ivan was already shooting, he could hear, while he was still fumbling with the gun with his useless hand. He heard Lisin yell, "Got one!"

"They are running away!" Komarov shouted. "Let's get them! Go, go, go!"

Yefim stepped from behind his cover and ran. Fifty meters ahead, a tall Lithuanian sprinted away. His silhouette stood out in a clearing in the trees. Yefim fired. Didn't have time to aim. Just fired in the man's general direction. The Lithuanian continued leaping forward. Then he stumbled and fell, holding his thigh.

Yefim reloaded and ran toward him. The partisan moaned on the ground, a stain spreading on the pine needles beneath him. He was trying to drag his body toward the Soviet-made rifle that he'd dropped. Yefim kicked it out of reach.

How different it was to shoot a bullet into real human flesh. Nothing like firing Uska at a tank. Nothing like it at all. Yefim felt a touch of guilt looking at this blue-eyed man with dirt smudged on his pale cheeks and a white armband on his right sleeve.

The partisan looked up at Yefim and spat out, "You Russian shit!"

Yefim's guilt disappeared. Instead, he felt annoyed and defensive. After all, he wasn't the one ambushing stranded soldiers in a forest. He wanted to tell him that he wasn't even Russian. He was Soviet, which superseded any ethnicity, unlike in Germany, which this fool was risking his life to defend.

Behind him, he heard Lisin's voice, "What are you babysitting him for? Shoot the fucker!"

"Lieutenant might want to question him first," Yefim said, surprised at how bloodthirsty Lisin turned out to be. Whatever happened to his dream of studying geology?

The partisan muttered something in Lithuanian as his face grew paler.

When Lieutenant Komarov reached them, he pointed the rifle at the lying man and asked, "How many others in this forest?"

The man didn't reply. His eyes were half closed and his nostrils inhaled desperately as sweat pooled above his pale lips.

"He probably doesn't speak much Russian," Yefim said.

"This should teach him," said the lieutenant as he pressed the nose of his rifle into the man's leg wound. "Where is the Red Army, you scum?"

The man groaned. He looked like he was about to pass out.

"He is useless," offered Lisin. "Let's shoot him."

"He'll bleed out soon enough," Komarov said. "I'm much more concerned about that one bastard who got away. We need to get out of here fast. Where is Ivan?"

Yefim winced. He hadn't seen Ivan since the shoot-out. He ran back to where he last saw his friend, past Gurov's body.

"Ivan!" His voice echoed through the pines, sounding more panicked than he'd realized.

There was a whistle from behind a tree. He found Ivan sitting on the ground against a tree trunk, holding his left shoulder and beaming like a madman. Yefim lunged toward him.

"Don't tell me you thought your fearless friend was kaput."

"Of course not," Yefim lied, leaning to inspect the bloody patch on Ivan's left shoulder. "How bad is it?"

"Just grazed me. Nothing I can't handle."

"Why are you grinning like that?"

"Because I'd feel like shit if I didn't get at least a little maimed in this war."

"You are crazy," he said and helped his friend up.

They joined the rest of the group that had gathered around Gurov's body. While Kosar and Pantyuk dug up a shallow grave, Yefim carefully cleaned Ivan's wound and wrapped it in gauze. Ivan didn't flinch, he just kept smiling.

"My own mother never fussed over me this much," Ivan said.

"Don't get too used to it," Yefim joked, though he was enjoying taking care of his best friend. Ivan could have been lying here next to Gurov, waiting for his grave, and where would that leave Yefim? There was no one in this group he trusted more than Ivan.

After the grave was ready, Lieutenant Komarov took out Gurov's military ID but left the photograph of his wife in his pocket. They placed his body into the fresh earth while trying to ignore the Lithuanian's continued whimpering in the background.

"Goodbye, mate," Komarov said. "The Motherland thanks you."

They threw fistfuls of earth and pine needles on top of the body. Then they headed east toward the Latvian border.

"Watch for any movement from the north," Komarov told them. "I have a feeling we aren't done with the Balts for today."

Soon the moans of the partisan faded, replaced by the silence of the forest. They didn't talk much, and every crunch of a branch made them clutch their rifles tighter. Yefim had trouble getting used to walking behind Pantyuk's thin frame. With Gurov gone, he worried they were doomed.

His neck ached from tension and he couldn't stop thinking about the partisan calling him a Russian shit. He kept imagining what he could have told him if the guy wasn't on the ground bleeding to death. If instead they'd met on the street, say. Yefim was sure he was on the right side in this war, but if the Lithuanian couldn't see it, he'd have to explain how they, the Soviets, were trying to build something that would ultimately be better for everyone, Lithuanians too. And yes, that dream came with sacrifices, sometimes great ones like the war between Reds and Whites, the famine, the frightening winter nights in '37, when he'd hear a car pull up and wonder if they'd come for his parents only to learn, gratefully, that it was one of his neighbors who was taken to the camps. But at least the price they'd all paid was for a brighter future of equality. And in Germany instead? The world was a serving platter for the master race, and at any moment officers with swastika armbands could parade you like a zoo animal with *Jude* smeared across your chest.

Yet the more he imagined their argument, the more something in it bothered him. He couldn't forget the hate on the pale face of the dying partisan. To have such conviction, against the USSR of all things, seemed inexplicable.

He remembered how, during the famine, he overheard his neighbors saying that Moscow was deliberately starving Ukrainian peasants to death—that they never should have become Soviet. They'd said it with the same kind of hate and it had shocked Yefim to tears. He remembered how he had run to Mikhail, who told him never to repeat it. Communism was good for the Jews, he said, good for everyone, because even though he, Yefim, was born a poor peasant, he could become anything he wanted.

When the sun was lower and their shadows grew longer, Ivan suggested they'd need to set up camp soon.

"We will, once we get out of these damn pines," said Lieutenant Komarov.

"How long until they end?"

"The pines? I don't know, but once they do, we'll be at the Latvian border."

A few minutes later Komarov shouted, "Watch it!" and jumped behind a tree.

Yefim dropped to the ground and waited for the commander's signal.

"False alarm," said Komarov in a more even tone, coming out of his hiding place. "Let's take a break. Kosar and Lisin on watch."

Yefim leaned on a pine and took off his boots. After weeks of walking, his feet were always eager for rest. He noticed a trail of ants crawling up through a deep groove of the bark. They were determined to get wherever it was they were going, uninterested in the human war raging around them. Yefim wondered what it would be like to join them on their oblivious march.

He knew it was bad to think like this. He had to focus on getting to Latvia, on rejoining the army and having his hands on a big gun again. Then he'd feel the power and the conviction. He was just cut off from reality, that was all. The lack of food was making everything blurrier.

It took more than two hours and three more false alarms before they crossed into Latvia. There were no signs, but according to Komarov's map, the border lay at the stream on the edge of the forest. Yefim was relieved. They had fought off the partisans and made actual progress east. The army couldn't be that far off now, he could feel it. And maybe Latvians would be nicer to them.

They filled their canteens, crossed the stream, went up a hill, and entered a leafy forest of spruces, birches, and alders that offered more cover. There, they walked until dusk and set up camp among the buckthorn bushes and cattails that surrounded a small marsh. They were tired, but despite losing Gurov, Yefim was feeling all right. Ivan was still with him.

"The marsh will help cut off anyone coming from the west," Komarov told them.

"It also has another advantage, *Tovarisch* Lieutenant," said Yefim.

"What's that?" Ivan asked, earnest as always.

"Killing our appetite."

Ivan chuckled, while Komarov sighed. The marsh stank, it was true, but it was the best spot they had come across to spend the night.

"Enough with the wisecracks, Shulman. You and Ivan are on watch duty tonight."

"Thanks, Commander," said Yefim, slapping a mosquito on his forearm. "I love watch duty."

"I don't," said Ivan.

"How can you not? Just think of the stars."

"Very funny," said Komarov. "You better be watching our backs, not stargazing. The Lithuanians are thirsty for our blood."

"Aren't we in Latvia now?" asked Lisin.

"Same shit. Latvians, Lithuanians, Estonians. None of them want us here."

For dinner, they had a few mushrooms that Kosar foraged along the way and which he said could be eaten raw. They ate quickly and went to bed. After a full day of walking and the adrenaline of the morning fight, everyone except Yefim and Ivan was asleep in no time.

The first half of the night was the hardest, so Yefim said he would take it.

"That's not fair, Fima," Ivan objected. "Let's just draw lots like always."

"Always with the fairness. You got shot today, man. You need to rest."

"I doubt I'd even fall asleep. Getting shot is quite a rush. Lots, please. I'm not backing down."

Ivan was as stubborn as he was. They drew lots and Yefim won, so he would get to rest for two hours until it was his turn to get up.

"Sure you'll be all right by yourself?" he asked Ivan. "We can still switch."

"Don't worry," said Ivan. "It will be your turn before you know it."

They said good night and Yefim nestled near a bush farther from the water. The frogs croaked peacefully and the stars above were spectacular in the moonless sky. But every time he closed his eyes, he saw the Lithuanian's pale face on the ground. So he kept his eyes on the sky.

It was August, prime falling-star season, and he thought of those hot summer nights when he and his brothers would lie on the hay and count the meteors to see who could spot the most. Naum, the second youngest, piped up every two minutes with "Did you see that one?" and then added it to his score, even though no one believed him. Basya slept inside on those nights, as their mother said the night air wasn't good for a girl. He wished he hadn't wasted his last letter to Basya talking about their base and describing the town. Had he known what was coming, he would have told her to grab their parents and head east to Kharkiv, if not farther into Russia. Now there was no sending letters from a swamp. His only hope was that Father had found a way to keep them safe, though he hated the idea of relying on his old man.

He wondered how his brothers had fared. He especially worried about Yakov. Yakov was a dreamer, read everything he could, and had married an artsy girl. Though he worked as an engineer, he also wrote poetry. He wasn't made for war. Even when they'd played Civil War as kids, Yakov always agreed to be on the losing White side and then walked off somewhere mid-game. It was Georgiy who always took their game seriously. Yefim still remembered how, when they were on the Red team together, Georgiy asked him if he wanted to see Moscow and lifted him by the ears. They were out in the sunflower fields, and

Naum, who was seven at the time, rolled around on the ground laughing, probably grateful it wasn't him hanging by the ears above the sunflowers. Now, Georgiy must have been very glad to fight the Germans. Yefim only wished he knew where he, Naum, Yakov, and Mikhail had been sent to serve.

Suddenly a star fell. As it made an unusually bright and slow arc across the sky, Yefim wished that he'd see his family again.

Before he knew it, Ivan was shaking him awake.

"Your turn, Sleeping Beauty," he whispered.

The stars had grown bleak in a bluish sky, and Yefim could already make out the cattails in the early light. As soon as he got up, Ivan collapsed into Yefim's spot and fell asleep.

Yefim walked up to the marsh and slapped his cheeks, forearms, and knees to get some circulation going. He kept an eye on the south flank, where Komarov said there was a village not far off. That's when he saw them: a pair of white cranes watching him from the other side. Their long, elegant bodies were reflected in the water, so it looked as though there were four of them standing watch.

He paced back and forth, keeping his eyes on the south edge of the marsh and the cranes. He knew they'd alert him if anyone was coming. Birds heard the smallest noises.

Yefim had always loved birds. His earliest childhood memory was of feeding chickens in the front yard. He remembered a sun-dappled yard and the rustle of the hens rushing toward him as grains spilled out of his fist. His mother always told him they weren't pets and that he shouldn't get so attached, but he didn't understand how you could live with a creature, feed and care for it every day, and not consider it your friend. And then collectivization came and everyone around them was starving and his family had no choice but to eat his feathered friends. Yefim cried when they slaughtered their first chicken, Bek-Bek, and refused to eat the meat. But his stomach had become so bloated from hunger that he had no choice but to eat the chicken soup his mother made. *Better than us eating you*, Mikhail had joked grimly, as by then everyone had heard the rumors of families eating their smallest members.

The cranes, which until then had seemed to be resting, stretched their necks to the south. Yefim peered into the darkness beyond the marsh. The birds waited for something, then took off. Yefim clasped his rifle. A moment later he heard the search dogs. He screamed, "Germans!" and rushed to wake up Ivan. Above him, the cranes moved like two white crosses against the sky.

Chapter 5

April 1955
Stalino, Ukrainian SSR

Nina knew something was brewing between Yefim and Claudia the minute she heard her husband's voice echoing from the landing below, followed by Claudia's coquettish laughter.

Now it appeared the cleaning lady at work knew it too. The gossipy broad had pinned Nina in the empty hallway of the Donetsk Industrial Institute, where she taught paleontology and the pretty redhead Claudia Mikhailovna taught crystallography. Nina felt nauseous as the old woman described how last night she had seen Claudia walk off with Yefim arm in arm. She wanted to get away from the moldy stench of the mop and the sloshing of the brown water in the metal bucket and debated whether to tell the hag to keep her porous nose out of their business. In the end she managed only "Thank you for informing me, comrade." Outside, the acrid stench of Stalino's big metallurgical and coke plants greeted her in the spring evening air.

Trudging home, Nina wondered if this was happening because moving here to the Donbas had been a mistake. She missed Kyiv. There, on the outskirts of the city, in a house on the edge of a forest, they had raised little Vita, and though that life hadn't been easy, either, there was much to love. She still remembered the head-spinning smell of the forest in the early morning as she and Yefim walked to the train station together, dreaming up a future for their baby girl.

Here, instead, Stalino was gearing up to be an industrial power-house, but while that seemed grand in propaganda posters, for anyone who actually lived there in 1955, there was coal dust that blackened the ceilings, hard water that barely sputtered out of the pipes, dry air, flies, too few trees, and ravenous packs of rats emboldened by overflowing trash bins. Stalino was no match for Kyiv's chestnut-lined boulevards, its cream-colored mansions, its ancient soul.

Kyiv was the reason Nina wasn't as jealous as she should have been about Claudia. It was where Nina had last seen the Professor. She had come by his office to thank him for getting her the job in Stalino, and his goodbye kiss landed on the crease between her cheek and her lips.

Nina stopped before crossing the tram depot, where several drivers were smoking and cursing. She didn't know if she could handle that special way they paused, long enough to let her know that she was a woman walking alone at night, yet short enough to make her feel that she wasn't that beautiful. On the other side of the depot, she could see the lights of her apartment building, where she and Yefim had received one room in a communal three-bedroom flat with another family and a young engineer. Claudia lived a floor below them.

Nina turned around and headed instead toward the stables. She told herself she couldn't blame Claudia for stealing her husband, given how few healthy men were left after the war. The only thing she begrudged her pretty colleague was the ability to be charmed by Yefim the way she had been before their first night on Lovers' Hill. That night, under a crescent moon, Yefim strong-armed her legs into indecent, angry angles. She never forgot the scratching of his stubble on her hot cheek when he collapsed onto her triumphantly, crushing her under his bony hips as if she was a felled enemy. If she hadn't immediately gotten preg-nant with Vita, she might have broken things off when they'd returned to Kyiv.

Instead, they got married. Abortion was still illegal then, and besides, Yefim had all the right qualifications to be a good father: he was kind, friendly, hardworking, and trustworthy. Yes, he had night terrors, occasionally disappeared without warning, and loved to make stuff up as a joke, but overall she had considered sex their main problem and had held out hope that with time she would stop being repulsed by their closeness. She had read that apparently it had taken Tolstoy's wife ten years of marriage "to feel like a woman." They were only on year five.

But now that Claudia had entered the scene, it turned out Yefim wasn't as trustworthy as she'd thought.

Nina approached the stables. The smell of horses always brought her back to her childhood in Kyiv, when automobiles were still a rare sight. Her idea of a happy marriage was modeled on that old world, the world of her parents. Reared in a wooden house filled with the busy swooshing of her mother's dress against the kitchen floor and the quiet, confident scratching of her father's quill on his students' papers in the study, Nina had her ear trained on the formal yet loving way her parents addressed each other—"Pavel Ivanovich, my dearest, would you care for some tea?"—and her understanding of romance was forever linked to the sweet smoke of the hot samovar and the lavish balls and duels she read about in the Pushkin tomes above her father's desk.

With Yefim, she found it hard to have anything similar. She blamed it on the irrevocable gap the Revolution had created, wider than any gap between previous generations of parents and children. Her mother and father grew up with the Romanovs; she and Yefim grew up with Stalin. How could their idea of romance—or even of life itself—be anything alike?

The Professor, on the other hand, smelled of that long-gone world before quotas, brigades, and red stars. There was a gallantry to him that was absent in Yefim, or maybe in all Soviet young men.

She looked at her watch. Claudia's evening class got out around this time. She imagined the cleaning lady watching Yefim meet Claudia outside the institute to walk home together. How the neighbors would hear their flirty voices on the landing, how he would drink tea in her kitchen and talk, really talk, as if they were the married couple and Nina the stranger. She felt like spitting.

As much as she hated confrontation, she would need to tell him he was being disrespectful to her and the children, and if more people at the institute found out, it could ruin her reputation at work. He knew just as well as she did that their family needed her income.

At home, she found the nanny, Mila, stirring ragout in the kitchen while Vita and Andrey were playing with the six-year-old girl who lived with her parents in the second bedroom. Vadim, the young engineer who occupied the third bedroom and often let all three kids of the apartment draw in his notebooks, wasn't home. In the kitchen, the radio droned on about the plenum.

"How were the kids?" Nina asked. As Mila proceeded to tell her about Andrey refusing to eat tvorog and Vita crying yet again when she picked her up from nursery school, Nina thought about who else besides the cleaning lady might know. She hurried to let the nanny go, and while Mila put on her boots, Nina listened nervously for voices on the landing.

Nina put the kids to bed and tried to work on her research paper but kept launching into an imaginary conversation with Yefim. She mulled over its many possible permutations, from telling him directly about the cleaning lady to hinting that she wasn't blind to asking how long he planned to continue this business with Claudia. In every instance, the conversation devolved into a fight, and so she'd try out a new approach. Finally, she decided she was too tired and went to bed. Yefim didn't get home until after ten, and by then, exhausted by the day, Nina was asleep.

In the morning, there was the usual rushing in an apartment full of people getting ready for work and school, then Vita's screams of protest as Yefim carried her off to nursery school—"Papa, if you love me even a little bit, don't take me there!"—while Andrey banged his spoon on the table, his little glasses sliding off his face. In the chaos, talking about Claudia seemed impossible.

It was only on her way to work that Nina realized how relieved she was that the confrontation had to be postponed. What she wouldn't give for none of this to be happening.

She thought she would have a hard time concentrating in class that morning, but as soon as she walked into the auditorium and saw rows of her students enjoying their last few minutes of liberty, everything else disappeared. She felt like a fish that had made it back into the water after flopping around breathlessly onshore.

When the students left and the auditorium was filled with silence, there was a knock on the door and a dark-haired face peeked in, asking, "May I?"

Before Nina could reply, Lena, an assistant professor from the geology department who taught some evening courses, dawdled toward her. Her green eyes drooped around her small, sharp nose in a mix of exaggerated pity and concern, and Nina knew right away why she was there.

"There is a private matter I wanted to discuss," Lena said carefully. "It's about your husband."

At first, Nina feigned surprise, but as Lena kept jabbering about how she'd seen Yefim with a certain colleague of theirs, how at first she wasn't sure but had now come to believe that they weren't just friends, et cetera, et cetera, Nina sensed a hint of womanly pleasure behind Lena's concern and it irked her.

"I heard he's been telling her about the war and his childhood and, let me tell you, Nina, it's never a good sign when a man starts confiding his past like that," Lena said, nodding professorially as if Nina were a freshman in a class on male behavior.

Nina packed her lecture papers quickly but calmly, trying not to look furious. She wished she could tell Lena that her husband had confided in her plenty, but that would be a lie. She couldn't remember the last time he'd talked to her about the war or his childhood. His past had become off-limits somehow, though she couldn't say when or why. She had thought it was he who wasn't interested in talking about it, but apparently not. Nina felt humiliated and, heaving her bag on her shoulder, made for the door.

"Awfully kind of you to tell me," she said, and hurried out.

Outside, she found a taxi. As they drove away from the institute, Nina wished they could keep going all the way to Kyiv so she could run back to the Professor and tell him that the job he had gotten her in

Stalino wasn't working out as they had thought. He would hug her and she would instantly know what to do.

Nina felt tears welling up. She didn't want to cry in front of the driver, so she focused instead on the window. The streets were abuzz with drilling, hammering, the whirring of different machinery, and the shouts of construction workers. On Universitetskaya, a crew of two dozen men was laying a wide new street through the heart of the city. Two blocks north, a bulldozer was leveling a hill that kids used to sled off on snowy days. Around the corner, a crane lowered a gray slab of wall onto the fifth story of an apartment building. Next to it, the side of a completed building was covered with a crimson poster that read THE FUTURE IS OURS.

Nina told herself she had to be patient. When there were finally enough buildings for everyone in Stalino, her family would receive their own apartment and they could build their private little life the way they had done in that house on the outskirts of Kyiv. Not all was yet lost. Even if romance wasn't in the cards for her, there could still be a good marriage. Wasn't that what mattered most anyway?

Over the next few weeks, Nina wasn't able to confront Yefim. Or at least that was what she told herself. Every evening, after a day of pitying looks and whispers from female colleagues at the institute, she got home infuriated and convinced she could take it no longer. Then she'd get busy with the kids and the next thing she knew she was falling into bed exhausted. Though Yefim continued coming home late, by morning her exasperation and the previous day's resolve to face her husband seemed like the desperate thoughts of a tired mind. In the sobering light of day, it seemed easier to pretend nothing was wrong.

One evening in the beginning of May, Yefim came home early. As he threw himself into bathing the delighted children and putting them to bed, she fried potatoes for both of them. She felt nervous but also strong like a sturdy coral that had outlasted the pretty fish. The relationship must have ended on its own. Now their family could get back on track.

When all their roommates were out of the kitchen, Yefim sat down and plunged into his plate of potatoes. She watched him: his sharp cheekbones, his muscular shoulders. She could see how a woman could be attracted to this man.

"So, this summer . . . ," Yefim started, a piece of potato still in his mouth.

"Let's go back to the Azov Sea," she said, glad he wanted to talk about their family vacation. "That house we stayed at last summer is available."

"Sure," he said dismissively. "But first, in June, I will head into the field with Claudia Mikhailovna. She'll be looking for crystals and I'll look for bryozoan fossils to start writing my dissertation."

Nina watched his fork stab another cube of potato. How did he lie like that without flinching? She could hear the sound of her blood pumping through her.

"Bryozoans?"

"*Da.*"

He was saying something about his theory on the microscopic sea animals, which they both knew were a useless thing to study for any meaningful dissertation in stratigraphy, when Nina walked out of the kitchen.

Lying in bed in their dark room, close to her sleeping children, she heard the clang of a fork landing in the sink and the apartment door shutting. Out of the window she could see a square of light that came from Claudia's room below. Nina willed herself to sleep, but the square of light taunted her from behind the curtains. On the wall, she could distinguish the bronze Roman numerals of the clock. Eleven P.M. Midnight. One o'clock. Claudia's light went out at one forty-five A.M. Yefim didn't come home.

This was an open declaration of war. The next morning she found him in the kitchen drinking tea in the same shirt he had worn the night before, now wrinkled. He was chatting with Vadim as if he hadn't just waltzed in after spending the night with another woman. Nina got ready and went to work.

But she couldn't concentrate on her lecture. The faces of her students seemed to undulate in their rows. She told them she wasn't well and needed to go home. When she walked out of the auditorium, the floor of the hallway swam away from her. She grabbed the wall to make it stop moving when someone caught her by the elbow. The familiar porous nose hovered above the funereal robe.

"Come with me," the cleaning lady said, and led her to the janitorial room.

Inside, the narrow room reminded Nina of a train conductor's compartment, except it smelled of suds. She was surprised to see that it must have been where the cleaning lady lived. She sat Nina down on the cot, gave her some valerian drops, and said, "Look at you. A professor and still clutching to a useless husband. What do you need him for?"

Nina stared at the yellow linoleum, feeling strangely ashamed.

"Lie down and rest," the woman continued. "We don't want any of these gossipy *baba*s seeing you like this."

Nina obeyed, lying down on the stiff cot. When the cleaning lady walked out, Nina looked around the strange abode: a closet full of mops and brooms, an orange curtain on the single-pane window, a small table with a teapot, a jar of honey, and a single cup. She felt as if she were at the house of Baba Yaga, the old fairy-tale witch who lived in the forest in a wooden hut that sat on chicken legs. *Turn your back to the forest and your front to me*, you were supposed to say, and the chicken legs rotated the hut so you could walk in. *That's how I'll end up*, Nina thought: alone in the woods, hunting for mushrooms and bryozoans.

When she woke up, she couldn't understand why she had been putting up with Yefim's behavior for almost two months. She snuck out of the cleaning lady's room and ran home. Everything felt bright and sharp like the day the Nazi tanks rolled into town. She had to move fast. At home, she threw some clothes for her and the children into her expedition backpack and packed a separate suitcase for Yefim. Then she locked the door to their room with the one key they shared, leaving Yefim's suitcase standing in the hallway. She picked up the children and, telling them they were going to visit Aunt Vera, went to the airport, where the three of them got on the four P.M. flight to Kyiv. It didn't matter that the ticket took a bite out of their savings. If things were reversed, Yefim wouldn't think twice about the money.

It was hot on the plane. During the descent, Nina felt dizzy. When she fainted, her body slid off the seat like a melting jellyfish. She came to when they landed but was too weak to get up, so the two stewardesses helped her and the kids get off the plane and into fresh air. There, on a strip of airport grass, Nina lay down, the kids by her side. She stared up at the sky, inhaling the sweetness of Kyiv's blooming chestnuts. In the taxi on the way to her sister's, she even chuckled, imagining the surprise that awaited Yefim at home.

Nina had written to her sister about the affair after the cleaning lady first approached her, so when Vera opened the door and looked at Nina's pale face, she didn't need an explanation. She hugged the children, sent them inside to play, and told Nina she was an idiot.

"What do you need in life? You've got a home, a good job, and children. Your husband doesn't love you? Big deal! My husband left me in an unfamiliar city without a home or money during the war. Meanwhile, here you are with everything except brains!"

Nina was too tired to argue. Her head spun and nothing made sense—except lying down. Vera gave her a sleeping pill and she spent the next twenty-four hours in bed dreaming of suitcases and mops.

The next day Vera woke her up and told her in a kind, stern voice that sounded just like their mother's that Nina would leave the children here for a week and return to Stalino to confront Yefim.

"But I don't love him," Nina said meekly.

"It doesn't matter," Vera said. "They do."

Nina looked at the children, who were trying to build a shoe tower in the hallway. Vita was a copy of her father: strong, ambitious, defiant. Andrey was softer, more hers, with his nearsighted gray eyes and the way he said "Mamochka" that made her melt. Nina tried imagining what children the Professor and she would have had, but she couldn't. These children, this husband, this life was the one she had chosen. No one had forced her. And now, no matter what happened, she needed to stop wondering about that night at the dig when the Professor, standing on his knees, kissed her hands and told her he loved her and she, making an excuse to use the restroom, ran all the way to the train station to return to Yefim and baby Vita. She had chosen her family then. She needed to choose it again now before her stupid husband ruined all of their lives.

In Stalino, Nina stopped by the institute first. She had left so suddenly she worried that she might be in trouble: a few years before, workplace desertion had been a criminal offense. As soon as she entered the professors' lounge, Lena dragged her into a corner and said the situation was worse than Nina had expected. Her sudden departure and rumors of the affair had caused a scandal that came to the attention of the Party committee. She was to go see the director in his office right away.

The director was a hefty man in his fifties with thinning hair that always reminded Nina of an amoeba. When she first met him two years earlier, he looked her up and down with a sigh that she interpreted as regret that he had accepted such a bookish young woman in scuffed-up shoes to work at his institute. Then, instead of making her a docent as had been agreed, he said that with her "lived-under-occupation" stain, he'd have to downgrade her to assistant professor. A rung below Claudia.

Now Nina had to discuss her personal life with this man. As she sat across from him, she focused on the paperweight of red granite with a small silver hammer and sickle on its side.

"Nina Pavlovna, I'm going to get right to the point," he said, tapping a pen on the desk. "All men cheat. The difference is in how a wife reacts. Now, a smart wife simply closes her eyes to such things."

That was when Nina began to cry. She had come to Stalino to build a career as a scientist and a professor, but instead turned out to be a pathetic little woman crying about her love life. Her tears quickly turned into a snotty mess and she started to hiccup, which embarrassed her even more. The director must have been embarrassed too, or maybe disgusted, because he gave up trying to reason with her and escorted her out, muttering, "There, there," then swiftly shut the door, leaving her alone with his secretary.

The secretary, a quiet woman with curled hair whom Nina didn't know well, handed her a clean handkerchief. Nina took it, grateful for the small kindness. The secretary glanced at the door of her boss, who was already on the phone discussing some prospective hire, and, leaning toward Nina, said, "You may like to know that Claudia Mikhailovna was fired yesterday. I've heard she is moving back to her hometown."

"Oh," Nina gasped. "I never intended . . ."

She wanted to tell her that she never intended for the poor woman to lose her job and housing and tarnish her employment record, that the fault for all of this was Nina and Yefim's. But then the secretary leaned closer and whispered, "Claudia brought a doctor's note certifying she was a virgin. I guess it didn't help."

Nina couldn't remember how she got home. There she found the door to her room off its hinges and Yefim's clothes piled on the bed. Nina looked around their small home—the children's metal beds, the kerchief remade into a lampshade, the aloe from their house in Kyiv on the windowsill, and the mirrored wardrobe that Yefim had stood all night in line to buy. Nina sighed and, not looking in the mirror, began to put her husband's clothes away in the middle drawer where they belonged.

Chapter 6

August 1941
Germany

Yefim tumbled out of the train car onto the soggy ground. He felt
light-headed. After two days packed so tight he could only
stand, his legs didn't obey him. But the guards were already yelling,
"*Schnell!*" as their dogs snarled. He scrambled up, holding on to Ivan,
squinting at the bright morning sky, and filling his lungs with the
smell of the rain that must have just ended, the wet earth, the grass.

He didn't know what awaited them here, but at least they were off
the suffocating train and out of the Tilsit camp, with its huge sandy
field encircled by barbed wire, where thousands of them had slept
standing in the rain as the cold Baltic winter pierced their uniforms.

When the train had emptied and Yefim knew, without having to
look, that only the corpses remained on the grimy floor of the cattle
cars, he saw he was standing amid an exhausted, filthy sea of overgrown
hair and putrid rags: hundreds of Red Army soldiers, many of them
wounded. They looked like the old vagrant men he used to see back
home during the famine. According to the flyers the Germans had
shoved in their train car, Stalin had issued Order No. 270, which deemed
Yefim and the rest of these men "malicious deserters whose families are

subject to arrest for violation of an oath and betrayal of their home-land." The order listed what they had failed to do: "selflessly fight to the last, protect matériel like the apple of their eye, break through from the rear of enemy troops, defeating the fascist dogs." Though many on the train said the flyers were just the enemy's creative way to demor-alize them, Yefim kept wondering if he could have done more to protect the Motherland and not incur Stalin's wrath.

Shots rang out. He clutched Ivan. A guard waved a pistol, passing them slowly. A few seconds later there was another shot. Then another. They were killing off the weak prisoners who couldn't get up. And he had thought this place was going to be better than the last camp.

They were told to march. Sluggishly, he moved his legs. He hoped that, wherever they were going, there would be water and food. He'd had nothing since the turnip he'd dug up three days ago.

They marched along the edge of a small town past a hotel and a dentist's office with German signs. For a moment, he felt reassured that the German he'd learned in school could help him and Ivan in what-ever awaited them next. A few locals came out to look. The street sweeper paused, staring with an expressionless face. A little girl in a straw hat pointed at them, asking something as her mother hurried her away. They must have been quite a sight.

After the town ended, they walked through a patch of forest. He told himself maybe he should try to make a run for it, but it was hard to think of anything but water.

Finally, they passed through the tall wooden gate of the camp. Inside, he could smell wood chips and manure and something else he couldn't identify. An eerie, muggy stagnation.

They arrived at a wide, oval dirt field. Four rows of pale green barracks radiated outward toward a guard tower. He noticed how barren the camp was, even in late August. No grass grew between the barracks, no trees were in sight. It was as if every living thing had been combed out of the place. He looked up at the nearest guard tower. The dark eye of a machine gun seemed to point right at him. Beyond the tower was a tall barbed-wire fence and then an open field where a running man would be an easy mark. No, he'd been a fool to tell Ivan they'd find a way to escape.

Soon an officer arrived to begin selections and someone whispered, "Straight is good; right is bad." But how did they know, and what did "bad" mean anyway?

The crowd around Yefim thinned as prisoners were sent in two directions. Before long it was Ivan's turn. He was sent straight and Yefim planned to run after him, even if they told him to go right. They had to stick together in this place. He tried to stand taller in case that mattered somehow, but the officer barely glanced at him.

"*Gerade!*" he said.

Relieved, Yefim ran to catch up with Ivan.

They walked to a small, windowless hut away from the barracks. Inside was a narrow room painted a morose blue. A naked bulb illuminated half a dozen prisoners. They filed past a large metal desk manned by a bald man with sharp, almost yellow eyes. Yefim could tell he wasn't a German guard. On the right side of his gray tunic was a red triangle with the letter *P*. A Pole, he guessed, though he didn't know if the man worked for the Nazis because he hated the Soviets or because he had no other choice.

"Name?" the Polish scribe asked the prisoner in front of him. "Ethnicity?"

Yefim's damaged hand tingled with pain. This was the question he dreaded. Under no circumstance could anyone here find out they were admitting eighteen-year-old Yefim Shulman from a large Jewish family into a Nazi camp. He tried to hold air inside him and concentrated on what must be done.

The line moved too quickly. The prisoners were all Russian or Ukrainian. One was a Kazakh. No one else here had his problem. Until now, he'd blended in. The soldiers around him all looked the same with their dirty bearded faces and their famished eyes. But now there was a merciless light bulb and a man who had probably been told to keep an eye out for any sneaky Jews.

"Next," the scribe called out.

Ivan stepped up to the desk. Yefim watched the greasy streaks of his friend's blond hair reflecting the stark light and tried not to fidget.

"Name?"

"Ivan Didenko."

"Ethnicity?"

"Ukrainian."

Yefim glanced back at the door. It was less than two meters away, half blocked by the prisoners lined up behind him. He could sprint for it. But then what? Guard towers, barbed-wire fence, machine guns. Ivan shuffled off to the next room, glancing back at him, a slight nod of reassurance.

"Next!"

Yefim approached the desk.

"Name?"

"Yefim Komarov."

Lieutenant Komarov's body had remained by the marsh, and on the train here Yefim had decided to use his dead commander's surname because it was simple, it was Russian, and it helped him remember there were good people willing to protect him. It felt like a small tribute.

Yefim watched his new surname appear in the thick notebook. At least he didn't have to invent a new first name. His brother Mikhail's real name was actually Moshe, but by the time Yefim was born, his mother—with incredible foresight—had given him a simple Russian name.

"Ethnicity?" asked the scribe.

Yefim steadied himself.

"Russian."

Back home, he thought of himself as a Soviet first, a Ukrainian second, and a Jew third. While he was no more Russian than an Englishman, here among the German guards and Polish secretaries he was as Russian as the rest of the prisoner lot. At least, that was what he needed to think if he was going to leave this room alive.

The scribe's hand paused in midair. His yellow eyes looked up at Yefim, studying his features.

"Russian, eh?"

Yefim was suddenly aware of his tanned complexion and his narrowly set brown eyes above his high cheekbones, inherited from his father. He'd always thought he and his brothers looked manlier than the Slavs, with their light-colored eyes and a feminine roundness in their cheeks, but now he'd kill for their downiness. Yefim held his breath.

A gunshot rang outside and everyone stirred nervously. Except the Polish secretary. He didn't even flinch. Just kept staring at Yefim.

The small room seemed to be closing in on him. He wanted to look down at his muddy boots but then remembered his mother had always told him: "Look people straight in the eyes, no matter who they are." Mother was neither beautiful nor rich, but she had such a proud, straight gaze that no one ever dared cross her. Yefim raised his eyes to meet the secretary's. The bald man looked away and called out, "Next!"

Yefim hurried toward the exit. Outside, he inhaled the happy air, wanting to hug Ivan. But Ivan wasn't among the gathered men. In the distance, a smaller group of prisoners was marching away when Yefim noticed a fresh trail of blood disappearing around the corner of the hut. What if . . . but he didn't let himself finish the frightening thought.

"Who did they shoot?" he asked an older man squatting nearby.

"Some young curly-haired guy. Probably a Jew," he said, and Yefim was both disturbed and relieved that at least it wasn't Ivan.

"And the rest? Where did they take them?"

"Hopefully a bath," the man replied, scratching himself. "I haven't felt warm water in weeks."

Yefim inhaled sharply. No, no, no. Not the bath. He could have the most Slavic name in the world, but the second someone saw he was circumcised, he was kaput.

"I'd rather eat than bathe," he said as casually as he could. "Not sure about your train car, but the waitress service in ours was pretty lousy."

The man laughed and squinted up at Yefim.

"Where are you from, funny guy?" He had a narrow nose and over-grown sideburns with a touch of gray, which made him look endearing, like an owl. An owl eager for a bath. Yefim sat next to him.

"Izhevsk," he said, naming the city in the Urals where the real Komarov was from.

He'd never been that far east, of course. All he knew about it was from the dead commander's stories, but he needed a town far from the front line in case records were checked. Plus, unlike the area around his native Vinnytsa, which had a lot of Jews, the Urals weren't known for Jewish settlements.

"Ah, the Urals," said the man with a reminiscing smile. "I doubt the Germans will get that far. They just got a head start, that's all, but we'll get them soon enough. I am Oleg, by the way. Oleg Stepanov. And you are?"

He extended his hand and Yefim shook it, hearing himself say, "Yefim Komarov."

He thought what an idiot he'd been to take a Russian name instead of a Tatar one. That way even in the bath he could say he was a circumcised Tatar. Now he needed to figure out how to avoid the bathhouse.

"I've been to Izhevsk once," Oleg said, and proceeded to tell him about a trip he took there when he was twelve.

Yefim half listened, wishing Ivan was here with him.

The guards approached and they were led along the barbed-wire fence to the farthest corner of the camp. Beyond the fence stretched an empty field with dead yellow grass that had been cut and was now in wet clumps with ravens picking at its seeds. Farther, Yefim saw the dark outline of a forest. He wished he could grow wings.

From the outside, the bathhouse looked the same as other barracks: long, pale green, windowless. But inside was where everyone would stare at his penis, dangling there exposed and unprotected like the fox's tail in the fairy tale his mother used to tell him. The tail was what gave the fox away to the hunting dogs. He shivered, feeling the traitorous member curled up inside his sordid underpants.

They approached the door, heavy with fresh paint. Inside, he heard many voices. He glanced back at the field beyond the fence, praying to a God he didn't believe in. "Please, let me live." Someone shoved him inside.

The bathhouse was poorly lit. Inside, he could taste the mildew mixed with sweat and fresh paint. Its bitterness coated his mouth.

Two lines of prisoners snaked past open shower stalls that lined the walls toward something in the center under the hall's only lamp. No one was naked. He didn't understand why.

"What's happening?" he asked the people in front, but they just shrugged.

He wondered if Ivan was somewhere in front. He rose on his toes to see but there were only backs and heads moving in the cavernous space. He had never felt so alone. His mangled thumb swelled with phantom pain. Then word got passed back that they were to be shaved.

"And that's it?" he asked, but no one answered.

Yefim crept toward the center. In a clearing between prisoners, he spotted two men in the same gray coats as the Polish scribe's. They were shaving prisoners' beards and heads. Beyond them, shaved men seemed to be exiting out the back of the barracks.

"Goddamn Germans," someone complained. "Can't they at least let us shower?"

Yefim was relieved. But then, looking at the barbers, he grew worried that without his matted hair and black beard, he might no longer easily blend in with the other POWs. What if they could tell he was Jewish?

He heard "Nächste"—"Next"—and stepped in front of the barber under the stark light. The man was thick-necked and looked more like a butcher than a barber. He worked quickly, gliding the hair clippers along his head, forcing his thick black hair to slide off him like a shield. Yefim felt naked and small, not at all like he had felt during his first shave in the army. Here he wasn't being inducted into an organization of power and discipline. He was being sheared.

The barber finished and sent him off without a word. Outside, he was blinded by the steely sky.

He found Oleg again and as they marched with the other shaved men back across the *Appellplatz*, he was glad to be part of a chorus of footsteps that resounded through the camp. This wasn't so bad, Yefim decided. He had a new identity and had survived the bath. Now all he needed was to find Ivan so they could stick together until the Red Army turned things around back home, which couldn't be that far off.

They arrived at the last barrack before the guard tower. Inside, the sharp smell of ammonia and disinfectant from the latrines made Yefim gag. In a long, dark wooden room with a low pitched roof and no furniture of any kind, he noticed a blackboard with the number 203 written in white chalk. Three small dirty barred windows illuminated the prisoners—all two hundred of them—sitting or lying on the bare floor, leaving almost no room to walk. Still, this was much better than sleeping in that freezing field in Tilsit.

"What are we, cockroaches?" someone yelled out. "You can't keep squeezing more in!"

Without answering, the barracks *Kapo* changed the number on the chalk board to 253.

"Almost as crowded as my house," said Yefim, and behind him Oleg laughed. His robust, infectious cackle reminded Yefim of Rabbi Isaac, who despite exchanging his rabbinical robe for a pair of pale green kolkhoz overalls, was forever known as Rabbi.

"Let's see how you laugh after a week here," someone hissed from the floor.

"Yefim! Over here, over here!"

Ivan waved from the corner of the room. Overjoyed to hear his friend's voice, Yefim squeezed through toward him. They embraced. Next to Ivan was a strange-looking youth with an oversized head and tiny blue eyes that sat above the baby fat of his cheeks. He looked like a gargantuan toddler.

"This is my friend Yefim," Ivan said.

"Welcome to paradise," the toddler said in a low voice. "I'm Bogdan. From Belarus."

"Yefim is from a neighboring vil—" Ivan started to say.

"Izhevsk," Yefim cut in before his friend could ruin his cover. "How long have you been here?"

"Three weeks."

Yefim lowered his voice. "Any successful escapes?"

If they could make it back east, he and Ivan could rejoin the army or locate some Soviet partisans.

"Don't get your hopes up," Bogdan said. "Even the French next door haven't made it out."

"What French next door?"

"There is a European POW camp behind ours. It's a different planet over there. You'll see. It will open your eyes to what the fascists think of us."

Behind them, the lock on the barracks door clanged shut.

He didn't see the other camp until a few days later. By then he'd stood for hours during senseless roll calls while the guards counted and recounted and recounted them again until their legs ached and the weaker prisoners began to faint. He'd learned what it was like to sleep with armies of lice crawling all over his face. He'd tasted the watery *balanda* made of rutabaga peels and a thin, almost translucent sliver of strange-tasting bread, the only meal of the day.

The European camp was nothing like that. Situated behind theirs, it was occupied by Czechs, Frenchmen, and Norwegians. While their barracks were the same pale green, they lit up at night because they had electricity and heat. Prisoners also had their own beds and even blankets. Yefim saw them hanging them on laundry lines. He bet they didn't even have lice. He'd also heard they received three normal filling meals a day with potatoes and grains. Occasionally, the Red Cross delivered boxes of other food. And one time, while he was dragging his tired feet to another roll call, he and Ivan saw them playing soccer. Soccer!

He couldn't understand why the Europeans got to live like humans next door while they were treated like flies.

"Aren't we both their enemies?"

"Yes, but the USSR didn't sign that special Geneva law," Oleg explained. "So technically they can treat us however they please."

"And the Red Cross? Somehow I doubt it's only the Germans who aren't allowing them to come in here," Ivan quipped. "We're 'malicious deserters,' remember? Our dear Motherland has no interest in helping us out."

"No, man, that can't be right," Yefim said. "I bet it's because we're the only ones actually beating the Fritzes, so of course they've got to treat us more harshly."

He really wanted that to be true. Every time he saw the other camp, his hands shook with rage.

Meanwhile, new prisoners brought bad news from home: the Germans had occupied almost all of Ukraine. No one would free them anytime soon. By late September there were so many arrivals that they had to sleep outside in trenches dug by hand. Bogdan said people were getting shot in the back room behind the bathhouse. Yefim didn't want to believe the rumor—shooting POWs was against all rules of war, a new low even for this godforsaken place—but he started seeing guards careening drunk in the mornings.

"Must be trying to forget their night's dirty job," Oleg said.

In October the rations were cut further. Now prisoners ate whatever they could chew, even leather belts. The temperatures dipped sharply. It was the coldest October he'd ever seen. Water froze in the pipes. During the day, all he wished was for nightfall. But at night, tucking his toes into the last remaining piece of his woolen socks and trying to sleep under a blanket of lice that fed on his shivering body, he couldn't wait for morning.

One day the Soviet army was bound to come for them. He just hoped they would come soon: he and his friends were rapidly growing thinner. The waist of his pants, which had long turned to cardboard from the dirt, seemed to increase a centimeter every morning. His face was probably a piece of work too, judging by Ivan's, whose cheekbones emerged, cutting sharply under his eyes and making him look feral. But it was Bogdan who had it the worst. He had lost all his baby fat and looked like a sickly sunflower with a giant head bobbing on his thinning frame. A few more weeks and they would all turn into *dohodyagi*, which in camp parlance meant goners—shadows of former men with vacant eyes and only one possible future.

He'd seen goners before, during that terrible winter in '33. One day he had come across a man slumped against a tree near his village. He had thought the man was resting, but then he came closer and saw he was dead. What shocked him was that he still had a piece of bread sticking out of his mouth. Someone must have offered help, but it came too late. What if the same thing happened here? What if the Red Army got to them too late?

When, one morning, Yefim woke up feeling hot and more tired than usual, he got worried. You didn't recover from illnesses at this camp, not unless you made it to the medical barracks, and that was the last place he wanted to be with his circumcision. But then a lucky break: the *Kapo* sent him to help bring the vats of soup from the kitchen. This was the best assignment Yefim could have gotten, and he shuffled his thin, stiff body through the frosty morning toward the promise of ruta-baga peels and stale sugar beet husk bread. He planned to steal whatever he could for him and his friends.

As he rounded the corner of a building, he heard, "Where are you running to, Russian swine?"

He turned. There were two of them. Eyes glassy and bloodshot. Rifles swayed from their shoulders as they pinned him against the wall. Their breath was rancid. One hit him in the stomach with the rifle, sending a hot wave of pain up to his chest. He coughed and slid down to the ground, trapped between them. Their hard boots kicked his ribs and hips as he covered his head, curling in like they'd taught him in the army.

"Don't hit me, please!" he begged, his throat on fire. "*Bitte hör auf!*"

But the drunk guards didn't stop. They punted him back and forth as he coughed his lungs out, coming apart at the seams. The sky grew white as if his mother were covering him with her woolen shawl.

One guard slipped and fell on his butt. The second guard hooted and chortled, spraying Yefim's face with his spit. The first guard scrambled up, put one boot on his chest, and opened his fly.

"You waste of skin," he said as hot piss soaked Yefim's neck and chest. "Even Stalin thinks you are a traitor."

Then the butt of a rifle struck his cheekbone and everything went dark.

Next he knew, he was in a green field. A young woman walked toward him. She had long, loose black hair and seemed to be almost gliding. She held something in her arms and he understood she was bringing him a gift. He moved toward her, full of anticipation, like that time his mother had made an apple crumble during the first good harvest after the famine. When the woman approached, he saw that she cradled a baby. The baby was dead.

He couldn't recall how he made it back to the barracks, only that Ivan teared up when he saw him. That night his fever rose and he was in and out of consciousness for he wasn't sure how long. All he remembered was Ivan's face hovering above him with a spoonful of water. By the time he regained strength several days later, Bogdan was dead. His body had already been carted off.

Oleg said, "Me, you, and Ivan are too stubborn to end up on that cart." But as typhus raged through the camp the first week of November, Oleg caught the illness and was on his last legs too.

That's when the news broke. The *Kapo* came in and announced that the next morning special SS units would arrive to select laborers for work in Germany.

"Didn't I tell you Hitler was in trouble?" a fresh arrival with ice-blue eyes and plump cheeks said to his buddy. "They've finally realized they can't trample the mighty Soviet Union. And now they need us."

When he'd joined their barracks the week before, this still-healthy man had introduced himself as Sergey Nikonov, an infantryman. But Yefim knew better. Nikonov must have gotten rid of his emblem-decorated coat because the Nazis killed Red Army commissars on the spot, but he had a much harder time getting rid of his bravura. Yefim was certain he was no mere private. There was a commanding officer's steeliness in his face and a patriotic sparkle of a die-hard Communist in his eyes.

"USSR is a tough nut to crack," another prisoner said. "If the winter is anything like it is in this hellhole, the Nazis are probably freezing their nuts off in Mother Russia."

"Let the fascists freeze!" Nikonov exclaimed, raising his canteen with a dashing white smile. "Now that they'll send us to work, we can finally do something for the Motherland."

Yefim felt his sunken cheeks flush. Sure, the fact that Germany suddenly needed laborers was a promising sign that their invasion wasn't going smoothly, and, sure, he also was itching to get out of this death pit, but working for Hitler? No, thank you. What would Mikhail say if he found out his little brother had aided the enemy? And it wasn't just Mikhail. His own conscience would eat him up.

Yefim turned to Nikonov.

"What are you talking about?" he said. "This is treason."

"Who are you to lecture me about treason?" Nikonov asked. "Laborers can sabotage, create diversions, steal weapons. We can make a real difference in the war instead of waiting here for slaughter."

"The only difference we'll be making is helping the enemy win," said Yefim.

"Feel free to rot here then. Komarov was it? You know, if it wasn't for your name, I'd think you were a Yid."

Ivan, who'd been sitting quietly nearby, jumped up with an energy Yefim hadn't seen from him in weeks. His eyes glistened with rage as he said, "He is Russian from Izhevsk. So shut it."

With his friend there, Yefim immediately felt stronger. But Nikonov, who seemed twice as wide as Ivan, ignored him. He came up close to Yefim and inspected his face. He was slightly taller and his dazzling smile with its perfect white teeth made him seem like royalty among dirty plebs. Nikonov continued to smile as he said in a low voice, "You can just tell the SS you're a member of the chosen people and they'll be happy to put a bullet in your head instead of sending you to work."

For some reason Yefim found this funny. Something about this Nikonov guy reminded him of himself when he had first arrived here, hopeful that with a new name he could outlast this camp, oblivious to what the guards, the hunger, the cold, and the ever-decreasing number on the barracks chalkboard did to your soul.

He smiled, raised his hand in an exaggerated military salute, and said, "Thank you for the advice, *Tovarisch Commissar!*"

Nikonov spat on the floor and walked to the far corner of the barracks.

Yefim couldn't relax for a long time. He sat in the dark, listening to Oleg's barely audible breathing and telling himself not to be afraid, but fear had lodged deep in his rib cage. Tomorrow, Nikonov or someone else would give him up to the SS and all the surviving he'd done would be for nothing.

He didn't want to die. Not yet, not here. If only Mother could wake him from this nightmare. She was the one who had saved him after his father—who always did as he was told "because God and Stalin are watching"—gave up all their family grain to the collectors. Mother had hidden some provisions. She had six kids and she didn't let a single one die. His poor, fierce mother. If there was only something she could do to save him now.

Yefim was suddenly overcome with an urge to leave something behind. A record. A name. He leaned close to Oleg's ear and whispered, "My real name is Yefim Shulman." But when his hand landed on his friend's chest, he realized Oleg was already dead.

It was five A.M. but as dark as midnight when they were rushed off to the *Appellplatz* for a special roll call with the SS. The snow that had fallen two days earlier had been trampled away, except for small icy clumps on the side of the road that were visible against the dark mud. Yefim had learned to half sleep through the roll calls, his shoulders propped by men on either side. But today, despite barely closing his eyes last night, he was wide-awake.

In the center of the *Appellplatz*, under the beam of the searchlight, stood a translator. Behind him were six men in long black leather coats: the SS. Yefim couldn't take his eyes off them. They looked like angels of death.

"Today is your lucky day," the translator announced, after one of the men stepped onto the short wooden podium that also served for hanging the camp's worst offenders. "Some of you will get to prove yourselves useful in the beautiful Deutschland."

Around him, there was a growing murmur until one of the guards behind the SS men shot a rifle into the air. Crows flew up from the surrounding fields, cawing. Everyone hushed. The wind whistled through the quiet rows and blew tiny sharp icicles into his face. It was beginning to snow. The translator went on.

"We will select the strongest of you to work in several industries. It is your duty to tell us if you've had special training or a previous occupation."

As the translator stepped back toward the SS men, Ivan, who stood to Yefim's right, gave him a reassuring bump on the shoulder as if saying, *We are going to get out of here.*

Just then Yefim heard, "First, we will take care of another business. Raise your hand if you were a political commissar."

The crowd fidgeted. Yefim didn't move. He thought of Nikonov.

"It is a crime to withhold information," the man continued when his first call didn't yield volunteers. "If you know who was a political commander or a commissar, you must point him out."

Again everyone shifted from foot to foot. Around him, Yefim saw dozens of shaved heads bobbing on thin necks. No one spoke up.

"You will be rewarded with a good job in Deutschland," the man said, and then, after looking over the crowd, added in a lower voice as if sharing a secret, "and a warm meal on your way to Germany."

Dozens of hands went up as people began to point and shout.

"He is a commissar, from my hometown!" someone hollered on the left flank.

"Him, him, Parovozov, over there! He came to the factory every month to give us political speeches!"

Then, right behind Yefim, a raspy voice: "Here! This is a commissar. I overheard him last night."

"I'm a private, you idiot!" Nikonov's familiar voice snapped, but before Yefim could turn around, one of the SS men headed their way.

"What's going on here?" asked the translator.

"This man is a commissar!" said the raspy voice, belonging to a thin ghost of a man with bulging gray eyes. He reached over and pulled on the back of Yefim's shirt, his frozen fingers scratching his neck: "This guy called him a commissar last night! I heard them."

Yefim turned and saw the SS man grab Nikonov's shoulder. The black swastika on his bright red armband rested close to Nikonov's face. His ice-blue eyes reflected the bright searchlight as he stared resolutely into the distance.

The translator asked Yefim, "Is this true?"

Nikonov didn't speak. Yefim tried to remain calm, but blood rushed to his face. This was his fault. He had no right to put this man in danger. He tried to think of what to do, but all he could think was, *Look them straight in the eyes.*

Then his mouth opened and he heard his own voice, which sounded oddly like Mikhail's: "I know for a fact that this man was never in any commanding post in the Red Army because my older brother was his commander in Crimea. Unfortunately, my brother died in battle and this private survived, though I wish it was the reverse."

The translator relayed his words to the SS man. The officer looked at Nikonov, then at Yefim. Yefim worried the German could read his thoughts.

The SS officer let go of Nikonov's shoulder and marched toward the podium. Below it, half a dozen selected "commissars" stood facing the crowd, glum and scared. Two other SS men guarded them with their rifles.

Yefim took his eyes off of them and looked up at the sky. If it would only start snowing harder, the SS officers might get annoyed and maybe dismiss them all. But the dark sky continued to sprinkle the *Appellplatz* with the tiny, hard icicles that felt sharp like the grains of buckwheat his father had made him kneel on after he had stolen sunflower seeds for the chickens from a kolkhoz field. *God and Stalin are watching.*

"Step forward if you are a Jew," he heard from the podium.

The hairs on his arms and legs bristled. He felt as if the SS pointed the searchlight right at him.

"If you point out a Jew, you will get half a loaf of bread," the man said next.

What is half a loaf of bread for a man who'd been reduced to chew on his leather belt? What is the hope of bread, of freedom, of life, especially if the price to pay is one little Jew? Yefim knew he didn't stand a chance.

Hands went up all around as voices shouted, "*Jude! Jude!*"

Ivan clutched Yefim's elbow. Then, behind him, the raspy voice: "*Hier Jude!*"

The man with the bulging gray eyes thumbed Yefim between the shoulder blades. "Say *kukuruza!*"

Yefim knew the infamous *kukuruza* test. Those who never lived next to Jews believed that *kukuruza*—corn—was a word Jews couldn't pronounce without butchering the Russian *r*. Yefim had no problems rolling his *r*'s, but he hesitated. Answering this man was beneath him, while not answering could mean he was trying to hide something. He didn't have time to deliberate. The SS officer was heading his way.

Behind him, he heard Nikonov: "Corn is clearly the only thing on your mind. You squeal every time the Nazis promise a meal."

Yefim turned and gave Nikonov a quick nod. But the SS officer was already there, bellowing, "You again?"

The German was huge in his long black coat and well-shined boots. He approached Yefim. His clean-shaven, square face smelled sharply of cologne. His lids, with long auburn eyelashes around the narrowed blue irises, didn't blink. There was a faint childhood scar on the right side of his jawline. Yefim never thought he'd get such a close look at his executioner.

The officer could probably see right through him to all the Jewish ancestors who had brought him onto this earth, his proud mother and his dutiful father, the aunts and uncles who had moved to America before the Revolution, his grandpa who'd died defending his house in a pogrom.

The sky above was black. The *Appellplatz* disappeared. And there was no more heaviness behind his rib cage. There was only this man with his swastika and a job to do. Yefim was his job.

The German's nostrils flared in disgust as he took a step back, his boots scraping the ground.

Yefim wished he had gone to Yakov's wedding. He wished he had seen Basya go to university, the first woman in their family. He wished Mikhail was here to remind him to stay strong. There would be no record of Yefim Shulman in any prisoner-of-war camp. They would never know how he perished.

The officer barked, "If I have to come back here one more time, I will shoot all of you where you stand!"

He marched away toward the podium, and Yefim took what felt like his first breath in minutes. But then the ground seemed to give way. He felt Ivan catch him and he held on to his friend through the rest: as the SS officers rounded up a dozen suspected Jews, as their miserable procession was led away in the direction of the bathhouse, as the *Appellplatz* echoed with gunshots.

Chapter 7

1961
Stalino, Ukrainian SSR

Yefim had been home alone only twice since they'd moved into their own flat the previous year, but both times he felt a jolt of joy at not having anyone to lie to.

It wasn't that he didn't love his family, but with them around, home was mined with potential slipups. Take last night, for example. As soon as he walked through the door, Nina ambushed him with an invitation to a lecture by some visiting POW.

"This guy escaped from a German camp by stealing their plane—imagine that!—and then of course spent eight years in the camps," she said, her gray eyes sparkling with excitement. "I thought we could go together."

How was he supposed to explain that he had no desire to go? That he'd worked too damn hard to sustain the myth of the brave soldier without divulging the pathetic truth to her or the kids? That he'd learned not to dwell on his memories and hadn't had a night-mare in months? He felt bad because he and Nina had been trying to do more things together ever since the Claudia mess, but this was an ambush.

"Why would you think I want to listen to some pilot?" he said. "It's not like he is Yuri Gagarin or anything."

"He isn't just *some pilot*, Fima. He stole a plane! From the Germans! I mean, what an adventure, don't you think? I thought you'd be thrilled to go." She sounded disappointed, as if she thought his snub was personal.

"Come on, Nina. The only reason this guy is touring the country is to help Khrushchev in his Stalin smear campaign. When it was convenient to them, they hid this poor schmuck away in Siberia. But now the winds have changed and they're showing him around like a prize monkey."

"God, you can be cynical," she said and waved him off. "Fine, if you don't want to go, stay with the kids and I'll take Tamara. I'm sure she'll appreciate my company."

Oh, this woman. She didn't know how difficult she was being. The only person who could understand was Nikonov. He'd know exactly why Yefim was horrified by the idea of having to sit through a lecture by a POW and then discuss it with Nina. Tomorrow he'd need to visit his "friend from the war," as he'd called Nikonov to his family.

He still remembered how sallow Nikonov had first looked after he was released from the Kolyma labor camps in 1956 as part of a wave of rehabilitations. The ice blue of his eyes was all that had remained of his once proud face; the rest had been stolen by the frost, the work in the gold mines, and the resentment toward the government that "rewarded" his suffering in Germany with ten years in the camps under Article 58.

"My homecoming gift," Nikonov had joked bitterly as they drank beer at a kiosk in Stalino.

And now this POW pilot who had received the same homecoming gift and who had now been rehabilitated by the newest benign ruler was touring the country so that suckers like Nina would gobble up preapproved stories of bravery by prisoners of war. Except it was all a show. While this pilot was touring, Nikonov and millions of POWs were snubbed by the government that had sent them to war. They weren't considered real veterans who deserved appropriate benefits, and every time they applied for work, they had to fill out a form that among many degrading questions asked, "Have you or your close relatives been captured or imprisoned during the Great Patriotic War?" They were shunned by society too. After all, they sat out the war in Germany while true patriots fought for the Motherland, so they must be cowardly and they sure as hell must be suspicious.

But not Yefim. For all anyone knew, he'd done his duty. Though if the KGB ever discovered him, his and Nina's life would be ruined.

So, no, he wasn't going to this ridiculous show of a lecture.

As Yefim walked up the stairs to the third floor, he imagined putting the kids to bed early, then drinking tea and reading something in silence before Nina got home. When he opened the door, Andrey and Vita ran up to greet him.

"Papa! Papa!"

They jumped on him on both sides, weighing the same even though Vita was almost two years older than Andrey. He always marveled at how different his children looked. Vita, who was thin, with wavy brown hair and narrowly set brown eyes, looked so Jewish that he worried about her future in this country. Andrey, instead, could have made a model Ukrainian child. He was cherub blond, with Nina's gray eyes and Yefim's athletic build. At their school, many didn't know they were brother and sister.

Just as they didn't know they were the kids of a clandestine prisoner of war.

They were clearly excited to see him as he was rarely home this early. He had always wanted to be a better father than his old man, but somehow he found himself not only working late at ArtemGeoTrust but also gladly taking on prospecting trips that lasted several weeks. Nina wasn't a fan of his long absences, but, frankly, it kept their marriage from overpowering him.

Before he had a chance to change his clothes, the kids were fighting.

"*Dura! I'm* supposed to tell him, not you!" Andrey shrieked, pulling one of his sister's braids. They circled around him, yelling, hitting, and grabbing each other while he tried to understand what on earth they were fighting about.

"What's the difference?" Vita yelped.

"It was my idea!"

"Stop fighting and explain what's going on!" Yefim tried, but they were just circling him, two unreasonable, scratching, hair-pulling monsters. If only they knew how good they had it.

It wasn't this bad when they were smaller, but now that Andrey was eight and Vita ten, it was never-ending. They'd even drawn a white chalk line down the middle of their writing desk to mark the border of their domains. Crossing into enemy territory with an elbow or the edge of a textbook was considered provocation and led immediately to war. Nina often resorted to spanking them with her slipper, but Yefim couldn't bring himself to use corporal punishment. That had been his father's method.

Instead, he grabbed Andrey and Vita like the two kittens that they were and shoved them into the bathroom to cool off.

"Stay there and sort it out," he said, latching the door from the outside.

He went into the living room, which doubled as his and Nina's bedroom, and tried to slow down his breath as Nikonov had taught him. He took off his work trousers and shirt, folding them into the middle drawer of the mirrored wardrobe that he'd procured after camping out all night in front of the furniture store. Sixteen years after the war and furniture was still hard to find. Since they'd received this apartment, the piano was the only other big item they'd been able to buy, and even that took five months on the waitlist. He and Nina thought it would be good for the kids to learn to play, but they didn't take to it, so now it just stood there, a big black curvy thing that Nina called "a reminder of the cultured family we could have been."

While he put on shorts and an undershirt he wore around the house, the kids, who scuffled at first, got quiet.

"Papa, we won't fight anymore," Vita called from behind the bathroom door.

"We'll be good, Papochka," Andrey echoed.

Yefim crept closer to the bathroom, unconvinced. He heard them whispering.

"Please let us out," said Vita in her sweet-little-girl voice.

"*Horosho.* Fine. But if you start up again, you'll march right back in there."

"We won't, we won't."

He opened the latch and pulled the door when something hit him on the head, a white light flashed, and he was drowning again like that night when the Germans had found them and he fell into the marsh. They shot from multiple sides, so he lost his balance and fell right into the water as the bullets whistled past and mud seeped into his boots, dragging him down into the murk, and he knew it was senseless to cry for help because everyone was busy saving their own lives, so he tried freeing himself from the boots, but his right hand, still bandaged, was of little use, and his left arm got caught in the gun's twisted strap, and he tried to swim up as his lungs burned, until Ivan yanked him out, gulping air like a fish.

The kids were running down the stairs, screaming their heads off. Yefim sat on the floor in front of the bathroom. His undershirt was soaked and water dripped down his face. His head rang. He could see what had happened: they had tied a string to the door handle and attached its other end to an aluminum pitcher full of water, which must have fallen from the ledge above the door when he pulled on it. He could see it all—the pitcher, the string, the puddle spreading on the tiled floor—and yet his eyes refused to focus on it.

The shooting had stopped. He spat out the marsh water, down on all fours. Lieutenant Komarov lay dead. Above them stood twenty enemy soldiers with torches and two German shepherds. They made a semicircle around their pathetic little group. Yefim rose and faced them, his pants dripping, his hands raised. Someone aimed a torch in his face.

"Commander?" a voice behind the light asked, and he shook his head, trying to ignore the trembling in his legs because he didn't know if it was from the cold water, from almost drowning, or from the suddenness of his life veering into the unknown.

The kids screamed below in the courtyard. He willed himself to get up off the floor but didn't go after them. Rather, he concentrated on the tasks at hand: untying the pitcher, mopping the floor, changing into a new undershirt and boxers, hanging up the wet clothes to dry. Focusing on the minute reality in front of him was the best way he knew to make the war ghosts retreat. He'd thought perhaps they were done haunting him. But no.

Outside, it was starting to get dark, and he went out on the balcony to call Vita and Andrey. At first no one answered, but after a few minutes he saw them below, emerging from the trees and walking toward their building's entrance. He went into the kitchen to warm up the chicken cutlets Nina had left. He barely heard them come in. They tiptoed, whispering like scared little mice.

Andrey pushed his sister lightly toward him and she, his firstborn, his scrawny girl with her funny eyebrows that danced just like Basya's, looked at the ground and said, "Are you mad, Papochka?"

He shook his head and noticed a dull ache. He wasn't mad. Not at them. No, it was something else.

"We didn't think it would hit you," Andrey said.

He expected them to start blaming each other for it, but instead Vita asked, "Why did you call us 'Germans'?"

"When?"

"When the pitcher fell."

"I did?"

"Yeah," Andrey said. "You screamed it in this wild voice. That's why we ran."

He stared at them, not wanting to believe he'd slipped up.

"Your little prank hurt like hell," he said finally. "I didn't want to use a swear word, so what came out was 'Germans.' "

He got through dinner and bath and even managed to read them a story despite his mounting headache. But when they were in bed, they were still agitated from the incident.

"Papa, did you know any pilots? Mama told me she was going to listen to one," Andrey whispered from his pillow.

"*Nyet*," said Yefim, though he remembered this one pilot in the barracks. He flew in the north around Leningrad before getting shot down and had some condition that made him bald, with no eyebrows. It made him look sick even when he wasn't. The last thing he remembered of him was his bald, shriveled head hanging off the morning corpse cart. "I was in the artillery."

"Which one is that?" whispered Vita from her bed.

"It's the big cannons that shoot at tanks and planes," said Andrey, looking pleased with his knowledge of war terminology.

"I bet you were a great artilleryman, Papa, since you made it all the way to Berlin," Vita said.

Yefim hated this war rubbish and never talked about it with the kids, but this wasn't the first time they'd mentioned their father had made it "all the way to Berlin" and he could see it gave them a misguided sense of pride. "Berlin" had become shorthand for victory over fascism for this generation who couldn't know what it was really like. And now that the Germans had started building the Berlin Wall, the strength of Berlin's symbolism would only grow.

"Time to go to sleep, guys."

His head pounded.

"One last question," Andrey begged. "Pleeeeease."

"All right, but then lights out."

"Did you ever have to eat anything gross in the army? Like mud or grass or, I don't know, rats?"

What a delicacy a rat would have been at the camp.

"Ate a raw onion once. Gross enough for you?"

"Yuck!"

"Good night," he said, and turned off the lights. He needed to lie down and put a warm compress on his head.

"Papa, wait," Vita said, getting up on her elbows. "So how exactly did you lose your fingers?"

"You are too little to know about such things!" he bellowed, just wanting them to shut up already. "Sleep. Not a peep more!"

He slammed the door and then immediately felt guilty. He was the one who'd called them Germans. But then, once he lay down and his head felt better under a warm towel, he thought it was good to have been rough with them. He shouldn't have even told them about artillery and the stupid onion. He couldn't afford to indulge the kids' curiosity. If someone got wind of his lie, he'd end up at the KGB and one didn't go anywhere good from there.

When somehow he finally managed to fall asleep, he had the dream, the one he hadn't had in almost two years. He and Ivan came across a pond. Its gray, murky water reflected the sun. They ran in. The water felt warm on his skin. He spotted a purple lily on the surface and wanted to pluck it, but as he approached, the flower moved away from him. He followed it, trying to catch it, but the lily seemed to move away from him as if someone down below wanted to lead him deep into the reeds.

"Let's climb out!" he cried out to Ivan.

He moved his heavy arms as fast as he could, trying not to think about who else was in the water. Something slipped by his left foot. Finally, he reached the bank and saw them: fat, slippery fish with big red ugly mouths, snapping at his ankles with their teeth. He gasped, waking himself up, sweaty and panting, on the sofa bed next to Nina.

In that second Yefim wanted to tell her everything. How he had been captured, what he had done to survive. She had lived under occupation, after all—she knew the compromises one made in a war.

In the darkness, he made out the curved edge of the piano and the mirrored wardrobe. His breathing slowed.

No, if he told her about being captured, she would also need to start lying every time she filled out a form with that damn question about a captured relative. She already had a stain in her record. He couldn't jeopardize her further. And even if she didn't mind lying to keep his cover, there was the question of fear. Was he willing to tell her how afraid he was that the KGB would one day find out? No, it wasn't good for a wife to see fear in her husband. He still remembered how differently his mother had looked at his father after the famine.

Only one person could know about his past: Nikonov. He'd go see him in the morning.

When he awoke, the kids were already up. Yefim walked into the kitchen and realized, too late, that he'd stumbled into Nina's retelling of the pilot's lecture.

"Conditions were horrible," she was saying. "Nothing to eat except *balanda*, this watery soup out made of peels, lice biting him every night, everyone constantly getting sick and dying. I can't even tell you all the things he said, it's too awful for children's ears."

"Good morning, everyone," he said.

"Fima, you really missed out last night. Such an interesting guy. I'm telling the kids because it's quite amazing how little they know about the war. You've really got to tell them more. Come, sit."

Nina loved nothing more than to tell colorful stories. Their kids probably knew way too much. Once she had even described villagers dying on the streets during the famine. He'd told her afterward that he didn't think children should know everything about their parents' lives, but she just said, "They also shouldn't know nothing."

Now Yefim said, "They got plenty out of me last night. I wish I could join for breakfast, but I've made plans to see my buddy."

He kissed the kids on their heads, then ran down the stairs. Outside, he got into the beige Moskvich that he had received from work and swept off the fallen October leaves with the wipers. It was meant for prospecting trips, but occasionally he used it for personal errands.

Yefim drove quickly from the city center, along the newly built section of Universitetskaya Street, where they'd opened a new candy store that Andrey and Vita loved. Soon, he had passed the outskirts and drove through harvested fields toward Yasinovataya, where Nikonov lived in a green-and-yellow hut.

He remembered the first time he'd gone to see him after their meeting at the beer kiosk. The one-room hut—which had previously belonged to Nikonov's cousin, who was missing in action—was cavernous, with low ceilings and a small window near the kitchen table. The window looked out onto an empty yard with an outhouse and a vicious mutt that growled at every noise, rattling its chain. The hut smelled of old wood and unwashed sheets from the metal bed in the corner. The beige flowered wallpaper bubbled in a few places near the ceiling and had scratch marks near the floor where the former owner's cat must have sharpened its claws. The only décor was Nikonov's wartime portrait from Crimea that hung near the window.

In the six years since he first visited, Yefim returned to the green-and-yellow hut every couple of months. The hut looked much better once Nikonov changed the wallpaper, made some stools from a birch tree, and planted a small vegetable garden. Nikonov had transformed, too, thanks in part to Yefim, who had gotten him out of his job as a custodian at the local hospital and into an assistant role at a mining trust where his gold mining experience from the Kolyma camps was appreciated. Five years later, Nikonov was still there and had even risen in rank. He'd bulked up, gotten himself some normal clothes, and though he'd never be as brash as when they first met, he was still a good-looking man in his forties. He had occasional flings with local women, though he always ended them when they started asking about his past. He said that if he wanted people to dig into his history, he would have moved back to Crimea, where plenty of folks would have been free to judge him.

When Yefim arrived in Nikonov's neighborhood, he parked the car a couple of streets away and walked the rest of the way. Nikonov's neighbors were nosy and a car would attract too much unwanted attention.

He knocked three times and reached over the familiar gate to unlatch it from within. Nikonov was happy to see him. Yefim had brought some dried smelt, a two-liter jar of kvass, and another two liters of beer. After he laid his provisions on the dining table, he jumped right in. "Have you heard of this POW pilot touring the country?"

"The one that Khrushchev is using to show off the gems that Stalin had locked away?"

"Nina wanted me to come to his lecture. I managed to get out of it. But then the evening turned into shit. The kids dropped a jug of water on my head—don't even ask—and I swear I was back with my unit the night we got captured. Apparently, I even called my own kids Germans. Totally spooked them. Of course, afterward they started asking questions."

"About the Germans?"

"The war. Sometimes I envy your quiet life here. You've got no one here to lie to."

Nikonov laughed. "I guess that's true," he said, pouring himself kvass. "But I certainly don't go around yapping about my past at work. I'm actually surprised you've gotten away with it. Didn't your wife ever ask you about the war?"

"A little, the summer we met. I just told her the things that I could and left out the rest. Since then, all anyone knows is that I 'made it to Berlin.' "

His hands were moist. He hadn't realized how disturbed he was.

"Whenever there is a thunderstorm, I dream about the camps, except Germany and Kolyma get mixed up," Nikonov said. "The snow, the soup, the roll calls . . . The key is to let it go afterward. If you start overthinking it, delving back into all that, it has a way of sucking you back in. At least, that's what I've learned."

Yefim didn't want to get sucked in. The Claudia fiasco was the last time he'd let the past get him in trouble. He had been having a hard time with the move to Stalino after he lied on his first work application. If his lie was discovered, he could be arrested, and even if, by some luck, they spared him, he and Nina would have lost both their jobs and the room in the communal apartment.

Back during those first months at work, he felt the KGB's eyes on him wherever he went. The only place to hide was at home, but there, roommates crowded the kitchen, kids were always fighting or getting sick, and Nina constantly complained about how much she missed Kyiv.

And so he'd found an escape in milky-skinned, redheaded Claudia, who hadn't chopped off her hair like Nina. Some vets drank, others beat their wives. For him, being in Claudia's cozy room that smelled of spring allowed him to pretend this was a different life—one without his past.

On all those mornings after, he had expected Nina to confront him, but instead she kept her eyes on the children, never saying a word. Here was her husband spending evenings with one of the prettiest girls at the institute just one floor below her, and she didn't seem to care. Sometimes she even looked relieved. Even when he told her he would be heading to the field with Claudia to collect bryozoans, all Nina said was, "Bryozoans?" as if that was what mattered. It made him crazy. He didn't know what to do with a wife who was more passionate about dead corals than about her live husband. And so, that one night he'd taken it too far and actually slept with the girl. Now he wished things hadn't blown up the way they had, with Nina fleeing with the children and poor Claudia getting fired. He didn't know what he would have done if Nina had left him for good.

Since then, he'd promised himself never to put his family on the line. Luckily, Nikonov reappeared in his life soon after and Yefim had put his energy into helping him. In exchange, Nikonov taught him what he had learned in Kolyma: how the KGB officers thought, the typical tactics of their interrogators, and breathing techniques he'd picked up from some former monk. Just in case Yefim's luck ever ran out and the KGB got to him.

"Do you ever wonder if it's worth it?" Yefim asked.

"What?"

"The lying."

Nikonov drank the last of his kvass and wiped the foam off his lips.

"Let me tell you a story. In Kolyma, about a year into it, I ran into this fellow. Barely recognized him. Ryazanov, one of my men in Crimea. He and his twin brother were in my command and I could never tell them apart until one of them got blown to shreds. Anyway, this Ryazanov sees me at the camp and starts yelling, 'You are why I am here!' And he was right. In Crimea, it was my job to inspire those boys to fight until death like Stalin ordered. But at some point I looked around and saw their scared faces and knew every single one of them would die. We were surrounded and outnumbered. We had already lost plenty by then, including Ryazanov's brother. We would have ended up like those poor bastards who died trapped in the Adjimushkay quarries. So I decided to hell with Stalin. I wasn't going to have those boys' death on my conscience. But when I saw Ryazanov that morning at the camp, all bones and circles under his eyes, I thought maybe I should have told them to fight the damn Germans till the end. At least we would have died with honor."

"What are you saying?"

"I'm saying that while we feel even a drop of shame, lying is our only choice."

On the way home late that afternoon, Yefim thought about how much a decade in Siberia had changed Nikonov. Back in Germany, he'd had no shame whatsoever. Maybe that was the didactic point of the camps, to put even the brash in their place. The German camps wanted to destroy your flesh. The Soviet ones wanted to break your spirit.

It was getting dark. As he drove out of Yasinovataya into the countryside, the fog was settling in. The chill air smelled of wet leaves. He drove past a small village with a few lit-up windows. They looked cozy in the darkness and made him think of Nina. He wondered, for the first time, if Nina had ever envisioned their marriage like this.

He turned right. The headlights weren't doing much good in the thickening fog. But in a few more kilometers there should be a sign for Stalino. How nice it would be if his city got renamed under Khrushchev's de-Stalinization campaign. They'd already gotten rid of the dead leader's statues and were rapidly renaming streets, territories, and cities throughout the country. He would be more than happy to live in a place called Donetsk.

Suddenly, an animal's eyes glared ahead. He slammed on the brakes. The car swerved. His hands tried to hold on to the wheel while the rest of his body left the seat.

He came to in a hospital. His head felt like a melon, hard on the outside, mushy on the inside. A nurse approached and told him he had been brought in that morning.

"You're in the Yasinovataya hospital. They found you on the side of the road. I don't know how you're not dead. A part of your scalp was torn off. But don't worry, the doctor has already sewn you up. You have a concussion, though, so you'll need to stay here for at least a week before we can get you home."

Home.

Crap, Nina was probably worried. He had to call her before she went to the police.

"Could I call my wife?" he asked.

"Yes, but first you've got to talk to the detective. He's been waiting for a while."

Detective. A nauseating wave hit his forehead. He'd be asked whose car he had been driving, where he was going, whether he had been drinking. Nothing out of the ordinary: it wasn't like he had killed anyone. Still, his heart quickened and he felt woozy. He didn't want some local detective asking Nikonov how they knew each other.

The detective turned out to be young, with smooth cheeks and a mole on his chin. He looked like someone who went into the police force because he didn't get into college. Yefim felt less intimidated.

"I'm here for the report," the detective said. "Are you able to tell me where you were going, at what time, and what caused the accident?"

"Absolutely. But first I need to call my wife. You know how women are. She'll put the whole city on alert if I don't call."

The detective gave him a vague smile that told Yefim he did not know how women were.

When the nurse brought over the red corded phone, he dialed Tamara, their only neighbor with a phone, and asked for Nina.

"Fima, is that you?" Nina said, more annoyed than worried. "What happened?"

The detective hovered two steps away and could probably hear every word.

"Listen, they're sending me to another job in Artemovsk. I should be back in a week or two at the most. There won't be phones there, so I wanted to call."

Yefim didn't need her knowing that she had almost become a widow, that his scalp was torn off. She would go crazy worrying and he hated when someone worried about him. It made him seem weak.

"Don't lie to me!" Nina screamed suddenly. "I know you're up to something."

He glanced at the detective, whose cheeks reddened as if he was the one getting yelled at.

"I would not want a wife like that," the young man said, a little too loudly.

"Who is that?" Nina asked, all suspicious. "Where are you?"

Before Yefim could get himself into more trouble, he hung up. He had no idea why she thought he was lying, but by the time they'd let him out of here, she'd calm down anyway. The important thing was that he gave her the courtesy of a call and now he could deal with the detective.

"Why didn't you tell her you were in the hospital?" the detective asked.

Yefim closed his tired eyes and exhaled.

"That, young man, is how you preserve a family."

Chapter 8

January 1943
Germany

Yefim loaded the wood onto a wheelbarrow. It was a gray, still day, cold and mean. Even the crows stayed away from the Müller Leinz farm. He couldn't remember the winter sky back home hanging like a cast-iron lid over the whole world. But here, in central Germany, it seemed to be how every winter passed. Maybe that was why they decided to conquer lands east and west.

A year earlier, when he, Ivan, and eight other prisoners had been brought from the camp here, to the western side of the Elbe, he had been baffled by the German landscape visible through the slits in the tarp of their truck. When he saw the neat fields and beautiful old villages with their huge houses dotted by garden gnomes, roads paved smooth, everything clean, no horse dung, no smoke from burning trash, he couldn't understand why these people had wanted to come to his country. Their life seemed beautiful, even in the dead of winter. He remembered being stunned into silence, trying not to cry—though perhaps that had been from exhaustion. He still didn't know how he had made it out of that camp alive.

Yefim rubbed his hands on his cheeks. What a cold day! The wheelbarrow was full of firewood, so he picked it up and wheeled it down the main road toward the mess hall. He passed the gate, where Herr Fischer, the middle-aged overseer who liked to wear a thick leather coat, had met them when they'd first been dumped at the gates, dirty and bruised like rotten potatoes.

He and Ivan had hoped the farm would allow them the familiar freedom of the countryside that they'd had in their childhoods. Instead, Herr Fischer explained that they'd be joining the other forty Polish and Soviet POW laborers who were guarded day and night by off-duty German soldiers. Then he pointed out the barbed wire that surrounded the farm's bleak buildings. Yefim immediately noticed the hanging tin cans that would rattle if someone tried to escape.

"And then we'd need to call the *Polizei* and you'll be sent back to the camp, where you'll be killed off faster than our hogs," he said, wagging his gloved finger. "So don't even think about it. Remember, we can always get more laborers to replace you."

Yefim remembered how Ivan had groaned, loudly and unexpectedly, almost collapsing onto his knees, and he had to pick him back up and tell him this couldn't be worse than the camp.

He had turned out to be right. Herr Fischer showed them the barn, where there were bunk beds covered with thin straw mattresses and— oh, miracle!—blankets. There were also wooden nightstands, though Yefim didn't understand what he was supposed to keep in there since all he had on him were dirty old rags. In the middle of the barn was a small potbelly stove. Later he'd learn that it was only useful when someone managed to sneak in some wood, since Herr Fischer never gave them more than ten minutes' worth of coal, which left them shivering under those thin blankets on the colder winter nights. But on that first day Yefim happily followed Fischer down this same road to the mess hall, where he slowly ate three thick pieces of moist rye bread with steaming ersatz coffee, a bitter hot thing that made him want to run circles around the farm.

Of course, the welcome breakfast turned out to be for show. The very next day the pieces of bread became much thinner and the dinner soup turned out to be only a grade better than the camp's. But they all occasionally stole some fresh milk from the cows and that made all the difference. Even without the milk, however, Yefim had been sure they wouldn't let him die here. He was useful to them, putting in ten-hour days to take care of cattle, fix machinery, chop wood, clean equipment, and work the fields.

Now, a year later, Yefim had definitely gained some of his strength back, but he was still thinner than when he'd first left home for the army. His body had simply hardened like a hazelnut shell. His mind had hardened too. He no longer waited for the Red Army to rescue him. No, he was here for the long haul and his only job was to survive. And so he had made himself get used to the strange, repetitive life between the barn, the mess hall, the tractor hangar, the cowshed, the equipment stall, and the fields.

Ivan seemed to be fine with the routine too, until recently when something in him had broken. His eyes grew vacant, his face listless, his cheeks no longer lit up with their signature rosy glow. He didn't laugh at Yefim's jokes and kept saying he was tired. This was shortly after New Year's, as if imagining another year in captivity had made Ivan give up. Yefim had seen it before at the camp and knew that those who gave up didn't last long. He'd had wisps of it himself, especially when bad news from the front reached the farm, but nothing like this.

Just the day before, while Yefim was telling a story about Bek-Bek, his pet chicken, Ivan barked, "Why do you keep blabbing about your village? It's probably a pile of fucking ash!"

So Yefim was keeping his distance, letting Ivan work through his malaise on his own. Meanwhile, he tried to figure out what to do.

The heavy wheelbarrow rubbed his hands and he took a short break by the tractor hangar. When he reached the mess hall, he parked the wheelbarrow and bent down to stretch his legs as Mikhail had taught him. That was the thing about Ivan: with all they'd been through together, he'd become his brother. When your brother was a jerk, he didn't stop being your brother. It was still you two against the Reich.

Yefim began to unload the firewood. He stopped when he heard the guards approaching around the corner. The younger one, Franz, a tall former soldier with a bad knee, was saying, "You think Vlasov could really raise an army?"

Yefim hid behind the mess hall to listen. Vlasov had been all the talk at Müller Leinz since his pamphlet was circulated two weeks earlier. He was a former Red Army general who had been captured the previous year and allied with the Germans to form his own army with the goal of ridding Russia of Communists. The pamphlet described how Vlasov had watched Stalin and his gang of Bolsheviks arrest the army's leadership in 1938, how they created a system of political commissars who spied on and corrupted the army, how Stalin mismanaged the war by letting his soldiers starve. Stalin was the true enemy of the Russian people, Vlasov wrote, and by aligning themselves with the Germans to get rid of him and his goons, they could build a new Russia. He urged Soviet POWs to join his Russian Liberation Army.

It wasn't clear how much support he was getting from the Germans or how sincere his cause really was, so naturally many on the farm called him a rat that should be fed to the Führer's dogs. However, Yefim was surprised to learn, some actually wanted to join Vlasov. Lev from L'viv said it may be the only chance Ukraine had to rid itself of "that butcher." He said it just like that, plain as day, and Yefim couldn't believe it. Back home, one didn't even dare think of overturning the regime, not to mention make open statements about it in front of witnesses. But out here, thousands of kilometers from the ears of the NKVD, some were apparently feeling bold. He had worried that Ivan might be swayed by the pamphlets, given his distrust of the Soviet leadership, but his friend didn't seem to care. As for himself, he figured it was best to keep his tongue, though of course he didn't trust Vlasov. Who in their right mind would be on the side of the Nazis? Plus the only way Vlasov would succeed was if the Germans did, too, and there hadn't been any news of major German victories since they'd reached Stalingrad back in August.

Keeping one hand on the wheelbarrow and trying not to fidget in the cold air, Yefim heard Günther, a balding, tired-looking Fritz in his fifties, inhaling a cigarette.

"Even if Vlasov can raise a small army from these POWs, it won't do jack if we aren't winning. And if they open a second front . . ."

There was a pause. Franz, the younger guard, must have been calculating how honest he could be. Hitler didn't like his soldiers speaking negatively of his army's efforts. The German newspapers, pages of which sometimes made it onto the farm, were full of propaganda.

"My wife's cousin in Berlin," Franz said in a quieter voice, "her husband was in Stalingrad's Sixth Army. Apparently, she hadn't gotten a letter from him since November and he used to write once a week . . ."

This was huge! If the Germans were worried about Stalingrad, it meant the Soviets must be putting up a big fight. And that meant, the Red Army would get here sooner or later and let them out of this damn farm. He felt himself grinning.

The guards were silent for a while. He could hear them blowing smoke.

"If Vlasov takes a few of these guys, we'll get some fresh blood in here," Günther said. "Maybe they know the latest from the front."

"Will he take whoever he wants?"

"Not sure. I heard they are searching for tank men and artillerymen."

Yefim heard Günther stomp a cigarette and say, "Let's go in. I'm freezing my nuts off."

When the guards went inside, he ran to find Ivan. They were the only artillerymen on the farm and apparently were about to get taken into the Russian Liberation Army. He had to warn him. This was bound to shake Ivan out of his malaise.

He found him in the hangar unloading hay for the cows. Yefim whispered, "We need to talk."

Ivan stared at him, his invisible eyebrows furrowing. He led Yefim away to the other side of the hangar where they wouldn't be heard.

"Vlasov's recruiters are coming to look for artillerymen. I just heard the guards. We have to get out of here."

"How the hell would we get out?" Ivan asked, blinking quickly.

"I have a few ideas I've been mulling over," Yefim lied.

"I can't believe you've been entertaining it seriously," said Ivan, a twinkle of mockery in his gray eyes. "Suppose we manage to leave Müller Leinz. We'll still be in the middle of Germany and on the wrong side of the Elbe. How far do you think we'll make it before they catch us?"

"Farther than you think," said Yefim with false confidence.

He had been so shaken by the news about Stalingrad and by the need to escape that he hadn't given much thought to how two men of fighting age, one of them Jewish and the other speaking only elementary German, would get around a country hell-bent on destroying people like them. He only knew that they'd been through too much together; he wasn't going without Ivan.

"This is the first time we've gotten a good piece of information and can act on it instead of feeding cows while the war happens without us," Yefim said. "The guards said things aren't going well in Stalingrad and that they are afraid a second front might open up. If we get out of Germany, we can rejoin the army or find some partisan group. We can finally live instead of just existing. If we stay here, we'll be dragged into Vlasov's army."

"So what? What does it matter at this point?"

"Have you gone mad? Maybe you want to fight for Germany now?"

"I don't want to fight for anyone. Not for Germans, not for Soviets. They are the same, don't you see? Neither of them give a shit about me or you or anyone. We're expendable. No, we're less than that. We are nothing."

Ivan was in a worse place than he'd thought. Yefim tried a different tactic.

"Don't you want to go back home?"

Ivan smirked.

"Home? To my drunk father and my dead mother? I don't have a nice, big family like you, Fima. I don't have anyone to defend. And I am tired. Tired of this life."

"You can't be tired of life yet. You're just in one of those weird states people go through when they turn twenty. My brother Yakov warned me about it. Like a little crisis where you feel old but you really aren't. We have a whole life ahead of us. We're going to get out of here. You'll go back to Ukraine and maybe my mother will even let you marry Basya."

Ivan lifted his head and Yefim thought he could see a hint of a smile. Then, Ivan suddenly laughed.

"Oh, I get it. You're just afraid of the medical exam."

In his excitement over the news, Yefim had forgotten about the upcoming exam, even though the last time the doctors showed up he almost got caught. He didn't like remembering how all the laborers had to line up stark naked while he hid under the bunks and Ivan went a second time under Yefim's name because there was no way he was going to show his circumcised member to Nazi doctors. Their plan almost flopped when that brute of a Russian from who knew what village asked Ivan why he was going again. There had been so many times when Ivan had saved him. Now it was he who had to be saved, whether or not he agreed to it.

"You're right," Yefim conceded, though he didn't love the idea of Ivan coming with him out of some sort of Jew pity. "I'm sick of dreading a bullet in the face every time they want to check us for venereal disease. Now, will you come with me or not?"

For a moment Yefim imagined Nikonov in Ivan's place and knew that he wouldn't think twice about leaving.

"I'm in no condition to traipse across Germany," Ivan said quietly, and Yefim felt bad for thinking of Nikonov.

The hangar door opened and the overseer headed toward them.

"Think about it," Yefim whispered. "I'm not leaving here without you."

"Any reason you two are standing around doing nothing?" Herr Fischer asked. "Get back to work."

Ivan went back to the cows while Yefim returned to unload the wood. Surely, Ivan couldn't say no now that he knew both of their fates depended on his decision.

There was a windstorm that night, and in the morning, before they had a chance to talk it over, Ivan went off to the fields to clear debris that had fallen while Yefim went to the hangar to clean and oil the harvester.

Yefim was thinking about how he could convince Ivan to leave when Piotrek entered the hangar, his left foot dragging behind him. Piotrek was a Polish Communist who had been transferred to Müller Leinz from a Pomeranian mine after his foot had been crushed in an accident. Though he sometimes used a big stick as a cane, he had the same sturdy build as Yefim and was always quick to smile. He often cheered Yefim up by calling the farm a *"pension."* He pronounced it in the funny French way, tapping his cane and lifting his worn-out cap as if it were a shiny top hat. He loved cars and dreamed of owning one if he ever got back home to Łódź. Over the past months Piotrek had taught Yefim a little about motors. He divided his labor hours between fixing tractors at the hangar and feeding the pigs in the pigpen.

Yefim called him over.

"Ivan and I are going to get out of here," he whispered. "Do you want to come with us?"

Piotrek looked at him, a crooked smile forming on his friendly face.

"Sure, I'll just limp my way home to Łódź. What are you, crazy? Have I not told you how good we have it here at the *pension*?"

"Vlasov's recruiters are coming to pick out artillerymen."

Piotrek froze while lifting his cap. His brown eyes began to shift back and forth the way they always did when he was thinking through a plan. Yefim had seen that shifty look before when Piotrek snuck out double rations from Vasilina, who worked at the mess hall, to help another Polish prisoner who'd been running a fever. Seeing Piotrek consider their escape made Yefim feel rotten. He realized he hadn't really planned on inviting his friend to join them—he wouldn't make it very far with his bad foot—and had told him only because he hoped for Piotrek's help.

"You can't escape in the dead of winter," Piotrek said resolutely. "That's suicide."

"What would you do?" asked Yefim.

"Hide here until April," said Piotrek, as if it were the most obvious thing.

"Here on the farm? Are you mad?"

"Shhhh," Piotrek said, looking around. "Think about it. This is the last place they'll look. Then, once they've forgotten all about you, you can make your move."

"And where do you suggest we hide?"

"The attic in the pigpen. The guards never look in there. Too stinky. There is a lot of straw to keep warm, and with all the hog noise no one will hear you. I can sneak food in for you when I'm working with the pigs."

It was not the worst plan, especially considering Ivan's state. Without having to waste all their calories on hard labor, they could recoup their strength for the long journey. That afternoon, Yefim approached Ivan.

"You told someone else about this craziness?" Ivan asked.

"It's Piotrek, not *someone else*."

"You're way too trusting."

"Oh, please. He is smarter than both of us; you know that. I figured he could help."

Eventually, Ivan conceded this plan was better than trying to run off now.

That same evening, while everyone was busy scarfing down their dinner rations of turnip soup at the mess hall, Yefim ate a few spoonfuls, then snuck out as if to take a leak. Dinnertime was their best chance to escape. The two guards relaxed in their shack near the farm's gate since prisoners weren't known to cause any trouble during dinner.

The sky was black and the lanterns that hung on the front of the main buildings—the mess hall, the barracks, and the guards' shack—left a lot of dark spots around the farm. Yefim went behind the mess hall to wait for Ivan, who was supposed to follow him out. He waited and waited, but his friend wasn't coming. Yefim wondered what to do. If Ivan chickened out, would he go by himself? No, he would not leave Ivan to be dragged into Vlasov's suicidal mission. He prepared to head back into the mess hall. He'd talk to him and they'd figure out another way to escape together.

As he was about to turn the corner, he heard the mess hall door open. Someone's footsteps hurried toward him.

"Ivan?" he whispered.

"No, it's your mother come to spank you," Ivan answered, and Yefim smiled, relieved.

When Ivan came closer, he said, "This is a bad idea."

For a moment Yefim wanted to punch him in the nose. Not too hard. Just enough to shake him out of his fear and selfishness. After all, he knew if he backed out, Yefim would have no choice but to stay here too.

"Don't back out now. Vlasov's men might come tomorrow, and then what?"

"Go alone. I'll only slow you down."

Yefim was about to respond when he heard someone else coming out of the mess hall and whispered, "Let's go." He pulled Ivan around the back, through the field, and toward the pigpen on the far side of the farm. He unlatched the door and they snuck inside.

It was pitch-black and smelled of manure and dirt. Yefim heard the pigs rustling in their hay beds. Piotrek had warned them the pigs might be spooked by unfamiliar visitors, so Yefim had brought some turnip peels. He held them out through the slats of their stall and waited. He heard one animal get up and approach him. A prickly snout brushed his hand and the turnips were gone as the pig chewed loudly, snorting. He heard the animal retreat somewhere into the darkness and plop back down. Then he and Ivan followed the wooden perimeter of the pen until they found a ladder leading to the attic. Piotrek had promised no one would look for them that evening, but Yefim felt as though every creak of the rickety ladder boomed like a megaphone across the farm. He thought of Günther and Franz rushing in with their flashlights, pulling them off the ladder and beating them to a pulp.

The attic was warm—warmer than their barn. Crouching in the darkness, Yefim felt a layer of hay covering the wooden floor. He and Ivan crawled quietly, trying to find a place to settle in. They didn't talk. In the corner farthest from the ladder, they lay down and quickly buried themselves in the straw. Yefim tried to lie as still as he could. He waited for someone to sound the alarm that they'd gone missing. The guards would run around searching, check the barbed-wire perimeter, maybe even call in the police with their dogs. Instead, Yefim heard the faraway noises of the other prisoners. Then the farm went quiet.

Still, he couldn't sleep. Something rustled in the corner. The wind howled over the fields. The wood of the pen creaked in the cold. And every time he had to tell himself it wasn't the guards coming to take them to the SS. In the upper corner of the attic he noticed a small window and wished he could look outside, but moving was too risky. He lay stiff, listening to Ivan's restless breathing and worrying about what his friend was thinking. How were they going to stay in this place for weeks? They should have just left the farm immediately or else abandoned the whole damn idea. What if Ivan got worse and needed a doctor? Of course, he hadn't thought of that earlier, had he? He was such a selfish prick sometimes.

He was starting to doze off when one of the hogs squealed and he jerked awake. Ivan's breathing was calm, though, and Yefim was glad his friend had finally fallen asleep. That was when it dawned on him that maybe he'd needed Ivan, not the other way around. What if all that talk about saving Ivan was a load of crap? Maybe he just didn't want to do this by himself. Or, rather, couldn't. He was still Fimochka, the baby of the family, who'd gone from his home to the army to the camp and was still afraid to do anything on his own.

Early in the morning Yefim was awakened by the panicked stomping of boots hurrying past the pigpen. He sat up. In the dim light he could see Ivan next to him, pieces of hay caught in his blond hair. His eyes were puffy and scared. He didn't say anything, just sat silently, staring at the wall. Outside, there was shouting. Then a motor revved up, chocking in the cold morning air, and the guard's truck skidded on the dirt road in the direction of town.

"We're screwed," Ivan whispered.

Yefim lay back down and didn't answer. Hopefully, Piotrek was right and they would never think to search inside the farm. He looked at the small window next to the hayrack in the top southwestern corner of the attic that let in a ray of light. It lit up a big spiderweb in the peak of the wooden roof, and Yefim found himself staring at the spider dangling in the web. He remembered how Mikhail used to sweep the spiderwebs in the ceiling above the brick stove where Mother couldn't reach. He closed his eyes and wished he was home.

It felt like hours before Piotrek showed up.

"The guards think you've escaped," he whispered from below, and Yefim was relieved to hear his friend's familiar Ukrainian mixed with Polish. "They went to report it to the police, but don't worry, they won't come here looking. They'll just search the surrounding villages."

Through the floorboards Yefim could see Piotrek's worn-through hat and his shoulders as he fed the hogs. Piotrek talked without looking up.

"You should have seen the hell they raised this morning. But I've spread the news about Vlasov looking for artillerymen, so now everyone thinks you ran off."

He brought them mashed rutabaga from the kitchen and hid it in the corner of the pen, away from the pigs. He told them to wait until dark before coming down to get it.

"Your only job is to make yourselves invisible," he said before leaving again.

After a couple of days, things on the farm seemed to go back to normal, and they worked out a system with Piotrek, settling into their strange new life in between. Though they were still at Müller Leinz, their days were completely different from the past year: they didn't have to work, they could sleep all day, the guards weren't yelling at them, and they didn't have to share quarters with dozens of other men, only with pigs, which were good at keeping their secret. But there were minuses, too: though the attic was tall enough to stand in and long enough to take a dozen steps, they couldn't walk around like they used to. Even worse, all they saw of the outside was through the tiny window, which they would have to climb on top of each other to reach. The window overlooked the back field, where there was a small outhouse. Occasionally they overheard bits of conversation between passing prisoners or guards, but they couldn't see them.

Yefim saw that a break from the daily farmwork was doing Ivan some good. His gray eyes came alive again and he was less grumpy. They discussed ideas on how best to escape, and once Ivan even admitted, "It would be good for me to get out of here."

He began following Yefim in his daily exercise routine of stretches, crunches, and push-ups, and together they built their strength for when the time came to make their move.

The most exciting part of their day was Piotrek's morning visit. Yefim's mood always soured as soon as he left. The long day stretched in front of him, sluggish and formless like fog. Before the pigpen, he had often fantasized about doing nothing like he used to on Saturdays as a kid, floating in the warm pond overgrown with duckweed or playing hide-and-seek with Naum and Georgiy among the sunflowers. Now, however, he often wondered if they should have left right away. It might not have been smart to go in the middle of winter, but waiting for spring to arrive was torture. Still, he saw it was good for Ivan and tried not to complain.

One morning, about three weeks after they "disappeared," Piotrek was telling them the latest gossip when they heard steps and then the voice of Günther, the older guard.

"Piotrek?"

"Ja."

Yefim heard Günther walk in. A shiver ran through him. If the guard found them, they were dead. Lying on the floor of the attic, he was afraid to exhale.

"Who are you talking to?"

"*Nein, nein,*" said Piotrek. "Just the pigs."

There was a pause. Yefim imagined Günther peering at the ceiling.

"You talk to pigs?" he finally said, sounding unconvinced.

"Sure. We always talked to our pigs in Poland."

"Maybe I should call you Polish swine," said Günther, and laughed, his laughter turning into a cough. "Come, Vlasov's men are here."

Piotrek wiped his hands on his pants and followed Günther out. Yefim lay there, unable to move.

They had to wait until the next day to hear what happened. Piotrek described how the two recruiters lectured the prisoners about the evils of Stalin's regime.

"They said the Russian Liberation Army has a very real chance to overthrow him. But they need more skilled soldiers to have a real effect. Most weren't convinced. You should have heard them booing and spitting. I noticed a few people who were sitting quietly. And then in the evening I saw the recruiters leave with Lev from L'viv and two others."

"So they didn't force anyone to go with them?" Ivan asked.

"We were strongly encouraged, but I guess the Fritzes didn't give them the authority to pluck whomever they wanted."

The rest of that day Yefim and Ivan didn't speak. Ivan curled up in the corner and pretended to sleep. He was clearly angry at Yefim for pulling them out on the fear that they'd be forced to join Vlasov. Yefim didn't know how to tell him that, even without that, making a change before Ivan wasted away was a way of saving his best friend. The silence made the attic seem even smaller.

The next morning Ivan must have changed his mind or acquiesced to their situation because things were back to normal. The question of Vlasov's recruiters didn't come up again.

Finally, April came and it was time to leave. Piotrek put the rest of their plan in place, and the next day around midnight they climbed down from the attic. The hogs slept in their stalls. Yefim waited for the signal. He knew Piotrek would come through. He just hoped he still remembered how to run. He turned to Ivan, who stood next to him, their shoulders touching.

"We're never coming back here."

"Never," said Ivan, and they shook hands in the dark.

Soon there was a commotion and they crept toward the door. Yefim shifted from foot to foot, warming up his muscles.

The farm erupted with screams. "*Pozhar!* Fire! Fire!"

"They're burning us alive!" someone screeched.

Yefim and Ivan burst out of the pigpen and darted toward the field with the small outhouse. Piotrek had said that panic was easy to spread in the middle of the night. He was right. While everyone was busy figuring out the fire was nothing but a small flame in the garbage bin behind the barn, Yefim ran. The fresh cold air rushed into his mouth. His eyes watered. The barbed-wire fence seemed incredibly far. Then, suddenly, it was right in front of him.

He got out a paring knife that Piotrek had lifted from the kitchen and began to cut the wire while Ivan kept watch. As his hands shook the fence, the tin cans jangled. He knew they would: that was why their plan relied on making a ruckus instead of escaping in the quiet of night. But the shrill noise alarmed him.

"Keep cutting!" Ivan said.

Except the knife wasn't as sharp as it could have been or maybe the wire was thicker; either way, it was slow. Across the field, he heard German barking mixed with Russian grumbling. He broke through the first wire and told himself not to get distracted. To the guards and the prisoners, they had long been gone.

As he cut farther up, the barbed wire scraped his hand and caught his sleeve. Ivan helped free him and he made another breach in the fence when the noise around the barn began to die down. They couldn't delay any further. He kicked the part of the fence that he had cut and together they pushed and pulled to pry an opening.

Once they were on the other side, they ran. First, toward the Elbe, which was closer than Yefim had thought. He could smell its fishy odor. Then they turned right and ran along the river's western bank.

His lungs burned.

At a bend where the river narrowed, they threw off their clothes and stuffed them in the potato sacks they had brought. Then Yefim took a big breath and stepped into the icy, gurgling darkness.

This was why Mother had forced him and his brothers to take all those cold baths. She said it would help them in life. If only she knew.

On the other side, they dried themselves with the sacks, scrubbing each other's numb skin with the rough burlap until it tingled and burned. After they had gotten back into their clothes, Ivan said, "There is no way I could have done this two months ago."

"Neither could I," Yefim lied.

Escaping had turned out to be easier than he thought. Still, he was glad he had allowed the extra time for Ivan to build up his strength. He couldn't imagine leaving him behind.

They hurried east, away from the river. The fields lay dark and motionless. Ivan kept turning around, thinking he'd heard something.

"They're chasing us!"

"No one's after us. Calm down. You're just on edge."

The truth was, at first Yefim also expected a guard to jump out behind them and yell, "Halt!" But the farther they walked undisturbed, the more he felt a space opening inside him, as if a breath he'd been holding for many months could finally be exhaled.

He hadn't realized how much he had gotten used to captivity. It was exhilarating and scary to be in a world that wasn't guarded or fenced off. The night was cold but he didn't notice. He was too overwhelmed by their escape, by the occasional darting of a bird, by the crunching of last year's leaves under his feet, and by the wind that carried the powerful, free smells of the countryside.

By dawn they had reached a forest. They thought it would provide cover in the growing light of day, but the forest turned out to be a thin woodland. Within an hour they emerged on the other side. There, fields surrounded a village, where ornate, neat German farmhouses with their crisscrossed brown beams glared at the two intruders from under the morning clouds. Once again he wondered why the

Germans risked their lives to come to Ukraine if they had all this back home. Why wasn't this enough?

They retreated back into the forest to wait it out until evening. Yefim wished they could light a fire and cook a warm meal, but fire was suicide. Instead, they each ate a small piece of a half loaf of rye bread, Piotrek's parting gift, which was supposed to last them two or three days before they had to find their own food.

He thought of the Müller Leinz farm. It was as hard to imagine being confined there now that he'd walked unguarded through wide-open land as it was to realize that they'd actually escaped. After breakfast, they dug a trench behind a bush, covered themselves with branches, and, to Yefim's surprise, fell asleep.

He woke up with the first drops of rain. Above, low spring clouds had gathered and the forest was dripping around them. They waited until it grew darker. By then the rain had stopped. They gathered their few things and walked north to avoid the village. But when they emerged from the forest, they saw a big patch of bright lights reflected in the clouds.

"Looks like we've hit a town," said Ivan. "We'll need to make a loop around it."

"Or we could stroll into town and say, 'We're two POWs looking for beautiful Fräuleins and some schnitzel.' "

Ivan's cheeks widened and he burst out laughing. Yefim realized it had been a long, long time since he'd heard that laugh. Those two slow months in the pigpen had been worth it after all.

"Aren't you glad you came with me?" Yefim asked.

"Yes. Just don't let it get to your head, my fearless friend."

They headed out, making a big loop around the lights of the town.

"What do you think your sister is doing now?" Ivan asked, and this, too, was a good sign.

It had started to rain again, and with his feet sinking into the mud it was hard to picture Basya. All that came was an image of her knitting, her slender shoulders bent over her work as her thick black braid cascaded down her back.

"Knitting," he said. "Somewhere in the Urals. But if you ever hope to see Basya again, we'd better hurry."

As they trudged through the hardening rain, they came across a railroad that led east. They followed it for a while. Soon they heard a train approaching and hid in the ditch.

Yefim watched the train cars thunder past and remembered not wanting to look at the bodies left in the cattle car that had brought them to the camp. It was the stench that he couldn't forget. He wondered how many people, dead and alive, had been squeezed inside this train above them.

Once it passed, they climbed out and continued walking east. Ivan said, "If they catch us, let's tell them we're *Ostarbeiters* who escaped from a transport train."

Ostarbeiters were usually from Ukraine and Belarus. Back at Müller Leinz, Piotrek had told Yefim about the young Ukrainian boys, some only fourteen, he'd seen at the mine. It was definitely safer to claim they were civilians. Germans were less likely to kill them than runaway POWs.

As they continued walking along the tracks, Yefim fantasized about coming across his brothers—especially Mikhail and Yakov, who had always been kind to him. At the farm any thought of his brothers was tainted with shame for being a German workhorse, but now that he'd escaped he didn't feel as guilt-ridden. He had a good story now: a heroic escape. He liked to imagine how they would head east all together. They'd talk all night like they used to when they were kids, passing whispered messages in a game of broken telephone as they lay on the floor of their hut while their father prayed in the corner and Basya, on the other side of the curtain with Mother, told them to shush. She was always jealous that she wasn't in on the boys' game. If they were here along with Ivan, they'd whisper about everything that had happened to them since they last saw each other back home.

For the next week, as he and Ivan hid during the day and walked at night, his fantasy grew and morphed. Once, he imagined finding all four of his brothers, collecting them like bread crumbs on his journey home. He pictured himself part of "the Shulman boys," as they used to call them in the village, strong and alive, with black hair and sharp dark eyes, sitting around a fire in their mother's woolen socks, a spoon in each hand eating, eating, eating.

"Hey!" Ivan shook him from his trance. "Did you hear what I said? We can't keep going like this. We need to find food or we won't last long."

He was right. It had been three days since they ate the last of Piotrek's bread, and though they'd had plenty of water, the hunger had had its effect. His muscles ached all over, and he'd grown more irritable and unfocused, like on bad days back at the camp.

They found the nearest village and waited until most of the lights had gone out. It was a moonless night, which made it hard to see if anything was growing. As Yefim inched along the rows of the first field they came across, he found no shoots. In hopes of unearthing a potato or some other bulb they could gnaw on, he dug into the cold soil with his hand. He felt himself getting jittery from the prospect of finding something edible. In the ground, there was nothing of use, just some seeds.

Next, they snuck into the garden of the closest house, which in a show of German honesty wasn't fenced off. Yefim searched the garden beds but couldn't locate anything except ceramic gnomes. He was growing frustrated when Ivan ran over and whispered, "Come! They've got radishes," and pulled him toward a patch on the edge of the garden. Yefim could feel them with his fingers, smooth and crisp. He hurried to dig one out. It was a tiny young thing, no wider than his pinky. Rubbing the dirt off of it, he shoved it into his mouth. The radish was crunchy and sweet, a dizzying reminder of the spring salad his mother used to make. Quickly, he dug them out one by one, trying to chew, but sometimes swallowing them whole.

The other rows had strawberries, though the berries hadn't grown yet. Instead, they tried some strawberry leaves, but they weren't any good. The next house on the other side of the garden was a big timber-framed building with an overhanging second floor surrounded by a fence. Its upper window was lit up and Yefim could see there was a big garden. They might as well try it. Radishes would get them only so far.

He moved toward it, but Ivan stopped him.

"Too risky."

"No one will see us," Yefim said, annoyed at Ivan's sudden back-tracking. "I've got a good feeling we'll find something there. Come on."

But Ivan wouldn't move.

"Do you want to starve?"

"This whole thing was your idea, Shulman, so you do whatever you think is best."

Ivan had never called him by his last name before. Yefim was too hungry to argue.

"Fine," he said. "Wait here."

He crept toward the big house, hopped over a fence, and entered the back garden, which had a row of trees and a small greenhouse. At first he couldn't find anything—just more seeds and some bitter shoots. Finally, he came across an onion patch. Yefim thrust his hands into the soil to pull up the bulb.

A dog barked from the other side of the house.

He froze.

In the quiet of the night, the barking felt as loud as if the dog were close enough to chew off his ear. It must have been running toward him. He yanked the onion and bolted. At the fence, he pulled himself up, but the dog grabbed the sole of his shoe, growling. He kicked. The dog yelped and let go. He leapt over the fence and ran.

He ran toward Ivan. Together they sprinted across the field. The dog barked on, waking up other dogs and what must have been half the damn village. They ran and ran until their lungs were giving out. When they were far enough away, they plopped down under an aspen tree, panting.

"What the hell . . . happened?" asked Ivan when he could finally speak.

"Damn dog . . . must have heard me digging."

"Did you find anything?"

"Yes! Here."

He took out the onion and carefully placed it in Ivan's hand. His heart still pounded hard.

"You risked your life for an onion?"

"Call me crazy." Yefim grinned.

"Crazy you are."

Ivan wiped the soil from the precious bulb, peeled off the skin, and bit into it.

"This is the best onion I've ever had," he said as tears ran down his face. Yefim looked at his friend and imagined them sitting like this back in Ukraine. Someday, he hoped.

For the next three weeks they walked and hid and stole whatever edibles they could. After the incident with the dog, they tried to be more careful. One time they dug out unpicked white asparagus. Another time, in the early morning, they caught a fish in a stream and ate it raw; that was a real feast. Otherwise, Germany wasn't as wild and overgrown as Ukraine. Its land rarely gifted untended sustenance, so more days than not, they went hungry and their eastward trek slowed almost to a halt.

Yefim began having frequent headaches and found it hard to focus, but he was still coping better than Ivan, who could barely walk. He tried to keep up their morale with stories from their time in the army, while Ivan usually kept silent.

"Remember that last dance we went to?" he said, trying to coax Ivan into talking. "All those Lithuanian girls? Before the brawl."

When Ivan didn't respond, he went on.

"I met Eva there. She really wanted to dance. I tried telling her that I didn't dance and kept thinking, 'Where the hell did Ivan learn to?' Can you please explain yourself?"

That seemed to do the trick.

"Mama," he said softly, pointing into the darkness as if he could see her. "She liked to dance with me when I was little."

Then a branch snapped underneath his foot and his voice changed. "Father hated it."

Ivan hadn't talked about his mother since before the war began. Yefim hoped his friend's mind wasn't getting stuck in dark corners of his past.

"You have to admit this may not be great, but it's still better than the famine," Yefim said.

Ivan didn't reply. They continued walking slowly through the forest when he mumbled something about fish.

"What?" Yefim asked.

Ivan stopped.

"During the famine, I managed to catch a fish once and was carrying it home. I was so excited to show it to Mother, so proud I would feed my family. But on the way one of the government men stopped me and took it."

"Prick. Maybe his family was also starving."

"No, Fima. He said, 'You'll die sooner without it.' Do you get what I'm telling you? The famine wasn't some natural tragedy. Stalin wanted us to starve. He has never cared about us—and never will."

"Why haven't you ever told me this story before?"

"Didn't think you were ready to listen."

"And now?"

"And now we're both fucked, so you might as well know in case you make it back home."

He didn't want to believe Ivan. They were kids back then; he must have misunderstood why that man took his fish. And now, in his famished delusion, he was ready to see evil everywhere. No ruler would starve his own people on purpose. That was just hunger talking.

That night Ivan found some unknown black berries and stupidly decided to eat them.

"You don't know what they are," Yefim warned him. "My mother told me never to eat things you aren't sure about."

"Your mother is smarter than mine. Mine just said, 'Survive.' And that's what I am doing."

He shoved a handful of berries in his mouth, looking pleased. But an hour later his stomach began to hurt. He doubled over while Yefim, who himself was feeling weak, tried to figure out what to do. By morning it was full-on food poisoning.

Liquids drained out of Ivan like bilgewater from a leaky boat. Yefim walked through the forest until he found a stream and kept bringing his friend water. At first Ivan took little sips with his pale chapped lips, but after a while his cheeks grew red with fever. He was in and out of consciousness. On the second day he stopped throwing up and just lay there with his eyes closed, taking shallow breaths.

Yefim knelt next to his friend, cupping his head and forcing his mouth open to pour small sips of water. He fashioned Ivan a bed out of fir branches to keep his body warm. As the sun set that day, Yefim fell asleep next to him, covering them both with branches. Every time he woke, he put his ear to Ivan's chest to listen for a heartbeat. He remembered how Oleg died right next to him before he even noticed. He couldn't let Ivan go the same way.

In the morning he went to look for help. East of the forest, there was a farm. He returned for Ivan and, gathering all the strength he had left, heaved him on his shoulders and carried him toward the farm's perimeter. There, he laid him down behind a bush and waited. After a while a group of ostarbeiter women and men came out to work the fields, and Yefim watched them closely from behind the bush, wondering whom to approach.

After an hour, one of the ostarbeiters came to till not far from where Yefim was hiding. He was young, sixteen at most, with a teen's thin blond mustache on a simple broad face. On his right breast pocket was a dark blue sign with white letters that said ost. He didn't look emaciated, which meant the rations were good at this farm. For a minute Yefim watched him. He tried to determine how trustworthy the kid was from the way he tilled. His father had told him that you could always tell a man's soul by the way he treated the earth, but Yefim never really understood what that meant. Besides, he didn't have the luxury of deliberating.

"*Hey, paren'!*" he called in a loud whisper.

The ostarbeiter looked in his direction and sauntered over, his face showing neither fear nor surprise, as if strangers popped out of these bushes on a daily basis.

"And who are you?" he asked.

"Ostarbeiters. The Germans were working us to death at a mine, so my buddy and I ran off," Yefim lied, figuring it was safer if the lad didn't know they were POWs.

"Where are you from?"

"Near Vinnytsa," Yefim said. "You?"

"Slutsk," said the kid, a Belorussian. "So what did you want?"

"My buddy got food poisoning and hasn't eaten in a week," said Yefim, pointing to Ivan, who was lying under a bush with his eyes closed. His face was pale, almost greenish. "Could you help us?"

The kid looked at them both for what seemed like too long a time. Yefim tensed up. Had he made a mistake trusting this guy?

"Shouldn't be a problem," the ostarbeiter finally said, and Yefim was relieved. "I'm sure I can find some extra bread or milk."

"Milk?" Yefim cried out. The last time he'd had milk was when Piotrek snuck some into the pigpen back in March. His mouth salivated at the very word *moloko*.

"Sure. They treat us pretty good here."

"Don't get into any trouble on our behalf."

"Don't worry," said the Belorussian. "I'll be back as soon as I can sneak something out."

Yefim watched him walk toward the barn on the opposite end of the field, then sat next to Ivan under a bush.

"Did you hear that?" he said, patting his friend's cheek. "*Moloko!*"

Ivan's lips moved, but no sound came out. Yefim remembered that first day of the war when Ivan stood over him saying something he couldn't hear.

"Just hold on a little longer," Yefim said, and propped Ivan up so he'd be able to drink.

The sun warmed them up. Yefim wasn't sure how long it would take the Belorussian boy to come back without being seen, so he rested his eyes while they waited. He remembered the milk swaying in a bucket that Mikhail carried from their neighbor Kateryna's barn and how he ran after it to make sure his brother didn't spill a drop. Their mother would then ladle it into a large mug and Yefim would drink it, still warm and deliciously musky, along with that morning's fresh black bread. He was still little then, before the famine.

"You guys here?" the Belorussian called from the other side of the bush. "I brought milk!"

Yefim jumped up so quickly that dizziness and the low sun blinded him for a moment and he couldn't see the kid. Then something cold and sharp poked him in the back. *"Hände hoch!"*

Yefim raised his hands and turned around. Behind him a German policeman pointed a rifle with the satisfied smirk of a bounty hunter. Next to him, the Belorussian drank a cup of milk.

Chapter 9

February 1965
Donetsk (formerly Stalino), Ukrainian SSR

The bright April sun shone right onto the chalkboard where Yelena Vasilyevna was writing out *Great Patriotic War* in her perfect cursive. Vita loved literature class. Partly this was because she got to share the desk with V.N. and smell his musk and orchestrate an occasional bumping of elbows that sent pleasant little shivers down her spine. But she also loved it because of Yelena Vasilyevna herself, a young and bubbly teacher who entertained them with gossipy anecdotes from the lives of writers they'd read, making them seem like more than just wise dead men.

Vita copied her teacher's words into her notebook and looked up as Yelena Vasilyevna wiped her delicate hands with perfect oval-shaped nails onto a small rag she kept on her desk. Today she wore one of her famous Ukrainian kerchiefs over a stylish midnight-blue dress, looking like she could have stepped off the pages of *Fashions*. Vita couldn't wait to graduate out of her brown cotton school uniform that no self-respecting fourteen-year-old should be forced to wear.

"Class," Yelena Vasilyevna said, her high cheekbones glistening with a hint of rouge. "On May 9, our country will be celebrating the twentieth anniversary of Victory Day. To prepare, we will be reading *The Young Guard* by Alexander Fadeyev, a novel based on a group of teenage partisans who fought against the Germans right here in the Donbas."

Vita had never read about anything that happened in the Donbas. Usually, books in their literature course were set in Moscow or Leningrad or some "town N" as in Gogol. To think their coal-mining, metallurgy-producing region was worthy of the written word almost gave her a chill. She glanced at V.N. to see if he was as thrilled as she was, but he was staring out of the window, his dreamy blue eyes focused on the tree swaying in the spring wind. The son of a steelworker, he wasn't much of a reader, but those gorgeous eyes made up for it. Plus he was still classier than any of the boys Lenka was sneaking out to see. Vita could hear Lenka doodling at the desk behind her. That girl was such a hussy that after her mother, who worked long hours at the salami factory, locked her in her room to keep her out of trouble, she still snuck out through the window but then fell five stories. Of course, if that was Vita, she'd be a corpse by now, but Lenka managed to snatch something on the way down and land in the bushes, walking off to see some boy. Like a cat. And now Vita was assigned to help Lenka with her homework and exert positive influence, even though it was clear as day that the girl was hopeless. All she talked about were lewd ideas of how Vita could get V.N. to notice her.

"Vita Shulman," Yelena Vasilyevna said, and Vita snapped to attention. "I will need to see you after class."

Vita felt everyone's eyes on her, maybe even V.N.'s, though she didn't dare look. Her chest grew hot in her uniform. Her cheeks, she could tell, were turning the color of beets.

After class, when everyone left, Yelena Vasilyevna closed the door.

"I've been told your father made it all the way to Berlin," she said. "Since this year marks an important anniversary of the war, I wanted to invite him to speak to our class."

Vita didn't know how much Yelena Vasilyevna knew about her father. She didn't remember ever mentioning him in class. What she did know with certainty was that Papa would not be pleased.

He never talked about the war, not to her or Andrey and, as far as she knew, not even to Mama. The only person he probably discussed it with was that war buddy he occasionally visited in Yasinovataya. But Vita had never even seen this friend, so who knew what that was all about? She certainly hadn't brought up the war ever since that brush-off years ago when he told her and Andrey they were "too little to know such things."

She wasn't sure when he would consider her big enough. Every February 22 on the eve of Soviet Army Day, she planned to broach the subject again. But on the morning of the holiday she'd get too queasy, as if prying into this forbidden topic might prove too painful for them both. Instead, she'd write him a card that said something vague about how proud she was of his service.

Meanwhile, what she knew about his soldier years she could count on one hand: he had been in the artillery, he'd lost parts of his fingers, he'd eaten a raw onion once, and he had made it to Berlin. There were no photographs, no letters, no mementos except for an ugly little brass mug he'd apparently carried with him to Berlin that now stood on a shelf. Even his medals were gone—stolen on the train.

"I will ask him, of course," Vita told Yelena Vasilyevna, already dreading it. "He travels a lot, so I don't know if he will be in town then."

After school, Vita walked home with Lenka. They pushed against the nose-pinching wind, which was always strongest on Lenin Square. The steely sky was slowly losing its light. Somewhere beyond the thick clouds the sun must be starting to set. The square was emptier than usual, with only a few figures battling the wind past the fountain. Even the pigeons were gone.

"Are you so excited to invite your dad?" Lenka asked.

"Wait, how do you know about my dad?"

"Oh, I was the one who told Yelena Vasilyevna about him. You know I love your dad! I wish I had a father like him."

Vita stopped near the fountain.

"You did this? Without even telling me? Why would you do that?"

Lenka's blue eyes widened. She blinked slowly, like a dumb doll.

"Why not? You have a dad who made it to Berlin and a certain boy you're trying to impress. Except you don't want to listen to my more . . . direct approach. So I found a way to make sure V.N. finally notices you."

"Because of my dad? You are such an idiot, Lenka!"

Lenka's cold lips pressed tightly together. Her eyes started to water. Vita felt bad for calling her an idiot. Lenka was just obsessed with boys because her own father had been gone since she was two. Her stepfather was gone, too, and now her mother occasionally brought a "friend" who'd last from a few days to a few months. No wonder Lenka didn't understand how fathers really worked, how if they didn't give you a green light to talk about something, you stayed the hell away from it.

"You may not know this, but my dad never talks about the war. Ever. And now, thanks to you, I have to ask him to talk about it in front of our whole class."

"Oh," Lenka whimpered. "I didn't know."

They continued walking past Vladimir Ilyich Lenin in silence. Vita wished Andrey was there instead of Lenka. He'd understand her dilemma better than anyone, even though he was only twelve and still such a kid sometimes. Anyway, he was at gymnastics and wouldn't get home till later.

At the end of the square where she and Lenka usually parted ways, they stopped.

"Your dad is a war hero," Lenka said gravely, her hand on Vita's shoulder. "That's a big deal. I bet he'd love a chance to make you proud."

"Right."

"It will be all right. I just know it. He is such a nice man."

Vita didn't disagree. Her father was nice. But considering Lenka only saw him in passing, she certainly had some exaggerated ideas of his benevolence. Still, there was something in this situation that gave Vita some hope. If Papa came to her class, she would finally get something out of him without appearing nosy.

"I am cold," Vita said, and quickly kissed Lenka on the cheek. "I'll see you tomorrow."

She hurried down a narrow alley flanked by brambles whose tiny buds looked like they were freezing. She couldn't wait to be in the warm kitchen, slurping Mama's soup. Mama would know how best to approach Papa about this school talk.

She could already see her apartment building up ahead, past the rectangular fountain and across the avenue, when a drunk in a torn military tunic meandered onto the path. He stopped a few meters in front of her, swaying. His face—red, puffy, with a large scab on his chin—was repulsive. Vita slowed but continued walking toward him, hoping he would disappear back wherever he had come from and let her pass. She could already smell his odor. When she was a few steps away, he suddenly spread his arms and legs wide like a spider and slurred, "Where are you heading?"

She froze. He began to advance toward her, scanning her body with his narrowed, puffy eyes. She didn't know what he wanted. Her breath was stuck in her throat. She took a step back, then another.

"Come here, my little Yid," he beckoned, his puffy red hands spread wide.

Vita turned and darted back toward the square.

She didn't turn around to see if he was following. Instead, she headed toward the granite Lenin as if he could protect her. Nothing like this had ever happened to her. At the square, Lenka was already gone. She tried to remember whether they'd passed any policemen on their way from school, but couldn't. Plus the drunk hadn't actually done anything except scare her. There was no way she was going to go up to a policeman and tell him some alcoholic called her a Yid. No, she just needed to get home another way.

Vita decided to make a big loop around the square and reach her apartment building from the side of her old daycare. She kept thinking how she should have turned around and said something to the drunk. But what? Lenka would know, she was of the streets. But not Vita. A professor's daughter, a perfect student, she'd never dare utter a nasty word out loud. As she crossed the street and headed north away from the square, his slurred, lascivious voice echoed in her ears: *my little Yid.*

She had never thought of herself as Jewish. She didn't even know what it meant. To her, the real Jews were foreigners who lived in the distant, exotic land of Israel. Instead, the Soviet Jews were just people with particular last names who otherwise could be just as studious as her or as immature as Andrey, but at the end of the day were simply Soviet citizens. Of course, she knew that Papa's family was Jewish, but it was another subject he never talked about. She had a sense that he also didn't know what being Jewish meant, even though his mother, Baba Maria, was the most Jewish person Vita knew. Baba Maria had a funny way of throwing Yiddish words into her Ukrainian, never ate pork, and, for some reason, was offended by rabbit. But mostly she had these stern, mournful eyes that made Vita afraid that if she asked the wrong question, a sea of sadness would spill out of them. Maybe that was what being Jewish meant. Vita didn't think she was anything like Baba Maria, so how could the drunk tell that she had Jewish blood? Maybe everyone else could tell, too, but just never said it.

She was grateful the sky was getting darker. Ahead, a crowded trolleybus screeched to a stop, releasing tired adults. They hurried past her, a blur of purses, boots, coats, and cigarette smoke. She wondered how Papa would take it if someone called him a Yid. And then it occurred to her that at some point someone probably had. Maybe when he was a kid in his mostly non-Jewish village. Or maybe in the army because guys said stupid stuff like that. It was hard to imagine what Papa did when he heard it and harder still to predict how he'd react if she told him about today's incident. Which was why she wouldn't. If he were to agree to Yelena Vasilyevna's invitation, she needed him in the best mood possible.

By the time Vita made it to her building, she was relieved to get inside. On the third floor, she could smell the soup—potato—as she rang the smooth metal doorbell that screeched for only a second before the door was flung open and her mother shrieked, "Where have you been?" Mama had gotten stricter with Vita's schedule ever since her figure got curvier. Normally, it gave Vita secret pleasure to scare the wits out of her mother, who theatrically clutched her heart like some senile babushka even though she was forty-one. But not today.

"I had to go to Lenka's after school," Vita said, nonchalantly taking off her fur-lined boots that Papa had brought her from one of his work trips.

"Since when do you go there on a Friday? Come into the kitchen. I'll have to reheat the soup for you."

Vita hurried after Mama. She could tell her original explanation wouldn't do. She decided to try a half-truth.

As her mother lit the stove with a match, Vita told her how she was hurrying home and a man blocked her path and there was no one around, so she ran away and took the long way home. She left out the part about being called a Yid.

"But where was Lenka?"

"She left before that." Vita hesitated, trying not to lose the logic of her story. "We had an argument on the square, but by the time I ran away from that bum, she was gone. If Lenka was with me, she would have known what to do."

Mama looked at her carefully.

"Did that man say something to you?"

Her question didn't surprise Vita. Mama was like a detective. Whenever Andrey got in trouble, she could tell either from his lying eyes or because someone had already exposed him; it could be a neighbor, a colleague, a student, or some other person because Mama knew half the city. But even without her informants, Mama had a freaky intuition for the truth. She always said she could feel it whenever Papa was in trouble during his trips, even if he tried to cover it up. Like that time when he got into a car accident and told her he was being sent on a work project, and she knew he was lying because she'd had a dream that he was covered in blood. Or so the story went. Vita didn't remember this incident, but Mama liked to bring it up as a show of her witchy powers.

Since Vita had never been good at covering anything up, she caved.

"He called me . . . 'my little Yid,' " she said, and—hearing the ugly words in her own mouth—began to cry.

Nina sat down on a stool, and when Vita looked up at her, her mother had teared up too, two tiny lakes in her gray eyes.

"Now, you listen to me, girl. This might not be the last time you'll hear some antisemitic comment. Ukraine has had a difficult relationship with its Jews and it seems to come and go in waves. Luckily, you were only a baby when it was really bad. I've actually been meaning to tell you something . . . My colleague recommended we change your last name before applying to universities. There are quotas for Jews."

Vita stopped crying. "But when I filled out the application for Komsomol, I put my ethnicity as Ukrainian. Isn't that what my passport will say too?"

"The admissions board won't look at your passport, darling. They'll see 'Shulman' and cross you out. I already discussed it with your dad. We'll give you my last name instead and you'll have no issues getting in, especially if you keep up your straight fives and receive that gold medal."

"So I guess universities also don't like little Yids?"

Mama sighed and ladled the soup into a bowl.

"Here, Vitochka, have some food and tell me about Lenka. Why were you arguing?"

Vita ate quickly, trying to calm herself. The Jewish quota wasn't Mama's fault. She just felt stupid for not having known. For thinking that good grades and her acceptance into the Komsomol guaranteed open doors to her future. But apparently her dad's last name trumped all that. With it, she was a second-class citizen. And yet Papa had carried that name his whole life and it didn't seem to have given him any trouble.

"Lenka told Yelena Vasilyevna that she should invite Papa to talk about the war. Without telling me first. You know how she idolizes him."

"Oh, it's always something with that girl," Mama said. "Your dad isn't going to want to do that."

"I know. But what am I supposed to do?"

Mama thought for a moment.

"I'm sure your father will figure something out. But don't tell him about the man on the square."

When Papa came home, Vita poured him soup while Mama was busy working on her students' papers in her room. To feel less awkward, she busied herself with cutting him bread and said, as casually as she could, "Papa, our literature teacher assigned us *The Young Guard*, and because it's the twentieth anniversary of victory coming up, she asked if you would come talk to our class."

"Talk about what?" Papa said between slurps as she handed him the bread bowl.

"About what you did in the war."

She stood nervously under the glare of the white kitchen lamp. Papa's hand paused above the bowl.

"Why would she ask that?"

Vita tried to keep her voice level. For some reason she didn't want to bring up Lenka's role in this.

"She said it would complete our understanding of the war. Maybe she wants someone to talk to us about how the army and the partisans worked together to kick the Germans out of Ukraine."

"But I wasn't in Ukraine."

"You weren't?" she said. She should have known that. Had he ever told her?

"I was in Lithuania," Papa said curtly, as if she had said something offensive. Her whole body tensed. "Besides, I can't just leave work and come to your school for a 'talk.' "

Vita decided she had no choice but to use her last weapon.

"But I just got accepted into the Komsomol, Papa. It would make me look bad if you don't show up. *Pozhaluysta!*"

He put down his spoon and looked out of the window. She followed his gaze. In the glass, among the yellow squares of the windows in the opposite building, she saw his sad, unseeing eyes and herself standing above him as rigid as a board. She felt guilty for forcing this upon him.

He said, "Did you know that Stalin got rid of Victory Day because everyone wanted to move on from the war? But now we apparently need it back."

He looked annoyed and she didn't know how to respond.

"All right, Vita, I will talk to my boss."

For the next couple of weeks Vita avoided crossing the square and took a longer route to school, passing instead by the newly built Hotel Ukraine. As she waited for Papa to confirm whether or not he could make it, she fell in love with *The Young Guard*.

She rooted for the partisans and seethed at the atrocities of the German fascists. But it was the cowardly, two-faced Ukrainian collaborators who shocked her most. How could anyone turn against his own people and work for the enemy? It boggled the mind. She carried the book from the kitchen to the bathroom to the bedroom, reading wherever and whenever she could. Never had she read a book—a war novel no less!—that was so affecting, so enraging, and that hit so close to home. Her parents had never explained to her what it had been like back then. No one's parents had. War had been something too ubiquitous to talk about.

The ending, when the Germans executed the partisans by throwing them alive down a mining shaft right before the Red Army returned, was so gut-wrenching that Vita had a nightmare about getting buried alive. She woke up screaming, and Papa rushed in looking like he was ready to kill whoever was hurting his girl. He held her for a long time against his chest. She listened to his heart and after a while was no longer afraid. After all, Papa had made it to Berlin. If there was ever another war, he would protect her.

As she was falling back asleep, she thought she'd need to write something very special on his Victory Day card to let him know how proud she was that he had risked his life for their country.

In the morning over breakfast with Andrey, Mama told her that she'd heard about her nightmare and not to take this novel so close to heart.

"Remember, it's a work of fiction, Vita. Don't repeat this at school, obviously, but it's . . . exaggerated."

Andrey said, "I heard there will be an organized trip to the Young Guard Museum next semester."

Papa rolled his eyes.

"Then you'll go and you'll look at this museum," he said. "But when you come back home, you'll move on."

In the following days, Vita tried to distance herself from the novel, but the images of the tortured young partisans weren't easy to erase, regardless of whether they were "exaggerated."

Then, on the last day of April, Papa came home and said, "That Yelena Vasilyevna of yours turns out to be our rector's niece. So it looks like I'll have to do your talk after all."

Vita had no idea what one had do with the other, but it didn't really matter. He was coming! She was relieved and excited. Her dad was a good storyteller and would surely be the talk of her class. Come to think of it, this would be a win-win. She wouldn't lose face in Komsomol, V.N. would be impressed, and she'd finally learn something about her father's past.

Two days before Victory Day, she and Papa walked to school together. The morning was sunny, and a warm breeze careened through the streets. They took the usual route through Lenin Square because she wasn't about to explain to him why she preferred the longer way. They passed the alley with the brambles—whose buds had now sprouted tiny leaves—and headed toward Lenin, when on the other side of the statue she noticed the familiar torn military tunic. The drunk was half lying on a granite step. Vita swallowed hard when Papa said, "Wait here," and beelined toward him.

"Papa, don't!" she called after him, but he was already approaching the man. To her horror, she saw Papa bending down toward the bum, exchanging some words, and then extending his hand to help him sit up. Even from where she stood, she could see the man's reddened face and almost hear "my little Yid" on his lips. How come Papa wasn't scared of this beast?

He pulled the drunk upright and handed him some money. When he returned to her, he said, "Now, that's a real vet. Yelena Vasilyevna would be better off inviting him to talk."

She didn't know what to say. She hadn't realized the man was a veteran. She'd assumed he was just some tramp who'd gotten his hands on a military tunic.

"But if he fought in the war, why would he be on the streets?"

"Why, you think all vets get medals, jobs, and apartments?"

"Well, I—"

"You know how many vets were on the streets when you were little? There were maimed men with medals all over Ukraine. Some had no arms or legs and moved on these boards with wheels. People called them 'samovars.' Then one day Stalin ordered the cities cleansed and they disappeared. All of them. Shipped up north, to an island."

That sounded horrible, but she'd be lying if she said she didn't wish this vet had been sent away too. Still, if Papa knew what the vet had called her, he probably wouldn't have rushed to assist him. They walked the rest of the way in silence.

As they approached the school, she noticed Papa's clenched jaw. Her palms immediately grew sweaty. What if he said something embarrassing or worse, something about Stalin or vets that would get her in trouble? He loved to make fun of the Party. Just the other day, he had brought home the latest political joke: "Brezhnev's eyebrows are Stalin's mustache, just on a higher level." Then, right after, he launched into a story about how he sweet-talked some official into giving him a permit he needed by complimenting Brezhnev's policies. When Mama had been forced to join the city council last year, Papa constantly made fun of her for having to raise her hand along with everyone else to pass the "correct" government initiatives. Neither he nor Mama had much regard for the Party. If Vita had to summarize, their family rules were: Don't kill, don't steal, and don't be a Communist. And don't repeat what Papa says in public.

They walked down the school's corridor and up to the second floor toward her classroom. In front of the door, she straightened his tie.

"Papa, you aren't going to say something wild, right?" she said, her voice coming out tiny and scared.

He looked at her and his lips curved into an impish smile.

"Do I ever? Come on now, let's get this show started."

When they walked in, she went straight to her desk, afraid to look at anyone, even Lenka. They were all staring at her dad, who was greeting Yelena Vasilyevna in a tone that told Vita he was also a little bewitched by her pretty teacher. Her dad was a charmer when he needed to be.

Vita slid behind her desk. From here, he looked imposing in his gray suit against the chalkboard, which said *Great Patriotic War* in an even bigger font than last time. He turned toward the classroom as Yelena Vasilyevna introduced him.

"As you guys know, this week we will be celebrating the twentieth anniversary of the day the Soviet Union won the war against German fascists." Her tone was celebratory and official. "As we're reading *The Young Guard* about what brave guys and gals were doing to combat the Germans right here in the Donbas, it's important to also hear what was happening at the front. Today, our guest is Yefim Shulman, a war veteran who has witnessed Victory Day in Berlin."

Though Vita had heard Papa make toasts in front of relatives and friends, this was different. Most of her classmates had never even seen her dad, since he was often traveling in some remote corner of the country. Whatever he said today was going to color how they viewed her, Vita, one of the best students, who was fun enough to be occasionally invited to the movies, poetry nights, and other social events. He'd better not disappoint her.

"The Great Patriotic War was long and difficult," he began, and Vita sucked in her breath. "We saw and survived a lot during those four years: there were days of bitter losses, there were days of rousing victories, again more losses though smaller ones, which were finally followed by a grandiose victory that shook the whole world."

She'd never heard Papa speak like this. The canned sentences, those words—"bitter" and "grandiose"—sounded bizarre coming from a man who never made grand pronouncements unless they were followed by a punch line. This was a performance. It was strange to watch it but also encouraging. Of course her father wasn't going to jeopardize her reputation.

"Today, I don't want to talk to you about victory but instead about what happened at the very beginning."

Vita tensed. She knew nothing good happened at the beginning because Ukraine had been occupied. Mama had told her a little about life under occupation: the hunger, the German street signs, waiting for the Soviet army to come while enemy soldiers walked around with guns. And then the burden of that "lived in occupied territory" stain in her passport. That whole early war period was an embarrassment that was rarely mentioned. Why wouldn't Papa talk about how he celebrated victory in Berlin?

"Our artillery regiment was stationed close to the Lithuanian-German border. Despite the pact between the Soviet Union and Germany, the air smelled of the coming storm. Still, we were certain that even if there was war, we would fight it on the enemy's soil and not give an inch of our own. In the evening, I remember, we walked around singing patriotic marching songs. But at four A.M. on June 22, the war began. The fighting spirit of the Red Army soldiers and commanders assured us that the enemy would be crushed quickly. None of us could have imagined that the war would last four years.

"When the German planes hit our camp, I was thrown under a pile of debris. And I will tell you that I wouldn't be standing here today if it wasn't for my closest buddy. He saved me. By the second day of the war, we were getting surrounded. The military situation was so dire that there was no possibility of an organized retreat. We had to retreat in small groups. So I, my buddy, and our small group headed east in hopes of catching up to the rest of our troops. It was a race against time: we had to get to them before the Germans got to us. But the belief that our situation would improve never left us. We suffered and we cursed, but still we believed."

The thing was Vita didn't believe. Not fully. Sometimes it felt as though Papa was talking from real experience but other times as if from a script. It was confusing. She noticed she was clutching a pen so hard, her fingers were going white from the effort. She needed to relax. The important thing was that her dad wasn't going to say anything scandalous. And at home she could ask him for a less phony version of this story.

"Then, one night near a marsh, we were ambushed by the enemy. We were outnumbered. We fought back bravely with all we had, but at the end . . ."

This part felt real and Vita wondered if he was about to tell them how he got caught or something terrible like that. She noticed Yelena

Vasilyevna cross her legs and glance nervously at the classroom as if she, too, was afraid her guest was going to say something inappropriate.

"At the end, my buddy and I were the only ones who made it out of there alive. The rest of our comrades perished. We continued heading east and eventually were able to locate and rejoin our troops. I can't tell you what a relief it was to be back with the Red Army. Now we could fight again and banish the treacherous enemy from our land."

Yelena Vasilyevna rose.

"Thank you for that," she said, and Vita felt waves of tension leaving her body. "Could you answer a few questions? I'm sure our guys—or perhaps Vita—have things they want to ask?"

Oh, no. She did not just say her name. Normally, Vita would be fine with being called on, but not for this. She had no idea what she was supposed to ask him. She was hoping someone else from her class would speak when her father said, "I'll tell you Vita's favorite war story."

He told them the story about an abandoned milk farm where he and his buddies found a cheese room and how the round cheeses kept rolling away. She remembered hearing about the rolling cheeses but had always thought it had happened in his childhood. The story felt like the least scripted thing he'd said and it dissolved the tension in the room.

Yelena Vasilyevna looked somewhere above Vita and said, "Yes, Lenka, you have a question for our guest?"

Vita turned to see Lenka rise behind her desk. Her cheeks were pink and sweaty and her eyes glistened with adoration.

"Could you tell us what happened to your buddy?" she asked.

Vita scoffed to herself. She should have been the one to have thought of that question. She turned back to look at her father. His jaw tensed again.

"He was awarded the Order of the Red Star and a medal for liberating Warsaw but he tragically died before getting to see the end of the war," he said, and then paused. "Before I go, there is one thing I'd like for you to remember. These are three most important things in war: courage, luck, and friendship. But friendship most of all. Without it, you are lost."

133

Vita heard Lenka behind her sigh loudly. It was gross.

"And now I'm afraid I must rush back to work," Papa said. "I hope I gave you a little slice of what the war was like."

"All right, class," Yelena Vasilyevna said. "Please get up and salute our veteran."

Vita rose to the sound of dozens of chairs scraping the floor around her and mouthed the salute Yelena Vasilyevna had told them the day before: "Happy Victory Day!"

Her father, looking either embarrassed or bewildered—she couldn't tell which—nodded at her classmates, grabbed his briefcase and coat, and, without meeting Vita's gaze, left the room.

The rest of the day she walked around in a daze. The school seemed smaller to her, as if Papa's story, or maybe just his presence, had shrunk her world. What bothered her was how unsure she was about what was true in his story and what was a show. She felt she should have known the real story. She was his daughter, after all. Instead, she knew only as much about her own father as her classmates.

After classes ended, Vita rushed out hoping to walk home alone. She was already out the door when she heard Lenka call, "Wait for me!" Vita rearranged her face to hide her annoyance.

"You all right?" Lenka asked as they walked toward Lenin Square.

"Of course. Why?"

"Must have been so amazing to finally hear your dad talk about the war."

"Sure. I mean, I've heard that stuff before."

"Didn't you say he never talked about it?"

If Lenka just knew when to shut up . . . It was none of her business what she and Papa talked about at home.

"What I said was that he doesn't talk *much* about it because there were so many gruesome things, but I've always known the story of how he avoided being captured. And much more."

"Oh, I didn't realize," Lenka said. "So you know about this friend of his?"

Vita looked around to see if she could find some distraction to get her out of this conversation, but there were only pigeons and a few boring passersby on the square. She switched her briefcase to her left hand and said, "He died right before they got to Berlin. Gangrene, I think."

She had no clue where she got the gangrene from, but having a specific detail like that made it sound like she knew what she was talking about.

"That's terrible," Lenka said.

Finally, they reached the end of the square and parted ways. It was only when Vita got to her building that she realized she had forgotten to be scared of running into the creepy vet.

That evening, when Papa came home, he looked different to her, the way he did when he came back from his months-long trips. She noticed lines on his forehead and that his shoulders stooped when he washed his hands.

He asked if Yelena Vasilyevna said anything about his talk and she said no, which was true.

"Excellent," he said. "Then hopefully that's that."

She wanted to ask him why he'd never told her and Andrey that story. Instead, she asked, "So that friend of yours . . . How did he die?"

He plopped down on the stool as if he'd been running all day and said, "There was no friend."

"What do you mean?"

"I made him up. You didn't really expect me to tell them exactly what happened?"

"But what about the retreat?"

"That was all true."

"So it was just you alone who wasn't captured?"

"That's right."

She was trying to figure out how to get more out of him when he picked up a newspaper and smiled. "I did your talk, Vita. But dwelling on the past will make me go bald, and frankly, I like my full head of hair."

And she knew the conversation was over. She went to her room, confused. She didn't know what to make of Papa's stories. It was as if he was protecting her from something, but she still couldn't understand why he needed to make up a friend.

She sat at her desk and took out a piece of thick white paper to write him a Victory Day card. Tomorrow there would be a big parade with fireworks in Lenin Square and the veterans were going to get some medals. She stared at the empty paper, thinking what to write. And then it dawned on her why Papa had invented a friend. He didn't want to appear like the only brave one who hadn't gotten captured. So he underplayed his courage, the way he often did.

Vita thought of *The Young Guard* and the Ukrainian snitch character who worked for the Germans and immediately knew what to write. Papa might not have wanted to appear like the only hero, but he couldn't deny that he was truly brave for not giving himself up to the Germans.

She sharpened a red pencil and wrote, "Papochka, Happy Victory Day! I am so proud that you fought the enemies instead of working for them like the snitch in *The Young Guard*. May you always have courage. Vita."

She stashed the card under her pillow. In bed that night, she thought of Yevtushenko's poem that she had recently copied into her journal. It was called "There are no boring people in this world" and had this stanza:

What do we know of our friends, our brothers,
Of our beloved, of our one and only?
What do we know of our own father?
Seemingly everything—yet nothing at all.

Chapter 10

April 9, 1944
Karow, Germany

Yefim fidgeted with his cap in the back of Karow's small baroque church. The Germans filed in, crowding the wooden pews, their perfumes adding to the already rich scent of Easter flowers wreathed in front of the church.

Yefim had never been to a church, and he had few memories of even their little village synagogue. He remembered it as a dim building that smelled of something ancient and made him feel like being there was somehow illicit. In this church, instead, light poured through the huge stained glass window onto a merry German crowd.

"*Frohe Ostern!* Happy Easter!" said the fat old butcher, looking oddly civilized in a gray suit rather than his usual bloody apron. The rations had been hitting Germany harder lately as Hitler's army was incurring losses, but one couldn't tell by the butcher's well-fed wife, whose feathered hat quivered as she proudly strutted past the pews.

"*Frohe Ostern!*" said the red-cheeked Frau from the village store, pushing a little freckled boy in front of her down the aisle as she looked for a place to sit.

Yefim tried standing tall, but what he wanted to do instead was disappear. He kept seeing malicious glances in his direction and was afraid that his lack of knowledge of what to do in a church would confirm what they must have already suspected: that he wasn't just a regular "Russian swine" but a Jew. After almost three years in Germany, he wondered how much luck he had left before he was found out.

He hadn't felt this nervous since last summer when he had first met the Burgomaster, his current owner—or boss, as he preferred to think of him. After the Belorussian kid had sold them out to the *Polizei*, he and Ivan were taken to a regional police station, where they claimed they were ostarbeiters who ran away from the transport train. They gave the police new names so they couldn't be traced back to the prison camp or Müller Leinz: he became Yefim Lisin and Ivan took the last name of Gurov. They were put in a freezing, wet dungeon and for the next week he was convinced they would never see daylight again. But one morning they were escorted out to a truck and driven to a large, empty building where thirty or so ostarbeiters, mostly fifteen- and sixteen-year-old Soviet teenagers, were standing wide-eyed in two rows, waiting to be bought. A sales manager sat at a small desk in the corner while a translator explained that they were to stand quietly and do as they were told when the customers showed up.

As he and Ivan had joined the second row, well-dressed German men and women came in to select laborers for purchase. The room was quiet, the proceedings orderly. An elderly couple had been the first to show up. They had glanced at Yefim but kept going, and, despite himself, he'd wondered why they didn't think him good enough. They selected two guys and one girl and left. Then an owner of a glass factory came in with a big order: he needed ten girls. He picked them out quickly, pointing at each one with his finger, then signed some papers, handed over a stack of German marks to the sales manager, and led the herd of frightened girls out, leaving less than two dozen ostarbeiters standing in the room.

Yefim had wondered what would happen if no one picked him. Though they didn't talk while waiting, he felt as though he could read Ivan's thoughts. Surely this human market was more proof that Ivan was right: that they were just expendable cattle. But no, that was the difference between Germany and home: the Soviet government would never do this to anyone. Human life wasn't for sale, that was the exact thing communism was built on. To which Ivan would probably say that people weren't for sale because they were worth nothing, and that was why soldiers in the "glorious" Red Army were left dying in camps.

Yefim was in the middle of this mental argument when the tall, burly Burgomaster barged in and announced that he was looking for three strong men for his farm in Karow. The Burgomaster sped past the teenagers, his plump red cheeks framed by an overgrown graying mop of hair, until he stopped in front of Yefim. He bent to look at his legs, then felt the muscles in his arms with his meaty fingers. Yefim couldn't stop himself from flexing.

"Open your mouth," the Burgomaster had told him, his voice booming in a hushed room. Yefim wanted to tell the big bastard to go back to whatever hellhole he'd crawled out of.

But then, he didn't really want to return to the wet dungeon, so he opened his mouth, feeling like one of the horses his father used to inspect at the stables. The Burgomaster examined his mouth so closely that Yefim could smell the beer on his breath. He wondered if he'd ask him about the gap from the upper tooth that had fallen out soon after he'd made it out of the camp. Instead, the Burgomaster looked up and asked, "*Jude?*"

Yefim felt as if everyone in the room—the sales manager, the translator, the teenagers from back home—could see right through him.

"*Nein,*" he replied, holding the Burgomaster's gaze. "*Russisch.*"

The Burgomaster turned to the sales manager.

"All right," he said. "I'll take this one."

Yefim stepped out of the row while the Burgomaster selected a wiry sixteen-year-old with a prominent Adam's apple, Anatoly. As he continued looking for a third, Yefim volunteered, "My friend Ivan, that one there, was a farmer."

The Burgomaster stared at Ivan.

"He's barely standing," he objected.

"Just needs some food," Yefim said.

"Quiet!" yelled the Burgomaster, his voice shocking the room. He moved toward Ivan for a closer look. He touched his arms and looked at his teeth as Yefim squirmed, watching his friend being inspected. Eventually the Burgomaster agreed, signed, paid, and the three of them were led out of the building toward a wagon that had brought them here, to Karow.

The Burgomaster turned out to be a moody sort. Whenever something wasn't to his liking, he gave them a kick in the shins, but once they learned to stay away from him, working at his farm was mostly all right, certainly better than at Müller Leinz. There were no guards, no barbed-wire fences, and even a daily glass of milk provided by the Burgomaster's daughter, who worked as the milkmaid. The work was familiar to both Yefim and Ivan: tilling, sowing, feeding the animals, building out the new barn so that it would be ready by harvest, cleaning the stables and the cowshed. In busy seasons, there was so much work that the three ostarbeiters, Mrs. Burgomaster, and her milkmaid daughter could barely keep up. They would have managed better, of course, if the Burgomaster sullied himself with the workings of the farm, but instead he kept himself busy "running the town," though it was unclear what that meant.

Yefim, Ivan, and Anatoly were housed in a repurposed toolshed, where they slept on thin mattresses. At first the Burgomaster used to lock them in every night, but after a while he stopped bothering. During the day he sometimes sent them on errands around the village, and at night they slept unlocked and unguarded. He didn't have to worry about them running away because the problem, as Yefim knew too well, wasn't how to run off but where to go. They were stuck in the middle of Germany, with no idea how far the Eastern Front was.

Ivan seemed to be gaining weight, and his cheeks had gotten their coloring back. Then, one morning, about two months after they arrived, the Burgomaster came for him. He said he needed Ivan to accompany him to the neighboring village to carry sacks of grain he was buying. Yefim wanted the boss to take him, too—he would have liked to see more of the area outside Karow—but he knew there was no point in asking. Instead, he went out to work the fields. He got a little concerned when the Burgomaster didn't return by lunch because he preferred lunching at home. By that evening Yefim knew something was wrong. He tried asking Mrs. Burgomaster but she repeated what her husband had told him. The Burgomaster returned late. In his truck was a new Polish laborer and no Ivan.

"Took your friend back to the market," he said when Yefim accosted him at the kitchen. "I told you he looked too weak."

He'd never actually whipped any of them, only threatened to, so Yefim pressed to know where Ivan had ended up.

"He's like a brother to me. Please tell me."

The Burgomaster yawned. "I barely convinced the salesman to take him back. I have no idea who'll buy him. Now leave me alone. I am exhausted."

Yefim went back to the shed where the Polish laborer was shaking out Ivan's old blanket.

He wanted to see his friend's round face with those invisible eyebrows one last time, to thank him for sticking by him these four crazy years and to hear his sarcastic reply. They would have come up with a plan for meeting if they ever made it out of Germany.

Instead, Ivan was just gone. Yefim couldn't even remember the last words they had said to each other. It was probably something banal. Gone was his last link to the past and the only person who knew his real name. For everyone in Karow, he was Yefim Lisin, a Russian laborer brought over on a cattle train to serve at the pleasure of German masters.

Standing in the church now, he wished Ivan was here. Instead, to his right, was Anatoly, his Adam's apple protruding, his arms folded, his narrow green eyes looking at the gathering villagers with a teenager's apathy. Next to him was Ivan's replacement, the bald-headed, round-cheeked Kuba the Pole, who had grown up going to churches in Lublin and now blushed with reverence at the prospect of witnessing his first Easter service since the war began.

Yefim looked toward what Kuba had whispered was called the altar. There, in the front pew, more pious today than ever, sat the Burgo-master. It was impossible to miss his Mozart-like mop, which shook in vigorous greeting whenever another prominent villager stopped by to say hello. He must have been saying, *Gut! Gut, mein Mann*, as he always did when he wasn't talking to his three Slavic workers.

The doors opened and more people squeezed inside. The men were in suits, the women in knee-length dresses with gloves and earrings peeking out of coiffed curls.

He recognized the limping postman, the pockmarked old barkeep who always reeked of beer, the red-haired boy who delivered the paper on his bicycle and who probably had little carefree time left if the war were to drag on much longer. Yefim had caught worry in their eyes as Italy switched sides, as chatter about the Americans sending more troops grew, and as the German army lost Stalingrad, then Kursk, then Kyiv. That joyous news about Kyiv's liberation arrived five months earlier, brought by another ostarbeiter who came to Karow to work for the farm behind the old distillery. Since then, Yefim thought more often about escaping, though this time he didn't want to make any plans until the Red Army got close.

When it seemed like all of Karow was packed inside, music began to play. Everyone hushed at the extraordinary sound. Yefim had heard the Burgomaster boast that this was the birthplace of one of Germany's most important organ builders, but that hadn't meant much to Yefim. The organ turned out to be a colossal golden beast made out of various pipes at the front of the church. And the sound it emitted seemed like it was everywhere at once: descending from the vaulted ceiling, pressing against the stained glass windows, then rising back up on the slender columns. He had never heard music like this, vivid and immense, its lingering, majestic chords leaving no room for earthly thoughts.

From the attentive way the parishioners—even the children—faced straight ahead, he felt that everyone was overtaken by the same awe. And although Yefim had never talked to these people and they had never acknowledged his presence except for the occasional repulsed or suspicious glance, listening to the organ along with them, he began to feel oddly familial, as if they were *his* villagers, not his enemies or his keepers. Then he thought of Mikhail and was filled with shame. What would his brother say if he saw him standing here among Germans in a church?

When the organ finished, the priest began his sermon. He spoke of how on Easter morning life awakens after the harsh winter, about goodness and regeneration. After his sermon, he called on the Burgomaster.

Yefim's boss got up and walked to the podium.

"On this morning of hope," he began in his signature operatic voice, "we believe in the victory and freedom of the Fatherland. Remember, God is with the brave. That has been proven again and again in our nation's times of need. The day is coming when our suffering people will rise victorious over the foe."

Suffering people. Yefim shook his head.

The Burgomaster sat back down and the organ started again. When the final triumphant chords sounded and the music ended, Yefim heard little taps of someone's feet emerging from behind the organ. A slender girl of about seventeen, her auburn hair glowing in the ray of sun, quickly bowed to the audience and fluttered away, like a butterfly in her cornflower-blue dress. Yefim had never seen her before and wondered how in the eight months he had been in this village he could have missed such a creature. As he craned his neck, she sat down in one of the front pews and the back of her head—crowned by a braided knot—disappeared amid the crowd.

When the service ended and everyone began to leave, Yefim stayed behind, keeping a close watch on the door. He thought he must have missed her leaving, but then he looked back toward the altar and saw her talking to the priest. The priest smiled gratefully, probably thanking her for a job well done. Yefim wanted to get a better look at her and made his way toward the altar, walking behind the colonnade along the wall, pausing as if to inspect the large painting of a woman in a crimson gown who stared up exaltedly at the sky as chubby, naked little angels played at her feet.

From here, he was close enough to see the girl's face in profile—the long lashes, the straight nose, the bow-shaped lips. She laughed at something the priest said and the chime of her laughter echoed around the nave as if it were a tiny organ of its own. For a moment she tossed her head in his direction, and Yefim's breath caught in his throat. She said something to the priest, but then, as if registering something unusual, she turned and her gold-speckled eyes stopped directly on Yefim.

"*Poshli!* Let's go!" Anatoly tugged on his arm. "The boss is looking for you."

He dragged Yefim toward the exit. Right before leaving, Yefim glanced back. But both the girl and the priest were already walking out of the side door.

"You better not be trying to steal anything in there," the Burgomaster lashed out. "I bring you out for a real German Easter and you make me wait for you? You Slavs are ungrateful."

The Burgomaster continued to berate him all the way back through the village, but Yefim was used to his boss's histrionics and didn't listen. Instead, he thought of the girl and how she looked at him—as if he was a man and not a stray dog.

The Burgomaster said he had to make an appearance at the Easter egg hunt, but when Yefim asked if he could come—he was sure the girl would be there—the Burgomaster said it was no place for ostarbeiters and walked off.

"What do you need to see German kids gathering eggs for?" Anatoly asked, but Yefim only shrugged, wishing Ivan was here to be his confidant.

"Actually, I'd love to see the egg hunt too," Kuba the Pole confessed meekly.

Yefim liked Kuba because his earnestness and mild temper helped offset Anatoly's caustic personality. Anatoly liked to act older than his sixteen years, but he often came off as pretentious, and Yefim didn't know how to—and didn't want to—play the older brother to set the boy straight. Even though Ivan grew up an only child, somehow he had been much better at handling Anatoly's remarks, putting him back in his place in a way that was authoritative yet not offensive. But Ivan wasn't here.

"That service was enough Easter for me," said Anatoly with a theatrical yawn. "So glad we got rid of that useless God-pining crap."

Kuba sighed. "In Poland, Easter was my favorite holiday . . ."

When the Burgomaster came home to have his Easter lunch and a few beers, his mood had improved. He even brought a small piece of the lamb roast to the laborers' table, a rare delicacy in these lean times.

"In Germany, we have many great traditions," he told them, waving his arms like a conductor. "I'm not just talking about our composers, philosophers, and military leaders, but the traditions that are in the blood of every man in the Reich."

The Burgomaster's beery eyes swam somewhere above their heads as if his audience were much larger than his three laborers. Yefim stared at him, his fingers waiting centimeters from the juicy lamb as the boss continued to sermonize.

"We're a refined, benevolent people and our role is to teach you Slavs what it means to live a life of work, purpose, and enjoyment. That is why I have decided that tomorrow . . ."

He paused, seemingly for dramatic effect but then burped heartily and went on.

". . . tomorrow you will join the rest of our village in communing with nature. It is our Easter Monday tradition in which we honor Christ, our Fatherland, and ourselves."

Yefim had no idea what "communing with nature" meant, but he didn't care as long as there was a chance to see the girl again. That night he felt he could still hear the sounds of the organ drifting in the wind.

The next morning the Burgomaster led his small flock of domestics and ostarbeiters out of his big two-storied house in the village center. It was a breezy day. Fat little clouds hurried past them, hiding and revealing the April sun. Down the main street, everyone had closed their shutters, giving the strange impression that the town's entire population had fled. Yefim wondered if that was what would happen if the Red Army ever made it into Germany.

They arrived at the lawn of the manor house that had hosted the Easter egg hunt the day before. Here and there, young blades of grass poked out in eager patches. Beyond the manor house was a wooded area with spruce trees. Yefim had never been out there and entering the wood felt as if he was crossing a foreign border.

Villagers sat on picnic blankets as children ran around and played among the trees. Some people strolled through the forest, others stopped to chat with friends. Several villagers biked past them and a couple of women in their forties speed walked, holding what looked like ski poles as if they were preparing for a race. Yefim now understood what the Burgomaster meant by "communing with nature," though the forest seemed so full of people that he wondered if the villagers were actually communing more with one another. Either way, Yefim had never seen this carefree, life-loving side of the German people and he couldn't decide how he felt about it. On the one hand, it made him angry that they had such luxury while no one was picnicking back home in Ukraine. On the other, the peaceful scene made him yearn for the end of the war so that everyone, here and there, could return to living their lives.

Trailing behind the Burgomaster, Yefim glanced around for the girl from the church. He saw the priest heading toward them.

"Hello, Friedrich!" said the priest.

"*Guten Morgen*, Father," said the Burgomaster.

Yefim moved a step closer.

"How are you enjoying the festivities?" the priest asked, his hands behind his back.

"Very much, very much. It's almost as if there is no war!"

"Every day, we pray for the end of the war . . . Did you enjoy yesterday's service?"

"*Ja, gut!* Your Ilse has grown into quite a talented young lady."

Ilse! Learning her name made Yefim blush.

"Yes, she's become a marvelous organist," the priest smiled.

"I'd like to talk to you about one matter," the Burgomaster said. When he turned around and found Yefim loitering behind him, he waved him off.

"Go commune," he told his three laborers. "Just don't stray too far. I'm not dragging you home from the police."

They hadn't left the village since they were brought here, but as soon as they walked off the dirt path toward the trees, Anatoly wanted to sit down.

"I can commune with nature from here," he said, and plopped near a bush.

"I'm going for a walk," said Yefim.

"I'll come with you," Kuba offered.

"I'd rather walk alone if you don't mind."

Kuba never seemed to take offense, so he shrugged and sat next to Anatoly.

Yefim walked off, weaving in and out of trees and looking around as casually as he could. The girl wasn't there. Perhaps she had come from another village to play the organ. And even if she was there, what then? He'd seen pamphlets warning German women to stay away from ostarbeiters because they posed a danger to their pure blood. What was he doing even thinking about her? He had been stuck in Germany too long if he dreamed of local girls.

He circled the wooded area and climbed a small hill. From there he could see the groups of villagers sitting or moving about. If he didn't listen closely and didn't pay attention to the absence of fathers and older sons, he could think there was no war. It was a strange, peaceful mirage, this Easter Monday, and for a moment Yefim felt as if he was looking at a postcard. But then the moment was gone and, with a sharp surge of guilt, he saw himself wandering aimlessly among his country's enemies while back home his four brothers and millions of Soviet men fought against them. How would he ever look his brothers in the eyes?

He went farther up and rounded a tall spruce. Beyond it, there were no villagers, just trees towering over sunlit patches of young grass. Birds sang in the wooded distance. Yefim walked toward them, letting his feet lead. Somewhere behind him, he knew, the Burgomaster was busy making his rounds while Anatoly and Kuba sat whispering jokes about the Germans. But he didn't let himself worry about what would happen if he kept on walking. Instead, he smelled the sharpness of the spruce trees and felt the April sun on his face as the voices of the villagers grew fainter. He hoped that, far off in Ukraine, his family was still alive. If they were, maybe one day they could all be together again, crammed into that little hut.

Someone coughed to his left. Yefim froze. Seated on a stump a dozen steps away from him was Ilse. She looked at him, her sun-dappled head cocked to the side. Spooked, he turned around and started back toward the villagers.

"Where are you going?" her voice rang among the trees.

He stopped, unsure what to do. He could feel the missing tips of his fingers though he knew they weren't there. He turned and took a few steps toward her, trying to look at ease as if he wasn't afraid of what she could do to him. After all, she had seen him walking away from the village. She might tell the Burgomaster he tried to flee.

"Do you understand German?" she asked.

"*Ja*," he stammered.

Ilse rose and took two steps toward him. He didn't move. She wore a beige coat over a yellow dress. Her hair was braided around her head, making her look almost like the girls back home. He noticed a notebook and pencil in her hand.

"Do you speak it, too, or do you just say *Ja*?" said Ilse as her heart-shaped face lit up with an ironic smile. She was mesmerizing. No, this girl wasn't going to tattle to the Burgomaster. At least, he didn't want to believe it.

What he didn't understand was why she wasn't afraid to talk to him. She must have seen the pamphlets. And yet she was so close now that he could see the tiny specks of gold floating in her hazel eyes, the soft down above her eyebrows, the beauty spot on her neck. Her cheeks were slightly pink from the cool spring air and he couldn't stop himself from wondering if they'd feel sleek like sea glass or velvety like a peach.

He looked around. No one could see them.

"I can say *Nein* too," he said, then feeling braver, added, "but never to Fräulein Ilse."

It was her turn to be surprised.

"So you've been spying around, I see," she said, tilting her head and laughing freely. Her laugh threw him off balance. "And what's *your* name?"

"Yefim. My boss, the Burgomaster, praised your organ playing and mentioned your name."

"The Burgomaster? I do my best to avoid him," Ilse said with a slight eye roll. Something in that gesture made Yefim feel like they'd known each other for a while.

"Why?" he asked.

"This war is the best thing that's ever happened to him. With all the other men gone, he is like a cock among chickens."

Yefim thought back to the Burgomaster calling her a "talented young lady" and felt a hint of disgust.

Behind them, a branch crackled. Before he knew what he was doing, he grabbed Ilse's arm and pulled her closer toward him to better hide behind the spruce. Her notebook fell on the grass, its pages rustling. Her arm felt slight but surprisingly strong, and he thought of her fingers making that music on the organ.

"Hey there!" Ilse exclaimed, freeing herself. A bird flew out from a tree, and he felt embarrassed for his forwardness.

He didn't want her knowing how overwhelmed he was by her and by this meeting.

"I was worried someone would see us," he explained. The suppleness of her arm was imprinted on his calloused palm. She picked up her notebook.

"If you're too scared . . . ," she said.

"Aren't you?"

"I don't care for their rules," she said defiantly. "Everyone in Karow can go to hell. They've gone nuts over this war. Did you hear what the Burgomaster was saying? 'Suffering people.' 'God is with the brave.' The Germans are starting to lose and suddenly we're a suffering people. Anyway, it doesn't matter. Weren't you leaving Karow?"

"No," he said quickly, a fear creeping back in. Would she report him after all?

"Oh, good. It's nice to talk to an actual human instead of only my journal."

"Don't you have friends?"

"That I trust?" she shrugged. "No one more than my journal."

He understood. He also had no one since Ivan left.

Ilse reached toward his mangled hand and asked, "How did this happen?"

Her thin fingers brushed the rough skin of the stump where his thumb used to be. Yefim hadn't been touched with such gentleness in so long. It gave him goose bumps. And in that state of defenselessness, he blurted out, "Our unit was—"

Ilse looked up at him in surprise.

He broke off, realizing his mistake. Panic burst through his chest. He'd been in Karow under the guise of an ostarbeiter, not a captured soldier. For Germans there was a big difference between the two. All this time, even after the Burgomaster resold Ivan, Yefim had managed to keep up the lie. He hadn't even told Kuba or Anatoly, and now, like a total idiot, he'd slipped up in front of a German girl. His fingers went numb. If she reported him, he was done for.

They stared at each other. Then Ilse spoke.

"I had a feeling there was more to you," she said quietly.

"Ilse!" they heard a man's voice calling from the meadow downhill. "Ilse! Where are you?"

"Father Otto," Ilse gasped. She turned in a hurry. "I'll find you. And don't worry, I'm good at keeping secrets."

Then she ran off. Yefim watched her, unable to believe that something so wonderful could be happening to him after so long.

A week went by with no news of Ilse. Nothing to even indicate that his memory of Easter Monday wasn't a dream—the most forbidden dream in the Reich: a Soviet Jew chatting up a German girl.

At first, all he thought about was whether she'd sell him out. Every time he heard someone walk through the Burgomaster's door, he feared it was the *Polizei*. After a few days, when no one came for him, Yefim let himself trust in Ilse, which, he realized, was what he had wanted to do all along. Then a week passed and trust became impatience. He wanted to see her again, hear her voice, feel her soft fingers.

Every night, resting on his thin mattress, Yefim dreamed of the things he could have told Ilse if they had met in a different time and place. He imagined her in his village, standing by the pond, running through the sunflower fields, swinging under the apple tree in their yard. He made her fit so well with his memories of home that soon, without noticing it, she was speaking Ukrainian as if she really were just another girl from his village.

Sunday came. The Burgomaster let them take every other Sunday off, so Yefim spent the afternoon walking up and down Karow's main street in hopes of seeing her, but after a while the villagers began to give him suspicious looks and he retreated back to the Burgomaster's.

The second week began at a crawl.

Then one evening Kuba ran into the toolshed, his eyes wide with excitement. "You won't believe what I just heard! The boss is getting drafted."

Yefim and Anatoly sat up on their mattresses.

"What do you mean, 'drafted'?" Anatoly asked.

"I was passing by the kitchen and heard the Burgomaster arguing with the Missus. He was saying, 'If they need me there, then they need me there, and that's final. No reason to cry your eyes out about it, woman.' And she said, 'But how am I to manage all alone?' Then he banged on the table and I got spooked."

"And why did you conclude he's being drafted?" Yefim asked.

"What else could they be talking about?"

"Kuba is right," hooted Anatoly, rubbing his hands with satisfaction. "Sounds to me like our dear boss is finally getting his fat ass drafted! And you know what that means: Hitler's boys are cracking!"

Yefim wasn't convinced. The Red Army may have reconquered Kyiv, but how desperate could the Germans be that they needed to draft a fifty-five-year-old in no shape to march or shoot?

Still, what if it was true? What if the Germans' power was waning and the Russians really did have them drafting every man they could find? That meant . . . that meant . . . Quickly, the excitement in the toolshed rose as all three ostarbeiters let themselves dream of returning home: Kuba to Lublin, Anatoly to Oryol, and Yefim to Ukraine.

All that night, Yefim tossed on his thin mattress. Maybe this was a sign that it was time to attempt another escape. If the Red Army was getting closer, he might have a real chance to link up with them. How great would it be to return home not as an ostarbeiter but as a soldier? In the darkness of the toolshed, he suddenly longed for the morning drills and the army porridge that he and Ivan used to slurp before the war. He wondered what he would be like if all he knew of being a soldier was the feeling of the freshly starched uniform against his chest, the swing of the rifle on his shoulder, the familiar curves of Uska in his fingers. Would he see himself as valuable or just another body to be used, as Ivan liked to say?

As Kuba and Anatoly snored on their mattresses, Yefim couldn't sleep. The army was so long ago that he hadn't imagined being a soldier again, yet suddenly there he was, in his mind's eye, driving Germans from Ukraine and then liberating his own village together with Ivan. Basya would run out of the hut to hug him, tearful and grateful for her brave brother. The images unfolded in front of him like the propaganda reels they used to show before movies, but he couldn't help giving in to the sweet pathos of what could have been.

Finally, his mind had exhausted itself and he was dozing off when there was a scratching at the door. Anatoly turned in his bunk and resumed snoring, while Kuba, always a heavy sleeper, didn't make a peep. Yefim sat up. The scratching stopped. Someone's footsteps retreated from the toolshed. He got up and tiptoed to the door. He opened it and looked outside. There was no one there. Then he noticed a slip of paper that must have fallen out of the slats near his foot. He picked it up and unfolded it. He could see it was a note, but it was too dark to read the words, so he hid it under his pillow and waited until morning.

When it was finally light enough, he opened what turned out to be a sheet of lined notebook paper and read, "By the eastern oak lies the truth of tomorrow's dawn. I."

For the rest of that day, Ilse—it could be no one else—was all he thought of. As he worked, he kept looking at the thick old oak tree that marked the Burgomaster's property on the eastern side, half expecting Ilse to be behind it. He couldn't believe her boldness sneaking around at night, slipping notes under ostarbeiters' doors. Was she just setting a trap? Some way to lure him out into the night and do what, exactly? He didn't know. Did her reappearance have anything to do with the news of the Burgomaster leaving? Again he didn't know. It was all very strange. Yet every time he began to worry about her intentions, he remembered her fingers on his mangled hand and told himself she couldn't mean anything bad. Still, meeting her tomorrow at dawn was madness.

Throughout the day, he snuck quick looks at the note hidden underneath his shirt and waited for the sun to set.

That evening he went to bed early, still unsure of what to do. He slept poorly, thinking it was a terrible idea engineered by a schoolgirl and then waking up afraid he'd missed the dawn and she was out there all alone, humiliated and surely planning to report him now. When the night's darkness finally began to fade away, he got up and slipped out of the toolshed.

A few birds chirped sleepily under a starless dark blue sky. Yefim walked toward the oak tree, trying to step lightly to avoid leaving a visible trail on the freshly raked soil. He looked hard for her shape, but everything was still murky. After a while he could make out the tree a few meters in front of him. Next to it he noticed something small and white. His pulse quickened. He slowed his step. What if this was a trap after all? Maybe he should turn and run. The toolshed wasn't too far. He hesitated. That was when the white shape turned into two, and as they approached, he realized they were the white stockings on the thin calves of what could only be . . .

Ilse ran toward him, grabbed his hand, and pulled him behind the tree. Her fingers were cold. She was breathing hard. Her heart-shaped face looked monochrome in the darkness. She giggled quietly, a nervous chime, then paused as if she realized she hadn't thought through what would happen next. And what happened next was that Yefim brought her delicate fingers toward his mouth and, cupping them in his rough hands, exhaled to warm them up.

"You came," she whispered.

"Your hands are freezing."

"Girls' hands are always cold," she said.

It was still too dark to make out the horizon. When her hands grew warm, he still held them in his.

"How did you sneak out?" he asked.

"Father Otto sleeps like a bear in winter."

"Did anyone see you?"

"No, no. Are you worried?"

"Well . . . ," he said, but didn't finish. "Let's sit."

He took off his jacket and laid it on the dirt behind the oak.

"Won't you be cold?" she asked.

"Not with you," he said, but then worried about how that sounded.

Ilse didn't seem offended and they sat down, their backs against the old tree. Their shoulders touched and he could smell the floral scent of her hair, which hung loosely over her jacket. For a moment they sat in silence. Yefim wasn't sure what to say now. He hadn't been this close to a girl since he had talked to Eva that night before life was turned upside down. Finally, he asked, "Why did you decide to meet me?"

"I told you: I needed someone to talk to."

"That's a lot of risk to take just to talk," he observed. "And why haven't I seen you before? I've been in Karow eight months."

"I try to avoid the village. I can't talk to these people after what they did to us."

" 'Us'?"

"My father and me. My mom died of tuberculosis when I was little, so I lived with my father. He was a schoolteacher. One night—I was eight—he didn't come home."

She spoke quietly, her tone more serious than he'd ever heard it. Yefim listened intently, afraid to move. He felt as if she was a magical bird—one he didn't want to spook.

"I didn't know this at the time, but he was a Communist and the Gestapo took him. I don't know who ratted him out, but Karow is small, so it must have been someone here, maybe some parent at school, I don't know. I was taken in by my mother's brother, Father Otto."

"What's he like?"

"He is . . ." She hesitated, then chuckled. "Let's just say he is afraid of the world. You'll probably find it ridiculous, given how far you are from home, but I'm seventeen already and I've never been outside of my county."

"Neither had I until the army," he said, liking that they had found something in common.

"All right, now it's my turn to ask questions," she said, and he tensed up. "Tell me what happened to your fingers."

He hesitated.

"I was stationed at the border and we came under attack," he said slowly, wanting to be honest with her but without making her feel any pity.

"What happened then?"

"Then we ran."

He felt awkward talking about the war with her, about how her people had captured his. She must have sensed it because she said, "I always wonder what it would be like in a battle. What I mean is . . . do you have to be male to endure it?"

He thought it was a pretty naive question, something a Soviet girl would never ask. Must have been Father Otto's protective parenting. It made him want to open her eyes to the world, just a little.

"There are a lot of women in the army too," he said.

"I know. We had a girl from Karow go to Berlin to work the radios last year. But I can't imagine participating in this madness. I am not cut out for it."

"Not sure most are cut out for it. Some people want to have a try at it; others have no choice."

"And you?"

"Both, I guess," he said, and shifted closer to Ilse.

Her body was pressed against his side and he could feel the rising and falling of her ribcage as she inhaled the cold morning air. He wanted to hug her tightly but didn't want to scare her off. Instead, he made his breath fall in unison with hers.

"They tell us so many things about how other people live, but I never know if I should believe them," Ilse said. "My father gave me this little globe shortly before he was taken. He told me he would take me all over the world one day. I love looking at it and dreaming about all the countries I could visit."

"I hope your Communist father hasn't taught you that the USSR is some sort of wonderland," he said.

"You don't love your homeland?"

"Oh, I do," he said, trying to ignore that he was imitating Ivan's aloofness to impress her. "But we have our share of problems."

"Like what?"

"It's just a different life over there. I bet you've slept in a bed all your life, right?"

"Of course."

"I grew up sleeping on a straw mattress thrown on the dirt floor."

"Is that why you don't mind this cold? Look at your hands: now they are freezing!" she said, taking his hands and bringing them to her lips.

Ilse's breath on his stiff fingers was like the first warm day of spring back home when the lilacs bloomed and the girls bared their delicate arms and everyone stayed outside late into the evening, singing.

"You know, the way you looked at me at the church . . . ," she whispered. "No one has ever looked at me like that."

She released his hands and put her head on his shoulder. It was so light that he felt he was balancing a rare bird's feather. Carefully, without disturbing his precious treasure, Yefim put his arm around Ilse. He felt hot now, though the air was crisp and the ground beneath him was frigid.

"I've never been gladder to attend a church service," he said, and lifted her chin with his finger. Then, as the first light glimmered on the horizon, he pressed his lips to hers.

For the next week Yefim and Ilse didn't miss a single dawn. For an hour each day before the outlines of the farm emerged with the first light, they huddled together behind the oak.

At first Yefim assumed she was attracted to him because, at twenty-one, he may have seemed a mature, worldly man who could tell her things she craved to know. But as they talked, he saw that what she needed most was a sympathetic ear. Her upbringing with a Communist, then with a priest, had left her with big ideas, which in this heart of Hitler's Germany she had nowhere to express. She told him about how senseless the war was and how their leaders had forgotten that beyond the language and the flags, they were all the same, just people eager to be clothed, fed, and loved. There was often a childlike wonder in her voice, as if her own ideas surprised her. He found himself agreeing with her and buying into her rosy vision. In their grim reality, her ideas were soothing. And while she talked, he was free to run his fingers through the soft strands of her unbraided hair and, closing his eyes, transport her away from the cold German farm to a warm sunflower field more than a thousand kilometers east.

"Don't you think when the war ends, our people could be friends?" she'd say dreamily, raising her head from his shoulder. And he, forgetting under her spell all that he'd seen her people do, would say, "Of course. We are more alike than different," and put her head back on his shoulder, squeezing her tightly.

If only Ivan could see him! He would have loved to brag of his conquest, even though, when it came down to it, physically he didn't progress much beyond kissing Ilse's shy, buttery lips. He got to caress the bumpy outline of her spine concealed under a jacket; he'd gotten close to her breasts; he'd inched his fingers from her delicate knee farther up her thigh while she talked. But at a certain point he'd stop. He was deterred both by her innocence and by the awareness that his punishment for going further was death and her punishment, according to one pamphlet he'd seen, was being walked through the village with her head shaved and a sign telling everyone she'd been defiled by an ostarbeiter.

From Ilse he learned that the Red Army was fighting well but was far from crossing into Germany. And so he abandoned his idea of attempting another escape and instead found himself being the listener Ilse needed him to be. Though an hour wasn't much time to spend together, with each passing day, leaving her became harder. With Ilse,

Yefim felt like a man. Without her, he was only a laborer with a secret.

On the morning before the Burgomaster's departure, Yefim sat next to Ilse, unable to muster the will to leave. He looked at the clouded sky that slowed the dawn's arrival and gave himself five more minutes. His hand was wrapped around Ilse, who had pulled her jacket over her knees, huddling into a ball. She had on a felt hat that smelled of candle wax, which made him melancholy for some reason.

"What will you do once the war is over?" she asked.

"Go to the university."

"What would you study?"

"I don't know. Something that lets me be outside. I need to move and breathe so I don't feel like a caged animal."

She turned away from him and, looking straight ahead, said, "Do you know why the Burgomaster is leaving tomorrow?"

Yefim wasn't sure what the Burgomaster's departure had to do with his plans for after the war.

"He is getting drafted," he said.

"Drafted? No. He is leaving on some sort of business to Genthin. I'm not sure what, but he's supposed to be gone for at least a week and I think . . ."

Here she hesitated, then squeezed his hand with renewed courage and continued. "I think this is your best chance."

"Best chance?"

"To leave."

Yefim felt as if a gunshot sounded in the quiet morning. The Burgomaster wasn't getting drafted and now Ilse wanted him to leave. Behind the wooden fence that marked the border of the Burgomaster's property, a scarecrow grinned at him with its hay mouth.

"I can help you," Ilse continued.

"Why would you want to help me leave?" he asked.

"Don't you want to go back home to study at a university? You said yourself—"

"Yes, but you still haven't answered why *you* want me to leave. Are you finally scared that we'll get caught?"

"Yes," Ilse said, looking at the ground and fidgeting with her jacket. "That too."

"What else?"

And suddenly he grew suspicious. What if she had never liked him at all? The flirting, the poetic note, the clandestine kissing—what if it was all a way to save her soul? Anger rose up his throat, coating his mouth, making him want to shout at this little church girl who had fooled him. He sprang up.

"You think, when the Germans lose, you won't have to feel guilty for this war because you helped one prisoner escape? Is that why you're here every night, letting me kiss you?"

She shook her head and, barely audibly, said, "You're not safe here."

He clutched her face, which looked bluish in the morning light.

"Did you tell someone I was a soldier?" he demanded, enjoying the feeling of this little enemy's fragile cheekbones locked in his grip.

He saw tears glistening in her eyes like molten amber and his hand fell powerless to his side. He plopped down next to the tree, overcome with remorse for wanting to hurt her.

Ilse quietly said, "As soon as the Burgomaster leaves, some villagers are planning to come here to prove you are a . . ."

"I'm a what?"

"*Jude*," she said, and tears rolled down her cheeks.

Yefim stiffened. There it was: his bane, his big secret, his fatal verdict. That rotten word, both tragic and sweet coming from Ilse's mouth, hung in the morning air, reminding him of who he was, to her and to all of them.

"Let them come! I've got nothing to hide," Yefim declared, but immediately he knew how unconvincing that sounded.

Ilse stared at the ground, rocking back and forth. Somewhere a rooster crowed. They sat in silence.

He was the one thinking of leaving before Ilse became part of his life, so why was he hesitant now? Yes, he knew his chances of making it to the Red Army were impossible. If he was lucky, this second escape would end at another police station and he'd be resent to an ostarbeiter market where some other enterprising German would buy him like a draft horse. If he was unlucky, then . . . well, there was no point thinking about that now. He'd just have to get lucky, that's all. Anything was better than being caught as a Jew in a German village.

Gently, Yefim turned her face toward his. In the brightening orange twilight, she looked older, like the wife she could have become. He wiped the wet streaks that were growing cold on her cheeks and said, "I will leave tonight."

Chapter 11

June 1975
Crimea, Ukrainian SSR

Nina sat on the sofa bed and cried. She couldn't understand why the authorities weren't letting her go to Poland. She was supposed to deliver her report on the worldwide paleogeography of coral fossils at the international conference at the Polish Academy of Sciences. It was going to be the most important event of her career. For months she'd prepared her documents for the exit visa and answered humiliating questions about her family and her time during the occupation to various government entities. Still, she'd had no doubt she'd get approved. They wouldn't put you through the wringer if you were going to be rejected. And so she had gotten carried away. She had imagined the applause of the leading scientists from Poland, England, France, and the United States. She'd imagined herself walking around Warsaw, enjoying her first-ever trip outside of the Soviet borders.

Nina looked around Yefim's room. She had thought of it as his ever since the kids flew the coop and she'd moved into their old bedroom. She and Yefim didn't even need to discuss it. Sleeping separately suited them both fine. But now, sitting on her husband's bed, she desperately needed companionship, his or her children's. However,

Yefim was at work, as always. Vita, suddenly an adult, had moved to a remote village in Uzbekistan to work at a geological expedition with Vlad, her tall, handsome husband she had met junior year. Andrey was in Moscow studying psychology, despite her and Yefim's pleas for him to get a more practical profession than listening to people's problems in a country where most people's problem was the country itself. But the boy ignored them. Apparently, he'd inherited Yefim's defiant streak.

Nina heard the squeak of the swing in the courtyard. The balcony door was open and the warm summer breeze brought the smell of the blooming acacia. A dove began to coo. It was all so peaceful. So dull. Warsaw was probably teeming with cosmopolitan life and here she was, home alone, not trustworthy enough to leave the country. An old orphan's fear returned to her: she was overwhelmed by the same loneliness as in those first months after her parents died and she was left to fend for herself in Nazi-occupied Kyiv. She tried to shake off the memories by heading out to the balcony where she could see which kids were on the swing. She had begun to calm down when she noticed Yefim rounding the corner. Nina hurried to the bathroom to wash the tears off her face.

When he opened the door, she wanted to ask him what he was doing home so early but instead blurted out, "They are not letting me go to Warsaw."

He threw his cap on the ground.

"Bastards."

"Maybe it's because Grandpa was Polish. Or because of all my quips in class. You know me, with my big mouth. But it's probably because I've cavorted with the Germans, so I must be a goddamn spy."

"Take it as a compliment," he said. "They think you're important enough to keep you close."

She looked up at her husband and wished he could somehow plead on her behalf, the way the Professor had back in Kyiv when they didn't want to accept her into the graduate school because of Stalin's directive not to take students from the occupied zone.

Instead, Yefim said, "Listen, forget Poland. Let's go to Crimea. They gave me ten days off."

Nina looked around, disoriented. Never in their twenty-five years together had they gone on vacation by themselves. They had Vita before they were even married and then their life was all about work, kids, long expeditions for him, and summer digs or paleontological conferences for her. They had spent more time apart than together. And now that she was almost fifty, Crimea, just the two of them? She didn't know how she was supposed to feel.

"Come on, pack your things," he pressed.

"You want to go right now?"

"Why not? There is a six P.M. train for Simferopol."

Why not? She looked at this husband of hers who never planned, who seemed to get through life by the seat of his pants. Her husband whom she knew intimately yet not at all. Her husband whose existence often seemed to run parallel to hers, without much intersecting. This could be interesting, she thought. It could be a new start for them.

As she packed their summer clothes, Yefim said, "But you have to promise me one thing. None of your planning, worrying, and organizing. Just this once, you have to follow my lead. *Ladno?*"

"*Ladno,*" she agreed.

When they arrived at the train station, the ticket counters stood empty. A bad sign.

"Tickets for Simferopol?" Yefim asked at one of two open windows.

"Sold out."

"What about—"

"For all directions," the saleswoman cut him off.

Nina resisted the urge to tell him that was what happened when you didn't plan. Instead, she wondered what they would do at home for ten days, just the two of them.

"Wait here," Yefim told her, and marched to the last ticket counter reserved for veterans and active military.

She watched him skeptically. He usually did everything to avoid his veteran's privileges, but this trip apparently meant a lot to him. His broad shoulders stooped toward the small window with the resoluteness of someone who always seemed to think the world would just bend to his will. When would he learn? They should go back home. They were too old for this spur-of-the-moment silliness.

Yefim turned from the window and walked toward her with a smirk.

"Got us two tickets for Simferopol," he said, as if that was the only possible outcome.

"What? How?"

"Some soldier gave them up."

Her husband's luck never ceased to surprise her. This man could get into a car accident on a country road and be bleeding to death when out of nowhere a policeman would magically appear and rush him to the hospital. He could fight through the worst war in human history and his only injury was damage to two fingers. As Nina and Yefim walked toward the platform, she knocked three times on the wooden railing for thinking these jinxing thoughts.

That night, after the conductor turned off the lights, Nina swayed in the lower bunk, unable to sleep. Tomorrow, she was supposed to be on a flight to Warsaw. She couldn't stop imagining the audience at the Polish Academy of Sciences applauding her colleague, Simonov, who would deliver her report. Simonov was evidently more trustworthy and less likely to defect or be turned into a spy or whatever the authorities feared. And all because three decades ago the young, orphaned Nina didn't have a way to evacuate from Kyiv. It was absurd that world events could be held against a person.

When the train arrived in Simferopol the next morning, Yefim and Nina took a trolleybus to the coast. The bus ascended the mountain road, and when they reached the crest, she saw cascading green slopes that ended in the shimmering Black Sea. Through the open window, the breeze brought the smell of the sea, cypress trees, and thyme growing in the hot sun. The smell of vacation.

"Why haven't we done this before?" she said, surprising herself. Yefim put his hand on hers and she felt the comfort of its weight.

With the kids grown and out of the house, they could give their marriage another try. Yefim's affair, the back-and-forth with the

Professor, the years in the communal apartment—they all seemed far behind her now. Perhaps she could even overlook Yefim's habitual lies or how he disappeared on his long work trips, never calling or writing, as if she didn't exist.

The bus arrived in the coastal town of Alushta in the early afternoon. At the bus stop, there were a few women with spare rooms and they followed one to a house with a yard that was shaded by vines with young grapes hanging within reach. Their room was in a separate building in the back, not far from the chicken coop, with two narrow beds and an outside washbasin.

They changed into their bathing suits, took their towels, and headed to the sea. The walk was longer than the woman had indicated, but Nina didn't mind. They bought sweet cheese vatrushkas and triangular packets of cold milk and inhaled them on the way, like they used to do when they were students in Kyiv.

Feeling full and happy, they walked the esplanade that stretched along the pebble beaches. On their left, the beaches were separated by concrete piers and were all identical: crowded with families eating, children splashing, people tanning, smoking, playing cards, and reading on the wooden chaise longues. Nina was getting hot and wanted to get into the water, but Yefim wanted to keep going. Nina followed her husband, trying to let him make the decisions. She was glad when he finally turned into one beach and they laid their towels on the chaise longues not far from the water. Later she would always remember that it was he who chose that particular beach.

Yefim ran into the water, and Nina walked in gingerly. He turned and threatened to splash her, but she waved her hands.

"Don't you dare!"

She wasn't a strong swimmer, so she stayed close to the shoreline while Yefim swam off into the shimmering distance. The cool water was a godsend after the hot walk, and for a moment she felt giddy to be in the sea. But after a few minutes she wished she were here after the Warsaw conference, not instead of it. She bobbed on the waves among the grandmothers in swim caps who faced the shore, their hefty bosoms floating on the surface like balloons as they kept a watchful eye on their grandkids, periodically yelling, "Don't throw pebbles!" and "Keep away from those waves!"

Clearly, these women weren't missing the biggest event of their career. Was that what the authorities wanted for her? To become just another babushka, cast off from all she had built?

Nina couldn't even imagine becoming a grandmother but with Vita now married she had to be ready. Life seemed to be accelerating. Maybe it was what happened with age or maybe it was that nothing around them changed anymore. They had been living under Brezhnev for a decade. Perhaps their country, too, felt tired of striving, of changing and reinventing itself. Maybe it also could use a seaside vacation.

Something grabbed onto her calves and pulled. Water rushed into her nose and mouth. Her arms flailed. The human sounds of the beach disappeared. She kicked until her legs were free. Popping back out on the surface, she coughed, her eyes and throat stinging from the salt.

"Got ya!" Yefim was laughing.

She spat out the seawater and brushed the wet hair away from her eyes.

"Are you crazy?" she yelled as soon as she could speak. Sometimes she didn't understand how this man had ended up as her husband. He was over fifty but still behaved like a boy who never thought about anything beyond the present moment.

"Loosen up!" Yefim said. "We're on vacation!"

Nina felt the curious eyes of the grandmothers. For a moment she considered heading in, but as much as she hated to admit it, Yefim was right. She had to get her mind off Warsaw.

"Loosen up, you say?" she cried, and, turning her back toward Yefim, began to splash him with all her might. He splashed back, and though she knew the grandmothers were still looking, she no longer cared.

When they came out, they lay down on the chaise longues. Her arms ached pleasantly. She covered her face with her hat and he put his shirt over his eyes. Soon Yefim dozed off, but Nina couldn't sleep. Her mind snagged on pieces of conversation around her, in Ukrainian and Russian. She sat up to look at the sea. Three seagulls cruised above the water.

Someone had once told her the best times to swim in the Black Sea were the first and last hours of the sun. When Yefim woke, she would suggest they return here at sunrise.

"Nina Pavlovna?" she heard a familiar voice say, and—not believing it could exist in this world of the sea, the pebbles, and the grandmothers—Nina clutched her husband's hand in panic.

Yefim sat up.

"What is it?"

Half hoping that she had fallen asleep and was only dreaming, Nina rose to greet the Professor.

He stood in front of her, not as tall as he once had been, looking strangely indecent in a T-shirt and knee-length shorts that exposed his thin legs. His wife, Olga Yurievna, her hair now almost all gray, held him by the elbow as if afraid he might fall.

"Of all the places, we meet in Alushta!" the Professor was saying as Nina was desperately trying to yank the towel from under Yefim's feet to cover herself up.

"My goodness, Osip Yefremovich, what are you doing here?" she stammered. "Olga Yurievna, I'm not sure if you remember me. It's nice to see you again. This is my husband, Yefim."

Nina wondered if she had misremembered the proper etiquette of who should be introduced to whom. She thought the less important person must be introduced to the more important one, but how she was supposed to decide which one of them was more important, she didn't know.

The Professor and Yefim shook hands.

"We just arrived today," Nina said, unable to look at the two men's hands touching.

Olga Yurievna looked from Nina to Osip Yefremovich and back, and for a moment Nina could see the scene through her eyes: the way her husband leaned a little too eagerly toward his former protégé, the way the younger woman fumbled with the towel, turning away from her own husband. Nina tried to relax her shoulders and act more casually. After all, she had nothing to hide.

The last time she had seen the Professor was over a year earlier. She came to Kyiv on a work trip and heard that he was in the hospital for an eye operation. She borrowed her doctor friend's white robe and rushed to the hospital. Inside, no one stopped her, so she ran into his room. His right eye was bandaged. As she squeezed his hand, he had laughed. "And Olga Yurievna couldn't figure out how to sneak in."

Nothing scandalous happened—they had long ago become friends, and they didn't speak of their previous passions—but she still didn't tell Yefim about her visit, and she supposed that the Professor never told his wife. It was their secret, innocent and precious.

"What are you doing here?" Osip Yefremovich asked. "Aren't you supposed to be in Warsaw? I may be retired, but I still keep my ears to the ground."

She heard a note of admonishment in his voice and felt as though she'd been caught cutting class with a boy. The Professor had put such hope in her over the years, guiding her through the research, graduate school, dissertation, her job in Donetsk—and here she was, frolicking on the beach, not good enough to be sent to Poland.

"The kids have flown the nest and I had some vacation days for once," Yefim intervened, and Nina felt grateful for his easy, cheerful tone.

"And the report?"

"Simonov will be reading it," Nina answered, hoping that maybe he had some way to intercede on her behalf the way he had so many years earlier. "They didn't let me—"

"The report is what matters most," said the Professor. "Everyone will know it was yours. Don't let this bureaucratic spanking get to you."

She laughed.

"I suppose the Crimean coast is not a bad compromise," she said, feeling less daunted by the sudden meeting. "My first time here. With Yefim's luck, we even scored two train tickets."

"I heard everything was sold out. Feels like the entire country is in Crimea."

"A soldier returned two tickets," Yefim explained.

"Oh, that's right, now I remember you were a veteran," Osip Yefremovich said, and turned to his wife, who still held his elbow as Yefim made his usual brushing-off gesture as if being a veteran was no big deal. "Olechka, Yefim was also a student in our department. Our star collector, as I recall."

His wife nodded in the kindly way of mothers who have something more important on their minds, and Nina again felt small in front of this woman with her thin, no-nonsense mouth, her gray hair in a bun à la Lenin's wife, her wary reticence. They had nothing in common. And looking at the grip of her aging fingers on Osip Yefremovich's elbow, Nina saw with an unprecedented clarity that she could never have been his wife.

"Where are you staying?" the Professor asked as Nina edged closer to Yefim. "We're in the Krymski Hotel, up the hill by the park. Shall we all have dinner? There is a cafeteria with a view."

"You need some rest, my dear," his wife said. "A little too much sun for one day."

"Sure, sure," he said. "Tomorrow, then?"

Nina nodded. The Professor and his wife said goodbye and walked off, pebbles crunching under their feet.

Nina and Yefim fell silent. Behind them, the sun rolled toward the mountains. The sea had grown quieter, the waves gently licking the shore. A thin strip of clouds hung on the horizon. Nina felt embarrassed, as if she had orchestrated the meeting. She was afraid Yefim would say something awful about the Professor. He might call him "that dirty old seducer" or, worse, ask if they had been seeing each other all these years.

"Tomorrow we're going to Lazurnoye," he said instead. "It's supposed to be a small village with a nice cove. Shouldn't be nearly as crowded as here. But if you want, we can stay here an extra night and meet them for dinner."

She kept her eyes on the sea, not ready to show him her face. He ran off into the water and disappeared.

They didn't stay the second night. Nina called the hotel and left a message for the Professor that they had to leave Alushta. She felt both guilty and relieved. Yefim never asked about the Professor. Perhaps he had forgotten that first fight of theirs the summer they met. Afterward she kept thinking how silly she was, a fifty-year-old woman still embarrassed by an old crush.

In the morning they took a bus to Lazurnoye and it was like Yefim said, a quiet village with a small cove. They ate crayfish and drank beer. Nina wondered if the Professor was angry at her for leaving or if, after some time, he, too, thought better of his dinner proposal.

There was no lodging in Lazurnoye, so in the afternoon they hiked up to a quiet mountain lake surrounded by a forest and huge, rounded boulders where they spent the night. It was a paradise of birds, crickets, croaking frogs, and fish that teemed in the emerald water. The mountain peaks surrounded the lake and were reflected in its surface. Yefim laid out their clothes in a spot not far from the water and said they could cover themselves with the towels when it got cooler at night.

They had both spent so many nights sleeping outdoors on their separate expeditions, yet never together. Lying next to him under the darkening sky, the Milky Way visible between the branches, Nina remembered their first summer together at that dig in Stany and thought how strange it was that twenty-five years had passed. A quarter of a century. And here they were, alone together under the stars.

They turned to one another and she felt the warmth of his breath tickling the tip of her nose, and then his hand slid down her hip and she felt herself at one with the pines and the crickets and the man who wasn't exactly as selfless or as honest as she'd thought but who *was* here, was hers, and, unlike that first night on Lovers' Hill, was languid and deliberate and tender. She didn't once think about the Professor.

Two days later, after visiting the palm-lined Yalta and mailing postcards to Andrey in his Moscow dorm and Vita in her Uzbek village, they caught a ferry to Kerch, an old city once occupied by the ancient Greeks. At the port, they picked up a brochure for the newly opened Adjimushkay quarries, where the Germans had surrounded more than ten thousand Soviet soldiers and civilians. She thought Yefim wouldn't want to see it, but, to her surprise, he agreed.

It was a hot weekday morning and there were four other people in their group. The guide, a young freckled fellow with a nasal voice, handed out flashlights and led them in through one of more than a thousand entrances the soldiers had used during the five months of the German siege.

The caves were cool and moist. Though after years of working at dig sites and quarries Nina was an experienced climber, here in the darkness she allowed herself to reach for Yefim's hand. They were led down some stairs and through a long, narrow passageway where they were forced to crouch. Their hard breathing echoed in the dark.

The hallway led them to a square-shaped room where the dark gray ceiling grazed the top of Yefim's head. In the center was a metal table with a map of the catacombs.

As Nina stood close to Yefim, the guide told them that the quarry was first used by the partisans back in 1941. Then, during the Crimean offensive in '42, the Germans surrounded a big regiment. From the first days of their defense, the Soviets' biggest problem was water. At first, they climbed out of the caves to get water from the wells above, even though the wells were heavily guarded and their attempts always ended with casualties. Then the Germans decided to fill the wells with dead bodies and broken equipment, so the trapped Soviets were forced to collect water from the walls of the caves, using pieces of German telephone cable to suck water drops out of limestone.

Nina stood there, listening to the intent, nasal voice of the guide as he told them about the thousands of people who had died here from suffocation, hunger, and rock falls. The horror of it all made it hard to breathe. Nothing could be worse than being buried alive in these caves.

She was still shaken up long after they climbed back out to the surface and took the bus back to the city, where they walked into a hotel and asked for a room. The receptionist said they were all booked, but then she must have noticed Yefim's injured hand because she asked, "Veteran?" and when he nodded, she magically produced a corner room on the second floor.

Nina was happy to finally put her feet up, but she couldn't sleep.

"Let's go see the Greek ruins this afternoon," Yefim suggested. "To cheer us up."

He sounded like he didn't need any cheering up. Nina couldn't help but think how callous his war experience had made him. He always lived in the moment. Never wanted to talk about the future or the past. Not his parents and siblings, not the war, nothing. Like he'd closed the door on it all and moved on. Even Andrey and Vita knew what they knew about the famine, the repressions, and the war from her, not from him. But she wasn't built like he was. She wanted him to linger with her in the suffering of those war years.

She stared at the fly crawling on the ceiling and said, "Have I ever told you the chicken story?"

"You mean about the black chicken that lived with you as a kid?"

"No, this was later, in '43. I was working at a poultry processing plant. The chickens went to the Germans, but we were allowed to take home heads, feet, and guts. The guard made sure none of us carried out a chicken under our dress. Anyway, right around then, my friend Vasya Varavva got involved with the partisans. Because I lived by myself, he used my place to hide secret packets in my closet. At night, someone would come pick them up. A few times the packages included German rifles. Where he got them and who he passed them on to, I don't know. One time, my friend Galina, who was in charge of handing out the chickens, said she wanted to help the partisans but didn't know anyone, so I mentioned her to Vasya. He said they could use some dressing materials. So you know what Galina did? Next time a German came for a pickup, she made up a story about how her sick mother really needed some dressing materials and that if he procured them, she would give him an extra chicken. Soon this German and several of his friends started bringing us medicine, bandages, and gauze, and she'd throw them a couple of extra chickens. Then we'd take all those things to my place and hide them in my closet. It was as close as I ever got to the partisans."

The fly took off from the ceiling and buzzed around the lamp.

"You've never told me you were involved with the partisans," Yefim said, sounding as disapproving as a parent. "That could have been dangerous."

"I wasn't really involved. I could have done more, but I didn't. I wasn't brave."

"What made you think of this now?"

"Because I know that Vasya and Galina could have lived in that terrible quarry, but not me."

Yefim fell silent, his face heavy, and she wasn't sure he understood.

What Nina really wished she could tell him was something that happened right before the poultry plant. After Nina's mother passed, her neighbor Zina helped her find work. Everything was run by the Germans, and though she was just short of finishing high school she managed to land a job as a secretary at a small construction firm. There were two German partners in the office and several Polish workers who went in and out. The main partner seemed to Nina a typical Fritz: his beer belly sat like a ball on top of his half a leg, which had been blown off in World War I. The job was easy since she had a good command of written German. Plus she got to eat a filling bowl of pea soup along with the Polish workers, a rare treat in those hungry months. All in all, it was a good job for an orphan girl.

When the owner brought in some pudding he received from Germany, Nina didn't say no. Sweets were an impossible rarity and she didn't think much of his treating her to it. She had been a good secretary after all. Then one day her boss brought a chocolate bar and when she took it his hand brushed her breasts as if by accident. The next day, as she was passing by him, he jokingly slapped her butt. Zina said that was how Germans treated their secretaries and to stick it out: the work was clean, the food was filling, and frankly Nina needed the money.

After a few weeks of this, however, the German confronted Nina. He told her he had received a letter from his wife back home in the Reich with permission to make Nina his mistress. He waved the letter nervously, and as Nina stood in front of him, she was certain she must have misunderstood.

"I wrote her that you were a good, polite girl, an orphan, and very hardworking," he said, and handed Nina the letter. As she read for herself, he stuck his hand under her dress and scanned her body, then smirked and told her to come back tonight when his partner wouldn't be in the next room and they could be alone. She ran home and told Zina. They decided she had to find a different job, but then, two days later, she received a summons to the labor exchange office. They were drafting her as an ostarbeiter to Germany.

She did not tell Yefim any of this. She didn't want him to imagine her being touched by that one-legged German while she stood there, too scared and hungry to bat his hand away. To think she was this close to becoming a "German sack," as they'd called the girls who went out with enemy officers. Nina still felt soiled by the memory.

Why had she ever thought the government would let her go to Warsaw?

Yefim sat up on the bed. His dark eyes darted as though she was forcing him to confess his own cowardice. Nina felt herself flinch because—and this realization distressed her—she didn't want to hear it. It felt as if their marriage depended on him not telling her whatever he was remembering.

Yefim got up and walked toward the window. He stood looking out at the back alley of the hotel, where a tree shaded a garbage bin.

Then he turned and said, "What you are claiming, Nina, is that you are a coward. But that's bull. Bravery is circumstantial. If you were forced to hide in that quarry to survive, you would have done it and not thought twice. Just as if your parents hadn't died, you may have done more for the partisans. Or maybe you would have been too scared for your mother and not hidden anything in your closet."

Relieved they were still talking about her, she persisted.

"You don't understand. You weren't a civilian. You were a soldier doing your job. But we . . . we were these helpless women waiting for the Red Army to rescue us while we cleaned chicken guts for our captors. And it didn't matter whether or not we were guilty of doing anything for the enemy because afterward the code in our passports told everyone we were."

"Doing our job." He smirked. "Oh, please. Things weren't that different in the army."

She wasn't sure how he meant that, but he jumped off the bed and said, "I'm not going to let you sit here justifying why you don't deserve to go abroad. Usually you see right through their crap, that's one of the things I've always admired about you. But this time you've let them get to you. I can see it: you're blaming yourself."

He extended his hands to her and smiled. "Enough. This is the last day of our vacation and you promised to follow my lead. We are going out."

"All right, but only if we promise each other one thing."

"What?"

"That there will be no more lying in our marriage," she said.

Yefim looked down at his feet. Then he knelt near the bed, grabbed her hand, and kissed it.

"That's a deal," he said, and she felt giddy with hope.

Outside, the wind had picked up, cooling off the city, and Nina found herself relieved to be out of that hotel room.

That afternoon they walked around Kerch's cobblestoned streets and ate watermelon. They looked at the ships going in and out of the busy port. They didn't talk of the caves or the war but instead wondered whether Andrey would like Moscow and also how long it would be until Vita and Vlad gave them a grandchild. In the evening they took a bus home to Donetsk.

Nina was glad to be home. She moved back into Yefim's room, where they shared the sofa bed. After years of living like two people parenting the same children, she felt she could confide in him and that made their bond seem more generous and more truthful.

With enthusiasm Nina hadn't felt since they had decorated their first home on the outskirts of Kyiv before Vita was born, she and Yefim threw themselves at cleaning out their nest. They sorted and put away Vita's and Andrey's old things, clearing room for their own books, clothes, and mementos from their expeditions. One afternoon, as she wiped the outside of the leather briefcase with Yefim's documents that had been collecting dust under the bed for who knows how long, Nina saw him come out on the balcony to beat the dust out of the carpets. His bare torso was tan and still strong and she thought, *What a reliable husband I have.* She could see this new life of theirs stretching comfortably in front of her.

But a week later Yefim came home and said they were sending him to the taiga. They'd discovered a new Siberian oil field and he had to map out the route for the pipeline. He stroked her cheek and said how glad he was that they'd gone to Crimea together.

Then he flew off and Nina didn't hear from him for the next two months.

Chapter 12

January 1945
Niegripp, Germany

Almost a year after Yefim fled the Burgomaster's, Ilse still came to him in his dreams. As he slept on his springy cot in the wooden shack behind Herr Mayer's mechanical workshop in the center of Niegripp, she would appear, her auburn hair loose, her voice hushed in the night. Her face was always shrouded in darkness and he knew, with the certainty that only happens in dreams, that if he could just see the amber of her eyes in the light, they would be happy and safe. But by the time he'd find a lantern, she'd be gone and he would wake up to find himself bundled up in an old moth-eaten blanket that his newest German boss was kind enough to provide.

Yefim didn't see Ilse again after she warned him it was time to leave Karow. Though he often wondered what would have happened with them if he had stayed, he didn't regret leaving. At first, after he fled, he headed toward the Eastern Front on the off chance the Red Army had crossed into Germany. He had thought that, in some ways, it might be easier to travel alone without having to worry about Ivan: he could move faster, stay quieter, and avoid having to make decisions that led to getting caught. But as he walked through central Germany, it turned out that the hardest part of fleeing alone was having no one to care for. Without Ivan's banter and the loyalty in his gray eyes, making it back to the army seemed almost pointless. After all, no one understood him as well as Ivan.

After three days on the road, Yefim was caught by the *Polizei*. Luckily, this time they didn't rough him up. Apparently, there'd been so many runaways, they'd stopped bothering with punishment. They sent him to the labor market, where he got lucky again. Instead of being chosen for a factory or mine, he was sold to Herr Mayer of Niegripp for his mechanical workshop, where he had been learning machinery skills for the past eight months. Here he was known as Yefim Lisin and no one seemed to question whether he was a Jew, perhaps because this late in the war an uncaught twenty-two-year-old Jew walking around Germany was unimaginable.

He still often fantasized about seeing Ilse again. After all, Niegripp was only forty kilometers west of Karow, and if both of them outlived the war, then maybe . . . Maybe what? Yefim didn't know. He tried to imagine some world in which being with Ilse was possible but couldn't. Still, if the war only ended, there was a *maybe*.

The Red Army, he'd learned, had already pushed the Germans out of Belarus, the Baltic republics, and even Warsaw. Meanwhile, the Allies had liberated Paris. The Germans couldn't possibly outlast those two surrounding forces, and he wondered when his army would get here, to this village on the Elbe.

While Niegripp had been relatively quiet when he arrived the previous summer, lately, in these first weeks of 1945, the honking of geese that wintered in this riverside area was increasingly replaced by the menacing whoosh of British and American bombers.

Luckily, Niegripp itself wasn't a target. With only three streets, a church with a high dark steeple, a redbrick school building with a bomb shelter, and a grocery where villagers stood in line with their ration cards, it wasn't of interest to the Allies. Yefim feared that Mayer's workshop, which was one of Niegripp's only businesses, could provoke their wrath, but his boss assured them they were too small for anyone to bother.

Mayer's workshop was a long one-story brick building that smelled of wood, oil, and tar. Located in a cul-de-sac, its three large windows looked out onto a courtyard surrounded by a brick wall, which made it feel like a small fortress. Inside, Yefim worked on the metal parts that would be shipped to another factory and assembled, no doubt by other prisoners—maybe even by Ivan, who knew?—into some type of machine meant for killing his compatriots. Maybe the machine was a tank, maybe a bomber. He was never told. In his hands, in the remoteness of Niegripp, these small parts seemed innocent, just chunks of metal. But he knew. Nothing made with such precision was going to be used for bicycles.

In three years of working for the Germans, this was the most dubious job he'd held. And yet, with the Red Army pushing the Germans back, he kept his guilt at bay by telling himself the small parts he made wouldn't change much. If Ivan was here, he'd agree. This was certainly better than working directly for Hitler's army or fighting with Vlasov against Soviet soldiers.

The Mayers lived across the street from the workshop in a house with a roof window that reminded Yefim of a giant eye. They were an odd couple. Herr Mayer was tall and wide in the shoulders, with remnants of youthful strength in his arms but with bushy graying sideburns and an unwieldy stomach that dragged him forward like a sail. His wife, Marie, was at least a decade younger and a lot smaller, with big gray maternal eyes.

They had two boys: two-year-old Wilhelm, who always sneezed and sniffled, and dark-haired six-year-old Marcel, who had a keen interest in the goings-on of the workshop. The only thing Marcel took from his father was his black hair; the rest—the mousy face, the small build—were all Marie's. Yet what he lacked in physical strength he made up for in tenacity. He kept trying to sneak inside the workshop, even though the Mayers had forbidden it—probably, Yefim suspected, because they didn't want their boy around Soviet laborers.

Though he never interacted with Marie or the boys, Yefim found himself following their lives with interest. The boys reminded him of his own childhood, when the big, scary events of the outside world would often be overshadowed by his private juvenile concerns. These days Yefim had a harder time remembering his brothers' voices, the exact faces of his parents, or the way Basya sang in the evenings, but watching the Mayers brought back unexpected memories. While Marie was brushing Marcel's tousled hair on the stoop one morning, he remembered how, when he had gotten lice, his mother sat him down and picked the bugs out of his hair before wrapping his head in a towel dipped in kerosene. He remembered the warmth of her hovering over him and the joy of the rare intimacy, just him and her.

Once, on a mild January day, Marcel came outside to kick a tanned leather ball against the brick wall of the workshop. As Yefim watched through the small dusty workshop window, he remembered playing soccer with Naum and Georgiy, how they had run around barefoot in the dusty potato field behind the cowshed. They kicked a ball made out of a twisted old work shirt caked in mud. Mikhail was in the army then and Yakov was reading something on a stump, refusing to join the game even though it would have been better with four. Now, watching from the window, he wished he could leave the workshop and play with Marcel.

Yefim heard the roar of plane engines approaching. Marcel looked up from the ball to a formation of two American B-17s and their escort of four fighter planes when suddenly they came under attack by the Luftwaffe. Yefim ran out into the courtyard. The boy stood mesmerized as the thundering planes tried to outmaneuver one another. Yefim urged Marcel to hurry home and the boy ran off.

The American formation quickly broke. Three of their planes tried to lure the Germans away from the B-17s toward the other side of the Elbe. It seemed to be working until Yefim saw smoke billowing from one of the bombers as it nose-dived toward the two small lakes east of the village. A moment later a figure fell from the bomber, a black dot against the light gray sky. A German pilot shot at the airman, but he was falling too fast, and as he dropped, Yefim could distinguish his arms and legs flailing helplessly in the air. He couldn't take his eyes off this man falling to his death when, no more than forty meters from the ground, the airman's khaki-colored parachute opened, yanking him up and carrying him toward the Elbe. He saw a few villagers run toward the river.

Later he heard they hadn't found the American and assumed he had drowned. Yefim hoped the airman had survived and escaped. Either way, it was the closest Niegripp had come in contact with the war, and it changed the mood in the village. The war was now fought directly overhead, and Yefim could see fear in the villagers' eyes.

To his surprise, he didn't enjoy seeing the Germans get a taste of their own medicine. He, too, grew jittery. For three years he had hoped to get out of the German snare. Now, instead, as the war was finally turning around, he might be blown to pieces by friendly fire.

In the following weeks Yefim began to hear the drone of planes almost every day as the Allies flew south toward Magdeburg or northeast toward Berlin and other targets. While the Americans had the day shift, the British flew at night, providing little respite from the chilling soundtrack.

One night in early February, the village siren blared. Yefim leapt off his cot, stumbling in the dark, heart racing. He rushed out of the shed. On the street, villagers were running toward the school with the bomb shelter. The siren wailed. In the distance, searchlights pierced the dark sky. He'd forgotten his shoes, but it was too late to go back. He hadn't survived three years in the Reich just to die in a raid. He rushed toward the school. Beyond the earsplitting shriek of the siren, he heard the whizzing of airplanes.

He ran faster. The frozen pavement scalded his feet.

As he rounded the corner, he saw the Mayers running ahead. His boss carried little Wilhelm in his arms, while Marie and Marcel ran hand in hand behind him. Then, he saw Marcel slip on a frozen puddle and fall, pulling his mother down with him. Herr Mayer, who was a few meters ahead of them, didn't notice. Yefim caught up to them, yanked Marie up by the hand, swooped up the boy, and, carrying him in his arms, sprinted toward the shelter.

They were almost at the entrance when the first explosions boomed in the east. The sky burst in an orange glow. Yefim thought, *Don't die now, don't die now.* He raced toward the entrance and a few seconds later leapt down the narrow stairs to safety.

Inside, it was cold and crowded. The low-ceilinged basement smelled of mud and fear. Yefim deposited the boy on the ground. The electricity had gone out, but the school principal held up a lantern, its light reflecting in the rim of her glasses. Farther in, he saw an old couple lighting a long candlestick. He made out villagers sitting on the floor along the rough brick walls, hugging their knees, exchanging panicked guesses about what was happening above. Yefim followed behind the Mayers, climbing over people's feet until they found a spot where they could fit. Marcel pulled him by the arm and he crouched next to his boss's family.

"*Danke*," said Herr Mayer.

Marie propped sniffling Wilhelm on her lap, swaying back and forth, her gray eyes wide and moist as her other arm wrapped around Marcel.

Outside, the siren howled, and though down here it wasn't as deafening, sitting buried beneath it made its shriek eerier. Squeezed between Marie and Yefim, Marcel wore white cotton pajamas and socks and Yefim could feel the boy shaking as the wall behind them gave off a humid, bone-chilling cold. He wished he had brought something to cover him, though he probably shook more from fright. Across from them, along the opposite wall, sat the gangly twin sisters who lived two houses down from the workshop with their aging mother. The girls were still in their long white nightgowns, their dark eyes shifting anxiously as other villagers ran in. He wondered why their mother wasn't with them.

Suddenly the wall behind him bucked and shook. He ducked as a shower of dust came off the ceiling. A dusty plume scraped Yefim's throat and he coughed violently. Wilhelm began to wail. The sisters clung to each other. What a way to go, he thought: Germans and Soviets all dead under the same bomb. For a moment he wished Ilse were here. He would hug her and kiss the tears on her face as she held on to him. Dying wouldn't be as scary together.

But, no, Ilse deserved to outlive this war and become one of those old German ladies who still looked refined at seventy.

The coughing subsided, but he could feel the grit of dust in his teeth. Marcel clutched his hand. The boy said something Yefim couldn't hear as the basement echoed with the scared cries of the villagers. He leaned closer.

"What?"

"The airfield," Marcel said, his little face ashen.

Yefim didn't know which airfield he was talking about. For a moment he wondered if that information had been purposefully kept from him, but then there was another explosion, farther away, and Marcel clutched his hand again as Marie shushed little Wilhelm.

They sat like that for a while until the siren stopped. The basement went quiet.

"Is it safe now, Mama?" Marcel whispered.

"I don't know," she said, stroking dust off his hair. "We have to wait."

The people began to talk, first quietly, then more boldly. One of the twins got up and, stooping under a low ceiling, shook out her night-gown as her sister sat still, her eyes vacant. Yefim heard bits of conversation all around him.

"Must have bombed the airfield," someone was saying.

"Wait till the Russians get here."

"Did you hear about the rapes?"

"If they take Berlin . . ."

The Red Army must have crossed into Germany, Yefim thought. In the voices around him, he heard fear and anger and also something else that sounded like regret. The war had humbled them at last. He felt sorry for them, for all of them in this shelter and all the people in similar shelters throughout this continent and beyond.

Marcel tugged Yefim's hand.

"What happened to your fingers?" he asked.

Yefim was happy to provide a distraction for them both. It was better than waiting for the siren to start up again.

"This is a very old wound. One day I was mad at my mama and ran away to the forest. It got dark and I couldn't find my way home. Do you know who I met there?"

Marcel shook his head.

"Herr Wolf," said Yefim conspiratorially.

"A wolf?"

"*Ja.* Herr Wolf was no ordinary wolf. He told me I was in danger from his wolf friends. He said if I gave him something of mine, he would show me the way home."

"What did you give him?"

"I didn't have anything, so Herr Wolf said, 'Give me your finger.' I said I needed my finger, but he said, 'You need your life more.' And so I gave him pieces of my thumb and forefinger. In return, he saved me from being eaten."

"Did it hurt?"

"Not too much. He said that when I learn to make great things with my hands, I can return to the forest and get my fingers back."

"*Boah!* And I thought you just lost them in the war," said Marcel.

He looked sleepy and leaned his head on his mother's shoulder. Yefim didn't know how long they sat there after that. He must have dozed off because at some point one of the twin sisters had morphed into that dark-haired woman with a lifeless infant he sometimes dreamt of. He shivered, wanting the night to end.

In the early morning, word came from above that it was safe to come out. Marie pulled up the sleepy children. Yefim rose, too, his joints stiff from the cold and the dread. The villagers filed toward the exit. A strange yellow light streamed from the door. The school principal led the way. Behind her, the twin sisters looked like a pair of ghosts floating in their nightgowns.

Outside, the morning sky was a dirty orange. The air smelled acrid, but there was no major visible damage to the village itself. At the workshop, a layer of brick dust covered everything and several of the tools had rolled to the floor. A pile of firewood lay in disarray. Near his workstation, Yefim heard a crunch and looked down to see a broken glass. He began to clean up the mess but soon felt too tired and went back to his shed to rest.

The Red Army had crossed the German border! He couldn't believe it. He had waited for this news for so long. Yet his relief was mixed with a strange ambivalence. In all the twenty-two years of his life, borders never felt permanent or secure: the Soviet Union ballooned, Ukraine changed shape, the neighboring Poland was tossed about like a ball, and the gluttonous Germany had tried to swallow half the world. What a mess it all was, and for what? If he ever got out of there alive, he'd want to understand what made land so desirable that people were willing to kill and be killed for it. He remembered Anton Lisin, whose last name he now carried. He'd made fun of Lisin for wanting to study geology, but maybe that was what he ought to do if he lived: go to Kyiv and become a geologist.

First, however, Germany would need to surrender. He had been here so long, it was hard to imagine what would happen to this neatly tended land and its people once his comrades arrived. He worried about Ilse and Marcel. He didn't want them to see the horrors of war. They didn't deserve that.

A knock on the door woke him. Herr Mayer entered the shed for the first time since Yefim's arrival. Yefim sprung up and faced his boss in the semi-darkness of the shed.

"I've come to thank you for your help last night," he said. "It was . . . kind." Mayer fell silent, looking in a corner awkwardly. To relieve the tension, Yefim asked about the damage.

"The airfield was leveled," his boss said in a grave tone, as if he didn't realize that an ostarbeiter might not see this as bad news. "Also, Frau Müller, the mother of the twins, was crushed under a fallen beam. There will be a funeral."

Over the next few days Yefim resumed his regular work and tried not to lose his nerve every time he heard the bombers approach.

Herr Mayer came into the workshop less often. Instead, Yefim usually saw him in his house, pacing back and forth in front of the window or carrying supplies to the cellar in the back of the house. Marcel was no longer allowed to dribble his ball outside.

Yefim still went into the workshop every morning. However, because the metal parts he made were no longer being shipped anywhere, he began to work on his own project, a small brass mug he hoped to take home when this was all over.

One morning in early March, he was looking for a wrench to fix the stalled electric saw that was filling the echoing span of the workshop's pitched roof with a toothachingly piercing screech. As he walked past the workstation closest to the door, he noticed that among the metal junk, the sawdust, the planks, the rods, and the sheets, something was out of place.

He stopped and retraced his steps. At the workstation, he bent down. There, Marcel was covering his ears with his small hands.

"What are you doing here?" Yefim asked.

Marcel looked at him with wide scared eyes, then glanced at the door as if assessing whether he could bolt for it. Yefim wondered if he was about to cry. Slowly, Marcel lifted his hands. Finally, he said, "I wanted to see the tools."

"I'd be happy to show you the tools, but both of us can get in trouble for this."

"Why?"

Why? Yefim thought. *Because even though we spent a night at a bomb shelter together, technically your parents are still my enemies, that's why.* Instead he said, "How about I talk to your father and see if he lets you come here to learn?"

"Will I get in trouble?"

Yefim had no idea, but he thought of his own father and quickly said, "Hopefully not once I talk to him. Now, run back home before they worry."

The next day, when Herr Mayer stopped by, Yefim said there was a private matter he wanted to discuss and could they step outside for a moment? The shift in the war was palpable, and Yefim saw no point in continuing to pretend they were anything more than two people in a world of greater forces. He wanted to act human, to feel human again. So, in the chill of the wind that blew under the archway, he said, "Forgive me, but I've seen Marcel looking at the workshop. Do you plan for him to take over someday?"

"I do," Herr Mayer said. There was surprise in his voice.

"I could teach him. Maybe it would help distract him."

"Distract him?" he asked. "Well, yes. Hmm."

Then Mayer turned to go. Yefim stepped back to give his stomach a wide berth and watched him sail back toward his house. He heard nothing the rest of the day and wondered if he'd been wrong to think he could transgress his status as a forced laborer. Perhaps he was "mixing paints," as Mikhail would put it: perhaps his employer wasn't ready for him to be a human.

However, the next day Herr Mayer came into the workshop leading Marcel by the hand. Marie followed them. The boy looked smart in black pants and a checkered vest over a white shirt. Herr Mayer informed Yefim that Marie would bring the boy for an hour each morning and Yefim would show him how things worked. He was not to put Marcel in any danger and was to warn them if the boy's behavior was of concern to his safety or the goings-on of the workshop.

Then Herr Mayer walked out.

"Today I'm going to stay here to make sure he is cooperative," Marie told Yefim, as her dainty fingers stroked the dark mop of Marcel's hair. "He is a very inquisitive young man and we don't want him getting ahead of himself, do we?"

She followed as Yefim led Marcel around all the stations. "This is where we solder metal," Yefim explained. "This is where we do the milling. The tools are kept here while the scrap metal goes there."

He tried to sound authoritative and felt a satisfaction at having a German boy follow him around as if he weren't some lowly foreign mutt working for free for his father. He led Marcel to the table with several boxes marked in German.

"Can you read this word?" he asked, pointing to a box.

"I'm still learning," he said.

"The school closed, you know," Marie said apologetically.

"That's all right. I am learning too. It says 'calipers.' And here you've got rods, gauges, fly cutters, carbide bars, and angle blocks that help us form metal into the shape we want."

While the boy examined the pieces, asking about each one, Yefim noticed the warm feeling of being next to a child. The feeling of peacetime he'd forgotten. When it was time for Marie and Marcel to go, he found himself hoping they'd be back.

As he drilled and sanded later that day, he wondered what it would be like to be a father. There was magic in a little loving face that looked at you as if you were everything: provider and protector. He fantasized about how, when the war was just a dark memory, he would marry Ilse and have children—not six like his parents but two, maybe three, but definitely two. He'd teach them to use tools. He'd carry them on his shoulders to a lake, where they'd splash and laugh, diving in and out of the sunshine. He'd show them how to dribble a ball, feed chickens, plant a tree. All the important things. And he'd finally be able to live without secrets.

His mother would love to have another grandchild besides Lyubochka, who by now would be—Yefim had to pause and think here—eight. Eight! Incredible. He couldn't imagine his little freckled niece as a second grader. He could still remember her plump, wiggly body on his back, her hands wrapped around his neck as he crawled around on his knees, trumpeting like an elephant. He hoped Lyubochka was still alive—that all of them were—but he worried about whether that was likely. There were too many of them and they were too Jewish.

The next morning Marie and the boy were back.

Yefim tested to see which tools Marcel remembered and the boy proved a good student, recalling the names of most of the tools he had seen. It made Yefim proud, the way he imagined a father should be.

At the end of their second visit, he was walking them to the door when Marcel asked, "Where did you learn to be a machinist?"

"Mostly here."

"So what were you before?"

"That's enough questions for today, son," said Marie and hurried Marcel out the door. But Yefim answered anyway.

"I was a farmer," he said. The lie floated to the boy like a weightless feather, and he felt a hint of a grown-up's satisfaction in saving a child from the harsh truth. "See you tomorrow."

For the next week Marcel and his mother kept up their visits to the workshop. Yefim wondered what Ivan would think of him getting so close to a German family. If they saw each other again, Yefim wasn't sure he would tell his friend about Marcel. Either way, at the end of the week, Marie came alone to tell him she wouldn't be bringing her son anymore. Yefim felt a sudden pang of rejection but tried not to show it.

"*Vielen Dank*," she said. "This has been a good distraction for him."

"For me too."

"Will you go home after this?"

Home. What a strange, hopeful word. That life with his family in the hut was distant like a half-forgotten dream. But Marie's question meant that even the Germans now thought the war was ending and he would go back home to restart his life, to be a free man again. Well, as free as his country would let him be.

"Yes, if it's up to me," he said.

After she left, Yefim rarely saw the Mayers outside their house. As massive swaths of ice flowed down the Elbe, everyone braced for what was coming.

Soon a stream of German civilians heading west began to pass by the village. They brought news of the Red Army advancing toward Berlin. There were rumors about revenge rapes, and Yefim cringed, thinking of Ilse and how scared she must be. He hoped Father Otto had found some way to keep her safe. He didn't want to believe his comrades were really taking the war out on German women. Many of them were crude, sure, but no one was that vicious. But then again, he had to admit that he thought more like a prisoner than a soldier now. Maybe the long war had made them vicious after all.

Yefim still went into the workshop, just to keep busy. The little brass mug needed improvement and trying to get the shape right kept his mind off what would happen once his army arrived. At the end, the mug came out a little too stumpy, with an uneven handle that resembled the shape of an ear, but he liked its imperfections. He decided it would be his good luck charm.

By early April, he could hear the distant whine of the Katyushas. The villagers scrambled like mice before a rainstorm. They packed their suitcases, nailed their shutters closed, and headed west, fleeing the Soviet forces. Those who had nowhere to go stocked their cellars with water and blankets. Behind the town hall, clerks burned heaps of documents. The sounds of shelling grew louder.

The Mayers hung on for another week. But by mid-April, when they could feel the ground shaking from the approaching tanks, Herr Mayer hid his tools and several machines that he thought would be commandeered by the Russians and chained the workshop's doors. Outside, he extended his hand and Yefim shook it, realizing with surprise this was the first time he'd ever shaken a German man's hand. If only Ivan was here to see it. His friend would have no choice but to stop saying none of them mattered. There was a way to live a life decently and earn respect, even in a war.

Mayer's handshake was firm, but his eyes looked embarrassed.

"Good luck" was all he said before he headed down the street toward his garage. Yefim had hoped he'd say he was grateful for his service or maybe even apologize on behalf of his nation, but Herr Mayer was never a man of many words.

From across the street, Marcel ran out of his house toward Yefim.

"Will the Russians kill us?" he asked, his eyes wide.

Yefim squatted down to Marcel's level and said, "No. They didn't come here to kill boys. They want the war to end."

"Father is taking us to our grandparents' house. He says we'll be safer there. Where will you go?"

"I will go with my army."

"To fight in Berlin?"

"Maybe," he said, wishing he sounded more certain about his own future.

With a wistful smile, Marcel said, "I wish I could go to Berlin with you!"

Yefim tousled the boy's hair and remembered his own hopes when he was just entering the army. The courage of the innocent. How misguided it was.

"Time to go, Marcel!" Marie called, setting down a small suitcase.

The boy turned and ran toward his house. Midway, he stopped, then rushed back.

"Will you go back to see him?" he asked.

"See who?"

"Herr Wolf, to fix your fingers."

Yefim smiled. "You know it."

Herr Mayer pulled up to the house in a beige Volkswagen. Yefim stood there as the family loaded into the car and drove off. Marcel waved from the back seat. A plume of dust trailed behind them. Then the village grew silent. All he heard were the explosions of the arriving Red Army.

Chapter 13

September 1984
Donetsk, Ukrainian SSR

He would never forget the way the ray of afternoon sun hit the black granite pen holder on the corner of his office desk when the phone rang. On the other end of the line, he heard the quiet, sinister voice of Zhdanov, the chief of the First Department at the Donetsk Design and Survey Institute of Railway Transport.

"Tovarisch Shulman, there is an urgent matter. Please come down without delay."

Yefim dream-walked through the corridor of the institute where he had worked as a land surveyor for the past eight years and down the stairs to the dreaded office of the First Department.

"Inconsistencies have surfaced in your record," Zhdanov said when he arrived, and handed him a small off-white paper with black borders.

A summons from the KGB.

Almost forty years he'd waited for this day. He had consistently falsified every employment and residency form, stayed clear of veterans' organizations, kept his tongue whenever anyone mentioned the war, and tried not to feel guilty for misleading his family. He'd almost convinced himself that his big lie wouldn't come back to haunt him. Yet here it was. He felt terrified, ashamed, and—this was the part that surprised him—relieved.

The summons said to report to the administrative office of the Donetsk Region of the KGB two days from now, on Friday, September 28, at nine thirty, in Room 104, for questioning by civil servant Kislykh. The appointment time and his name were filled in by hand in black ink. Underneath, the summons read, "In accordance with Art. 73 of UPK of the USSR, your presence is mandatory."

The day of reckoning had finally come.

In a way, he was surprised it took them this long: he was sixty-two, almost retired. For years he'd expected the KGB to catch him. Yet the more time passed, the more it seemed that it must have gotten buried. Now the almost forgotten fear returned, and Yefim's mangled fingers tingled with forgotten intensity. He folded the summons and put it into his shirt pocket. When he turned to go, Zhdanov said, "Could I make a suggestion?"

Yefim nodded. Twenty years his junior and still in the thrall of career making, Zhdanov didn't seem like a bad man despite working in the loathed First Department.

"Most people wait until the questioning to see how much *they*"—he tilted his head up toward the all-knowing gods of the KGB—"know. Don't do that. Prepare a statement and bring it in with you. It will make a good impression."

In his office, Yefim swallowed his blood pressure pill, then went for a walk along Universitetskaya. He walked fast—fast for a man in his sixties—his legs trying to gain speed as if he could outrun *them* (here he thought of Zhdanov's gesture directed upward). He felt watched in the same way an unsuspecting ant is watched by a boy with a magnifying glass.

It was an annoyingly beautiful morning. Yefim noticed every detail, the way he had during battle. The autumn sun filtered through the poplars' yellow leaves, casting everything in gold: the Volgas and Zhigulis wheezing by, the laundry hanging in the balconies of the five-story apartment buildings, the benches encircled by pigeons picking at the sunflower seed shells someone had left, the ice-cream cart where the bored vender was waiting for the season to end, and the colonnaded movie theater where three gardeners were cleaning up marigolds planted in the shapes of Gena the Crocodile and Cheburashka.

While Yefim's eyes darted from place to place, his mind was busy trying to solve an unsolvable puzzle: What did the KGB know? While he was willing to follow Zhdanov's advice and confess preemptively, he didn't want to land himself in more trouble than he was already in. If he only knew what they knew, he could frame his statement more carefully. But of course, they were too smart for that. "Inconsistencies" was their way of being purposefully vague, a classic interrogation technique.

As he walked toward the park where Vita used to bring her kids when they were smaller, Yefim worried what confessing would do to his family. He wasn't too worried about himself: he was an old man now, and as far as he knew they'd mostly stopped sending ordinary citizens to labor colonies. Even though he'd just read an article about a writer and his wife who got arrested for keeping "slanderous" manuscripts of their dissident friends, he hoped he wasn't as big of a fish. They could still stick him in jail, but hadn't he lived through worse?

His family was another story. They would be under suspicion as the relatives of someone who had falsified military, state, employment, and residency records and covered up his wartime whereabouts in a way that cast suspicion on his loyalty to the Motherland. The state didn't like being fooled, for four decades no less.

They could take away Vita's family's ninth-floor apartment, which Yefim, as a veteran, had received in the city center on Universitetskaya Street. They could make sure Andrey wasn't able to defend his dissertation and become a professor of psychology like he wanted. There were also four grandchildren to think about. They were still too young to see direct repercussions, but Yana, the oldest, was going to graduate within the decade. If she kept up her good grades, she should have no issues entering any university, but with a tarnished family record she could get stuck in some technicum studying to be a bus driver.

But worse than all that was that he'd pass on his shame to them.

Yefim ran out of breath as he reached the park, where the last of the bloodred roses were still in bloom. He sat on a bench and wiped the sweat off the back of his neck with a handkerchief. It was lunchtime, but the greasy smell of the fried meat piroshki wafting from the kiosk on the corner only made him nauseous.

He imagined the shock in Nina's eyes when she learned about the summons. She would be angry at him for putting them all in danger—and right when their relationship was settling into a warm companionship, which had begun on that Crimean vacation. Yet Nina's reaction would be nothing compared to his children's. His stomach churned at Vita and Andrey's disappointment and humiliation. Every year, they had written Red Army Day cards for their father who'd made it to Berlin. They didn't deserve to know their hero was really a lying prisoner who sat out most of the war. They didn't deserve the indignity of having to explain to their own children that the war hero story they'd proudly told about their grandfather had been a hoax.

A gardener arrived and began clipping the roses along the main alley. Soon, heaps of them lay on the asphalt. Their syrupy scent filled the air. As Yefim looked at the doomed mounds of red petals and thorns all around him, he realized that his only hope was to tell the KGB as much truth as he could spare and in return ask—beg, really— that they not tell his family. It was one thing for the authorities to know who he really was. It was another to see his disgrace reflected in the eyes of his family.

Yefim asked the gardener if he could take a few flowers. Tomorrow was Nina's sixtieth birthday, as if he didn't have enough troubles already.

"Be my guest," the gardener said. "We'll be throwing them away."

He picked five roses and headed back to the office. There he waited until everyone went home, locked himself in, and wrote his confession letter. The following day he would need to skip work and go to Yasinovataya to show the letter to Nikonov. Nikonov had been through plenty of interrogations in his time and could advise him the best way to talk to the KGB. Unfortunately, he'd have to lie to Nina again—and on her big birthday at that. But what choice did he have? This was as much for her safety as for his own.

Nina woke to find Yefim kneeling next to her bed with a dozen red roses. He'd never brought her roses before. For a moment she was confused. Then he said, "Happy Birthday, Ninochka," and she remembered: today she turned sixty.

When he kissed her on the cheek, she noticed that he had already shaved and was wearing a suit.

"I was hoping you'd help with the party," she said. "It's at six."

"Today is very busy at work," he said apologetically, picking up his briefcase and hurrying out of the bedroom. "But you've got Andrey to help. I'll try to get out as early as I can."

"Can you pick up *salo* at the bazaar?" she called after him.

"Sure," he said, and then, looking back in from the hallway, winked. "Anything for a birthday girl."

Then he was out the door.

Nina didn't get up. There was a lot to do, but she wanted to stay in bed a little while longer to honor all the people who weren't here to celebrate with her. Papa and Mama had never made it to the age of sixty. Vera and Yefim's mother had both died from a stroke. The Professor passed earlier this year. The last time she'd seen him was at a colleague's funeral in the fall of '81. Afterward, he came up to her and said, "I am next." Everyone she had known when she was young seemed to be gone. Now Nina was the matron of the family, a position she still wasn't used to.

She got up and stretched her calves. Her friend Tamara, the pediatrician who lived below them, had told her the stretches were supposed to help with her toes, which were starting to curl, climbing on top of each other like wrestling children. At least her back didn't bother her today. And yet there was no way around it: she was officially an old woman. She wished her parents were here, wishing her a happy birthday, saying her name: Ninochka.

She went to check on Andrey. He was still asleep. Her poor son was probably exhausted after months of juggling the new baby, Masha, and the dissertation. Moscow was a grueling place. She was glad he was able to get away to celebrate with her.

Quietly, Nina closed the door and went to the bathroom, where she inspected her face in the mirror. It was rounder than ever, just like the rest of her. Her mother would be proud: Ninochka was no longer the skinny, hungry orphan worried about being pretty enough to be liked by a man. She had so much more now. She was a professor, a renowned paleontologist, a grandmother. And compared to other Soviet babushkas her age, she was more energetic and had money saved up for traveling once she retired in a few years. Sixty was looking pretty good.

The doorbell rang. Vita stood in the hall wearing a magenta blouse that accentuated the contrast between her tiny waist and her wide hips, which had expanded after two kids. One day Nina would need to tell her daughter to start watching her figure unless she wanted someone like Claudia stealing her husband. But then again Vita and Vlad seemed much more in love than she and Yefim had ever been, so perhaps she needn't worry.

"Happy Birthday, Mamochka!" Vita squealed, and handed Nina a bouquet of sunset-colored sword lilies.

"These are marvelous, Vitochka! *Spasibo.*"

Nina may not have had her parents or sister, but she was grateful Vita had returned from that godforsaken village in Uzbekistan and now lived just a few blocks away with a nice sunset view of the slag heaps. Nina would have considered herself a failure of a mother if both of her kids had settled far from Donetsk.

"I made Olivier salad," Vita said. "I figured you won't have enough room in the refrigerator, so I'll bring it after work along with your gift. Will you manage without me until then?"

"It would have been easier if your father hadn't run off, but Andrey and I will manage."

"I thought Papa was going to take the day off."

"So did I . . . ," she said. "As you know, no one can tell your father what to do."

Vita patted her shoulder. "I'll see you this afternoon," she said, and left for work.

Yefim glided his mangled index finger along the edge of the confession letter in his pocket as he dialed his work from a pay phone on the corner of Universitetskaya. Coughing masterfully, he said he wasn't feeling well and would be staying home. Then he dialed Nikonov, but the line rang and rang, so he had no choice but to show up unannounced. He took the bus to the train station just in time to catch the ten o'clock train to Yasinovataya. Yefim calculated that he should be back in Donetsk by the start of Nina's dinner party.

Yefim hadn't been to see Nikonov in over a year. He'd been too busy with work and his trips to Moscow to help with little Masha while Andrey worked at a psychiatric clinic and wrote his dissertation. But now he really needed his buddy. Nikonov was the only one who knew the truth about him and the only one who could tell him if what he'd written in his confession was a good idea. As the train wobbled slowly down the tracks, Yefim hoped he'd find his friend at home in his green-and-yellow hut the way he had on every visit for the past thirty years.

In Yasinovataya, he passed municipal buildings near the train station, an inn that had appeared a few years ago, and a grocery store that had appealing drawings of bread and meats on the windows, but mostly empty shelves. The streets were empty, too, and the only movement was that of a stray cat dashing into an overgrown yard.

Yefim crossed the street and turned right. The asphalted part of town ended and here on the outskirts, Yasinovataya looked the same as in the '50s: like a large village with dirt roads and barking dogs. The air smelled of burning leaves. At the corner fence, an old woman in a white kerchief glared as if he was trespassing.

When Yefim arrived at the wooden gate of Nikonov's fenced off house, he wiped the sweat from his forehead and took off the woolen cap to comb his graying hair, carefully avoiding the lipoma that had sprouted on top of his head in recent years.

Then he knocked three times and reached over the familiar gate door to unlatch it from within as he'd done a dozen times before. Instead, his hand found a new, complicated lock that required a key. That was strange. Yefim looked at the front yard and noticed the absence of the wooden doghouse and the mutt that Nikonov lovingly called Fashistka. In their place was a row of tomato plants. Then he noticed white lace curtains in the windows.

He stepped back from the gate to make sure he hadn't come to the wrong address. But, no, this was number 17, still marked clearly on the rickety fence. He looked again at the lace curtains. There was no way his friend could have moved. Not without telling him.

The other, grimmer possibility loomed in the growing stuffiness of the late morning. Nikonov had seemed healthy, but he was also almost seventy . . .

Yefim hadn't felt this alone since the war. Even getting lost in the taiga wasn't as lonely as standing in front of Nikonov's house and wondering if the only person in the world who knew the truth about him was gone.

He wondered if he could ask the neighbors, but Nikonov hadn't made many friends in the village. Yefim was about to leave when the green door of Nikonov's hut opened and a woman in her forties walked across the front yard toward him, squinting. She was on the slim side, with a bun in her hair and plastic slippers on her bare feet. She wore gray track pants and a plum-colored shirt. Behind her, a small, silly dog wagged its tail and looked to its mistress, unsure if they were dealing with a friend or a foe.

"Sorry to disturb." Yefim waved his cap from behind the gate, trying to thwart suspicion.

"Do you need something?" said the woman, without letting him in the front yard.

The dog looked at its owner for a cue and, seeing that she'd put her hand on her hip, barked. Yefim ignored it and went on.

"You see, I wanted to pay a surprise visit to an old friend. He's lived here for a long time, but I'm not sure what happened to him."

She stared at him from behind the low gate with a mixture of suspicion and disinterest. He tried to look more grandfatherly. The dog kept barking.

"And who might that be?" she asked.

"Comrade Nikonov. Perhaps you knew him?" Yefim tried.

"You mean Seryoja?" said the woman, and a smile broke on her face like a sunrise after a stormy night. "Oh, I know him all right!"

It took Yefim a moment to realize that his friend wasn't dead. He'd never heard Nikonov called by a diminutive and had no idea who this woman could be. Nikonov didn't have any children and she seemed too young to be a companion to a man pushing seventy.

"We've been friends for a very long time," Yefim offered, in case she needed more convincing, but she was already unlatching the new gate lock and gently shoving the dog to the side with her slippered foot.

"Seryoja went to the store, but he should be back shortly," she said, inviting him to follow her to the house. "I'm Svetlana."

Inside, Yefim hung up his jacket and cap on the hook near the door. The front room was transformed. A murky cave under Nikonov's direction, the room had become so light that it seemed to have doubled in size. A lace tablecloth matched the lace curtains and a bouquet of marigolds crowned the table. Nikonov's wartime portrait from Crimea still hung on the wall near the window, but now there were also other decorations: a cuckoo clock, an embroidered still life, and a rooster baba that covered the teapot.

Svetlana was already putting out three teacups, a bowl of baranki, and a rose-petal jam.

"Homemade," she said, clearly pleased by the appearance of an unexpected guest to appreciate her cooking.

"How do you know Seryoja?" she asked as she put the kettle on the gas stove.

"From the war," he said, expecting that she'd leave it at that as people usually did.

"From Crimea or Germany?"

Yefim was stunned. Germany? Never in the four decades that he'd known Nikonov had the man told anyone about his time in the Reich. In fact, he'd never met a self-proclaimed POW or ostarbeiter. The whole country liked to pretend they didn't exist. And yet there'd been millions of them, which meant they were everywhere. They just kept quiet, as he did. Posterity had no need for their truth.

Svetlana must have seen his hesitation because she said: "Seryoja told me quite a lot about the war. I find that it helps him to talk about what happened."

Her voice grew buttery, as if she were inviting Yefim to also confess all his secrets. Maybe she was a psychologist like Andrey, he thought, and decided to turn the conversation to her rose-petal jam. Then they heard the bell. There was a short ring, then a slightly longer one, and Svetlana said, "That's him. What a splendid surprise this will be!" Outside, they heard heavy steps and the door swung open. Nikonov looked shockingly frail. His neck skin was folded like an accordion, and his once wide shoulders were stooped and uneven. A brown avoska with potatoes and a loaf of rye bread swung from his right hand.

"Yefim?" he wheezed, almost dropping the groceries.

"Tovarisch Commissar," Yefim said, rising up and saluting his friend with a smile.

"Oh, sit, sit," said Nikonov, then he turned to Svetlana and raised his voice. "Woman, why didn't you warn me someone was here?"

"You said the warning was only for suspicious characters, and this gentleman didn't seem . . . ," she started.

"Nonsense! I never said such a thing! How can you judge who is suspicious and who is not? This is my house and I want to know if someone is here, damn it. That's why I created the warning system."

Nikonov launched into a coughing fit. His ice-blue eyes grew red and watery. Svetlana gave Yefim an apologetic glance and led Nikonov to a chair. Yefim felt uncomfortable for causing a scene, but soon the coughing stopped and Nikonov said, "Sorry about that, pal. It's good to see you. I'm just trying to teach Sveta to be careful. She hasn't seen what we've seen and is much too trusting."

This last phrase he said with what sounded like tenderness.

"But she's been a great help since the stroke."

"You had a stroke?" asked Yefim. It explained why Nikonov had aged so much in such a short time.

"About a month after your last visit. My left arm is still not fully operational, but otherwise I'm in tip-top shape. Thanks to Sveta. She was my nurse at the hospital and I decided to keep her."

Svetlana smiled at this, and Yefim was relieved the storm was over.

"So, what brings you to Yasinovataya?"

Yefim reached into his pocket but then hesitated, embarrassed to speak in front of Svetlana. Nikonov must have caught his hesitation as he quickly said, "Svetik, give us a few minutes, will you?"

After she left, Yefim explained that he had received a summons.

"Took them long enough," said Nikonov, taking the paper that Yefim handed him. "What's this?"

"My confession letter. Someone advised me it was better to prepare a statement. Tell me what you think."

As Nikonov read the letter, the paper trembling slightly in his spotted hand, Yefim drank his tea. He listened to the noises of the house: the teapot exhaling, someone's saw whining outside, the ticking of the cuckoo clock in the corner. Then Nikonov looked up and handed back the letter.

"They will ask you to name names," he said. "Stick with the ones who are dead."

"And otherwise? Is the letter fine? Am I saying too much?"

"It's fine. What concerns me is this line: 'My children and grand-children love me very much and it would be a big psychological trauma for them to find out what I'm about to report.' You're asking the KGB to keep this from your family, when what you should really do is see this as a sign that it's time to tell Nina and the kids."

Yefim pushed the teacup away from him. It rattled unpleasantly on its saucer. How dare he! That line, which had been the hardest thing to write, sounded almost pathetic in Nikonov's mouth. How many times had they both sworn never to share their burdensome past with another soul? And now he, who had no wife and no children, told him to do the opposite? The stroke must have made him senile.

"You want them dragged into this?" Yefim asked.

"They'll find out anyway," Nikonov said, in a tone that to Yefim sounded condescending. "You can't possibly believe the KGB will keep them out of this."

"I'll take that bet."

"At this point the only thing you're protecting them from is knowing you. The real you."

"This isn't about me!" said Yefim, getting up to pace the room, which now seemed as small as it always had been before Svetlana. They had done a lot of discussing and pondering and remembering in this house and now—just as when they'd first met in the camp—Yefim felt like they didn't share the same view of the world after all.

"I don't want them spending the rest of their lives embarrassed by me and keeping their mouths shut the way I've had to," Yefim said. He hated that he had come here for advice and was now defending himself instead. "So, yes, I've lied. But my lie has done them no harm. It saved me and it saved them too. No one has suffered."

"Except yourself," said Nikonov. "I've told Svetlana everything that happened to me. And you know what? I finally stopped feeling like a goddamn leper. Now I'm at peace. Maybe one day you'll understand."

Nina surveyed the dining table. Vita had brought a big bowl of Olivier salad and eggplant caviar, her specialty. On the opposite ends were two bowls of pickled cabbage, which Yefim had been fermenting on the kitchen windowsill for the past week. The plates and glasses were set, and a carafe of Nina's favorite homemade cherry liqueur presided over the table. In the center stood the crystal vase with Yefim's roses.

There was only one thing missing: salo. She had no time to get it herself and didn't want to be seen around town. Lately, she'd had a strange feeling she was being followed. It was most likely nothing, certainly not concrete enough to mention to Yefim or the kids, but she still didn't want to worry about it on her birthday.

"Where on earth is your father?" she asked Andrey while Vita was in the kitchen. "The guests will be here any minute."

"Mamochka, I'm sure he'll turn up soon," her son said in a calm voice.

Andrey was always a sweet boy, but ever since he'd become a psychologist, he had adopted this serene, patronizing voice that made her feel like she was constantly overreacting. She didn't understand how he could think his father's absence half an hour before the party was no big deal.

She had hoped Andrey would be more helpful. That morning she'd sent him down to the courtyard to get the dairy from the milkman. When he came back up, he told her that he wished he could play soccer like in the old days, stretch his muscles a little, be less of an adult, but "the dissertation isn't going to write itself." She could see he was trying to get out of helping, but she refused to have yet another man skip out on her to do "more important things." Not today.

"The rules of this house haven't changed: chores first, fun later," she said.

He'd always been an efficient worker like her, so once he finished the chores, he locked himself in the bedroom, where she'd spotted a smuggled pocket-sized Bible among his papers. Where did he get it and what was he thinking bringing it on the train? A student of hers had just been kicked out of university after it was discovered he had gotten baptized. Was that what Andrey wanted? But in his calm voice, he said that he was very careful, but he needed it for his dissertation. He told her he hadn't meant for her to see it.

"That's just great!" she said, though now she saw she was taking her nervousness about the party, Yefim, and possibly being followed out on her son, who now emerged dressed for the party, looking handsome in a checkered shirt tucked into gray trousers.

Nina had decided to wear her navy dress with white rhombuses. She had bought the dress the year before, during the international paleontology conference in Yalta, and had saved it for a special occasion. The cut minimized her hefty upper arms while accentuating her waist and bosom, and the color deepened the gray of her eyes. Over it, she put on a white river pearl necklace, one of her most prized possessions. She was putting on lipstick—the only makeup she ever used—when the doorbell rang. For a millisecond she thought, *Yefim!* Then she realized he wouldn't ring the doorbell. She heard Andrey open the door.

"I know I'm a little early, but I could no longer stand the delicious smells invading my apartment," Tamara laughed.

"Tamara Aleksandrovna, welcome," said Andrey.

"Oh, look at your mustache! That's quite something, Andrey! Don't even tell me how old you are, I couldn't stand it. I remember how our ceiling shook when you'd jump down from the piano when you were just yea high."

Nina heard Vita join them and came out of the bathroom to greet her friend.

"Ninochka, happiest of birthdays! You look lovely!"

The doorbell rang again. It was Irina, Nina's closest friend at the university, arm in arm with her husband. Nina couldn't help but think that Irina's husband would never disappear on her birthday, but then reprimanded herself for comparing. Instead, she asked her son to accompany everyone to the table.

"Andrey will entertain you with stories from the psychiatric clinic where he works," she said, staying behind in the hallway by the beige rotary phone. Once they were out of hearing, she dialed Yefim's work.

"Can I speak to Yefim Iosifovich?" she asked when a secretary picked up.

"He is not in."

"Do you happen to know what time he left?"

"He hasn't been in all day. I believe he called in sick. Would you like to leave a message?"

"No, thank you," Nina said, and hung up.

In the big room, she could hear Irina exclaim, "Andrey, you look so strapping with that mustache!"

Nina hadn't caught Yefim in any lies in a long time, not since Crimea. She thought he was done with that. Her trust had been restored, allowing their relationship to morph into a camaraderie of grandparents. But now this. What on earth would he have to hide this time?

Maybe she should have worried, but it wasn't like he could have gotten lost in Donetsk. She remembered that time he'd flown to Siberia and disappeared. How his colleague had called her asking if she'd heard from him and she screamed into the receiver, "*What did you do with my husband?*" It turned out they had lost him in the taiga two days earlier. Some miscommunication, though Nina wasn't convinced. She had then spent the rest of the week imagining Yefim's dead body being picked at by Siberian birds until they called to say he'd made it out safely on his own.

But today he wasn't lost. He was just being selfish. She felt the familiar old bitterness returning.

In the past, she would have thrown the red roses he had given her into the garbage, but she was too old for such drama. Instead, she picked up a stack of congratulatory postcards lying next to the phone. The cards had arrived from friends and colleagues living in all corners of the USSR—from Vilnius to Vladivostok. They were full of good wishes and reminded her that, in that world, she commanded love and respect.

The doorbell rang again. *Yefim*, she thought, despite herself.

Instead, it was her son-in-law, Vlad. Nina walked into the kitchen and told Vita to forget about salo.

"I swear, all that pork fat will give us a stroke one day," she said.

"Mom! Phew-phew-phew," said Vita and knocked three times on the wooden underside of the kitchen table.

Nina stirred the pot of ragout. This was going to be a marvelous dinner, with or without her husband.

Yefim was running. The train was due at the Yasinovataya station in six minutes. If he made it, he'd be right in time for the birthday dinner. If he didn't, it would be years before Nina forgave him. Hell, with her memory, she wouldn't forgive him until one of them was in the grave.

Though he tried moving his legs forward, he wasn't as fast as he remembered. Damn old age. It was almost as if the gravitational pull of the earth itself had intensified over the past decade.

His boots fell heavily on the dusty street. He had taken off his cap and folded it in his hand. A few passersby stared at him, an old man running. Soon his heart thumped like a wild animal and his chest spouted fire, sending him into a coughing fit. Up ahead, he could see the red-and-white-brick train station. A rusty Lada pulled up to him.

"You need a ride?" asked the middle-aged driver.

"Yes, the station," Yefim muttered, trying to catch his breath.

"Hop in!"

Yefim got in the car and in less than a minute he was in front of the train station.

"Good luck!" said the driver, parking the car to wait for new passengers.

Yefim ran into the station and saw a crowd of people milling about the waiting hall. Someone grumbled behind him, "Did they say why it's late?"

"Issues with the tracks," a young woman answered.

"Also known as the conductor was too drunk to come to work," a tan man with a drooping mustache pointed out to his friend, who wore round glasses. They sniggered.

Yefim looked at the board and saw two white hyphens where the arrival time should have been.

Just then, from the loudspeakers, the nasal female voice bellowed, "Attention! Attention! The train to Donetsk Central Station will be skipping Yasinovataya station due to mechanical issues."

The entire population of the waiting hall gasped in unison. The speaker crackled, went dead, then a few seconds later reawakened. The passengers perked up their ears.

"The next train will arrive at . . ." The announcer paused dramatically, said something indistinguishable to someone else in her booth as if to toy with everyone's nerves, and then finished. ". . . at seventeen fifty."

Yefim crumpled down onto a nearby bench. Normally he'd go to the administrator's office and find out what was going on. After all, he hadn't spent eight years doing cadastral surveys for the railway for nothing. But he had no strength for it now. He knew he'd be two hours late to his wife's sixtieth birthday and he'd never hear the end of it.

But what was worse was that he'd have to lie. Again. How could he tell them why he went to Yasinovataya today or why tomorrow morning he would be questioned by the KGB?

Peace, Yefim scoffed, recalling Nikonov's last words. Must have been Svetlana who knocked all sense out of the old man. Didn't he understand that peace was precisely what Yefim had had all these years? His secret hadn't deprived his family of anything. So what if they didn't really know him? What did it mean to know someone, anyway? The only thing that mattered was that they were safe. If Ivan was here, he'd understand.

And yet Nikonov's words bothered him.

The train station's loudspeaker didn't crackle again. Yefim sat glued to the bench, trying to think of a story to explain why he had to stay late at work. Around him, the hubbub had subsided as some passengers exchanged their tickets and went back home while others awaited the late train. They settled in, unwrapped their bread and baloney, peeled their hard-boiled eggs, skinned their potatoes and dipped them into tiny mounds of salt that rose from the greasy furrows of yesterday's *Pravda*.

Then he thought back to how Svetlana had looked at Nikonov, her eyes both deferential and protective, and thought: *What if I tell Nina that tomorrow morning I will confess something to the KGB that I've never confessed to her? Would she understand? Would she sympathize?* Maybe the truth was his only way out.

Nina had a shot of cherry liquor to calm any remaining nervousness and even told a joke to ease everyone about Yefim's absence.

"An earl shows his new lackey around and says, 'Dinner is served promptly at eight.' The lackey responds, 'If I'm running late, feel free to start without me.' "

They all laughed and the matter seemed to be put aside. They'd all gotten used to Yefim's absences and strange misadventures over the years. Tamara even said she couldn't wait to hear what happened to him this time.

Still, Nina found herself enjoying the dinner. Her children were there, her closest friends in Donetsk were there, and without her husband she felt that she was in charge of things, the way she always was in her classroom. She told jokes and made sure everyone was sampling all the dishes.

They were about to clear the table for dessert when she heard Yefim's key in the door. Her mood immediately soured. When he walked in, his forehead glistened as if he'd been running.

"Looks like I'm right on time for cake!" he said as everyone got up and exclaimed, the din taking over the party.

"Where on earth have you been, Papa?" said Vita.

"You do know your wife turned sixty today, right?" quipped Irina.

Yefim spread his hands and said, "Believe me, I would have rather been here with you all. They called me into the First Department. Today of all days! Would you believe it? It's like they wanted to give my wife a reason to kill me."

There were a few laughs, then Irina exclaimed, "First Department? My goodness, for what?"

Nina said nothing, busying herself with the dirty plates around her.

"But before she does," Yefim continued as he bent down toward the cabinet where he kept his old leather briefcase and pulled out a small blue box, "I shall give her this."

He squeezed past the guests and presented Nina with a bottle of Climat by Lancôme, a French perfume that was hard to get in Ukraine.

"Happy Birthday, Ninochka!" he said, and gave her a kiss on the cheek.

She thought he smelled vaguely of the train—a mix of creosote and starched sheets—and wondered if she was imagining things. Either way, he'd saved face in front of the guests and at the moment that was what mattered most.

"Now sit down and eat something," she said. "You've got to catch up before we clear everything for dessert."

"Take my chair, Papochka," Andrey offered, moving out his chair. "I'll get you a clean plate."

"Now tell us, what could the First Department possibly want with you?" said Tamara, whose late husband had run into trouble with the First Department after his brother immigrated to the States.

"Turned out to be nothing—some ridiculous misunderstanding," said Yefim. "Some map disappeared and they thought I'd taken it out. Et cetera. You know how paranoid they are about maps. I won't bore you with it. Today is about Nina!"

Then he made a toast that Nina barely listened to. She wondered how he did it. How could he make stuff up without even flinching?

The guests left at around nine. Nina finished washing up, said good night to Andrey, and went to bed. Yefim came into the bedroom, undressed, and lay next to her. She was curled away from him, facing the wall.

"Nina?"

She wished she didn't have to listen to him lie. She thought they were past that.

"Are you asleep?" he kept trying. "I didn't mean to ruin your birthday. Really. Something strange happened today."

Nina tried to breathe steadily as if she were sleeping. She didn't want to be disappointed. That wasn't how she wanted to remember this day. After all, everything in her life was going well: Andrey and Vita were both married and had children of their own; she and Yefim were relatively healthy; her research in paleontology had been widely recognized; she had tons of friends and received a mountain of postcards. In short, she was loved. Maybe all of that was more important than her husband breaking his promise?

And yet she still sounded resentful when, without turning, she said, "You lied to me and you're about to lie again. I'll spare you the trouble if you tell me one thing."

"What?"

"Would you forgive me if I did it to you?"

"You mean miss my birthday dinner?"

"No, I mean lie after we promised not to."

He was silent for a long time.

"I don't know," he said, his voice full of hurt that pleased her. "You don't usually break your promises."

"I wish you didn't either," Nina said.

They didn't speak after that.

The next morning Yefim fidgeted with his hat. He sat on the wooden chair in the narrow, subterranean room 104. His knees bumped against the empty wooden table. Above him, a yellow light bulb made everything look jaundiced. The officer who'd led him from the passport checkpoint, down two flights of stairs, along the corridor, and into this narrow room had said Civil Officer Kislykh would come soon to begin the questioning, but Yefim had sat here long enough for his back to start aching. The room's dampness seemed to creep in through the walls.

With his letter in the pocket of his jacket, Yefim thought about fear. About how this place, its walls, its lighting—the very letters KGB— were meant to intimidate whatever lab rat was unlucky enough to end up here. Today, that lab rat was him. And though he knew that the waiting was intended to rattle his nerves, create confusion, and induce penitence; though he'd read enough illegal Solzhenitsyn to know their interrogation techniques; though he'd assured himself that in 1984 even the KGB were unlikely to sincerely believe in the bright future of communism, he was still afraid. It was as if they'd pumped a fear-inducing chemical into the room.

And yet, as afraid as he was, a part of him was eager to finally let out his secret and beg that it never left this building.

When the thick metal door opened and a tall, sandy-haired officer walked in, Yefim had to keep himself from springing up. Civil Officer Kislykh was in his forties and had a weary, reptilian face with round hazel eyes and plump, overly large lips. He slid into the chair on the opposite side of the table and plopped down a file.

"All righty, then," he said, licking his forefinger and opening the file's flap. "Yefim Iosifovich Shulman, *tak*?"

"*Tak*," agreed Yefim, trying to peek at the papers under the man's arm.

"In reviewing your military record for the upcoming veteran's pension—you are nearly retired, aren't you?" Yefim nodded. "It has come to our attention that there are certain discrepancies."

Here, he poked his bony finger at the papers and paused. Yefim stared at him. Forty years he'd been looking over his shoulder, and it took his retirement for them to look at his falsified record? What irony.

"So, illuminate me: Where exactly were you between June 22, 1941, and May 9, 1945?" Kislykh asked.

Though it was the exact question he'd expected, Yefim suddenly felt an urge to bang on the table. What right did this schmuck have to ask him that? He was probably a tadpole when Yefim was trying to survive Germany.

Of course, this man had every right to ask why he'd found artilleryman Yefim Shulman serving in Lithuania at the beginning of the war and private Yefim Shulman fighting in Berlin four years later, but no Yefim Shulmans in between. Yefim's anger curled back into a tight ball. He swallowed hard.

"I've prepared a statement," he said.

"Ah. Have you?" Kislykh said, licking his large lips. "Let's see it."

Yefim reached into his pocket, then hesitated. What if confessing was the wrong decision? No one ever confessed to the KGB—not unless there was no other choice. Didn't he still have a choice? Couldn't he make something up? Or feign memory loss?

But somehow the folded letter was already moving from his pocket toward Kislykh, who had extended his long arm to take it.

The KGB officer unfolded the letter and began to read. Yefim shivered as if he were standing stark naked in front of a medical examiner, the way they had at the Müller Leinz farm, poor Ivan having to go twice to cover for him. His heart bucked like a frenzied horse. He imagined himself having a heart attack: how he'd clutch his chest, then slump over the desk, his face landing on its cold, laminated surface right next to his confession.

But, no, it wasn't his time to go yet. First he needed to make sure his family never learned of his past.

When Kislykh finished reading the letter, he got up and began to pace the room slowly, his hands behind him like a professor. Yefim didn't dare turn. Instead, he listened to the scuffle of the officer's shoes against the concrete floor: one, two, one, two.

"Let me get this straight. You, Citizen Shulman, sat out the whole war and then lied about it for nearly forty years, but now you are asking us to keep this disgrace of a life from your family. Do I have that right?"

Yefim's moment had come. Nikonov had warned him that the KGB were used to the lies, avoidance, jokes, insanity pleas, and every other trick in the book employed by citizens who didn't want to confess whatever the agency needed them to confess. What they were not used to, he told him, was an honest, unsolicited declaration of guilt.

"Can I be frank, Tovarisch Kislykh?" Yefim asked, putting his hat on the table.

"I can't think of a better time for frankness," he said, continuing to pace the room on Yefim's left flank, slightly out of view.

"I was younger than yourself when I took the opportunity to change my war story. It seemed simple: omit a few details and voilà, your future is fixed. That's how young people think, don't they? But what I was too young to understand was the unintended consequences of lying."

He could hear Kislykh stop two steps behind him.

"Such as?" he asked, and the scuffling of his shoes resumed their rhythm.

"I don't mean lying on official forms. No, you've got me there. That's not what I'm talking about. I mean the lying I've done to keep the truth from my family, the way so many of us men are forced to do. We don't want our wives and kids knowing certain ugly things about what we've done in the past or what we do at work, or the compromises the state has made to get to where it is today. It would create private pockets of doubt, and as a geologist I can tell you little fissures quickly grow into big cracks. We can't let that happen to the holy memory of victory over fascism. It's the one thing every Soviet citizen firmly believes in. If we start telling the truth about millions of POWs and ostarbeiters, what would happen to the morale of our families, of our nation? You've got to agree, in these uncertain times, we simply cannot afford it."

Kislykh returned to the table and sat down. He looked straight at Yefim for what seemed like the first time. The whites of his eyes were yellow in the light.

"So your deceit is now a patriotic duty, eh? Very clever. Is that why you haven't left for Israel yet, because you're such a patriot?"

Yefim looked at this lanky, yellow man with a funny last name, who once must have been a boy with dreams of becoming brave and strong—a firefighter perhaps, or the captain of the Shakhtar soccer team—and who instead climbed the Communist ladder until he found himself in this dungeon questioning an aging Jew about what he'd done forty years ago.

"Israel? No. That's because I've been to the desert on assignment and didn't like the climate."

Kislykh blinked.

"They should have left you to rot in Siberia when they had the chance," he said, and Yefim's knee jerked from the mention of the taiga.

The officer slid the confession letter inside the file.

"Do you understand there will be no veteran's pension for you, Shulman?"

"I understand," Yefim said, though he didn't yet know how he would explain it to Nina. "What I care about is will you tell my family?"

"Your family is your business. Our department has better things to do than dig through your dirty laundry."

He got up and walked toward the door. As he reached for the handle, he turned and said, "But then again, we know all about Nina . . ."

Then the door slammed shut, its echo ringing in Yefim's ears. He sat, unmoving, as dread came over him, filling the room like thick smoke. What if they brought in Nina for questioning? Or dragged Andrey to the Lubyanka? He looked down at his hands and noticed a tremor in his fingers.

He listened for any sounds: a conversation from the next room, the heavy footsteps of the guards, the clang of handcuffs, even—anything that would tell him what would happen next. But the walls were purposefully thick. He didn't hear anything except his own heavy breathing.

Yefim got up and steadied himself. He couldn't afford to panic, not right now. It was essential to remain clearheaded. He walked back and forth across the narrow room and soon began to feel more like himself. He even felt a certain lightness: after fearing being caught for four decades, he couldn't deny that a part of him now felt relieved that he'd finally come clean.

The door opened and Kislykh walked back in. He seemed surprised to see Yefim on his feet. He handed Yefim his confession letter.

"Keep this copy," he said. "You will hear from us if we have other questions. For now, you may go."

Before Yefim knew it, he was walking down the long corridor past heavy metal doors that could open at any moment and swallow him. He slowed his steps as if to assure whoever was watching that he wasn't running, that he wasn't afraid. Yet he looked only straight ahead toward where the staircase would take him up and out of this building.

Somehow, he made it outside into a warm autumn day. Inhaling the bittersweet smell of fallen leaves, he felt such space in his lungs that instead of going home, he went to sit at a leafy plaza with a small playground. Two boys were climbing a ladder, a girl was swinging with a stuffed bunny, and another girl was collecting yellow maple leaves into a bouquet. Their little voices echoed in the plaza. Yefim sat down on a bench, took off his hat, and cried.

Chapter 14

April 1945
Niegripp, Germany

For the first time in five years, Yefim was free. Until the Red Army marched into Niegripp, he had nothing to do and nowhere to be.

The April day was misty. Wearing a small knapsack with his brass cup inside, he took the cobblestone path from the village down to the river and sat on the cool grass, watching the wind ripple the water, listening to the geese squabbling downstream, waiting. Waiting to be absorbed back into the Soviet fold. If Ivan was with him, it would be easier to face the looming change. He missed Ivan. At least now that the army was coming, he had a real chance to find him. And then after the war ended, they could go home together.

Yefim tried thinking of home but he couldn't get ahold of the image. It felt slippery, like a fish, like a dream. There were only snapshots: Basya pinning her braid, Mother lighting the stove, the scent of a spent candle as his body settled in between his brothers' on the floor. The rest was a mix of worry and anticipation, which, like the river in front of him, bubbled and swerved.

He should have been looking forward to going home, but the idea of returning in his ostarbeiter overalls made him feel as if a stone were lodged in his chest. His mother would be relieved to see him no matter what, but his father . . . He could see his father's narrowed brown eyes as the old man muttered, "*Shande*," through his beard. Shame. His youngest son, a prisoner who sat out the war, a Jew who worked for the Germans. He tried to reason with himself, but the closer the Red Army got, the more he felt the familiar fear: unless he came home a true soldier who had fulfilled his duty, he would forever be good-for-nothing little Fimochka. Making it to Berlin, and staying alive in the process, was his only way to avoid disgrace.

The geese had waddled closer to him, their black beaks nibbling. They were big, serious things, and he remembered how he had once walked his neighbor Mykola's flock to the lake. That must have been before the famine, so he must have been around seven. He still remembered how proud he'd felt commanding the flock all by himself. Even Father had said, "You might turn into something worthwhile yet."

If Ivan were here, he'd remind him why nothing that had happened to him was his fault, that in this war they were caught between two forces that didn't care whether they lived or died. Maybe he'd even make a wisecrack about making sure not to earn any medals so that he didn't get stuck going to dreadful Red Army veterans' meetings and parades after the war.

But Ivan wasn't here. What was here, or would be soon, was the Red Army itself. And though he felt no strong desire to kill anyone—it was harder to kill people he'd lived among—Berlin was his last chance to regain at least a little dignity.

He wondered what it would be like back in the army after so long. To march through the forests again until his feet ached. To sleep to the chorus of snores. To wake up to the taste of army porridge. He didn't know if he could ever blend in with the soldiers again. After the last four years, he had none of their conviction. He'd seen good people and bad people on both sides of this war. But in the army you couldn't think like that. There was no room for nuance. The objective—to crush Hitler—was bigger than all of them. Would he be able to think like he used to, to throw himself into battle "for Stalin, for the Motherland"? He was certain the soldiers in the Red Army thought of themselves as conquerors, heroes with medals that awaited them back home, while to them he was a no one if not worse: a slacker. And he couldn't blame them. The old him would probably have looked at him with disgust: a laborer sitting on a German riverbank, waiting to be rescued like a goddamn fairy-tale princess.

Yet, when Nigriepp finally filled with the Soviet soldiers—mud-caked, with listless eyes—Yefim was surprised that they didn't look like heroes. Berlin was two days' march from here, and he could see that all they thought about was getting there and catching their breath before the last big battle. They didn't give one damn about Yefim or the other ostarbeiters and POWs they picked up along the way. They, too, were just trying to survive.

He found it easy to join them. The unit of "repatriates," as Soviet citizens on enemy territory were called, was placed between two infantry echelons. Like a sardine blending in with its school, Yefim simply matched his steps to those around him, following them out of Niegripp and out of a prisoner's life.

————

That evening they arrived at an empty village, where he had to report to SMERSH, the mobile counterintelligence office that screened all repatriates. SMERSH was an abbreviation of "death to spies." The very name made him uneasy.

He didn't know if it was better to be an ostarbeiter or a POW in the eyes of the Soviet spy hunters. A part of him wondered if maybe it was best to hide behind his latest assumed identity and tell them he was "ostarbeiter Yefim Lisin." But then they wouldn't know he was an artilleryman, and if he hoped to fight, he needed them to know of his training. Lying to the Germans may have worked, but it was a bad idea to try to outsmart the Soviet intelligence.

The SMERSH office was stationed in an abandoned German family home. As Yefim approached the door, he was both nervous and resolute. He took off his cap and knocked.

Inside, an officer with bags under his eyes sat at a dining table covered with paperwork. His assistant milled nearby, stamping a stack of papers. The house smelled of recently fried cabbage.

Yefim approached the table. The tired officer pointed to a wooden stool and continued to write. Above the table, three moths flung themselves at a hanging lamp. When the man finally looked up, he let out a small sigh and, putting a new piece of paper in front of him, said, "Name, year and place of birth." His voice was coarse.

"Yefim Iosifovich Shulman. 1924. Nepedivka, Ukraine."

It was so strange to say his real name after three years that he almost thought they wouldn't believe him. The officer rubbed his right eye and said, "A Jew ostarbeiter?"

"Not exactly."

"What's 'not exactly'? Not exactly a Jew or not exactly an ostarbeiter?"

His voice sounded more tense than before. Yefim felt flushed. He was a prisoner of war, a forced laborer, and a Jew who had survived four years in the Reich, which was either very lucky or *very* suspicious. How did he not think he'd have "collaborator" written all over him? They were going to bury him. He could feel it.

"Explain yourself!" the officer barked. His assistant looked up.

Yefim tried to steady himself. He just had to explain everything, that was all. Then they'd believe him. There was no reason to panic.

"I was a Red Army artilleryman, Regiment 96, stationed at the border and captured in August '41."

He told him about the POW camp and the work farm, keeping it short and factual. No emotions. He tried not to get unnerved by the interrogator's pen moving as his story appeared on some form.

"In early '43, there were rumors that Vlasov was searching for artillerymen for his army, so I ran away."

The interrogator stopped writing and looked up.

"Alone?"

Yefim hesitated. He hated naming names, but he couldn't afford to lie.

"I had a friend with me, Ivan Didenko, another artilleryman from my regiment."

"Where is he now?"

"I haven't seen him in almost two years," Yefim said, wishing Ivan could corroborate his story.

"All right," the man said, writing down Ivan's name. "Then what?"

"We were caught and decided the best way to avoid a bullet in the head was to pretend we were ostarbeiters, and so . . . well, here I am."

As Yefim's story hung in the mothy air of the German hut, he felt oddly guilty, though for what he didn't exactly know. He wondered if they would believe him. The interrogator scratched with his pen behind his left ear, as if unsure what to write in the report.

Just then the assistant, who all this time had been busy with stamping and hadn't said a word, rushed up to Yefim and grabbed his collar.

"Why did you survive?"

His sudden breathy presence threw Yefim off. Why? Was he not supposed to? Did they want him to die? He grew so hot that his throat felt like it was closing up.

"Did you collaborate with the Germans, you fucking Yid, while our boys were dying for the Motherland? Talk!"

His mind became cluttered with all the ways in which his story could be reframed as collaborating. He had forgotten about that Soviet art of reframing, insinuating, twisting your words into a new meaning. He needed to think fast, to give them something bulletproof. But then, out of a corner of his eye, he noticed the main interrogator covering a yawn with his hand.

This whole thing was theater.

He composed himself and, looking the assistant straight in the eyes like his mother had taught him, said, "At the camp, I used a fake name. Afterward, since there aren't many Jewish ostarbeiters, no one suspected me."

Here he paused, looked at the main interrogator, and continued in a voice calibrated somewhere between frankness and bravura, "I got really lucky. But I also have four brothers in the army, so the whole time I sat here like a schmuck, all I wanted was to fight. That's why I tried to escape. Twice. I don't like the Germans any more than you do. In fact, I'd love a chance to give them hell in Berlin. I'm sure the army could use another artilleryman."

The assistant let go of Yefim's collar and walked back to his stack of papers as if nothing had happened.

"Who can corroborate your story?" the main interrogator asked.

Yefim named some boys from his regiment, though he knew they were dead, and a few ostarbeiters he'd met in Karow and Niegripp. He felt dirty uttering their names but hoped that no harm would come to them because of his confession.

"All right, Shulman. You still owe the army eighteen months of service, so I'm assigning you to Division 22 in the storm battalion. You're to report to their commander immediately."

"I was hoping to be placed with the artillery."

The man turned to his assistant with a scoff.

"You hear that? He was hoping. I'm giving you a chance to redeem yourself, Shulman. Count yourself lucky you're not on a train to Siberia. Now get out of my sight."

"Thank you," Yefim said.

"Thank your Motherland that she still needs you," the assistant said grimly.

Outside, Yefim looked up at the first stars appearing in the sky. The cool air felt good on his hot face. The questioning had gone pretty well, even if they didn't assign him to the artillery or show any empathy for a surviving Jew. None of that mattered now. They needed soldiers and he needed a battle, so their goals were aligned. He'd get to go to Berlin, and then, once he returned home, he'd restart his life and forget all the horrors and the nonsense of the past four years.

He went to check in with his assigned division and noticed that while the "real" soldiers wore updated Red Army uniforms with newly epauletted green tunics, green helmets, and tarpaulin boots, there were no uniforms for the new soldiers like him in the storm battalion. Instead, he was handed a gray German overcoat, Soviet pants, and worn-out ankle boots.

An hour later he was standing in line for supper. The line was long, snaking hungrily through the empty German village, but Yefim didn't mind the wait. He was reveling in being among his countrymen. His ear had been tuned to German for so long that he had forgotten how nice it was to hear familiar jokes, complaints, even curses. He kept smiling to himself like a fool, wanting to hug them all as if they were his brothers. Most men spoke Russian, but occasionally he overheard the softer melodic sounds of his native Ukrainian. He hadn't heard it since Ivan. His heart squeezed at the thought that perhaps now he would finally get a chance to find his friend.

The line turned the corner and his stomach rumbled at the prospect of food. He looked forward to eating and falling asleep. Tomorrow they would march many kilometers in the direction of Berlin. Suddenly his knees buckled from the force of someone's boot. Behind him a low voice said, "Beat the Jews, save Mother Russia!" as heavy steps ran off into the darkness. By the time he straightened himself and turned to look, those around him only stared in silence. Yefim shook with rage. Somehow word had spread about who he was, and now, with the familiar language, came the familiar slurs. He felt like a white crow among his countrymen. The guy in front of him quietly said, "Don't mind that idiot. He's drunk." The line inched forward toward its evening grub.

————

His division was stationed in Teltow, southwest of Berlin, and though it was a huge camp with several thousand soldiers, he had no one to talk to. After the previous night's incident, he missed Ivan more than ever. Ivan had never let such things slide. He would have helped him find the bastard. All night Yefim tried to shake it off, but the bad taste in his mouth wouldn't go away.

When he rose in the morning, everything felt gray and endless, as if he was back at the camp. He moved like an automaton, trying not to think. He was handed a rifle and he and the other newly minted soldiers were sent off toward Berlin without a moment of training.

Yefim marched down the road, his rifle swaying from his shoulder. His fingertips yearned for the reassuring metal curves of Uska. He wished he was farther ahead with the artillery boys. They would have accepted him as their own and no one would harass him like last night.

Instead, he was in the back with the cannon fodder. He could sense in the determined stomp of the many boots their desire for vengeance. But he'd lived among the Germans for too long to see them as just the Enemy. Yes, there were drunk guards and sadistic bosses, but there were also people like Ilse and the Mayers, regular people with their fears and a desire to provide for their children and a national rhetoric that made their heads spin. Just like back home.

The sun was high in the clear sky when he arrived at a large field surrounded by farms behind which, rising above a line of trees, Yefim saw the shell-damaged steeple of a bombed-out church. The field was full of soldiers sitting in groups on the fresh spring grass. Some were smoking; others chewed their rations. Except for the distant roar of bombers over the German capital, the field reminded him a little of the Easter Monday in Karow when he first talked to Ilse. If he saw the end of this war alive, he would need to find her.

Yefim approached a group of four men in Red Army uniforms and asked them why everyone was stopped here.

"They've cleared a path across the Teltow Canal," one of them said, squinting up at Yefim. "Now we've got to wait for the engineers to put up a bridge."

The man looked up at him carefully and said, "You one of those repatriates?"

Before Yefim could answer, his neighbor spat out a cigarette butt and said, "Got to relax while we fought our asses off?"

Yefim wanted to tell him that he'd been an artilleryman, that he'd run away, twice, and that he wanted to end this war as much as anyone there. But the man wasn't wrong. So instead he said, "Some relaxing that was," and walked back.

"Komarov, is that you?" someone shouted from behind. Yefim started. He hadn't used that name since his first escape.

Then a man was standing in front of him.

"Nikonov," the man reminded him.

His ice-blue eyes brought Yefim back to the *Appellplatz* where the SS were scouring the crowd for Jews. Good old Nikonov had survived after all.

"*Jivyokhonkiy!*" Nikonov shouted as if he had risen from the dead. "And I wagered a bet you wouldn't make it more than a month."

Around them the field was abuzz with chatter over the rumble of artillery.

"What happened to you?" Yefim asked.

"Long story. You've got a smoke?"

Yefim shook his head and Nikonov sighed with disappointment. They sat down on the grass away from the others. From his knapsack Yefim took out a piece of bread.

"I was sent to a mine," Nikonov began in a slightly lowered voice. "What a shithole. Rations almost as bad as at the camp. The guards escorted us back and forth through a village to the mine and as we clog-clog-clogged down the street, village kids threw rocks at us, little fuckers. They had me work the day shift at first, then switched me to the night shift and I decided I'd had it. Me, a goddamn Soviet officer, slaving like a serf. So I ran away. With another two guys. We dug a tunnel under the barbed wire and were off. But we didn't last long. Got busted by a pair of teens on bicycles. Imagine that? Just stumbled upon them one evening. Couldn't run away fast enough, us all thin and weak. Anyway, I rotted in prison for a month. That's where I lost these"—he tugged at his lip and Yefim saw a gap in his lower teeth— "but at least they didn't shoot me. Eventually, they sent me to another camp. There was a whole underground life there, its own rules, a black market, even a resistance."

"How long were you there?"

"Until our army showed up. Well, actually, the fucking Germans marched us out west when they heard our boys were coming."

Yefim was surprised at how frank Nikonov was being. He seemed a different man. There was no haughtiness, no propagandist zeal. He talked as if they were equals.

"Did you have any problems with SMERSH?" Yefim asked.

"I'm here, ain't I?" Nikonov shrugged. "The facts of my capture checked out and, well . . ."

"What?"

Nikonov quickly glanced around as if to make sure they couldn't be heard. A strange gesture for a commissar.

"I skipped the part about the mine. That way they don't have me on record working for the Germans."

Yefim wondered if Nikonov remembered how they'd argued about becoming laborers when they first met. Either way, it seemed like he'd changed his tune.

"So what about you, Komarov?"

Yefim drank a few sips of water from his canteen and told him about the farm, his two escapes, and parting with Ivan, whom Nikonov couldn't remember. He didn't mention Ilse or the Mayers or anything else that he hadn't already revealed to the SMERSH officers.

When he finished, Nikonov asked, "And they cleared you too?"

"I'm here, ain't I?" Yefim repeated his line.

"You and I are two lucky birds, Komarov. They could have easily sent us you know where."

"You think? I figured they needed every man they could get right now."

"What, you haven't heard? They sent a train of repatriates to Russia last night."

"Must have been collaborators or young boys who don't know how to shoot."

Nikonov looked at him as if trying to decide which one of them was naive.

"Tell me, Komarov, what do you think is the purpose of the Red Army soldier?"

"To defend the Motherland," Yefim spouted the answer a commissar would expect.

"Oh, come on! Don't feed me that bullshit. I'm not a commissar anymore, and after all you've seen, you should know better."

Yefim didn't understand what Nikonov wanted.

"I'll tell you, then. A Red Army soldier has only two purposes: shoot bullets into enemy chests or absorb enemy bullets so they run out of them quicker. I'm telling you this as someone who's seen how the Party thinks. When this war ends, it will be cast as our country's greatest act of bravery and sacrifice, and people who don't fit into that storyline will be inconvenient. People like you and me. And I don't need to tell you what our Motherland does with inconveniences . . ."

Yefim stared at Nikonov. He couldn't understand how a former commissar could say such things. There was only one possible explanation: Nikonov was a provocateur. He was testing Yefim to see if he'd been turned by the enemy. It made sense that SMERSH would send tons of these scum around to reveal who was who. He needed to get away from him, and quickly.

"Still don't believe me?" Nikonov asked, with that beguiling smile of his. "Well, don't. They've given us a chance to fight, so if we come back from Berlin alive, maybe they'll spare us. Who knows?"

There was commotion as someone commanded, "Move out!" All around them, men began to get up. Yefim rose quickly, trying to hide his relief.

"Time to go," said Nikonov, rubbing his hands with anticipation as if he hadn't just talked gloom and doom. "Can't wait to fry those fascist pigs. You be careful out there, Komarov. We've made it this long. Let's get back in one piece."

Then he winked. Yefim walked off to join his division, not noticing where he was stepping or who was around him. As he waited to cross the Teltow Canal up ahead, his arms hung by his sides, heavy and long. If he wasn't being pushed toward the narrow pontoon bridge by the men around him, he would have liked to lie down. Nikonov's words sloshed like acid in his stomach. He wished he hadn't run into him.

Then he remembered that Nikonov still didn't know his real name and felt a lot better.

Slowly, the traffic of men moved across the pontoon bridge. Yefim looked down at the water. Charred pieces of timber flowed down the wide canal like ice in the first days of spring. When he reached the northern bank, the shattered houses of a small riverside town still exhaled smoke from a battle that ended earlier that morning. Huge lumps of concrete and broken masonry littered what had been a street. Out of a window, a pair of motionless legs in German boots hung like drying laundry.

On the right was a medical tent where, through the open flap, he could see three nurses and a doctor attending to two dozen wounded. A general moan was occasionally broken with cries of the staff rushing back and forth. Farther off, men were loading corpses onto a truck. Someone ran by with a stretcher. On it, a soldier's pierced lungs released bloody bubbles with every intake of breath. Yefim and the others fell silent as they passed. He felt guilty knowing that while he was talking to Nikonov, these advance troops had fought for this canal town, clearing the way for him and the rest of his division. The words "absorb German bullets" echoed in his head.

Soon he came across a clearing in the buildings and saw the blackened sky on the horizon where planes raged in the fog of dust above Berlin. Looking at that fog, he grew anxious. Tomorrow morning he would be fighting in the city.

That night they camped on a field just beyond Berlin's outskirts. Yefim worried he would see Nikonov again, but it was dark, and as soon as dinner was over, everyone made beds on the ground, exhausted. It wasn't easy to sleep with the weeping whine of the Katyusha rockets and the deep-throated rumble of the shelling. Under his German overcoat, Yefim worried about what tomorrow held for him. His mind kept flipping between the first battle back in Lithuania and Nikonov's words. He'd see himself shooting at an enemy only to realize his mangled fingers weren't able to pull the trigger and then he'd think, *Useless, inconvenient.*

As he was finally settling into a deeper rest, the call to get up sounded across the field. He opened his bloodshot eyes. It wasn't dawn yet. His calves were sore from the new boots. His fingers were stiff from the cold. He poured water from the canteen into his brass mug for good luck and drank it.

When daylight broke, smoky and charged, his battalion entered the southwestern outskirts of Berlin. Five-story apartment buildings lined the wide streets, which were spliced by a tram line. After three years in rural Germany, this vast man-made world dwarfed and astonished him. He couldn't shake the feeling that he was a fly crawling through a model city like the one he and his brothers drew in the dirt behind their house when they played Reds and Whites. Except here Katyushas had left their mark: many buildings stood decapitated, with large gaping wounds, their guts indecently hanging out.

Yefim's feet crunched the broken masonry that had been pounded into dust by the bombing. The streets ahead echoed with gunfire and explosions. He clutched his rifle.

After a block, they broke into smaller groups and fanned out toward different streets. Grenades were exploding closer now, just around the corner, and it became harder to hear. Yefim's squad commander, who reeked of vodka, indicated they go left. As Yefim rounded the corner, his eyes fixed on a white apartment building billowing smoke and he tripped on something. When he jumped back up, he saw that it was two bodies lying crisscrossed on top of each other.

Suddenly, a torrent of grenades rained all around them. His teeth rattled and he froze, no longer hearing what the commander was yelling. The explosions ricocheted deep in his bones. Everything around him moved in rapid bursts. The street broke into fragments:

a wild-eyed soldier sitting under a sign that read FR SEUR

blink

a grenade making an arch across the sky

blink

hot specks of dust and brick biting Yefim's skin

blink

the soldier slumped like a sack, ears oozing blood

Yefim squeezed his gun hard, knuckles taut against the skin. He tried to concentrate.

"Look out!" someone shouted.

From the higher floor of the burning apartment building came a burst of machine-gun fire. He ran.

The spatter of bullets followed him. He heard another man from his squad on his heels, but then the back of his neck was splattered with the man's blood. He continued to run, alone. Reaching the opposite intersection, he swerved toward a flipped German scout car, burned and crushed by a tank. Yefim hunkered behind it. He breathed in the carnal odor of someone else's blood and brains and, trying to suppress the nausea, wiped his neck with his sleeve.

When his knee caught on something he looked down. A scorched arm stuck out of the scout car's window. A gold wedding band shone on the blackened finger.

Careful not to stick out his head, he studied the street through the car window. The body of the man from his squad was splayed in the middle of the asphalt. He tried to locate the others but couldn't see anyone. The gunfire, which was now less rapid and more probing, told him his unit was either dead or hiding. He traced the shooting to a second-floor balcony of the white apartment building and aimed.

He fired, steadying the rifle with his right hand, when suddenly the scout car was rattled by an explosion and he was lying on the asphalt staring up at the yellow-gray sky. His ears rang.

He'd thought this battle would be his redemption, but he was just another body between Moscow and Berlin. Yefim pushed the thought away. He had to focus on staying alive. *Get up*, he thought. *Move.*

He slithered toward the nearest building. The machine gun began to rattle again, but he continued moving. The building was no more than a bombed-out shell, four walls filled with rubble and no roof. Still, it was cover. Here he felt a deep, dull pain in the back of his head. His hair was wet from blood. *Just a scratch*, he told himself. *I'm fine.*

As soon as he peeked out from a jagged edge of a window, he was met with a barrage of bullets. Someone must have spotted him. He ducked and crawled toward the farther corner of the building. He needed to find a different way out of this trap. A crate peered out with *Kart* written in black letters. Potatoes. This must have been a produce store. Yefim kept crawling over the wreck that had been formed by the blown roof and several floors, when after the cold hardness of rubble his fingers landed on something warm, fleshy. He yanked his hand back. Camouflaged by the dust was the thin thigh of a German boy with red stains on the gray shorts of his Deutsches Jungvolk uniform. The boy's left arm was pinned under a large piece of cement. He stared at Yefim with wide, scared blue eyes.

The boy couldn't have been more than twelve, his hair a bright blond mop sitting on top of shaved sides. When Yefim looked at his white knee-high socks, he thought of Marcel and got angry. This was no place for boys in socks. How desperate were the Germans to send children into this hell?

The boy tracked his every movement, glancing with terror at his rifle. Yefim leaned toward him and said, "I'm going to get you out."

He wrapped his hands around the piece of cement and began to lift. The boy groaned. Scared to drop it back down and crush the boy, Yefim lifted and pushed the heavy slab until it finally slid off to the side. He saw the twisted, bloody remainder of the boy's lower left arm and felt the forgotten pain of his own fingers. He grabbed the boy's good hand and pulled him up. The boy whimpered. Yefim thought the poor boy could use some luck, so he opened his knapsack and poured water into his small brass mug. The little German looked from the water to Yefim and back, blinking uncertainly. Then he drank it.

"Get out of here," Yefim told him, pointing toward the other edge of the building, away from the corner where he came from.

The boy scrambled in that direction, his left arm hanging like a broken wing.

Yefim reoriented himself. He heard a boom that sounded a lot like good old Uska somewhere beyond the rear of the building. He crawled toward a row of windows, keeping his head low.

Carefully, he looked out of the window, whose glass had been broken. Below was what must have once been a lovely garden that opened onto the next street over. In the middle of the garden stood a newer version of Uska. The gun was positioned under an apple tree, and every time the three Soviet artillerymen fired, raising great palls of smoke and throwing stone and timber into the air, the apple tree quivered, shedding white petals onto the grass.

For a moment he stood transfixed by this odd sight. He thought of last spring, of Ilse. If only she could see him right now, a real soldier, not some poor Jew she had rescued. Feeling a surge of strength, he jumped down onto the ground.

Right as he landed, there was gunfire and two of the artillerymen fell to the ground. Yefim spun around and fired into the window where he thought the gunfire had come from.

"Where is he?" the third artilleryman hollered from behind the wheel of the big gun where he took cover.

"Third floor, second window!" Yefim yelled back.

Just then the shooter's head popped out and instinctively Yefim fired. It was only after the head with the familiar mop of bright blond hair hung, bloody, on the window frame that Yefim realized he had killed the boy he just saved.

For a moment he had a feeling of sinking right through the ground, but then he found himself sprinting toward the artillery gun and the motion of running helped block what had just happened. Under the tree, the surviving man, his face red, was shaking his two friends by the lapels. "*Sergey! Dimon! Vstavayte!*"

Yefim grabbed at the sight of the gun.

"What the fuck are you doing?" the man yelled.

"I'm an artilleryman!" Yefim said, finding the familiar shape of the gun's sight.

The gun was aimed at a three-story brick building with large arched windows that must have been a store or a factory. Yefim didn't care what was in there or why it needed to be destroyed. It was all sense-less anyway.

They loaded the next shell and Yefim fired.

Next to him, the apple tree shed its petals.

———

He didn't see central Berlin until the first days of May, when the most brutal fighting had died down. By the time he walked the winding streets of the city, they smelled of petrol, horse shit, and burned cars.

He wasn't sure what exactly he was hoping to find here, now that he wasn't being shot at. Helping to conquer the German capital was supposed to give meaning to his useless drifting around the Reich. But while he saw in his fellow soldiers the satisfaction of revenge, he couldn't share it, just as he couldn't share all they had gone through to get here. To him, the battle had been noise and destruction, and he could find no reason why he was the only one in his squad to survive.

Now he walked freely around Berlin. The wrecked enormity of the city's bridges, train tracks, subway stations, cathedrals, brick factories, colonnaded palaces, and shops overwhelmed him. In the farther neighborhoods where his unit had fought, Berlin had seemed to him not too different from Vinnytsa, the closest city to his village that he'd visited before shipping out. But now that he'd made it deeper into the city's core, he saw that while Vinnytsa's streets begun and ended, Berlin's never seemed to. Even despite the rubble, one street simply became another, slightly changing course and widening like a meandering river.

Perhaps he wouldn't have been so confused by this city had the Berlin streets not been completely motionless in those early May days. No trams ran, no shop doors swung open, no smoke blew out of the factories, no trains whooshed out of the subway stations. As the last vestiges of fighting moved west, the southern neighborhoods sat empty and still, their shattered buildings shedding rubble like skin. The only signs of life were the white flags, bedsheets, tablecloths, and rags draped from windows and balconies. Behind them, he knew, were thousands of Berliners, mostly women, hiding in cellars and attics, trying to survive on food supplies that had dwindled long ago. He couldn't decide what was eerier: the chaos of the battle or the silent shards of a city it had left behind.

At one point he turned into a dead-end alley and saw a swirl of leaves floating through the air. He thought it strange to see leaves falling in May and moved closer. That was when he saw they were German marks landing on the cobblestones and gathering in the ditch. As he looked at these former riches, he felt a little like them—worthless.

On the night of May 8, Yefim woke up in his camp to a shooting uproar. He grabbed his rifle and darted out of the tent. German paratroopers must have landed to retake their capital.

Instead, he saw soldiers gathering from all sides, firing their guns and rifles into the sky, no longer worried about sparing bullets, as their commander ran toward them, waving a Soviet flag and screaming, "The war is over!"

That night, everyone hugged and danced and drank vodka until the morning, the joy so enormous it felt like it could never end. In the middle of the celebration, Yefim walked to find a quiet dark spot behind a tree. He sat down and raised his little brass mug. The war was over. He—a prisoner, a laborer, a Jew—had outlived it. Somewhere, he hoped, those he loved were also celebrating.

———

In the following days, Yefim was only permitted to return to Berlin once. On his way, he passed by a train station where a Soviet colonel directed soldiers as they loaded an oak cupboard, a piano, chandeliers, a bicycle, and rolls of carpets onto a freight car. A shiny black Mercedes awaited its turn to be loaded onto the platform car.

The brazenness of the colonel's greed shocked Yefim. Was that what they had fought the war for? So that those in power got a shiny Mercedes? When he returned to the camp that day, he found out that the looting had been legitimized by the Red Army commanders, who announced that all Soviet soldiers could send spoils of war to their families back home. Privates like Yefim were allowed a five-kilo package. The camp was abuzz as soldiers gathered wristwatches, textiles, canned beef. When someone asked him if he was planning to send something, he shrugged. Yefim was sure that after four years of not hearing from him, his family believed him to be dead. Canned beef wasn't the right way to tell them he'd made it.

So, a week after Germany's capitulation, he wrote a short letter telling his parents he'd made it to Berlin and asking about their fate. He went to the camp's post office tent to drop off his letter home and ask whether they knew the best way to locate Ivan. On the way, he tried to think of some covert way to contact Ilse when he heard, "*Zdorovo,* Komarov!"

It was Nikonov. He was crouched outside, smoking. His left arm was bandaged. For a moment Yefim thought of turning the other way, but Nikonov was already beckoning him.

"You got hurt out there?" Yefim asked, pointing to Nikonov's arm, hoping to steer clear of politics.

"Yeah, shrapnel. Not so bad, really. Now I'll look like a real war hero back home. The girls will love it. Ha ha!"

"Home?"

"A bunch of us are shipping off tomorrow," he said with a note of sadness. "Not you?"

"From what I've heard, our unit will be here for a while. Plus I owe them eighteen months of service," Yefim said. "You're heading straight to Crimea, then?"

Nikonov adjusted his bandage and looked to the side as if embarrassed. Yefim had never seen him like that. It was as if all the blood had drained from his face.

"It's not home they're sending me to, Komarov," he said quietly. "Didn't I tell you we were useless to them? Inconvenient?"

Siberia, Yefim thought. He squatted next to Nikonov, feeling terrible for thinking he did dirty work for SMERSH.

"But if they've reinstated you into the army, doesn't that mean you've been cleared?"

"That's what I hoped until I was back in the SMERSH office this morning, writing out my whole damn story again: how I was captured, where I've been, et cetera."

"Oh," Yefim said, wondering why he hadn't been called back. "Does this mean they'll send me there too after my tour?"

"Don't know. I was a commissar, though. It's different for you. Maybe they'll spare you," Nikonov said, but he didn't sound convinced.

Yefim didn't know what to say. How could their own people punish them for surviving? The injustice of it fogged his mind. He sat next to Nikonov, who stared into the distance.

They may have outlived the war, but peace wasn't going to be much easier. For the first time, he was frightened by what awaited him back home.

A bicycle bell rang and a private rode past them, weaving and trying to keep from falling.

"You know how to ride a bike?" Nikonov asked with a strange levity.

"No," said Yefim, looking up at the biker. Bicycles had been a popular thing to loot.

"Maybe you'll learn if you stay here long enough. Better yet, go west. It's probably your last chance to escape."

Yefim didn't look at Nikonov. What he was saying was heresy, and yet Yefim felt oddly honored that the man cared enough to suggest it. He'd heard of other Soviets who weren't too thrilled to be repatriated and had gone west. Maybe he'd think about it. He had some uncles in America who had left long before he was born.

He wanted to do something nice for Nikonov. He was a strange fellow, but maybe life had brought them together for a reason.

"Hey, listen," he said, "will you write me once you get there? Let me know where you end up."

Nikonov was silent.

"Sure," he finally said with a shrug. "If I am allowed."

"Please do. Write to Yefim Shulman. That's my real name."

Nikonov stared at him.

"No shit! So I was right about you being a Jew all along?"

He laughed hard, his eyes watering, until he accidentally yanked his arm and swore from the pain.

"You are one lucky son of a bitch, Shulman."

Chapter 15

November 1989
Moscow

Andrey was running late. He was supposed to meet his parents at the Paveletsky train station ten minutes ago and he was still one metro stop away. He scratched his beard, wishing he could push the train along. Mama and Papa were probably waiting on the cold platform, annoyed that they took an overnight Donetsk–Moscow train and their son couldn't even pick them up on time. Considering he'd basically tricked them into coming to Moscow, he wasn't off to the best start.

He was tired and agitated after a restless night next to Lina. His wife had slept annoyingly peacefully—but then again, she wasn't the one who had to lie to her parents. The reason his parents thought they had been summoned to Moscow was to help with the kids while Lina was away at a conference. But though his wife had indeed flown off to a conference, Andrey's real reason for calling them here was to tell them he and Lina wanted to emigrate.

Lina was the one who had first brought up the idea. It had caught Andrey completely by surprise, though it shouldn't have. Leaving made sense for Lina: she spoke decent English and had never felt much love for the Motherland. Her father, who had spent the war in the Gulag, had brought her up on smuggled samizdat publications, so she knew many of the country's dirty secrets long before most, certainly before Andrey. She was also Jewish, which made her eligible for emigration. Jews were now leaving in droves, some to Israel but most to America, which, she liked to point out, was the hotbed of modern psychology. A psychologist herself and the pragmatist of their marriage, she told him she was sick of food lines, cockroaches in their kitchen, and the crowded, hour-long bus ride to the nearest sensible school that wouldn't feed their kids Communist bullshit.

Arguing that things in the country were changing didn't sway Lina. According to her, glasnost may have begun to open the people's eyes to the full horror of Stalin's rule—from the Ukrainian famine now called Holodomor to the millions of POWs sent to labor camps after the war—but it wouldn't make any difference. The long denial of these truths only confirmed that the Soviet Union was rotten to its very core and had nowhere to go but down.

But Andrey didn't see it that way. He felt more honesty and less fear in the air. All that exhumed history ought to cleanse people's souls, to help them heal and rebuild. Of course, his father hadn't survived a labor camp like Lina's, so maybe he was being naive.

They always discussed emigrating in their home office, which was the farthest from the kids' bedroom, and only at night. The last thing they needed was for the kids to overhear. The walls of the office were lined with books and it hurt to look at them, the dozen shelves that his father had helped him hang. They had gotten this apartment only two years earlier and moving had been such an undertaking—with the kids, the cat, the books—that just the thought of abandoning those shelves and moving again exhausted them both. Or maybe only him. Lina often seemed full of wound-up energy, like a panther on the prowl.

While Lina talked, Andrey temporarily bought into her vision: Move to America, practice American psychology, give the kids a better future. He nodded along to her reasons and told himself he had never felt at home in Moscow anyway. He was still an outsider with his Ukrai-nian last name, his softened way of speaking that contrasted with the pretentious Moscow accent, the holes in his knowledge of Moscow neighborhoods, cultural figures, and references that only the locals understood. He missed the smells and freedom of the steppe, where his parents had often taken him when he was little. And yet, under Moscow's elitist pressure, he didn't advertise that he was from the Donbas. Of course, in America he'd be an outsider, too, but there the details wouldn't matter. He'd simply be a "Soviet psychologist." A fresh start, an adventure. Or so Lina made him believe. But at night, while she slept probably certain she had finally convinced him, he tossed and turned with the truth: he didn't want an adventure. He was satisfied with the life they had.

After a while their discussions had begun to loop in maddening circles until Andrey finally put his foot down and said he wasn't emigrating without his parents. Mama and Papa may have lived an overnight train ride away in a different Soviet republic, but at least they could see each other whenever they wanted. Emigrating meant they might never see each other again.

He suspected that his parents wouldn't want to emigrate. It wasn't that they were patriotic—not at all. But they also didn't fit in with the type of people who were leaving: the ones who'd been miserable here because they felt repressed or discriminated against; the ones who thought the country was going to shit and America was the only path to happiness; and the ones who were happy to scrap the past for the sake of the future. People like Lina.

Once he told her he wasn't going without his parents and he was sure they weren't interested, he thought that would put an end to their discussions. But then his shrewd wife came up with a solution. "Let's tell them we will leave with or without them," she said, "and I bet you they'll start packing right away."

At first he balked at this. It seemed treacherous and he wasn't well practiced at deceiving his parents. They'd always been honest with him. Still, he agreed. It was the only way to resolve the matter once and for all. And so, he lured them to Moscow since it wasn't safe to discuss emigration over the phone.

Finally, the metro swooshed into the station, the doors opened, and Andrey ran along the arched platform with its gilded hammers and sickles, up the escalator, and through the long halls connecting the metro to the Paveletsky train station. The station smelled of luggage and sweet tea, and he could tell the crowds from the Donetsk train had already dispersed. He ran through the doors leading to the platform and bumped right into Papa, almost knocking him down. Mama exclaimed; they laughed as Andrey apologized; and they all embraced.

On the metro back to Andrey's apartment, he sat between them. His father had stopped by the newspaper kiosk and was now showing him an article about East Germany's government deciding to open its borders to West Germany while his mother said the harvest at their in-laws' had been good this year. They'd brought some homemade jams and pickles for the kids.

"We live in interesting but hungry times," his mother said.

"Have you heard this joke yet?" his father quipped. "At the store: 'You wouldn't have any meat?' 'No, we don't have any fish. The meat department is where they don't have any meat.' "

Andrey wondered if maybe his parents were more amenable to emigrating than he had assumed.

Leading them from the metro to his apartment building, he felt even more like a foreigner in this fast-paced city. His parents didn't walk as fast as the Muscovites, and people kept bumping into them, grumbling under their breath. He remembered how, when they had first come to visit him fifteen years earlier when he was a student, he tried to show off Moscow to make them see why it was so much better than Donetsk. How callous he'd been, making them feel that Donetsk, where they had given him the best life they could, wasn't good enough. He wondered if that was how his children would feel about the USSR if they were to move to America: a mixture of arrogance, pity, and guilt.

In the evening, after the kids went off to bed, Andrey set out tea in the kitchen. Lina had baked a heap of cinnamon rolls, her one contribution to Andrey's difficult task.

He skipped saying the prayer out loud so as not to make his parents uncomfortable and simply crossed himself before sitting down. He hadn't forgotten how shocked they were when he first told them about finding God and invited them to his baptism. He had thought it would be a treat, especially for Papa, who had never experienced the magic of a Christian service. Instead, his father tried talking Andrey out of getting baptized. At first Andrey thought Papa was offended that his half-Jewish son had chosen Christianity, though it wasn't like he'd ever showed any attachment to Judaism himself. But it wasn't that. He and Mama were apparently worried because Christians were often oppressed by the authorities and their careers cut short. What they couldn't understand was that Andrey didn't really care about that. It seemed like a small price to pay for the private blessing he felt. It was as if he'd found something that had been missing his whole life. In a country where he had to say one thing while thinking another, turning to God was a remedy from feeling like his whole life was a fraud. If only his parents could see that. He didn't blame them for being atheists as in their time that had been the only choice, but now that things were freer, he wished they, too, would cast off decades of antireligious ideas they'd been fed by the Party and open themselves up to the divine. They had both survived incredible hardships—Holodomor, the purges, the war— and yet they never thought to thank God for watching over them.

Now, as they sat down to tea, his throat tightened. He was a Christian who was about to lie to his parents.

"This East Germany situation is quite interesting," Andrey said, knowing his father would appreciate some political talk before he launched into his real conversation. "My friend Ignas told me the Baltics are heading for some sort of independence. What are you hearing in Ukraine?"

"They've just made Ukrainian the official language of Ukraine," his father said, an ironic twinkle in his eye.

"Only took a few decades," Mama added.

"Don't think we'll go independent," his father continued, grabbing one of Lina's cinnamon rolls. "But you might want to brush up on your Ukrainian next time you come visit."

Andrey looked from his father, who was sipping tea the way he always had—as if cherishing every drop—to his mother, whose thick round glasses sat on her grandmotherly cheeks. It was hard to believe they would be seventy in just a couple of years. He hated springing this emigration business upon them, but it had to be done.

"Listen, Lina and I have been thinking . . . that maybe it's time for us to leave."

"Leave?" His dad looked at him confused and then put on his bifocals as if they helped him hear better.

"Emigrate," Andrey spat out, feeling awkward at the word.

Mama gasped as if she'd been slapped. Papa launched into a coughing fit, making Andrey wince at the terrible deep-sea sound.

"You really ought to have a doctor look at this coughing, Papa."

"Only if you have a doctor look at your head," his father finally replied.

"Emigrating!" Mama scoffed. "Where would you go?"

"America or maybe Europe," he said as calmly as he could, glad that they were past the initial shock and could turn to details. "We have friends and colleagues in the States, in Belgium, Germany, England. But we want you to—"

"Definitely Germany," his father interrupted. "They have a fondness for half Jews there."

There was an unfamiliar bitterness in his father's voice, and Andrey realized his dad had never said anything good or bad about the Germans. He couldn't have thought well of them, considering that he'd fought them for four years, but it wasn't like he'd been in a concentration camp either.

His mother began to cry in that dramatic way of hers: from nothing to full bawling. Wide streams of tears covered her puffy cheeks as the ball of her nose grew red. Andrey had to turn this conversation around, and quickly. Lucky Lina at her conference not having to see all this.

"Please calm down," he tried. "We want you to come with us!"

This seemed to shake his mother out of her hysteria, and through the tears she sniffled as stoically as she could, "We are too old to go anywhere. Plus there are Vita and her kids too."

"They could also come."

"Our life is here," his father said sternly. "We are not going to give everything up and move who knows where."

"Your life is here too," his mother said with a resolute shake of her head. "Emigrating is for traitors."

That he didn't anticipate. It was a phrase often thrown at those who were leaving, but he never thought he'd hear it from his own mother. She was rational—a skeptic, even—not some staunch Communist who believed in traitors.

His father banged on the table, making his teacup jingle on the saucer.

"You know how I hate that word, Nina," he said, and Andrey tensed from a hint of a childhood fear that some limit of his father's had been overstepped. "Point is, your mother and I have seen this country go through much worse than what is happening now, and we're still here."

Mama said, "There has probably never been a better time to believe in the future. It almost feels like it did after the war, doesn't it, Fima? The hunger combined with knowing that the worst is behind us?"

But his father didn't reply. He was looking intensely at the table, the ball of his lipoma glistening under the kitchen lamp. He picked up the newspaper with the East Germany article. Then he lunged for something in the far corner behind the teapot and smacked the paper on the tablecloth, exclaiming, "Gotcha!"

It was a cockroach. His father got up and took the newspaper with the squashed insect to the garbage bin under the sink. It seemed as though his father was making a show of the whole thing to demonstrate that this conversation wasn't worth his attention. Andrey turned to his mother.

"Mamochka, didn't you always want to go abroad?"

"Sure, but going abroad is not the same as emigrating," she said, wiping her face with the kitchen towel while Papa returned to the table.

"Unlike you two, I've actually been abroad," he said. "I've seen Germany with its fancy buildings and bicycles and watches. And you know what? For a moment I considered what it would be like to stay and live in the West."

Andrey was surprised to hear his father confess thoughts of defecting that in Stalin's time would have been treasonous. Judging by his mother's look, she also had never heard that before.

"Why didn't you?"

"Because I had experienced what it was like being a foreigner—not like you, a Ukrainian in Moscow, but a real foreigner—and I realized it is committing yourself to a lifetime of dissatisfaction, of homesickness, of loss of identity."

It was strange to hear his father, always so practical and down-to-earth, talk about "loss of identity." Andrey fell silent. Outside, he could hear the windy November night roaming through this huge city full of towering apartment buildings where millions of people sat in kitchens discussing what was going to happen to this country.

Then he said the phrase he had rehearsed many times. "I can understand this is hard for you, but we've decided to go . . . with or without you."

According to Lina's plan, this was supposed to get them in line. But now he really did feel like a traitor. He studied his parents: his mother's plump arms in her plum-colored dress, his father's still-handsome face looking sharper, more Jewish than he'd ever noticed. Andrey wondered if there was a chance they would succumb to his blackmail.

Papa jammed his hands under his armpits and asked, "Why are you sure they'd even let us out?" His eyes darted nervously. His voice was shrill and unfamiliar. Andrey realized he'd never seen his father scared before.

"Why wouldn't they? It's not like we know some state secrets. At least, *I* don't."

"Maybe *you* don't, but I know a lot about the Soviet gas and oil reserves, coal-mining operations, railroads. Not the highest level of state secrets, maybe, but still . . . I mean, do you know what records they check? Or what they consider in the exit visa?"

Papa was agitated, talking fast, his voice rising.

"Your father is right," Mama said. "You and Lina will need to quit your jobs to apply, and if they deny you, you'll end up like the refuseniks—all those doctors and teachers sweeping the streets."

Andrey wished he knew more about the refuseniks or exit visa procedures to calm his parents' paranoia. Lina should have prepared him better.

"I haven't heard of anyone getting denied," he said. "I don't think we should worry about that."

The radiator clanged behind him. He was suddenly very tired. They must be exhausted too.

"Let's sleep on it, all right?" he said. "This isn't a decision to take lightly. We can talk more in the morning."

His mother nodded, her face sullen as if she was already mourning her son's departure. His father got up and left without saying good night. Andrey stayed behind. This had been the hardest conversation of his life. Harder even than when he'd told them about his faith.

And yet that night he lay in bed relieved: his parents were against emigration. While Lina had often made him feel foolish for not wanting to leave—"Only idiots can hope things will get better here"—his parents' refusal reaffirmed the validity of his feelings. Yes, places like London, Paris, New York, even Berlin, might brim with sophistication, worldliness, and a bright, open future for the kids, but that didn't mean their future here was doomed. Things here were changing, really changing. They lived in the era of the Great Confession and, just as in Christianity, facing their country's history would inevitably bring forgiveness and renewal. His mother was right: this was the time to stay.

He woke up to some rustling in the hallway. When he opened the door he saw his parents, already dressed, packing up their suitcase.

"What are you doing?" he whispered, as the kids were asleep.

"If you want to go, that is your right," his mother whispered back, closing up the suitcase with jerky movements. "But we aren't emigrating. Fima, help me close this thing."

He had not expected his parents to be so dramatic.

"No, leave it," he pleaded, approaching his father, who had stooped above the suitcase. "No one is emigrating."

His father looked up at him.

"What, you changed your mind overnight?"

"I . . ." Andrey didn't know how to explain. "I was going to tell you this morning. I guess I changed my mind, yes. Leave your suitcase. Let's go talk in the kitchen."

Lina was going to be very disappointed, but that didn't matter. He wasn't going to let his parents go home without telling them the truth.

"I never wanted to emigrate—certainly not without you," he said once everyone sat down. "I suppose you called my bluff."

"Then why did you have to put us through all that?" his mother asked. "We aren't that young, you know."

"I'm sorry. I needed to be sure. I didn't know how you were going to react."

"This was Lina's idea, wasn't it?" his father asked.

"How did you know?"

"The cinnamon rolls. She was clearly trying to sweeten the deal."

Papa smiled with that ironic smile of his. There was no more fear in his eyes as they lit up with a kindness that had always made Andrey feel his father would never do anything to hurt him.

"We were really going to go, you know," his mother said, still hurt.

Andrey came up to her and kissed the top of her head. "I'm sorry, Mamochka. This must have been very hard."

"Morning!" came the little voice of his six-year-old daughter.

Masha swooped into the kitchen, followed by Denis, who was still groggy. Their grandparents swept them into a hug and Andrey's chest expanded with warmth at the sight. How could he have threatened to take them away to the West?

Once Denis was free, he picked up the newspaper folded to the East Germany article, which was still lying on the table.

"What language is this in?" he asked, pointing to the German signs held up by protesters.

"You can't read that?" Andrey joked, trying to cast off the last shadows of their argument from the room.

"I could if it was English," said his son, who at twelve already spoke better English than he did, which was yet one more reason it was a bad idea for Andrey to emigrate. "Oh, I guess it's German."

"What's it say, Deda?" asked Masha.

"Grandpa doesn't speak German," Andrey said as his father nodded absentmindedly. "Here, it says, 'Protesters in Berlin hold up a sign, "Talk is silver; action is gold."' East Germans are now allowed to freely travel and move to other countries if they want to."

"Why would they want to?" Denis asked. "I thought the GDR was cool. Artem from our class said his mom has been there."

"Maybe they don't want 'cool' anymore," Andrey ventured, feeling his parents' eyes on him.

"Grandpa would know! Is Berlin cool, Deda?"

Andrey felt a familiar nervousness. Ever since he was little, he knew—though no one had ever exactly told him—that you shouldn't ask Papa about the war. That part of his dad's life was mysterious and sacred, like something that you simultaneously wanted to know and were afraid to find out.

"I saw it a long time ago, my dear," his father said. But the kids didn't give up. Andrey envied them for not sharing his trepidation.

"Oh, tell them something, Fima," his mother pressed.

Andrey wondered if his father would continue to resist. Instead, Papa's eyes lit up the way they did when he told jokes.

"Berlin is a big city, a capital, almost like Moscow. I remember these really wide streets with tram lines, metro stations, and beautiful apartment buildings. But you know the most incredible thing I saw? German paper money floating in the air like falling leaves. No one was picking them up because the reichsmark—that's what the German money was called—had become worthless."

"What's 'worthless'?" asked Masha.

"It means that to buy one egg, for example, you'd need to bring a truckload of money," Nina explained.

"A truckload?" The kids giggled.

Andrey had never heard this story and it struck him as odd that he'd never asked about Berlin. Perhaps even in his family there was room for glasnost.

"Papa, maybe you ought to write down your memories," he said carefully.

"For whom?"

"For the grandkids. For posterity. For yourself, even. In the spirit of glasnost, you know?"

His father grabbed a cinnamon roll and said, "I'm sure posterity will have better things to think about than some old geezer's past."

Then he stuffed the pastry in his mouth and grinned.

Chapter 16

October 1946
Poland

He was going home. The place he loved, the place he feared.

As the train of demobilized soldiers rolled east along the Polish countryside, Yefim wondered what he would see once they reached Ukraine. He stared out the dusty window at the fields and yellow-leafed forests that seemed so orderly and neat he knew, even without looking at the signs, that they were still in Europe. He regretted that they went past Warsaw at night as he'd heard rumors it had been leveled. He couldn't really imagine a big city like that razed to a pulp. Occasionally they passed a village with burned houses or a brick building lying in ruins, and Yefim yearned for the hour when they would get to Ukraine and he could see his own village.

During the day, the soldiers fantasized about what they'd find back home. Some had girlfriends or wives. The fellow in the lower bunk said he'd left a two-year-old son back in 1942 and now was bringing him a school notebook and a shiny new pen.

Yefim didn't talk much. He didn't know what awaited him back home. His letter to his family had gone unanswered. Perhaps they had evacuated east to Russia and hadn't returned. He would get to his village and ask whoever was still there and then go find them. There were seven of them, plus two sisters-in-law and Lyubochka. It wasn't like they all could have disappeared.

When night arrived, it was cool and quiet. As the train moved east, its whistle was the only sound in the dark. From the upper bunk, Yefim bobbed along, his forehead pressed against the cool windowpane, where he watched the moon rise above the blackened landscape. In his rucksack, tucked behind a net on the wall, was his brass cup from Niegripp next to a thick bar of chocolate, a loaf of white bread, and a kilo of butter from Berlin. He didn't know if these were the right things to bring for his family, but he was determined not to show up at his home empty-handed. The relatives of the other men in his unit wrote letters hinting at the hunger back home, so as soon as they arrived in Berlin for a one-day stopover before being discharged and shipped home, he went shopping.

After a year serving on a Soviet base on Germany's wild Baltic coast where the breeze ate through him, leaving holes in his chest, Berlin looked surprisingly cozy, even inviting. There were still a lot of ruins, which stuck out like broken teeth between intact buildings, but far fewer than a year earlier, certainly fewer than he had expected. Unlike that day when he had wandered the streets at the end of the war, there were plenty of Berliners going about their business as if nothing had ever happened. Men in coats and hats, with newspapers rolled under their arms and purposeful looks on their faces, waited for trams. German girls sat in cafés and giggled at the young soldiers gawking at them from the outside.

Yefim went to a post office and mailed a postcard to Karow. He didn't know Ilse's address, so he sent it to the church. Maybe the priest would throw it out, but he had to try. "Fräulein Ilse," he wrote, "I am going home to Ukraine. One day I hope we will meet again." He signed it simply "Yefim."

Afterward, he had wanted to return to that corner where he had almost met his end, but it was in one of the Allies' quarters where Soviets weren't allowed. Instead, he wandered the streets, looking at the stores and barbershops that had reopened behind rickety, bullet-ridden facades. At first he could hear the echo of the guns ricocheting between the balconied buildings, but after a while the echo disappeared and he began to soak up the feeling of rebirth that filled the city. Once again he wondered if he should have listened to Nikonov and gone west, perhaps even all the way to America. But just as before, he knew if he did, he would never see his family again.

Now, on the night train heading home, he saw flashes of postwar Berlin scenes jumbled like a stack of postcards—the newspaper sellers, the café girls, the facades—and soon, as his lulled head slid from the cool window onto his arm, he dreamed he was walking into a barbershop with Ilse on his arm, finding that inside it was his parents' hut. His mother must have just scolded his brothers because they were all sniggering and elbowing each other at the table. Basya carried a large, steaming pot toward the table, walking right past him and Ilse. "Go," Ilse said. "I'll wait outside." But Yefim just stood there, watching them, afraid to cause chaos.

The train jolted and came to a stop with a clang. Yefim opened his eyes and saw a sliver of an empty platform yawning under a yellow streetlamp. He craned his neck and up at the tail end of the train saw two guards, each one leading a German shepherd on a leash. The border.

He heard their boots and the dogs' breathing as they boarded the train and inched toward his bunk. Soon a flashlight paused, scanning his face as the dog sniffed around. They checked everything quickly. It was all soldiers heading back—not much to check—but Yefim was still tense. Afterward he and the others gathered their things and walked to a different train that sat on the wider Soviet tracks. Yefim couldn't fall asleep again for a long time even after they had left the border. He thought of how he was going to get from Kyiv to his village, who would be there to hug him, and how to find Ivan.

In the morning it was drizzling. Yefim and the other soldiers were glued to the windows, straining to see their country beyond the whirling drops. They passed a forest. The trees had lost most of their leaves in the October rains and now swayed, their branches slender and exposed, waiting for winter to clothe them in snow. The chatter in the train car was growing more and more excited as they neared their destination.

"I better see my Maria waiting on that platform."

"I don't care if it's Maria or Katya or Alena. Happy to kiss them all!"

"Wish Kyiv was my last stop. I still got to make my way down to Kharkiv. My mother and little sister are down there."

"When did you ship out?"

"Winter of '42. Been so long, my little boy won't recognize me."

"Don't worry, as soon as he sees your uniform, he'll follow you around like a puppy."

The train whooshed into a clearing and everyone fell silent. It was a burned-out village. Yefim saw a row of a dozen large brick stoves, each just like the one at the center of his family's hut. They stood like lonely tombstones on scorched, fallow earth.

"Poor Ukraine," someone said.

It was late morning when they finally arrived in Kyiv. The once grand new train station, from which he'd left the country in 1940, was marred by war. But the platform was filled with people, mostly women, half running, their hands waving eagerly, their eyes searching. No one knew Yefim was coming, yet for a moment he imagined that Basya was there to greet him.

He jumped onto the platform and inhaled the sad sweetness of fallen chestnut tree leaves, the chalky smell of the train station, the warm breath of the eager, smiling women. Their eyes searched his face for recognition—*Is that my Petro?*—and he lowered his head, knowing that among the gathered crowd he wasn't anyone's husband or son. He squeezed past them toward the exit, where he was met with a huge poster of a Red Army soldier proudly standing guard underneath WE WON! written in all caps. Right below the poster, a girl in a kerchief stood begging for change next to her father, a vet with multiple medals on his chest but with only one arm and no legs.

———

It had stopped raining by the time Yefim approached his village that afternoon. On the way, he saw burned houses and gray, hunched villagers wrapped in rags. The dock on the pond where Mikhail had taught him to fish had fallen in. Even the school he and his brothers had attended in the nearby kolkhoz lay in a pile of beams and trash. The amount of destruction was shattering. He was a fool for thinking a few days of fighting in Berlin could make up for staying so far from all this.

Now he better understood the Red Army soldiers he had met in Berlin: they had marched through hundreds of kilometers of such ruins on their way to Germany with its immaculate two-story houses, its cars and bicycles, its well-dressed people. No wonder they had wanted to pillage the place. Perhaps they had earned the right to loot, a small payback for what they had lost. But then he remembered the shiny Mercedes being loaded onto the train in Berlin and again had the feeling of disgust. No, Ivan had been right all along. Even their Soviet regime that purported to care about the common man didn't care one bit. The only way to live within it was to figure out how to use its rules to get what he needed.

When he rounded the last bend in the road and saw the huts of his village in the distance, Yefim stopped, picked up a stick, and scraped off chunks of mud that had caked his army boots. He'd need to look presentable to whoever was there to greet him. He could imagine his mother opening the door, a ladle in her hand, then yelling for Basya to come quick because her brother who they'd thought had perished was alive! His letter had never arrived, she'd tell him once they all calmed down. He slicked his hair under his cap, heaved his rucksack on his back, and hurried toward the village.

The wide dirt road, pockmarked by large puddles, was empty. As he approached the first houses, he was spooked by how quiet the village was. His chest constricted. He passed the well, still intact, from which he used to help Mikhail carry the water in the mornings. He wondered what Mikhail had felt when he returned after his tour in '35, medals jingling on his chest. Yefim's return was certainly nothing like that.

He passed the house of Rabbi Isaac: windows boarded up, a pile of debris in the yard. Yefim looked ahead for the thick chestnut tree that marked the center of the village, where all the kids used to play in the hot summer afternoons. Instead he saw a stump. An old man sat on it. His dirty bare feet dangled above the ground. Was that Father?

When he approached and saw the man's face—ashen and wrinkled—it took Yefim a minute to recognize him as Matveyich, the carpenter.

Yefim remembered how, when he was nine, his father had sent him to Matveyich to borrow a saw. When among the many small and large saws hanging on the wall of his shed, Yefim pointed to one at random, Matveyich kicked him out of the barn empty-handed, as apparently he'd picked the nicest saw the man owned. Yefim had tried to avoid him ever since, but now, looking at this shadow of a man, he couldn't understand his childhood fear. It was good to see a familiar face.

"*Zdorovo*, Matveyich," Yefim said, but the man only nodded absently.

"Yefim, Shulman's son," he tried again, thinking his soldier's uniform and the close-cropped hair under his cap must have made him hard to recognize, especially for an old man who'd seen God knows what in the past five years.

Matveyich just nodded again, his hazel eyes staring through Yefim. Probably gone senile, Yefim figured, and walked on. If Matveyich was alive, that was a good sign. He couldn't be the only one here.

On the left was the green house of Baba Klavdiya, who hadn't been the same since her son Vasil died from choking on a stale piece of bread during the famine. The chickens that normally roamed her yard weren't there. That was when Yefim realized why the village was so quiet: there were no dogs running around, no roosters crowing, no geese honking. Only the wind blowing through the broken windows of the ramshackle huts. What if his family had left after all and there was no one here to tell him where they'd gone? His breath grew shallow.

As soon as his parents' house came into view, Yefim froze. The roof was half caved in, the wet straw sagging inward. The front window, where his mother always kept a jar of pickled cabbage, was broken. Only the old apple tree still towered over the untended yard. What if they were all . . . but he stopped himself. It couldn't be.

He walked toward the front door and knocked, just in case. When no one answered, he tried opening it, but the hinges must have rusted in the rain. He put down his rucksack and pushed the door with his shoulder. It budged a little and, after a few strong shoves, finally swung open with a screech.

The smell of mold and dust hit him. The empty hut looked tiny. The floor was covered with straw, dead leaves, and broken glass from the window. The dining table and the bench where they'd squeeze together to slurp their mother's kasha were gone. All that remained was their *pich*, the whitewashed brick stove like the ones he'd seen from the train. Decorated with sunflowers and mallows by Basya when she was twelve, it had heated their house, cooked their food, and provided a warm place to sleep on its top ledge. Now it stood gray, with soot lining its oven door and mouse droppings in place of chopped wood on the bottom sill.

Yefim stepped outside into the fresh, humid air and closed the door behind him. They couldn't all be dead. No. He refused to believe it. There had to be an explanation, something reasonable and obvious: his parents probably got evacuated, his brothers worked in the city, and Basya, well, she was old enough to have gotten married by now. A lot could have happened in the six years since he shipped out.

He walked through the village searching for someone who could tell him anything about his family. Up ahead, he spotted two boys poking sticks into a big puddle on the side of the road. They were about six or so, skinny as hell, barefoot, in rags. They reminded him of how he and his brothers looked during the famine. When they spotted him, they stared and he felt self-conscious in his soldier's uniform.

"Whose are you?" Yefim asked.

They glanced at each other.

"Rudenko," one of them said. The other boy didn't answer.

"Kateryna?" Yefim asked, remembering the girl's wide-set brown eyes and how he'd kissed her once while she was milking her cow. A silly kiss, never repeated.

"*Da*, that's my mama," the boy said, as if surprised that the stranger knew his family. "Who are you, soldier?"

"I used to live here before the war. Can you take me to your mom?"

Without a word, the boy turned and began walking toward his house on the other end of the village. The second boy followed, gazing up and down at Yefim's uniform.

Then Yefim stopped and asked, "You boys hungry?"

Before they answered, he opened his rucksack, dug out the wrapped loaf of bread, and tore off two pieces. They grabbed the bread with their dirty fingers and shoved as much as they could into their tiny mouths, leaving them almost unable to chew.

When they arrived at Kateryna's house, the boy yanked the unchewed bread out of his mouth and ran in, calling, "Mama! A soldier is here for you."

Out popped Kateryna. Her hair was tied in a white kerchief, making her wide-set brown eyes stand out even more than he remembered. She wasn't even married yet when he left and now she had this hungry boy on her hands.

Kateryna looked at Yefim hesitantly, trying to read his face. Then, suddenly, she exclaimed, "Shulman?"

It was a strange relief to hear his family's name coming out of this woman's pale, chapped lips that stretched into a bewildered, warm smile, revealing a gap between her front teeth.

"Reporting for duty," he said, putting his hand to his cap's visor.

She kissed him the old Ukrainian way, three times on the cheeks, and he felt himself blushing.

"Come in, come in," she said as her son went inside while his little friend ran off.

"I was looking for . . . ," Yefim began, edging into her warm house.

"Your family, *da, da*," she said, moving quickly, clearing things from the table for her guest. Then she noticed her son and asked sternly, "What's that in your mouth? Better not be another mystery root."

"*Khleb*," he tried, though it was impossible to understand him with his mouth full.

She looked at Yefim.

"Figured he'd want to taste German bread," he said, trying to sound casual, as if this didn't mean anything about their poverty.

Her eyes began to water and she turned away to feel the samovar with the back of her hand.

"Still warm," Kateryna said, not looking at him. "Some acacia tea?"

"Would love some."

As Yefim looked around, he noticed a photograph of Mykola, who was a year younger than Yefim, and asked, "Is he Mykola's son?"

"Yes," she said. "We got married before they shipped him off and, nine months later, out came little Mykola here. We got a missing-in-action notice before he turned one. And you know what that means: dead in a ravine somewhere."

She put a pinch of dried acacia flowers into a cup and pointed for him to sit down.

"I can't believe you're alive!" she said. "You don't know what happened to your family?"

"*Nyet*, nothing," he said, bracing himself for whatever she was about to say. "Do you?"

"Your mother moved to Ivankivtsi after the occupation ended."

Yefim exhaled with relief. Ivankivtsi was the next village over.

"You'll be able to find her at the butcher's," Kateryna said.

"The butcher's?"

"Yes, well . . ." She paused, setting the cup under the faucet of the samovar and pouring the hot water. "Your father . . . he went to the ghetto. Your mom was alone and I think she got work at the butcher's. I don't really know."

He could see she didn't want to upset him. What she was really saying was that his father was dead and his mother was living with another man. Yefim's hands began to itch.

From behind, the boy tugged on his sleeve and asked, "Tovarisch Soldier, you've got more bread?"

Kateryna swatted a kitchen towel at the boy, yelling, "How dare you! He's come all the way from conquering Germany and here you are begging! Leave him alone before I whup you."

Mykola retreated to the corner as Yefim blushed. Conquering Germany. Was that what everyone was going to think?

"Don't mind him," Kateryna said, but Yefim was already taking out the loaf from the rucksack.

"It's for you," he said. "Better eat it before it gets stale. There is some butter as well."

She began to object, but he interrupted: "Hand me a knife."

When she did, he sliced off a piece of butter and transferred it onto a plate. Mykola crept closer to the table. Kateryna spread a paper-thin sliver of butter on a piece of bread and told her son to sit down. She poured him warm water from the samovar and warned, "Now, eat slowly or you'll get sick."

As the boy ate, Yefim asked if Kateryna knew anything about his siblings.

"I don't know anything about your brothers, Yefim. But Basya . . ."

Here, she began to cry. Yefim saw he'd been foolish to hope for his sister.

"She was shot."

Yefim stared blankly at his pale yellow tea.

He spent the night at Kateryna's house and in the morning took his rucksack and headed toward Ivankivtsi. The bigger village lay a few kilometers away, through the narrow forest, past the sunflower field, and across the Big Road, which despite its grandiose name was only a dirt lane pockmarked by cow-sized potholes, narrower than a small Berlin alley. The day was blustery and he had to watch his step to avoid puddles.

He had thought he was prepared to hear that not everyone in his large family had survived, but now he couldn't believe that his father and Basya were both gone. Basya, with her soft voice, her long black braid, the way she'd wrap him up in a kerchief when he was little and roll him around in a pushcart as if it were her pram and he was her baby. She should have gotten married, had babies of her own. Had he been here, he would have made sure his father didn't go to the ghetto and his sister was kept safe.

In the fragrant silence of the familiar forest, he remembered how Basya had played hide-and-seek here with him and their brothers. He was eager to find his mother and ask her where his brothers were. Mikhail was probably back in Kharkiv with his wife and little Lyubochka. Yakov would be in Vinnytsa with his Ida. Georgiy and Naum could be working somewhere. Once he saw his mother and sorted things at the commissariat, he would go visit them, ask them where they'd fought.

Yet, as he walked out of the forest onto the sunflower field, he became unnerved by the sight of the ripe sunflowers' droopy black faces silently swaying on human-sized stalks. There were rows and rows of them, flanking the road like dead troops, eyeing him resentfully, the man who walked through the land he hadn't had to defend.

By the time he arrived in Ivankivtsi, Yefim felt dreadful. He knocked on the door of the first house and asked where he could find the butcher. The old woman who opened the door eyed him wearily and he felt her gaze on him long after he turned and walked toward the house with the red roof that "you'll miss only if you're blind," as she'd told him.

The house with the red roof was indeed hard to miss. It was in the center of the village and looked well tended. Smoke surged from the chimney and a cat lounged on the windowsill. A cage with rabbits stood to the side of the small veranda. Clearly, the butcher wasn't suffering from the hunger that gripped the rest of the region. Did his mother really live in this house?

Before Yefim had a chance to knock, the front door opened to reveal a middle-aged man with a strappy corn-colored mustache who was busy tucking his shirt into his pants as if he'd just been caught on a john.

"What is it, soldier?" he asked, like someone who was used to constantly being bothered by the needy.

"I'm looking for Maria," said Yefim, half hoping the man would tell him she lived somewhere else.

"And what do you need with Maria?"

"I am her son."

"Son?" the man said with a strange smirk. "She never told me about no son."

"She has five sons. Now, where is she?"

The butcher stood there, calculating something, his eyes scanning the road behind them. The cat came to the door and went straight to Yefim, rubbing itself on his dusty boots. The butcher pointed to the back and said, "She is out there, probably by the chicken coop. Don't give her a heart attack. I need her strong and healthy."

Something in the way he said that last sentence made Yefim feel as though he were back in Germany, an ostarbeiter talking to his master.

He walked behind the house and saw Mother in the yard, stooped over a tub of laundry. She was smaller than he remembered. He watched her as she picked up a man's beige overalls, wrung out the water, her hands red from the effort, and stood on her tiptoes to hang them on the line strung between two trees. Gray speckled her raven hair. It was twisted into a bun, and he remembered how every night she'd let her long hair down, brushing it in a silent ritual none of them dared to disturb. And now here she was, his mother, the proud woman with a straight gaze, wringing out a butcher's overalls.

As she picked up another garment, Yefim called, "Mother."

She turned. The wet cloth in her hands plopped back into the tub. He watched her sharp eyes take him in. Her youngest son, her Yefim.

"Alive!"

She ran toward him, holding up her long apron, tears already streaking her angular cheekbones. He leaned in to embrace her, plunging into the smell of unfamiliar laundry soap and the bready, slightly bitter smell of his mother that he thought he'd forgotten.

"Let me look at you," she said when they separated.

While she inspected his face, Yefim saw, with a mix of pity and shame, how much his mother had aged in six years. Wrinkles radiated from her deep-set brown eyes, which had acquired a glassy veil. There was a lot more gray in her hair than he had first noticed. Her skin, once tan and vibrant, was now tired and sallow, with fragile spider veins stretching across her left cheek.

"I am an old woman, I know," she said, turning away from his gaze. "And you've turned from a boy to a man."

She took his hands in hers, lifted them to her eyes.

"Shrapnel," he said before she had a chance to ask about the fingers. "Could have been worse."

She began to cry again.

"Your brothers . . ."

"Where are they?"

"Oh, son, you're the only one left."

Gone? All four of them? Yefim's throat went dry. Out of six siblings, he was the only one left? Impossible. Even on the worse nights in Germany, he had never felt such crushing emptiness.

"What happened to them?" he finally asked.

"Mikhail, Yakov, and Georgiy were killed. Naum went missing. His missing-in-action notice came in '41. I got one for you, too, around then."

All dead. His mind went blank. Then, he heard himself ask, "What about Basya?"

She sighed and sat him down on a bench behind the house.

"Your father went to the Berdichev ghetto in the summer of '41. He asked me to come too, but I told him someone had to stay outside in case our sons came back maimed, who'd take care of them? Plus, you know him, always did what he was told. So Basya and I hid in the swamps. Your father would drive a German officer from the ghetto and back and whenever he passed by the spot where we hid, he'd throw us some bread. Then, one day in October, he didn't show up and soon we heard everyone in the ghetto had been . . . So your sister and I went begging door-to-door. Sometimes kind people took us in together, but usually we'd have to split up. That's how it happened. Basya got a job sewing for a family in Kozyatyn—you remember how good she was on the Singer?—and I was staying two houses away. One day a local policeman walked in while Basya was sewing, said, 'Ah, you Yid, hiding out, eh?' and shot her before she even got up."

Yefim winced. He could see it all in detail. And yet he couldn't believe his sister had been executed point-blank—by a Ukrainian no less. His mother began to howl and sway back and forth.

"Why couldn't he find me and shoot me? Why her, so young, so . . ."

A part of him wanted to hold her, but for some reason he couldn't bring himself to touch this lonely old woman. He wanted to yell at her for choosing such a spineless husband. His father was the man in the family, he should have protected them when all of his sons went to war. And here she was blaming herself when she should have been blaming her husband for abandoning them. He clutched his fists hard and stared down at his army boots, not wanting the guilt of being away from all this to swallow him.

"Where is she buried?" he finally managed.

"The host family took her to a field. They told me the spot and I went to put a boulder there. I go there whenever I can. I will take you. We must give her a proper burial."

"We will," he said, putting his hand on her knee.

He heard the heavy footsteps of the butcher in the house behind them and asked, "Why didn't you go back to our house?"

"What was there to go back to? Memories of everyone who's gone? If I had known you were alive, I would have stayed there, but I had no one left. And what would I eat? Good thing Nikolay Ivanovich was kind enough to take me in, a widow."

He thought he heard reproach in her tone. As if he'd had a way to let her know he was still alive.

"But tell me, how did you survive?" she asked, and Yefim clammed up at the dreaded question.

"I'll have to tell you next time," he said. He told her that he needed to go back to their village to sort out his papers. He had no documents and needed to get a passport and report to the regional military commissariat tomorrow morning to check in within the obligatory three days of arrival.

"Our house is too run-down," his mother said. "Let me ask Nikolay Ivanovich if you can stay here. I'm sure he won't mind for a few days."

"Don't. I'll manage."

"But there is nowhere to sleep. And the mice—"

"I'd rather go home," he said sternly.

She sat silently, letting the word "home" hang between them. She clutched his hand and he could feel her cold rough fingers on his two stumps. He promised himself that as soon as he sorted out his affairs, he'd get his mother out of this house.

She did not want to let him go, but he promised that he would return here as soon as he was done at the commissariat. Before kissing him goodbye, she took his face in her hands as if trying to commit it to memory.

"I cannot believe you are here, Fimochka. I knew God wouldn't take all seven of my children."

"You mean six, Ma," he corrected her.

"No, seven," said his mother, her cold fingers on his cheeks. "I never told you this, but two years before you were born, there was a baby girl. She came out stillborn, a tiny blue thing. The doctor said we shouldn't have any more children, that it was dangerous. But soon I got pregnant and couldn't bear the idea of getting rid of another baby. Your father didn't want me to have it. He was terrified I'd die in childbirth. But I didn't listen. I prayed every day to let this baby live. When you came out, you were strong and healthy, with a roar of a voice, and I named you Haim."

"Haim?" said Yefim, taking her hands off his face, confused.

"You were Haim for a year until the repressions made us change our Jewish names. That's how you became Yefim, but now it's clear you are Haim."

"Why?"

"Because in Hebrew *haim* means 'life.'"

Chapter 17

August 1995
Donetsk, Ukraine

Tomorrow, September 1, was supposed to be Masha's first day of fourth grade back in Moscow. Instead, Papa was taking her on an overnight train to Donetsk to visit her grandparents. And all because of the stupid cockroaches.

That was what Mama had said: that the exterminators needed to spray a deadly chemical that wouldn't evaporate for several days, so everyone had to evacuate the apartment. Masha hated cockroaches—the way they scurried off in all directions as soon as she turned on the bathroom light—and yet something about the story felt off. Maybe it was that her mother used the word "evacuate" or maybe it was the urgency with which she packed Masha's things. And then, there was also Papa's strange phone call. As the train approached the Donetsk station, Masha looked at Papa, who stared out the window onto the parallel tracks.

He didn't call the house much since their divorce, but two days earlier he had called in the middle of Mama's birthday dinner and Masha ran to answer. When she heard Papa's voice on the other line, it sounded off. He didn't say anything special, just asked if everything was all right, then told her to call Mama to the phone so he could tell her happy birthday. But his voice didn't sound like the voice of someone who wanted to wish his ex-wife a happy birthday. Besides, he hadn't called the previous three birthdays. And then, boom, and she and Papa were on the train back to Donetsk, even though she had already been there for her annual visit just two months earlier.

Deda was waiting for them on the platform, looking sharp in a vest over a collared beige shirt that made his round stomach, which she liked to call his *arbuz*, his watermelon, less visible. She jumped down onto the platform and kissed his tan, clean-shaven face, quickly inspecting his nose. Usually she'd find a hair growing from its tip that she could pluck, but today he'd taken care of that.

Grandpa took Papa's bearded face in his hands and said, "Let me look at you."

Masha watched Deda's fingers, mangled in the war, on her father's reddish beard and for some reason the gesture made her heart squeeze. The tenderness of it. The way her papa looked like a son instead of a father, with his big glasses sitting a bit crooked on his small nose, his gray eyes twinkling with embarrassment at being so closely inspected.

The bus took them across the river into the city center. Masha had never seen Donetsk so close to autumn. The poplars along the road were already yellowing, a mother was carrying a new purple backpack she must have just bought, and kids raced bicycles, looking like they were trying to squeeze the most out of their last day of freedom. She wondered what her classmates would think when she didn't appear at school tomorrow.

In the courtyard, Baba Nina waved to them from the balcony. Inside the apartment building, it was cool and clean. Masha's Moscow lobby reeked of fried onions, cigarette butts, and cat piss, while the elevator was defaced with curse words and rock band names. Here at her grandparents', there was still a sense of order, as if the mess of the USSR's crumbling hadn't quite reached them.

On the third landing, Grandma, in her flour-dusted apron, was already waiting by the open door as if she wanted to quickly hide them in the safety of her home.

"Come in, come in," she said, clutching Masha to her bosom and sniffling.

"Why are you crying, Babushka? You just saw me in June."

"No reason, *detochka*. Just happy to see you. Now, go wash your hands and head to the kitchen. I made your favorite!"

Lunch was oddly tense. Masha wanted to tell them about the Jewish kids' camp that Mama had sent her to last month, but she couldn't talk about it in front of Papa. He was a super Christian who took her to church and often quoted stories from the Bible. She knew he wasn't happy about the Jewish camp, though he'd never said it.

So instead she told her grandparents how last semester her school got humanitarian aid from America: flour, canned orange slices, frozen chicken thighs, and Swiss cheese.

"If you're going to send someone a wheel of cheese, why choose one with such big holes?" she asked, and they all laughed, the strange tension easing slightly.

Finally, when they finished, Grandma asked her if she wanted to go see if any of her friends were around. Usually, Masha was the one to ask, always feeling a little guilty, but today she felt they wanted her out of the house. Another mystery.

The courtyard was empty. She wandered to the next apartment building, where there were Ping-Pong tables, but those were empty too. She came back to the courtyard and sat on the bench, near the place where her grandpa had planted an apple tree. She could go knock on the door of the twins or Lida, one of her closest friends in Donetsk. But how was she going to explain why she was back here at the start of the school year? There was no way she was going to tell them about the cockroach exterminator. None of the neighbor kids had any cockroaches. Her whole reputation for being the Moscow girl would be ruined.

She swung on the swing, then walked around the block, past the kindergarten that Papa went to and the bakery on the corner. She considered walking further to Aunt Vita's, but she was probably at work. Feeling lonely and unwanted in this city she didn't know well,

Masha returned to the apartment. The front door wasn't latched, so she opened it quietly. The adults were still in the kitchen, unable to see her hovering by the coatrack. Masha heard one of them stirring something in a cup and imagined it was probably Papa because then the stirring stopped and he said, "She told the police I drove a new car. You know what they said? 'Then he is a goner.'"

Masha crouched by the shoes, afraid they might hear her breathing. She knew the second she walked into the kitchen, they'd change the subject.

"How did they figure?" Grandpa asked.

"From experience," Papa said. "Moscow has gotten wild. It's not just gangs shooting up each other anymore. Now everyone is a target. My friend Saplin got mugged on his way home last month. Someone hit him over the head and took his wallet. Poor guy ended up with a concussion."

Masha knew Saplin. He had dressed up as Santa a few years ago when her parents were still together. She remembered how afterward he took off his beard and drank vodka in their kitchen.

Why couldn't adults just tell her what was happening? It wasn't like she was blind and deaf. She knew perfectly well that things had been rough in Russia. There were oligarchs in their magenta jackets and empty store shelves, and last year a dead body had washed up in the river by their school. She didn't go down to see it, but the rumor was that it was decapitated.

She felt she was on the edge of finding out what this sudden trip was really all about. If only they could return to that thing Papa had said about his car and being a goner.

Instead, Deda said, "It's not just Moscow. I almost got mugged myself in Kyiv."

"What?" Grandma exclaimed. "How did you not tell me?"

"Didn't want you to worry."

"You old fool," she said. "Haven't you learned that whatever you hide usually comes out anyway?"

Deda began to talk about how he couldn't find some banquet hall and had asked a decent-looking young man for directions.

"He didn't look like a hoodlum," he said. "But once we turned into a dark alley, I began to get a bit nervous."

"No wonder your blood pressure had been spiking lately," Grandma said.

"Is that true, Papa?"

Before Grandpa got a chance to answer, the phone rang right behind Masha. Quickly she opened the front door and slipped out onto the landing, her heart pumping.

————

When the phone rang, Yefim went to answer, still in shock about Andrey's story. To be kidnapped just like that for no reason by four hooligans with knives and then tied to a tree in a bloody forest . . . like in one of those telenovelas that Nina loved. Imagine if they had kidnapped the grandkids too! Where did they even get such ideas, these wild beasts roaming Moscow? Not that Donetsk was much better. Just last month he saw two new, foreign cars pull up to an old green Moskvich and block it. There was some yelling, then the drivers got out, in their Adidas pants and leather jackets of the nouveau riche hoodlums who thought they were in charge now. They ripped the mirrors off the Moskvich and beat the driver. How naive everyone had been to think that once Ukraine was out from under the Soviet grip, there would be freedom and happiness. Now freedom was getting beat up in broad daylight.

On the phone was Andrey's new wife, calling from Moscow. Her voice was jumpy and shrill. Yefim handed the phone to his son. Afterward, Andrey announced, "They've caught them!"

"Unbelievable!" Nina exclaimed.

"I thought no one ever catches these lowlifes," Yefim said.

"So did I," said Andrey with a shrug.

"Must be your father-in-law's connection."

Andrey's new father-in-law had served in the KGB before he retired and Yefim had been wary of this connection. When, last year, he had briefly met the new in-laws in Moscow—the KGB father squinting at him suspiciously while the mother sat morosely, clutching her cup—Yefim couldn't help wondering if they had looked through his file. Sometimes he wished they had, so they could tell Andrey about his past and spare him the trouble of confessing.

"I have to go back tomorrow to ID them," said Andrey.

"Then call my buddy at the railway. He'll exchange your ticket by phone so you don't have to go to the station right now."

While Andrey was calling about the ticket, Masha came back. She said none of her friends were around, so Nina sat her down to help make vareniki. He couldn't imagine what would have happened if the kidnappers had gotten her too. What had this country come to? For decades they'd lived in communal apartments, worked long hours, stood in lines, sacrificed for what was advertised as a happy future just within reach, and then *poof*, the future and the past were gone overnight and now bandits threatened children and Americans shipped them cheese.

Yefim watched as Nina and Masha took out a bowl and the linen bag of flour and began to mix the dough.

"Your papa needs to return to Moscow tomorrow because of work," Nina told the girl. "But don't worry, we'll figure out how to get you back next week. Meanwhile, since you're missing a few days of school, we'll be doing math, Russian, history, and science here. And later this week we'll celebrate Rosh Hashanah, the Jewish New Year."

He watched Masha roll the dough into a long sausage. Earlier, Nina had suggested that maybe it wasn't good to lie to Masha about why she was here, but Andrey cut her off: "She is too young for such things. And anyway, children shouldn't know everything about their parents." Flat out, just like that.

Andrey was right, of course, and yet that phrasing bothered him. Had Andrey overheard him saying that at some point?

Masha cut the dough into small pieces to be boiled.

"Baba, since when do you celebrate Jewish holidays?" she asked.

"Since she started working in Sokhnut," Yefim answered.

Last year, Nina had become bored with retirement and decided to sub as a daytime guard at Sokhnut, the local Jewish organization. Soon she—the Slavic girl who'd never showed a particular interest in Jewish culture—became the family's main Hebrew expert, much to the amusement of their friends.

Yefim couldn't stand it. After all, what good did being a Jew ever do him? In the past few years, as Jewish communities were beginning to enjoy a post-Soviet rebirth, he'd avoided reading about the Holocaust and listening to news about Israel, and he certainly wasn't keeping track of Rosh Hashanah on his calendar. Even with Nina's prodding, he neither wanted to nor knew how to be a Jew. He'd spent six decades avoiding all it entailed. But now it seemed that she had decided to rope their granddaughter into her Jewish crusade.

"Considering you're Jewish on your mother's side, my dear Mashenka, it won't do you any harm to learn some traditions," Nina said. She dumped the small pieces of dough into the enamel pot.

"Sure, Baba. Did I tell you how Mama took me to Purim this spring? It was like a carnival, with puppets and costumes, very fun!"

At that word, "Purim," Yefim saw a long-forgotten glimpse of his brothers dressed up as robbers while his sister wore a crown made of wheat. He remembered fidgeting during Rabbi Isaac's preaching and then music, lights, and those sweets, whatever they were called.

"Hamantaschen," Nina said to Masha. "Did they have those triangular cookies?"

"*Da*, with raspberry jam," Masha said.

"For Rosh Hashanah, we will try making challah from a recipe I got from a friend at Sokhnut," she said, and then winked slyly in the direction of the hallway where Andrey was still on the phone with the ticket office. "And since your papa is heading to Moscow, we'll be safe to celebrate."

Andrey had been taking Masha to church, and though Yefim didn't like him brainwashing the girl—if Andrey had seen what he had seen in Germany, he wouldn't be swayed by any God—he also hated that Nina was now going behind Andrey's back to introduce the girl to Jewish culture. It seemed like a vicious cycle: Andrey keeping things from Masha; Nina keeping things from Andrey; Yefim keeping things from them all. He saw the damage that all this concealment could do:

sure, secrets kept your loved ones from worrying, but they also shut them out of your life, leaving you to combat your ghosts alone.

Lately, confessions were pouring out all around him as if the fall of the USSR had popped some sort of cork and the once obedient Soviet people refused to keep silent. This summer old Jews had started coming to Sokhnut to share their stories of surviving the Nazi occupation. Now that Germany had started giving out reparation money, they needed counsel on how best to prove what happened to them fifty years ago. It often fell to Nina, who had moved up from a security guard to a librarian—organizing a growing collection of books left by emigrating Jews—to offer them advice.

Once, Nina had told Yefim about a woman from a nearby village who was four years old when the entire Jewish population was gathered, shot, and buried in a mass grave. When the men who did the shooting noticed a child's hands sticking out of the dirt, they pulled her out and kept her hidden in their barracks.

Then, there was the story of a ten-year-old boy who lived in the Donetsk ghetto, located behind where the circus now sat in the sand quarry. He told Nina how one day he'd left the ghetto to go for a permitted walk, and when he returned that afternoon the ghetto was completely empty. He didn't know what had happened to them. In tears, he'd wandered back into the city, where a German officer picked him up and kept him hidden until the end of the occupation.

These stories irritated Yefim. He'd find himself arguing that if everyone came out with their grievances, there'd be not enough reparations to go around. The whole country suffered. Should he get a check because all his siblings were killed? What would he do with that money? Buy himself salami? He told Nina it was better if stuff like that were kept under wraps. Then, minutes later, he wondered why he had gotten so upset. Was he resenting that he had chosen to keep silent?

After Andrey successfully exchanged his ticket, Nina brought him into the kitchen and said, "Before you leave, would you talk some sense into your father and convince him to take the new pension?"

"I can decide for myself!" Yefim said, feeling ambushed.

"What's this pension?" Andrey asked.

"Veterans with disabilities are entitled to a bigger pension. Our neighbor—remember Ilya Vulfovich, the one on the second floor?—he's got the same injury as your father, with the phalanges of his two fingers missing, exactly the same, and he is receiving his disability money. All your father needs is a simple note from the doctor, but—"

"But nothing!" Yefim cut in, angry that after pestering him for weeks she was now trying to involve Andrey. Worse yet, this was happening in front of Masha, who looked from one adult to another while dipping the fluffy dumplings into a pool of sour cream on her plate. "Don't be ridiculous. How are my fingers a disability? They're a man's distinguishing feature. It's like asking for money for a scar. I won't hear of it."

Yefim had to control himself not to yell out, *There is no veteran's pension!* Instead, he got up and left the kitchen. He was so sick of all the little ways in which he'd had to evade the truth. Sometimes it took all his self-restraint to protect the many things they didn't know about him: that he spoke German and cringed whenever Nina mispronounced a German word; that he'd lied on every bureaucratic form until the questions about the war had been removed three years ago. His family didn't know about Nikonov, who'd passed away last year, or that he'd recently sent a letter to Karow, Germany, addressed to an Ilse Becker. Just as they didn't know how overwhelming it felt when earlier this year Russia's President Yeltsin ordered full rehabilitation of POWs. After five decades, people like him were finally considered legitimate war veterans entitled to the same benefits. He expected Ukraine to follow suit soon, though he wasn't sure he'd want any pension then either. He couldn't forget how his mother, who was eligible to get money for her four dead sons, said, "I don't want any money from this government for my sons' blood."

For now, though, he had to con Nina so she wouldn't find out he wasn't a valid veteran. All these games tired him. Dealing with Nina's nagging was often the hardest, while Andrey and Vita were usually too busy with their own lives to notice all his wheeling and dealing. But the grandkids . . . well, the grandkids were a different story. Especially Masha.

In 1984, when he had met with the KGB, Masha was just learning to crawl. By the time she'd started school, the portraits and quotes from Communist leaders had been erased from textbooks, the brown-and-white Soviet school uniform had been retired, and the weekend cartoons produced by Soyuzmultfilm were largely replaced by Disney's Chip and Dale and Donald Duck. While the Great Patriotic War was still a major event in the culture that she absorbed, for Masha it bore no personal significance and her young brain seemed unburdened by the particularities of Soviet morale that had told her parents and grandparents what was honorable and what was shameful.

Looking at her across the table, it occurred to Yefim that, for her, finding out that her grandfather had been a prisoner rather than a war hero would mean . . . he didn't know exactly what, but something much less potent than for his kids, who would have been ashamed. And so he wondered if his youngest granddaughter was the one he could safely talk to.

———

The next day, while all her classmates were at school—dressed up, tan, catching up on all the summer gossip—Masha was cross-stitching with Baba Nina. Papa had left that morning, her local friends were at school, and Grandpa had gone out to the store, so they were alone.

"We'll embroider a traditional Ukrainian pattern with red crosses," Baba Nina said. "And while we're working on it, I'll tell you about history. That way you'll be done with your history and homemaking and you'll only need to do math and reading."

"Deal!"

If lying on the couch with Grandma counted as school, she didn't really mind. Babushka's ample body, blubbery and warm, was an island of calm that didn't exist in Masha's frenetic life in Moscow. Grandma always told interesting stories and, unlike other adults, had time and a willingness to tell them. She was a window into a very different world, of an old Ukraine Masha knew little about. It was only a couple of years ago, when their TV switched to Ukrainian, that she learned that

Baba and Deda's native language was Ukrainian, not Russian, which blew her mind.

Grandma handed her a plastic ring with taut white fabric and showed her the stitch, a tiny cross on a tiny square. With a red thread in her needle, Masha began to work, slowly and carefully.

"At your summer camp, did they tell you about the Jews who were killed during the war?"

"No. They told us stories about Israel and the old temple and different holidays. And we had lots of parties."

Grandma smirked.

"Well, listen, then. This will be your history lesson for today. When the Germans came to Ukraine—and that happened very quickly after the war began—they decided to get rid of all the Jews. We had many Jewish neighbors in Kyiv and some of them hadn't evacuated. One day, the Germans posted a notice that all Jews had to appear at one intersection the next morning. Many went voluntarily; some left their children with non-Jewish families. We hid a beautiful girl named Ada who was a few years older than me. Everyone who showed up was taken to a ravine called Babi Yar and shot. There is a haunting Yevtushenko poem about it that you can read one day."

Masha tried concentrating on her needle diving in and out of tiny holes in the white cloth, but the horrors Grandma was sharing made her fingers moist and the needle kept slipping. She gripped it tighter.

"Why haven't I ever heard any of this? Will they be teaching that in history class when I'm older?"

"I don't know, Mashenka. There is a lot they don't teach at school and a lot I am just learning myself. All these stories I hear from Jewish witnesses who were there, they've kept to themselves for decades. Your own great-grandfather, Deda's father, was also killed in a ghetto, and for years I didn't know any details because Deda doesn't like talking about his past."

This surprised Masha. Grandpa seemed very open, although now that Grandma mentioned it, she realized she knew almost nothing about his childhood, his family, or the war.

"Why doesn't he like talking about it?"

"I suppose because he doesn't want to remember the bad things he's seen. We were taught not to ask many questions, only to adore our country and fear its leaders. It's hard to explain how pride and fear can coexist in one's heart without contradiction. I was there and still can't explain it. But because of that, we never talked about the really terrible things, especially if those things were done by our own government. There have been things I also never talked about."

"Like what?"

"Have you ever heard of Holodomor?"

"No," Masha said, turning the word in her mind, the very sound of which was chilling and weighty. "Was that also during the war?"

"No, that was earlier, in 1932, when there was suddenly very little food and everyone was starving. I had to stand for hours to get some dense black bread and was always hungry. But in the villages, things were even worse, so the peasants would come to the city at night to try to find something to eat in the garbage bins. In the mornings my dad wouldn't let me go outside because villagers often died next to those trash bins."

Masha didn't understand.

"How could there be no food? Didn't the peasants grow things in the villages?"

"The government took their harvest. It's hard to explain. Our country had a lot of secrets and we're only beginning to learn about them now. I'm sure it will take many years to unearth everything."

Masha looked down at her embroidery and noticed she had made a mistake in her pattern.

"Do you think Grandpa would talk about his past if I asked him?"

"You can try. Maybe he'll tell you something since you're his favorite."

Masha figured this was her chance to also ask about Papa.

"What's going on with Papa's car? I heard something about the police."

Grandma gave her a funny look and waved her arm in dismissal.

"Oh, his car was stolen, but don't worry, they already found it," she said. "No big deal. Now let's go set up your desk so you can do your math homework."

Masha had a hard time concentrating on her math. What Grandma said about Papa's car getting stolen made sense. That was probably why he'd called Mama on her birthday to tell her the police may be coming to her for questions like in that French spy film she saw on TV recently. What she didn't understand was why he hadn't told her himself. It didn't seem like something that needed to be a secret. It also seemed odd that he took her to Donetsk two days later, though of course the cockroach spraying must have been pure coincidence.

Masha put away her math and took out a blank piece of paper. She had the urge to draw something. Something small and orderly. Something that would shake her out of the feeling that there was a huge dark ocean of things she wasn't supposed to know. She drew the wall of the Kremlin with its toothy reassuring spires. Then she drew a road. On the road was a car, boxy and red, just like Papa's. She could still hear Papa's voice saying, "New car? He is a goner."

She was trying to decide who to draw inside the car when Grandpa walked in.

"Guess what?" he said, holding his hands behind his back. "Dyadya Volk stopped by earlier this morning and when he heard you were visiting, he asked me to give you something."

The invisible appearance of Dyadya Volk—Mr. Wolf—during her every visit was their favorite game. Masha didn't really believe in him anymore, but she didn't want to hurt Grandpa's feelings, so she smiled and played along.

"What is it?" she asked.

From behind his back, he brought out a Red Riding Hood, a chocolate wafer that was her favorite candy even now that Snickers and Mars crowded the Moscow kiosks.

"Please thank Dyadya Volk for me next time he visits."

———

Yefim asked Masha if she would like to play cards, but she told him she was about to go meet her friends in the courtyard and asked if they could postpone cards until later. While she was gone he tried reading the paper, but when he noticed his eyes were scanning the words blindly, he got up and went to oil the hinges on the balcony door that had become squeaky, then found a couple of leaves on the windowsill plant that needed trimming, then, running out of things to do, turned on the television, all the while wondering how he would tell her. He worried that Masha wouldn't understand or that she would acciden-tally spill his secret to someone else in the family, but the urge to tell had acquired a life of its own and was now rolling him toward the cura-tive relief that he hoped confessing would bring.

Masha returned right when the news came on and sat next to him to watch the armed campaign being launched in Chechnya. He knew she didn't understand Ukrainian and was glad she missed the details of the news story. When the news ended, they positioned themselves on the sofa bed to play *durak*, using his stomach as a table for the cards, while Nina was heating up dinner.

"Deda, did they say there will be a war?" Masha asked, sorting the six cards in her hand. He wondered if this could be a good entry point.

"It's hard to say."

"There is already that other war in Bosnia, right? I don't understand why there is so much squabbling between neighbors."

"Being neighbors is often the easiest cause for a war. Just imagine that one neighbor has something and the other doesn't and they can each see what the other one has and one gets jealous."

"My neighbor Lenka has a hamster and a snake in a terrarium and I think they're neat and all, but I don't want to kill her for it."

He laughed.

"You know," she continued, glancing over her cards as if they were a shield, "sometimes I try to imagine what it would be like to be in a war and have to shoot somebody, but I just can't. I know when you or Papa take me fishing, we kill these live animals, but as long as they're pretty small, that doesn't feel so bad. But a person who looks at you and speaks to you? I just don't understand it."

Yefim was tense, waiting for something that was on the tip of her tongue. She laid down a jack of diamonds. Then she said it:

"How did you go through the whole war? I know soldiers have to, but I can't imagine you killing anyone, Deda."

There it was, his chance. He had contributed little to win the war, but now, looking at his ten-year-old granddaughter's apprehensive eyes, he realized that, to her, those puny soldierly deeds would seem monstrous, and for the first time in his life he was grateful for how little fighting he had done.

He lowered his cards toward his chest and quietly said: "I was taken prisoner right after the war started."

Masha looked up at him. Her eyes softened with relief, as if now she no longer needed to reconcile the image of her grandfather with a killer. She opened her mouth to say something when Nina called from the kitchen: "Come eat! Dinner is ready."

Masha put down her cards but didn't move, looking uncertain about the right thing to do: continue the confessional or go to the kitchen. But Nina didn't like asking twice, and a few seconds later she appeared in the door with "Dinner is on the table! Come now."

"Coming, Baba," Masha said, and jumped off the sofa, extending her hand to help Yefim.

He put his hand with its mangled fingers in her palm and let her pull him up.

On the way to the kitchen, he went into the bathroom and latched the door. He turned on the faucet and splashed cold water on his cheeks, where stubble had grown.

He had done it. He'd finally told someone. Yefim wanted to look in the mirror to see if anything had changed, if he had excised the malignant growth, if the tension he had hidden for five decades was gone from his eyes. But he couldn't bring himself to look. Instead, he tucked his face into a towel and realized that he was angry at himself. He didn't know what he had expected from a child. Why was she supposed to care about the shame of being a Soviet prisoner of war? Her father had just gotten kidnapped. This was no time to think about the past—his or anyone's. They first had to survive the present.

As if to confirm his feelings, Masha didn't mention anything at dinner and afterward joined Nina to watch her favorite soap opera, *Santa Barbara*. He didn't know whether she understood the significance of what he'd told her or simply didn't think it was worth probing deeper. But for the next week, while he half expected her to ask more about the war, she was busy with homework, courtyard friends, and cooking with Nina for Rosh Hashanah, and didn't ask him any more about his past. Then she returned to Moscow and a year later emigrated with her mother to California.

And all the while Yefim wondered whether he had told her anything at all.

Chapter 18

October 1946
Ukrainian SSR

Returning to his village after finding his mother, Yefim dreaded going to his old house. He considered staying at Kateryna's again but couldn't force himself to pass his family's hut. Going inside felt like penitence.

Their house had never been this quiet. With eight of them squeezed into the small hut, it was always filled with loud, joyous, cantankerous banter in Yiddish, Ukrainian, and Russian. In the evenings, when everyone got ready for bed, Basya sang, her voice lulling him, making him less afraid of the night outside. Even when they slept, the house wasn't quiet. There were snores, scratches, sneezes, yawns, whispers. And now, nothing. Even the mice were gone.

After sweeping up the broken glass and patching the broken window with a rag, Yefim lit the oven in the bottom of their *pich* and climbed on its top ledge in hopes of getting some sleep. After the past few years he thought he could fall asleep anywhere. But tonight he was haunted by the family that wasn't there.

Mikhail, Georgiy, Yakov, Naum. Gone. Why didn't they survive? They were stronger, braver, smarter than he was. Naum, the handsomest of his brothers, could have married any girl in the village. Yakov could have had children—nice Jewish children his mother would have loved. Georgiy, a tank of a man who'd had no qualms eating a pet like Bek-Bek—how could someone like that perish? And Mikhail, his favorite, who'd practically raised him. He should have made it back. They all should have been here in this house. Instead, he'd lived and they hadn't. Why, why, why?

And then there was Basya. He tried pushing away the image of his sister but it kept returning, her delicate hands on the Singer, her head topped by a black braided knot, then the shot, blood splattering the sewing machine and the chair, her head nodding, her body slumping. He could see it all through his mother's eyes. It made him want to break the walls, the roof, the village, the whole world. He told himself to calm down, that there was nothing to be done. But the reel of her death played over and over.

There were no comforting places for his mind to go. If it wasn't Basya, he'd see his brothers, their stiff bodies scattered in some nameless field. And if it wasn't his brothers, he'd circle back to his father driving off to the ghetto for the last time, dust settling behind his wagon. The father who never wanted him because he was afraid to lose his wife, the father who abandoned her and took himself to his own death, the father who was—he had never before wanted to use the word—a coward.

At least his mother had survived. He should be thanking whatever gods had kept her on this earth, and yet, instead of relief, he felt the weight of responsibility tinged with guilt. The way she'd clutched his face when she called him Haim—he couldn't get it out of his mind. A grieving old woman grasping the last vestiges of her life. How was he supposed to tell her that the child she had risked her life for, the one offspring who'd survived the war, had done so by working for the Germans? The same Germans who'd killed the rest of her family. For now, he knew she was glad he was alive. But what would happen once she found out how he'd made it?

Yefim tossed on the top ledge of the *pich*, then got down and paced back and forth. There was no getting out of it. Tomorrow morning he'd have to report to the regional military commissariat, where he would be issued a new military ID that would forever seal his reputation as a prisoner of war, one of millions of worthless soldiers who did nothing to save the Motherland. And then, in the lucky event they didn't send him—like Nikonov—straight to the camps, he would have no other choice but to tell his poor mother the dreaded truth.

The house was getting cold. He threw another log into the stove and climbed back up on the ledge. He was sure he'd be awake until morning. But then he saw the familiar shape of the woman with the long black hair walking toward him through the field, a quiet, still infant in her arms. He had never properly seen her face before and now as she came up to him he recognized his mother, younger, as he'd remembered her before the war. Her dark eyes glistened, either from tears or from joy, he couldn't tell. "Haim," she said and extended the infant into Yefim's arms. He took it, afraid to look at its dead face. As he stood there cradling the bundle, he felt its warmth and, looking down, discovered the child sleeping peacefully.

He woke up just past dawn. The embers in the oven had burned out and the hut, cast in the first gray light of the October day, now seemed unfamiliar. He felt stiff and agitated. His body craved movement. Quickly, he gathered his things and walked out of the house. He couldn't wait to get out of this village, which he'd spent six years longing to return to. The only way he was going to save his sanity was if he started fresh, away from here. He dreamed of heading to Kyiv and entering any university that would take him. At twenty-four, he'd be the oldest freshman there, but what did it matter if he got to stop playing soldier and start a new life? The only question was whether the military would believe him.

As he left his village for the commissariat in Kozyatyn, it seemed to him that he was heading to purgatory, where his fate would be decided once and for all. Though he had already told his story to SMERSH, they had needed him then for the Berlin battle. No one needed him now. In fact, there were probably several articles of law that sought punishment against Red Army soldiers who were captured by the enemy and then, voluntarily, became ostarbeiters. He felt as though he was walking into Stalin's maw.

His only consolation was that the commissariat would have the latest record of Ivan's whereabouts.

The road to Kozyatyn lay through Ivankivtsi, but once he saw the first houses of the village where his mother lived, he turned off the dirt road and headed for the back fields. It felt cagey, but he couldn't face her until he knew what they would tell him at the commissariat. From across the field, he recognized the red roof of the butcher's house and saw a faraway figure in the yard that might be his mother. He steeled himself and kept walking.

He remembered how she had looked at him as she said, "Now it's clear you are Haim." She sounded so sure of herself. His illiterate, superstitious mother. So what if "Haim" meant life? That name—that strange, foreign name—wasn't why he had survived. If anyone had known he was Haim, he would have long been a pile of ashes settled on some German field.

After Ivankivtsi was behind him, Yefim turned back onto the road. Kozyatyn was another hour's walk, and though he hadn't slept much, he didn't want to rest. He needed to know what the rest of his life would look like. He heard a horse-drawn cart approaching from behind and stood to the side of the road to let it pass. The driver slowed down.

"Where are you headed, soldier?" the driver asked. He was an older man with a thick graying mustache driving a thin horse.

"Kozyatyn, but I'm fine walking. Shouldn't be too far."

"No reason to dirty your boots. Hop in."

Something in the way the man held the reins reminded Yefim of his father and he found himself unable to say no. He climbed in.

"You heading to the commissariat?" the man asked when they began moving again.

"I am. How did you figure?"

"You look like you've just arrived from over there," he said, pointing west as if toward Europe. "And I've seen a bunch of youse heading to the commissariat to check in. My sons didn't make it."

Yefim took off his hat and asked where they'd served.

"One died in '41, the other in '43. Only kids we had."

Yefim didn't know what to say, but the man continued without waiting for a response.

"When did you ship out?"

"Summer of '40."

The man whistled and looked at Yefim.

"That long you survived? Well, if I ain't riding with a real hero! What's your name, soldier?"

"Shulman. Yefim."

"A Yid? You're either the luckiest son or . . . Wait a minute, you didn't get into some funny business with the Fritzes, did you?"

The man was pulling on the reins to slow down his horse.

"I heard Germans burned all the Yids, but here you are with all your arms and legs," he said, stopping the horse. "You better get off here. I don't want any trouble."

Yefim jumped down and the old man hurried off, the horse kicking up dust on the road. Was that what they all thought around here: that a Jew who survived must have been some sort of spy? Would the officers at the commissariat ask him the same question: "Why did you survive, Yid?"

His back stiffened with worry. If his plan didn't work, there would be no university and no Kyiv, just ore somewhere in Siberia.

It was early afternoon by the time he arrived in Kozyatyn. The ornate train station from which he and Ivan had shipped off that summer of 1940 still stood, looking less grand than he remembered. The commissariat's wooden building where his military career had begun and where he first met Ivan was only a few blocks away. As he walked there, he remembered how nervous and excited he had been when he first headed there, a green seventeen-year-old seeking glory in the Soviet army. How naive he'd been to think the military would make him into someone his country would value and his family would admire. His country didn't care. His family was gone. But maybe he could at least finally find Ivan.

When Yefim reached the building he'd been instructed to check in at, he found that it had burned down. He stopped by a nearby pharmacy where the salesclerk told him it was now up the street in the two-story brick building that had been a textile baron's mansion before the Revo-lution. He followed her directions and quickly found the mansion. With two Soviet flags flapping out front, it looked distinctly municipal.

Next to the building was a wooden fence plastered with handwritten notices. He paused and read, "Missing Red Army soldier Petro Stasyuk, 22 years of age, last seen in October 1941. Grieving mother and sister grateful for any information." There were dozens of these notices: "Looking for our father," "our beloved sister Valentina," "our only son Rodion." Several were clipped out of the regional newspaper's missing persons section and one even contained a portrait. All were missing, missing, missing. Now just names on a fence.

With a heaviness in his chest, Yefim climbed up the steps of the commissariat, swung open the metal door, and went inside. The air smelled of office paper and fresh paint. Echoing across the long hallway was the leaden clang of a typewriter. He felt his hands go cold.

The invisible typist must have been recording the various fates of Red Army soldiers into a weighty book of records. As Yefim approached the third door down the hall, he imagined his name appearing in that book, a mark of his military failure kept for eternity.

Inside was a brightly lit room with a large desk where the typist turned out to be a young woman in a gray wool dress and a corn-colored bob. When he told her he had been demobilized and needed to receive his new military ID, she went to the closed door of an internal office and, after peeking inside, returned to her typewriter.

"Boris Vladimirovich will see you once he is free," she said casually, as if Boris Vladimirovich wasn't an arbiter of fate.

Yefim sat on an upholstered chair and listened to the staccato of the keys, broken up by the trill of the return lever until, as at the end of a military march, the secretary would finish with a bang, turn the roller knob, and seize the paper out of the machine.

"Come in," a man's voice boomed from behind the door.

Inside the narrow office, he found a broad-shouldered, heavyset man in his fifties writing at his desk. Yefim offered a proper salute.

"At ease," Boris Vladimirovich said, putting down his pen. "Returnee?"

"That's right," Yefim said. "Arrived in Kyiv two days ago."

"Good job making it on time," he said as he showed him to a chair while his left hand remained invisible on his lap. Behind Boris Vladimirovich was an old-fashioned standing clock no doubt left over from the days of the textile baron and an unnerving portrait of the Leader hung on yellowish wallpaper. "Many miss the three-day mark and then we make them jump through a bunch of hoops, and who needs that, am I right?"

He had a jowly, tan face and mirthful green eyes.

"I am Boris Vladimirovich Boyko, the officer in charge of regional records. Now, what I need you to do, son, is to take me in detail from the day of your recruitment to three days ago when you returned home. You think you could do that?"

Yefim didn't know if it was the kindly "son" or the conversational manner of this man, but he felt like this was someone he could talk to, someone in whom humanity outweighed, at least slightly, the call of patriotic duty.

He told Boyko when he was recruited and how by June 1941 he'd ended up in the artillery unit on the border. Boyko took a few notes, but mostly he listened, his eyes half closed as if trailing Yefim in his imagination.

"They bombed the barracks. We were able to hold them off for almost two days but were quickly getting surrounded, so my commander, Komarov, told us to retreat."

He recounted how they ran east and fought off the partisans. He wanted this man to know that he'd tried, that in those days rejoining the army meant everything to him. Then he hesitated.

"And then you were captured, weren't you?" Boyko said, as if he'd heard the same story a hundred times before.

Yefim nodded, glad not to hear reproach in the man's voice.

"We tried to fight them off, but there were only eight of us. We were outnumbered," he said, then stopped, remembering the swamp he'd dove into when a bullet pierced Komarov's forehead. He bristled and tried to regain focus. He needed to get this man on his side.

"Where did they take you?" Boyko asked.

"A camp near Tilsit, then another camp further in Prussia. In November they picked out a few of us and sent me to a large work farm. In the spring of '43 I ran away, but got caught." He decided to leave Ivan out of this. "I told the police that I was an ostarbeiter."

He felt himself getting into the story, weaving it carefully but quickly as if he had no agenda besides telling the truth.

"And they believed you?"

He spat out the rest of it in one gasp.

"They must have, because I was sold to a village burgomaster. About a year later, I ran away once more but again got caught. This time I was sent to a different village where I worked until our army came. I talked to SMERSH and they let me join the infantry, so I went to fight in Berlin. Then our reserve unit was transferred to the Baltic coast. That's where I've been stationed until three days ago when I returned to find my family, except that . . ."

Yefim trailed off here, not wanting to launch into the story unless the man asked for it himself. He noticed the ticking of the clock above Boyko. Next to the clock, Yefim tried not to look at Stalin's twinkling eyes and bloodcurdling mustache. How could he ever have thought Stalin was counting on him to defend his country? What a child he'd been then.

"Except what?" Boyko asked.

He began to speak quietly.

"Except I found only my mother has survived. My four brothers are all gone, my father died in the Berdichev ghetto, my sister was shot by a policeman."

Here he paused and then, trying to ignore the sickly feeling of using his dead family to help him, he pleaded.

"I am the only one my mother has left and, to be honest, Boris Vladimirovich, I can't bring myself to tell her I sat out the war in Germany. The shame of it, with all the deaths . . . it will finish her. She'll feel like she can't count on me in her old age."

"*Mda* . . ." Boyko considered, and turned to stare at the window that faced some leafless shrubbery. It had begun to rain. The clock ticked.

Yefim watched the man's jowly profile, worrying he'd leaned too much on his mother's feelings. After all, what concern was she to an officer in the commissariat? But it was the only card he had. Boyko would need to be a monster to send a mother's last child off to Siberia.

When Boyko turned back to face Yefim, he said, "Here is what we'll do. Put the dates of your captivity as the dates of your army service."

Yefim stared in shock. This man, who was supposed to be a recorder of truth and an arbiter of fate, was suggesting the impossible. To lie. Lie to the army—lie to Stalin himself. That was not what he'd come here for. He had hoped to avoid being sent to the camps, but Boyko was offering something entirely different: a way to completely erase the stigma of being a prisoner of war. Tabula rasa.

"That way it will look like you served in the army the entire time and you won't have to tell your mother," Boyko went on. "As I see it, it's your only way out."

What if this was a provocation, some sort of test of his patriotic duty? He had to tread carefully here, to cover all his bases.

"But I've already reported my capture to the SMERSH office back in Germany," he said earnestly. "Won't it be inconsistent?"

"Even better that you told them the truth," Boyko laughed conspiratorially, crow's-feet around his green eyes. "Less likely you'll get shot."

Yefim wasn't sure how he figured, but the man's levity made him see this wasn't some elaborate Soviet ruse. Boyko knew the bureaucratic procedures of this system and decided Yefim had a real chance of avoiding being smeared as a POW. He must have calculated his own risk of what would happen if this ever came to light. With his right hand, the officer pushed a blank form and a pen toward him.

"Here, fill this out and we'll have Lenochka type it up."

It all suddenly seemed so easy: a form, the permission of an older officer, Lenochka on her typewriter, and in minutes his whole shameful history would be erased. He would no longer be *inconvenient*, as Nikonov had called it. He would be a soldier who'd made it to Berlin. His mind felt foggy, his body exhausted by the tension. He was being offered a rare chance to stop worrying about the past and start fresh. The price of that chance was a lie.

The clock ticked on the wall. Next to it, Stalin's portrait waited.

"Don't worry, son," Boyko reassured him with a warm smile. "It will all be fine."

He put his left hand, which had until then been hidden on his lap, on the desk and Yefim saw that it was missing the forefinger. Maybe that was why he'd been so kind, Yefim thought.

He filled out the form, skipping the dates of his capture and erasing four years of his life in Hitler's Germany.

When he finished and got up, Boyko shook his hand and said, "Forget the past, Shulman. Go live your life. And if anyone asks, your medals were stolen on the train."

He was disoriented and elated. He had walked in a lowly prisoner and walked out an honorable veteran. Then he remembered something.

"Before I go, could I check on my friend?"

"Ask Lenochka on your way out."

The girl was adjusting her hair when he came out. If she couldn't tell him anything, he'd still have time to go to Ivan's village and ask there.

"Could you check your records on my buddy? Last name Didenko."

Her eyes widened and she smiled.

"Ivan?" she said.

"Yes! You've seen him? Is he back?"

"No, no. I knew him before the war. We were at the orphanage together not far from here."

"That must be someone else. The Ivan I knew lived with his father."

He named Ivan's village. The girl lowered her voice.

"I'm sorry to tell you this, but Ivan's father died—drank himself to death after his mother was arrested. He'd been at the orphanage since he was six."

Yefim didn't want to believe her. He and Ivan hadn't had any secrets.

"Why wouldn't he tell me any of this? We were very close. He saved my life more than once."

Lenochka looked at him with what seemed like pity.

"That kind of past makes friendships complicated. He probably wanted to protect you."

Yefim didn't know what to say.

"But I'm sorry to tell you, Ivan was reported as deceased."

He thanked her and walked out of the commissariat office into the damp air. Passing the flapping, wet notices of the missing, he quickened his step.

Chapter 19

March 2007
Donetsk, Ukraine

Somewhere here was the barn with straw that smelled of milk and home. Yefim remembered emerging right onto it after he scrambled out of a thicket between the woods and the farm fields, a day's walk from Karow. If this was the same thicket, the barn should be just on the other side. There, he could swaddle himself in the warm straw and finally stop worrying. He'd scratch his hands and face all day long just to stop worrying, stop glancing back.

"You there!" he heard, and knew he'd been spotted.

He flung himself into the thin branches, but, instead of clearing a path, they entangled him. He ignored the thorns ripping through his shirt, lacerating his arms. Pain was no new thing.

"*Tovarisch!* Grandpa, you can't go in there."

Someone's fingers grabbed the back of his shirt. Yefim half turned and a thick branch whipped the grabbing hand. Freed, he plunged deeper into the thicket, but he wasn't moving fast enough.

"Where are you going? Someone help me get this old man!"

Yefim twisted toward the straw, toward peace. He already sensed he wouldn't make it to the barn, but he couldn't quit trying.

"The old geezer must have lost his marbles! There is nothing but a fence back there."

"Someone go after him! He's hurting himself in there."

"Why don't you go?"

"Can't you see I've got my son with me? Let this big fellow go."

"Let's wait for the police. What if he fights back?"

"Fights back? He is at least eighty."

"Just go after him! Where do you think we are, Zurich? Our police are too busy counting bribes to get some old crank from the bushes."

Damn police, Yefim thought. They'd take him back to the camp if they didn't shoot him first. He jolted left. A branch flogged him across the forehead and he fell.

"*Tak.* That's it! I'm going in there."

Yefim saw the blue of the sky between the leaves and tried to get back up, but his arms didn't obey. He couldn't understand why he was so weak.

Someone lifted him as if he weighed nothing, and Yefim shut his eyes. He didn't want to see his captors. Otherwise, he'd dream of them for years, this menagerie of faces snatching him, questioning him, betraying him. He was tired of running, of hiding, of carrying his lie. He hoped this was the last time he got caught.

"Here we go, Pops, out of the bushes. You must be lost."

Yefim kept his eyes shut while someone hushed him like a baby.

"Do you know where you are?" a woman's voice asked.

He shook his head without opening his eyes. Next she'd be questioning him about how he, a Jew, had managed to survive.

"He doesn't know where he is," she reported back to someone. "He is lost."

"Where do you live?" a man asked.

"Izhevsk," Yefim answered quietly, but no one heard.

"Must be dementia," someone else said.

Then a woman hollered into his left ear as if he were deaf, "You are in the Forged Figures Park! On Universitetskaya."

Universitetskaya Street was where Vita got an apartment on the top floor with the sunset view over the slag heaps. This woman was lying. He must be in central Germany.

"Where is your home?" she probed again, but Yefim didn't want to answer any more questions.

He kept his eyes closed even though tears tickled his lids. He didn't believe that he was in Donetsk—that the war had been over for decades, that Nina's left eye had gone all crooked and milky after her stroke, and he thought she'd be the one to go first. But no, it was he who was weak, confused and crying, when all he wanted was to wrap himself in straw and rest in peace.

———

The bystanders who brought him home told Nina and Vita that before finding his wallet with his address, Yefim had said he was from Izhevsk. "He's never even been to Izhevsk," said Nina, looking at him with her one good eye. It was the closest he'd ever come to slipping. Luckily, Vita quickly diverted everyone's attention to how to prevent her wily father from escaping and getting lost again.

Once he was thinking clearer, the embarrassing incident told Yefim that his Parkinson's—which had until then been stalling his body in frustrating, unpredictable ways—was now eating his brain. At eighty-four, after evading death many times, he could feel it looming around the corner like a deadline. And he knew the time had come to make the final decision: confess to his family or take his secret to the grave.

The first thing he resolved to do was dig up his documents, the only remaining evidence of his lie. For decades he had fiercely guarded his ancient leather briefcase that contained his private papers, which had moved with him from Kyiv to Donetsk and, after he'd had the second stroke a few years ago, into Vita's apartment, where it was stuffed under his bed. The household rule he had established long ago was that no one was to touch his papers, and as far as he knew, no one had. The children never cared to dig through their father's dusty documents. And Nina? Well, she had respected his privacy both because she didn't know what she didn't know and because, he suspected, she'd always been too preoccupied with her own secret to notice his. Yefim knew perfectly well that she had never quite let go of her youthful crush on the now dead Professor. First love, especially unconsummated, was like that. It never died. The reason he had allowed Nina to have her secret was out of fairness, but also out of guilt.

Now the time had come to reckon with that guilt.

On one of his better mornings in March, when he felt lucid and strong, Yefim slid the briefcase from under his bed, unclicked its metal latch, and took out a thick stack of folders tied with a cloth string.

The folders smelled of time. Many of the papers had yellowed, acquiring the preciousness of museum relics. Yet, unlike real relics, much of what he'd saved had been made worthless by time: records from hotels he'd stayed at during his work trips, requisitions, a geological survey on the bogs in Siberia that he never finished, some research on beekeeping, a library card from 1951.

Then there were other papers, which, as his sinewy fingers took them out one by one, made his heart squeeze into a ball of nostalgia, shame, and regret. A photograph of Mikhail, Georgiy, Yakov, and Naum. His military ID. Nikonov's letters from Siberia. And finally the large sealed beige envelope.

Yefim had told himself that he'd kept this briefcase full of documents *just in case.* He didn't know in case of what, exactly, but one thing he'd learned was that in life, especially in a Ukrainian life, one never knew what could come next. Next door, Russia was now run by an ex-KGB man. Who was to say that the KGB couldn't return, that evidence couldn't be requested; it was always prudent to keep your own record of things. But now, as he looked at the papers in his shaking hands, he saw that the real reason he'd held on to them was because they were the only evidence that he had lived the life that he had. After all, the war was over; the country that he had served had fallen apart; Nikonov, the one friend who knew the whole truth, had long since left this earth; and Germany had become a desirable emigration destination for those who didn't believe in Ukraine's prospects or were scared of Putin's tightening grip. Time was erasing things, making them irretrievable, yet here it was: ink on paper, proof of what he'd done.

Proof that his family must never see.

Before opening the beige envelope, Yefim looked at Nina, who seemed to be dozing. He listened for the voices of his daughter and son-in-law in the kitchen. Vlad was too polite to barge into the bedroom. Vita, however, moved fast. He decided it wasn't safe to remain in the bedroom.

He grabbed his military ID, Nikonov's letters, and the beige envelope and trudged toward the bathroom. Unlike many recent days when his body was stalled by a disconnect between his brain and muscles, today he glided like a free man. He turned on the bathroom light, locked himself inside the narrow, wallpapered room that was always a few degrees warmer than the rest of the flat, and gingerly put his papers on top of the toilet water tank. Then he opened the cabinet he had helped hang two decades ago, where his son-in-law kept his tools. After rummaging for a while, he found what he was looking for: a box of matches. A red poppy was drawn on one side. On the other was a figure of a little boy in a Ukrainian *vyshyvanka*, standing in a field of wheat. Above him, Yefim read KEEP OUT OF REACH OF CHILDREN.

There'd been days when Vita treated him like a child. He supposed she had to, though he didn't like thinking about those moments when, after the second stroke had made him bedridden for some time, she'd had to lift him out of bed and transfer him onto the plastic "throne" in the middle of the room so he could relieve himself. Though he laughed it off, the whole thing had reminded him of the camp, where the privacy of one's bodily functions was replaced by the communal defecating, shared lice, typhus's spreading rash, oozing foot sores, and the hair-raising odor of human decomposition that hung in the cold German air.

Now, standing above the toilet bowl, Yefim opened the matchbox, took out a match, and lit it. The first to catch fire was the military ID. Its inside pages burned quickly and with them—on page 5—went the original lie of when and where he'd served. Soon the flimsy burgundy jacket with its faded Soviet star was also burning. Yefim watched the flame eat up his young face and the black curls that stood almost upright on top of his broad forehead. These days he only had wisps of white hair left, but they still stood stubbornly upright. Once the flame got too close to his fingers, he let the blackened pieces of the ID fall into the water, where they hissed and soaked into clumps. *Goodbye, war hero Shulman.*

Next were Nikonov's letters. Yefim had received the first one while he was still in Germany, so he had destroyed it before heading back to the USSR. The others found their way to him a few years later, starting in 1953 after Stalin's death. By then Nikonov had been released from the main camp and sent to work at a nearby town. Yefim had kept two of his letters. In the first, Nikonov had talked about how "the muddy place where we met" wasn't much different from where he was now, only about twenty degrees warmer, which had made Yefim shudder when he remembered the bone-freezing winds in the POW camp. He couldn't imagine how a human being could survive anything colder than that—for years, no less. In the second letter Nikonov had reminisced about Berlin and how surprised he had been to find Yefim there. Neither directly spelled out that Yefim had been captured—Nikonov was too smart to compromise him like that—but Yefim still put a match to the two folded letters. *See you on the other side, old friend.*

The toilet water was now full of black paper scraps that swirled like a downed armada. Yefim flushed.

Finally, he carefully tore open the beige envelope and took out its contents. The first was the 1984 summons from the administrative office of the Donetsk Region of the KGB requesting that he appear for questioning and reminding him, lest he had other ideas, that "your presence is mandatory." He recalled the thin face of the officer who had questioned him. He'd never forget the whites of the man's eyes, made yellow by the dim lamp.

Yefim suddenly felt very tired. He had wanted to purge these memories, but he hadn't considered how hard it would be to erase himself.

He leaned on the bathroom wall. His strength and clarity were leaving him, and he was no longer sure that destroying everything was what he wanted to do. With a shaking hand, he leafed through the stack of papers: the KGB summons, the deposition, the confirmation that he was not entitled to a war veteran's pension, and then, at the very bottom, his confession letter. The document that explained how he became a prisoner of war, his escapes, his liberation, and the way he was able to hide it once he returned.

It all came rushing back: the first morning of the war, Ivan, the *Appellplatz*, Ilse, Berlin, his mother, the commissariat.

Yefim slid down the wall, tears in his eyes. The war had ended sixty years earlier. Even the confession letter itself was now more than twenty years old. His children had gotten their own gray hairs; his grandchildren had grown up and started having children of their own. Yet here he was still hiding the truth.

Someone rapped on the door.

"Are you all right?"

His heart thumped and for a moment he wasn't sure where he was. He struggled to get up, but his legs refused to listen. They knocked again.

"Papa!" the familiar voice screeched.

This was Vita's bathroom, he realized, the voice his daughter's.

"I am fine!" he snapped.

"Why does it smell like something is burning?"

"I am getting rid of some documents. Don't disturb me!"

He heard her walk away in a huff. A few moments later, two pairs of footsteps approached the bathroom door. Why couldn't they leave him alone? Yefim held his breath. There was a more hesitant knock.

"What is it?" Yefim whimpered.

It was his son-in-law this time.

"Yefim Iosifovich, please, come on out," Vlad said, in his gentle voice that always counterbalanced Vita's crescendos. "We don't want you to hurt yourself."

"Or burn down the apartment," Vita butted in.

"Don't worry, I am just . . . ," he started, and then gave up, feeling caught and defeated.

He looked at the confession letter in his shaking hand. He didn't want to admit that what started out as a way to protect his family from harm had become a way to protect himself from his family. For a brief moment he saw himself: a toothless old lunatic hiding in the bathroom.

He picked up the beige envelope and slid the letter inside. He'd have to finish this another day.

———

But another day wasn't coming. In April, everything turned off-kilter. Despite full nights of sleep, Yefim was always tired, and had no appetite even for salo. He couldn't understand why the world seemed to have lost focus.

Every morning he woke up feeling that there was something important still left to do, but couldn't remember what. It had to do with the war, he knew, but whenever he tried to think about it, images and fragments meandered through his mind, one morphing into another like an exhausting military parade. He watched his mother become his sister become his daughter but couldn't catch any of them long enough to ask if they knew what he had to do.

One morning he woke up on the ground. Two figures were leaning above him, yelling. Their tongues clicked and hissed. He was terrified. Why did the guards pick on him again? He tried to get up, to run. But they were much stronger than him, fascist bastards. One, with thick round glasses, grabbed him by the ankles, shushing him. They were going to beat him, he knew, beat him until he was raw and oozing and no more alive than those stiff bodies piled up on the cart.

"Don't hit me! Don't hit me!" he begged, covering his face.

"Shhh," the round glasses said menacingly.

There were footsteps, then a stout female guard screeched, "Drink this!" and forced his jaw open and poured in the poison. He tried to spit it out, but the liquid had already trickled down his throat. It was too late. Maybe it was for the better. He could take his secret to the grave. But no. NO! He had to survive. He always survived. His name was Life.

Yefim tried turning onto his stomach to make himself throw up the poison, but he was leaden, weighing as much as Uska, impossible to lift. He heard the thump of his head on the floor. The monsters began to fade. The light also.

There was nothing for a long time. Then he woke up and found a priest with a reddish beard and glasses sitting next to him.

"Who?" Yefim whispered.

"It's me, Papa," the priest said.

Yefim strained to remember who this was. He could fake it, of course, but he felt guilty for some reason, guilty that he couldn't remember this bearded man. Maybe he wasn't a priest. It was probably some young colleague of his, from the railway institute or maybe earlier?

"Andrey," the preacher said. "Your son."

A son? Yefim had four sons, but they all died in the war. The daughter died, too, shot by a policeman. Yefim closed his eyes to let the familiar image of blood splattering on the Singer pass. Then he opened his eyes again, straining to find something in this Andrey that would give him a clue.

"Which son?" he asked.

A woman began to cry somewhere above his head. Andrey turned to her and said, "I'm glad you called me, sis."

"I told you he wasn't doing well," the woman's voice replied.

Yefim tried to lift up to see who the woman was, but he felt dizzy. He fell back on the pillow. Then there was nothing again for a while.

Nothing.

Nothing.

Nothing.

When he opened his eyes again, it was sunny in Vita's apartment. He saw Nina's thick back curled away from him on the bed across the narrow bedroom. She wore white socks on her feet, whose toes, he remembered with pity, had twisted beyond what human feet should allow. His poor old wife.

Yefim sat up. At first he was dizzy and the room grew whiter, but then it passed. He felt very hungry.

"Nina, you awake?" he asked, his voice coarse.

"Nina!" he tried again louder, but was overcome with his usual cough that ripped through his chest.

Nina turned and a moment later Vita ran in.

"Papa! Papochka!" she said, tears streaming down her plump cheeks, though he wasn't sure why she was crying.

His cough subsided but sat there crouching in his chest, waiting for him to take a big breath.

"Water," he whispered, trying to keep it in.

"Yes, one second," Vita said, and ran to the kitchen.

Meanwhile, Nina squeezed her feet into her slippers and asked, "Rise and sing, Fima! How are you? You were gone for a while. Andrey is here, too, from Moscow. He just went to the store."

Yefim nodded, glad to hear his son was there, though he wondered why he'd come all this way. Was it Nina's birthday again?

When Vita brought him water, he drank the full glass, then said, "How about some breakfast?" and Vita laughed through her tears.

———

A few days later, his oldest granddaughter, Yana, came to visit with her two sons. She brought flowers.

"Happy Victory Day, Deda!" she said as his great-grandsons, seven and four, stood awkwardly near the bed while he tried to sit up.

Yefim looked at the flag-red carnations interspersed with white roses. Sickly sweet, pompous reminders of what he wasn't. He didn't want to take them. It had been Nina's idea to create a war veteran cult around him once they had great-grandchildren. She made sure they congratulated him every Victory Day: a way to pass on the memory, she'd said, though he wished he could tell her that it wasn't memory that was being passed down but a myth. He wished everyone would just let him be.

As the boys ran to the kitchen, where Vita must have prepared some sweets for the occasion, he told Yana, "This isn't my holiday. *You* know the truth . . ."

Didn't she remember what he'd told her? She was little then, sure, but she was the only person he'd entrusted his secret to. Didn't she understand the shame of being told Happy Victory Day and handed flowers when neither the flowers nor the victory belonged to him?

"What truth, Deda?"

Yefim panicked. Had he muddled things? Maybe it wasn't Yana he'd confessed to. Who, then? He could still see the cards laid out on his stomach and a pair of cherry eyes looking at him. Masha! Of course. It was Masha, his youngest granddaughter, now in California. Yana would have been much older then, she would have questioned him more.

Feeling embarrassed, Yefim took the bouquet. Yana sat down next to him on the bed and held his shaking hand.

"Deda, Victory Day is about ending a terrible war," she said, her voice soothing. "It's a celebration for everyone who was there, no matter what they did."

He felt himself relax. *No matter what they did.* Perhaps she understood after all. Perhaps they all would, and he'd been wrong to think he would disappoint them. What if, it occurred to him, the morals of who did what in the Great Patriotic War had changed around him and the people of today knew how to see it without dividing its partici-pants into heroes and traitors? Wasn't that the job of time after all, to put history in perspective?

"True," he said at last, his mangled hand shaking in his granddaughter's.

For the rest of the day, Yefim was compliant, taking the congratula-tions, offering his toothless smile, glad that this Victory Day as a war hero would be his last.

———

Though in the following days he continued going through his other documents, the confession letter remained undisturbed in its beige enve-lope. Yefim was no longer keen on destroying it, though he also hadn't decided what he would do with it. And so it lay there, in the purgatory of his briefcase, awaiting the final resolution of its fate.

By June, even if he had wanted to burn it, the task became insur-mountable. He could no longer make it to the bathroom as his legs wobbled underneath him like reeds in the wind until he inevitably crumbled back down on the bed. The plastic throne was reinstalled in the middle of the bedroom. When soon even that became too much of an effort for everyone, he was thrown into the ultimate ignominy of adult diapers.

It was in those bedridden days that Yefim finally arrived at his decision. He needed to come clean; the confession letter would do it for him. He told himself he was no longer capable of retelling the whole story or answering the questions his family would have. The letter would do a much better job. Not only did it describe what had happened to him and how he'd covered it up, but it also explained why he'd kept it a secret. He still remembered writing that last line: "I beseech you not to let my family find out what I have written. Their peace is more important to me than my own."

The following afternoon, when Vita came in to change his diaper, he said, "Vitochka, I need your help."

She leaned closer to him.

"Did you need something, Papa?"

"I am leaving something in the briefcase for you to open after I am gone."

She looked at him with confusion.

"Say it again, Papa. I can't understand you. What do you need?"

He pointed downward in the direction of the briefcase, trying to get out of bed to show her.

"Do you need to go to the bathroom?" she asked. "No?"

With a surge of strength, he lifted himself up on his hands and wrestled with the blanket, which seemed to have ensnarled his feet. Vita propped the pillow behind him.

"Maybe you just wanted to sit up?" she asked, looking at him like a mother at an infant.

He shook his head, growing frustrated.

"My briefcase," he tried again, his throat coarse. "There is a letter."
"What?"

Had she gone deaf? Her ear was so close to his mouth that he could smell the chamomile shampoo in her black hair, which revealed its gray roots.

"*Pis . . . schka . . . port . . .* ," he repeated, trying to speak loudly and enunciate.

But there was no use.

"I am sorry, Papa, I don't understand what you're saying."

Exhausted from the effort, he turned away and lay back down, closing his eyes. His thoughts drifted from Vita to the newborn Vita sleeping in Nina's arms to Marcel in the workshop to Masha who liked Mr. Wolf to Yana who said victory was for everyone. They were all interconnected somehow, these people who led to other people who would get to stay here while he took his leave.

The letter would remain in its purgatory. One day after he was gone, they would find it and maybe they'd understand. Or maybe they'd judge him. Either way, he wasn't going to be there to find out.

He was heading for his final escape.

Chapter 20

August 2015
Donetsk

As the August heat melted the streets of Donetsk, the shelling intensified. From her sofa bed, Nina asked Vita to open the balcony in hopes of catching the morning breeze, but instead all they got was the roar of the blasts in the northern part of the city.

Since Russian-backed separatists appeared in town last spring, Donetsk was no longer a booming city of new condo towers, open-air restaurants, and a fancy arena built for the UEFA Euro 2012 right under Nina's window. Instead, it had become a war zone with dumb, young militants running around in balaclavas and old ladies like her with nowhere else to go. Stores were boarded up, banks and the post office shut down, the ATM unplugged. There weren't many cars on the roads, and in the evenings after curfew Nina heard the streetlights humming in the stillness between the explosions.

At ninety, Nina wasn't perturbed by the war itself but by who was waging it. When the Germans had marched into Kyiv, their invasion made a certain amount of sense: they were foreign enemies set on occupying her homeland. Now it was her own people who were the enemy. Backed by Russia's ample resources, local separatists were trying to make her city into a republic. Nina thought the idea ridiculous. What did they think Donetsk was, the next Monaco?

But what she found most disturbing was how quickly this conflict was turning families, friends, and neighbors into enemies. Even her own son didn't seem to understand how this war forever changed the relationship between Russia and Ukraine.

Several months earlier, on the seventieth anniversary of Victory Day, a parade called the Immortal Regiment took over the streets of Moscow and other Russian cities but also Donetsk. The internet was flooded by images of people carrying enlarged photographs of their parents and grandparents who had fought in the Great Patriotic War. Though it was supposedly a grassroots movement, the news showed Putin walking among the people, carrying a photo of his father.

That day Andrey sent Vita a photo of himself holding a poster of the young Yefim and his four brothers. Behind him, the thick Moscow crowd was peppered with Russian flags. Nina and Vita were livid.

"I do *not* want my Jewish Ukrainian father and uncles carried around Red Square!" Vita told her brother.

"Calm down," Andrey said. "This isn't a political thing. There is such unity here. It's not just for decorated heroes, Vita, it's for everyone."

"Right, everyone and Putin. If you were here getting shelled, you'd understand. We had a parade today too, you know. And the same photos of veterans were carried right next to photos of separatists as if they're also heroes. The idiots in our so-called government can't make up a solid reason for young men to die fighting Ukraine, so they are shouting nonsense about some Nazis and trying to link these two wars to rouse patriotism. They even found a theater troupe to put on *The Young Guard*. It's ridiculous! So please don't talk to me about unity, Andrey. It's bullshit."

Nina was baffled that her son couldn't see how the Great Patriotic War was being used for Russia's agenda. Donetsk was full of billboards styled after Soviet posters that showed soldiers hugging children against the tricolor background of Russia's flag. Their slogans read

OUR GRANDFATHERS WON VICTORY AND SO WILL WE and WE MADE IT TO BERLIN. IF NECESSARY, WE'LL DO IT AGAIN.

Andrey apologized for not consulting them before going to the parade with the pictures, but Nina saw that, although her son claimed he never became Russian despite living in Moscow since the '70s, he wasn't Ukrainian either. Despite the war tearing apart his native Donbas, he was still living under the ghost of the Soviet Union, where Russia and Ukraine were inseparable.

Unlike him, Nina felt her Soviet identity shift. She began to speak Ukrainian. She regretted never teaching her children and grandchildren her native language. She wondered how different their lives would have been if she and Yefim had stayed in Kyiv.

And yet she also couldn't make herself leave Donetsk, which had been her home for seventy years. When Masha called from California to try to convince her to flee before the shelling accidentally hit their apartment building, Nina told her she was too damn old to run.

"I don't care anymore," she said, though she didn't really expect twenty-one-year-old Masha to understand what it was like to be waiting for death during a war. "Let them come and get me."

Finding herself under occupation once again, Nina performed her own small acts of resistance. When someone called from the institute about a special Great Patriotic War pension—allotted for helping clean rubble off Kyiv streets back in the 1940s—she refused to accept it because the money was coming from the new separatist government. When Lenka, Vita's old high school friend who called to check in on them, said she thought Donbas was better off with Russia, Nina told her she was an idiot and not to call again until she smartened up. But of course, besides this, there was little she could do.

She saw that, for Vita, the war was difficult to accept. After all, she was born in the 1950s, when the Soviet Union promised its postwar children eternal peace. Life's main slogan was "As long as there is no war." Now Vita had gone completely gray from the war and stopped bothering to color her hair. For Nina, it was strange to have a gray-haired daughter and still be alive. It felt wrong somehow. When Vita's kids,

Yana and Igor, fled to Kyiv, Vita said she didn't want to start over as a sixty-something refugee. Nina chose to believe her, though she suspected that her daughter would have also fled if it wasn't for her.

Now she was driving Nina crazy with anxiety.

On this sweltering morning, after opening the doors to both balconies to create a breeze, Vita sat down at her computer to read the news, when Nina heard a gasp.

" 'Shelling Hits Cemetery,' " Vita read out loud, then turned to Nina.

Her brown eyes, a copy of her father's, were wide with horror. Nina immediately knew that the cemetery in the headline was the one where they had buried Yefim eight years before. The man deserved to rest in peace. Instead, war seemed to have come for him again.

"Who does that?" Vita cried, sitting on the edge of Nina's bed. "Who shoots at the dead?"

"Bastards, that's who," Nina said, taking her daughter's hand. Maybe they should leave after all, for Vita's sake.

She wondered what Yefim would have done. From the confession letter he had left behind, she was certain he'd know what to do.

Eight years earlier, when they had found the letter, Nina asked Vita not to tell anyone but Andrey. It was too shameful of a secret to share with anyone else, even the rest of the family. She could see embarrassment in her daughter's eyes as Vita tried to adjust to this new image of her father.

That evening they called Andrey in Moscow. Vita asked if he was alone in the room and he said, "Yes, what's happened?"

"It's about Papa," Vita said. "We found a letter."

Nina butted in, "It's probably better if we read it to you."

By then Nina had memorized some of Yefim's sentences, and as she listened to her daughter's shaky voice rereading the letter, she wished she could see her son's eyes.

Nina had understood why Yefim had hid such a thing. Having had her own documents marked with "lived in occupied territory," she knew the stigma that followed him. But even though she understood his reasoning, she wondered if it had been worth it.

Her friend Irina had once said that Nina had a family but not a marriage. The letter made Nina wonder how much his past was responsible for the wall that had always seemed to stand between them.

She thought back to when they'd met, trying to recall what he had told her then about the war. She remembered he had talked about his family and a little about Berlin. He had probably stayed vague, while she hadn't asked questions because she had met enough returning soldiers, grieving widows, and childless mothers to know not to press for more. But what if she had?

Or what if she'd put together the clues: his night terrors; the reappearing bronchitis that he must have gotten from the freezing months at the camp; his erratic, escapist tendencies; his sudden spurts of anger; how he'd avoided the veteran's pension; how he'd evade whenever Andrey or Vita pestered him about writing down his memories; how he had never talked about the war? It all spoke of a pain she hadn't recognized in almost sixty years of living together. She felt guilty and foolish, but mostly she felt sad. Sad to think they could have had a better marriage.

After Vita finished reading the letter to Andrey, he said, "Our poor Papochka." He was finding it hard to process what this meant, he told them, and needed some time to think. But Vita didn't want him to hang up just yet. It seemed to Nina that she was ridden with guilt and needed her brother to share it.

"Remember how I made him give a talk at my school?" Vita said, tears in her eyes. "I can't imagine how he must have felt talking in front of all those kids while I sat there gloating like, 'Look at my papa, the warrior who'd made it to Berlin.' "

Andrey must have asked how Nina was taking it because Vita looked at her and said, "Better than me, I think."

A week after that, during the final cleaning of his side of the room, Vita had stumbled upon another paper. It was a small square notepad sheet, no bigger than a thumb, and in its center a shaky, Parkinsonian handwriting spelled out one word: *Haim*.

Nina didn't know what to make of it, but she was convinced it signified something important that her husband had wanted to record before it got erased by his weakening mind.

"Maybe he had a son in Germany," she told Andrey on the phone. "He was there for five years, anything is possible. Who else's name would be important enough to remember on his deathbed?"

"Why would this son have a Jewish name?" Andrey objected. "You've watched too many telenovelas, Mama."

"Maybe it was a friend," said Vita. "Someone from the camp or maybe someone who helped him escape."

Andrey tried running a web search for Haim in the Russian war veterans' database but didn't find any clues. Eventually, they had no choice but to put the notepad sheet together with the KGB letter and stop guessing.

By then Vita's initial shame had changed to anger. She told Nina she was furious at the Soviet system that had made a good man too mortified to open up to his loved ones while brainwashing those loved ones into believing that his shame was deserved.

Andrey's reaction was more proactive. He took some vacation days and drove to the part of Lithuania where Yefim had been stationed. He called Nina from a nearby town to tell her he had found no remains of their army base but he still liked seeing the land and the pine forests where his father ran from the Germans.

"I was standing in a forest, imagining him, this Jewish boy running for his life, trapped between the advancing army and the partisans. Remember that cheese story he told sometimes? He even said it happened while he was running from the Germans. But somehow it never occurred to me to ask what happened after: Did he outrun them or get caught? Why didn't I ask, Mama?"

"Don't kick yourself," Nina told him. "None of us asked."

That fall, they finally decided to tell the rest of the family. Nina was nervous. She wasn't sure Yefim had left the letter intentionally. What if he'd meant to take his secret to his grave, and the letter was simply forgotten? Now everyone he loved would know he wasn't the man they thought. She felt the weight of responsibility, as if she had abetted him in keeping his secret.

The reaction of the grandkids surprised her. Yana said she wished he had told them so he could see they didn't love him any less. Igor, who was struggling to rebuild his life in Kyiv, sounded impressed by his survival. And Masha said she wasn't shocked, though she couldn't explain why.

"I feel like he tried to tell me something once, but it was a long time ago," she said.

It had been a relief to Nina, this reaction. Perhaps Yefim had been wrong to keep silent after all. Maybe their whole generation was wrong to be so secretive. Maybe what they needed to do was talk about all the complicated ways in which they had survived. About the nuances of real life that weren't pretty enough to make it into history books.

Yefim used to say she told the kids too much, that she needed to be more careful, but maybe it was the opposite. Maybe she didn't tell them enough. Now her memories of the war and the famine seemed to acquire a new urgency. She had told her kids about the villagers who had died on the streets during the famine, but what she didn't say was that there were guards who were trying to prevent them from sneaking in to find food. A small change with big implications. She also didn't tell them about the time Mama chanced upon a rare chunk of meat at the market, but when she boiled it, the smell was so unusual that she poured it out and buried it in the backyard. Back in the Soviet days, she didn't want her kids to know that their mother almost became a cannibal or that the country, which promoted equality and brother-hood, often pitted its people against each other.

Soon after, Nina began dictating her memories to two of her former students who volunteered to type them up. She didn't want to die like Yefim, his life an enigma. She wanted her descendants to know what she had seen. She felt like a vessel for the twentieth century. Three decades from now, who would remember what life in the USSR had really been like? The horror of the famine, the terror of the war, the joy of mattering as a scientist, the stupidity of the paranoid regime, the mix of relief and disappointment when the country she was helping build dissolved into chaos, freedom, and greed.

For the next eight years, on Yefim's birthday and on the anniversary of his death, Nina visited the cemetery. But last year, when the war in Donetsk started, she'd been forced to stop. There were days when the shelling was quieter and they could have gone, but Nina had gotten much weaker by then and spent most of her time in bed. Making it from the bedroom to the kitchen for breakfast was a feat she could accomplish only on the best days. She slept a lot, and her dreams were filled with those who were gone: Yefim, her parents, Vera, her friends Tamara and Irina, the Professor. Nina's weakness was different from the past twenty years when she had felt old and afraid of death, falling asleep each night in hopes of seeing another morning. Now every night she went to bed hoping it would be her last.

When Vita told her about the shelling that hit the cemetery, Nina felt a surge of energy she didn't know she still had. There was one last thing to do before she left this life.

"We're going to the cemetery," she said.

"Mama, you're in no condition to go anywhere," Vita objected.

"This is my last wish. You have no choice but to take me."

She needed to know if Yefim was safe.

Vita got busy procuring a wheelchair for the trip, which turned out to be no small task in a war-torn city where pharmacies had been shuttered and few functioning hospitals were left. After two weeks, she was able to get one, and right before Yefim's ninety-third birthday, they took a taxi to the cemetery.

As they drove through streets that Nina hadn't seen in more than a year, the gregarious middle-aged cabbie shared the latest news.

"They hit a nine-story apartment building near where we lived," he said. "Then they shelled the bazaar where my wife worked. I managed to get her out in time, but a shell hit her friend at the next stall. Scorched on the spot."

Nina clutched her purse.

"So we moved to a different neighborhood, but it seems they are following us. A week after we moved in, I heard an explosion. In the morning I found my car covered in broken window glass from the apartment above ours."

Vita joked, "Whatever you do, don't move near us."

"Fair enough," the cabbie said.

Soon they were creeping along the gravel path toward the cemetery's gates. They got out and Vita wheeled Nina along as the sound of the taxi receded.

There were no cars parked in their usual spot and no flower seller with wreaths and bouquets. The cemetery appeared empty. They could hear the occasional shelling going off in the distance. Probably over Yasinovataya, Nina figured, trying to imagine how much of that small town was left intact. She remembered Yefim going there to visit some old friend from the war, though she never pried into who it was.

The sky was hazy from smoke, and the October sun cast an unsettling orange glow over the thigh-high dry weeds that swayed between the untended graves. The once tidy cemetery now looked like an abandoned field littered with headstones and crosses. Nina grew anxious. The damage was worse than she'd thought.

They didn't speak. Vita tied a plastic bag with a hand rake and a small shovel to the wheelchair's handle, and in the silence it clinked as they moved. Up ahead on the main path that led from the gate, something shimmered. Carefully they approached and saw the end of an unexploded artillery shell stuck in the ground. She remembered seeing one like that in Kyiv at the start of that other war.

They made a big loop around the shell and continued past the cemetery's first, older section, watching the path more carefully. On the right, Nina saw a tall gray obelisk she had remembered from past visits. It lay in a pile. Farther up, an exploded shell had turned two plots into a scorched no-man's-land. Melted wrought iron fencing drooped around it. Small and large pieces of tombstone with letters and dates littered the untended grounds.

Maybe the newer section where Yefim rested wasn't as bad. Maybe he had gotten away with a chipped headstone. She'd take that over this total annihilation, a death after death.

Finally, they turned right toward Yefim's section. Usually, many of the graves there were marked with fresh flowers from recent visitors. Today there were only dead leaves and more scorched earth. Despite her hopes, this section hadn't been spared.

If something had happened to the gravestone in normal times, they could have made repairs, but with the war, it was impossible. She told herself they would need to make do with whatever was left of their plot, but knowing that she would also soon be buried in this denigrated place where no one was resting in peace, she felt a wave of despair.

As they took the path that led to their plot, a raven landed on the chipped granite head of a decapitated bust. The black bird cawed loudly. Nina clutched her heart.

"You all right, Mama?"

She nodded, unable to speak.

"Please," she prayed silently.

Their plot was up ahead. As they got closer, they almost ran over a chunk of a coral headstone with the icon of Mother Mary that had been blown onto the path. Vita pushed it to the edge so the wheelchair could pass through. Then they rolled on and Nina finally saw their family's small tiled plot.

It was littered with small chunks of stone. In the middle, Yefim's shiny black tombstone stood unharmed.

"Papochka!" Vita cried, running to touch the stone.

Nina looked at the black monolith standing defiantly amid the destruction and smiled to herself. What luck, even in death.

While Vita swept up the rocks, pulled dried weeds out from between the tiles, and wiped the dust off the tombstone, Nina silently talked to Yefim. She told him about this new war, how it was dividing people, how lucky he was that he hadn't lived to see it.

"We shouldn't have been so afraid, Fima. We should have been telling our truth all along."

When they were leaving, she placed a pebble next to the tombstone and said, "I will see you soon."

When they returned home, she asked Vita to read Yefim's confession letter aloud again. It had been a while since they had looked at it. As Vita reread the words written by a scared man to the faceless authorities, Nina put her hands behind her head the way she used to as a kid when she dreamed up plots for stories she would never write. There were almost no personal details in his confession, but this time she wanted to fill in what he had left out. Those things that made him into the man she had known and loved.

Nina lay in her bed thinking of her husband. Outside, the air rocked with explosions.

AUTHOR'S NOTE

I hope you enjoyed *Your Presence Is Mandatory*. This story is very important to me, as it connects the past to the present and tells a story of one family that stands for the story of many.

I began writing this book in 2017, three years after the Russia-Ukraine conflict destroyed my grandparents' city of Donetsk, but long before Russia's president ordered a full attack on Ukraine in February 2022.

Having a war happen in the same place and to the same people who bear the scars of an older war makes one look to the past for any signs that were missed or lessons that weren't learned. For me that missed sign was the life story of my grandfather, a kind, jolly, generous man who made the world's best latkes and who never talked about his years as a soldier in World War II.

Your Presence Is Mandatory was born out of a real KGB confession letter my grandfather had left when he died. Just two pages long, the letter described where he served, how he was captured, the names of the German camps and villages where he was a forced laborer, his escape attempts, and his return home to his heartbroken mother. The letter was a shock to our family, both because it upended all we knew about him and because he was no longer there to ask questions or let us hold his hand.

At the time, I was a young journalist and budding novelist, so I was immediately intrigued. Though I had studied World War II in school both in Russia and in the United States, I'd never heard any mention of Soviet prisoners of war or ostarbeiters. My grandfather's letter was my first window into the fate of millions of survivors who got caught between two totalitarian regimes. In particular, I wanted to understand three things his letter didn't address: how a young Jewish man could have survived four years in Hitler's Germany, how it felt to keep silent about such trauma for seven decades, and how historical memory and mythmaking played a role in Russia's attack on Ukraine.

In my research, I learned that the Nazis captured almost six million Soviet soldiers and deliberately killed more than half of them. Those who survived were then put through a ruthless Soviet filtration system that sent many of them to labor camps in Siberia and turned them into social outcasts for life. Their rights as veterans were not legally reinstated until 1995, when most were in their seventies.

Some of these POWs had the added misfortune of being Jewish, and less than five thousand of them managed to return home alive. You're reading these words because my grandfather was one of them. I would have never pieced together how he managed to survive if it wasn't for the extraordinary Russian-language research of the historians Aron Shneyer and Pavel Polian, who had collected data and interviews with Jewish POW survivors, a group that no one else cared much about.

In the Soviet Union, where history was constantly gilded and where people never reckoned with the past the way Germans had, restoring the truth is both tricky and vital. The oral histories of Svetlana Alexievich and the work of Memorial, an organization that has documented the victims of Stalin's repressions, were beacons of light as I wrote this novel. (They are also both Nobel Peace Prize winners, and for a good reason.) My grandmother's memoir was also a key source on what it felt like to live in Ukraine from the 1920s until the 2010s. Today, in an era of misinformation, witness accounts continue to be essential in documenting the illusive present. Stanislav Aseyev's *In Isolation: Dispatches from Occupied Donbas* helped me round out the stories of my family members in Donetsk as well as what I saw there myself during a visit in the first years of the Russia-Ukraine conflict.

My main goal with *Your Presence Is Mandatory* was to describe the events of the past half century not as they appear in history books, but as they felt to the people who lived through them. I hope the story of Yefim and Nina has given you a glimpse into that world. A world where war never really left and where, despite that, love and forgiveness can prevail.

ACKNOWLEDGMENTS

This book would not exist if it weren't for my agent, Michelle Brower, who immediately recognized the value of this story, and my brilliant editor, Grace McNamee, who patiently nurtured it as only a co-parent could. Their relentless support of me and my work during the hard months of war has meant everything.

I am grateful to the rest of the Bloomsbury team who took such amazing care of this novel: Barbara Darko, Jillian Ramirez, Rosie Mahorter, Lauren Moseley, and Katya Mezhibovskaya, who understood exactly where I was coming from when she designed the cover.

I also couldn't have done this without the support of the Trellis team, including Allison Malecha, who fulfilled my dream of being an international author, and Natalie Edwards and Khalid McCalla, who took care of all the essential things.

This story found its footing thanks to the encouragement and feedback of the Leporines, especially Alia Volz, Jacqueline Doyle, Caryn Cardello, Frances Lefkowitz, and Luke Miner. A huge thank you to my first readers: Rose Andersen, Katie Worth, Sarah Van Bonn, Michael Denisenko, Robert Morgan, and Oleg Kaushansky. I also received support from my fellow post-Soviet writers: Olga Zilberbourg, Masha Rumer, Maggie Levantovskaya, Yelena Furman, Ruth Madievsky, Katya Apekina, Vlada Teper, and Tatyana Sundeyeva. Marian, thank you for giving me the break I needed. Marie, danke for your help with all things German.

Shortly after starting this book, I lost both my father and my grandmother, who could have been an immense source of support and knowledge. These days, the internet makes it seem that any history can easily be dug up, and yet, there remains a distinctly human memory of emotion, attitude, sensation, hunches, grudges, smells, and secrets that no technology can replace. I'm grateful that my grandmother had left a memoir full of details both vital and unnecessary, which became a treasure trove for this story. I also relied on interviews with survivors and historical research into the lives of Soviet POWs and ostarbeiters. But the one person I truly couldn't have written this book without is my aunt. She has been my eyes and ears in war-torn Donetsk, my sounding board, my fact checker, my gossip provider, and my keeper of memories lost. Dyakuyu!

Thank you to Mama and Vova for hauling our entire Soviet-era library to America. Soon after our arrival, when I was about thirteen, I told my mom that one of the books in that library was crap. It was a French novel in Russian translation. She looked at me with new eyes and said, "You've got good taste." That one phrase is largely responsible for why I dared to start writing a novel at all.

I began writing this story right before the birth of my son and continued through the birth of his sister two years later. Finding quiet time would not be possible if it wasn't for the childcare help of my mom as well as Lyudmila, Olga, Inna, Valentina, Irina, and Ilaria.

Finally, the one person who was there daily—through family deaths, transcontinental moves, pregnancies, the pandemic, and the gut-wrenching months of war—and who never, not even for a second, doubted that I could finish this book and release it out into the world was my husband, Richard. I love you.

A NOTE ON THE AUTHOR

SASHA VASILYUK was born in the Soviet Crimea and spent her childhood between Ukraine and Russia before immigrating to San Francisco at the age of thirteen. She has an MA in journalism from New York University, and her nonfiction has been published in the *New York Times, Harper's Bazaar, Time*, the *Telegraph, Narrative, USA Today*, the *Los Angeles Times*, and elsewhere. She has won several awards, including a Solas Award for Best Travel Writing, a North American Travel Journalists Association (NATJA) Award, and a Berkeley Art Museum and Pacific Film Archive (BAMPFA) Fellowship from UC Berkeley. Vasilyuk has lived in New York City, Warsaw, Berlin, and Bologna. She currently lives in San Francisco, California, with her husband and children.